The Hunger Winter

The Hunger Winter

Johanna M. Selles

RESOURCE *Publications* · Eugene, Oregon

THE HUNGER WINTER

Resource Publications
An Imprint of Wipf and Stock Publishers
199 W. 8th Ave., Suite 3
Eugene, OR 97401

www.wipfandstock.com

PAPERBACK ISBN: 979-8-3852-3979-5
HARDCOVER ISBN: 979-8-3852-3980-1
EBOOK ISBN: 979-8-3852-3981-8

VERSION NUMBER 02/21/25

This is a work of fiction. Unless otherwise indicated, all the names, characters, businesses, places, events, and incidents in this book are either the product of the author's imagination or used in a fictitious manner. Space and time have been rearranged to suit the convenience of the book. Certain long-standing institutions, agencies, and public offices are mentioned, but the characters are wholly imaginary.

To the memory of my parents
and
with gratitude to my siblings:
Marian
Bert (d. 1972)
Rein
Geraldine
John
Otto

"Just remember that love created you, and love tended you as you grew up. There was always love, and it is up to you to continue to bring love to all that surrounds you."

—Tante Gerda to Ada, Chapter 52

Contents

Acknowledgments | ix

PART I: Fall 1944 | 1
Chapters 1–24

PART II: Winter 1944–45 | 125
Chapters 25–43

PART III: Spring 1945 | 211
Chapters 44–59

PART IV: Late Spring–Summer 1945 | 291
Chapters 60–79

Epilogue: Amsterdam 1990 | 381

Appendix A—Reading Questions | 389
Appendix B—Topics for Further Research | 391

Acknowledgments

I WOULD like to thank my managing editor, Matthew Wimer, as well as the rest of the team at Wipf and Stock.

Heartfelt thanks to my editor, Jessie Steffes, whose careful guidance helped bring this story to life.

Writing mentors, including Kim Echlin, Diane Terrana, Helen Humphreys, Barbara Radecki, and Kim Abrahamse, provided useful advice at just the right time. Thank you for your generosity.

To Martha Smalley, a huge thanks for carefully reading the manuscript (more than once!) and providing editorial suggestions. Anne Howland gave both feedback and encouragement on earlier versions of the story and hospitality to the author. Jill Sauer, thank you for being the first and last reader and never doubting that it could be done.

When words fail, it is helpful to have visual artists revive the imagination. Thanks to Dee Van Dyke for sharing her work. Her series titled "Sealed/Revealed" was a solo exhibition of open and closed scrolls at IAM (International Arts Movement) in New York City in 2009. Earlier (2005) an individual scroll, "Anointed" (eighteen inches wide, eighteen feet long), was included in a group exhibition at the Museum of Biblical Art, New York City. Photographer Otto Selles (www.ottosellesphotography.com) helped me understand the technical and aesthetic challenges of both portrait and landscape photography. Landscape painter Geraldine Selles-Ysselstein (http://www.birchtreegallery.ca/) paints nature with a quality of attention that inspires reverence—an essential prerequisite for the creative process. Her landscapes help me picture how Lina used memories of natural beauty to survive her jail experience.

Librarians, archivists, and curators are essential to the writing of history and historical fiction. Many thanks to Curator Maartje van den

Heuvel who provided guidance on the Emmy Andriesse photography collection as well as relevant collections held at the Leiden University Libraries and elsewhere. I also acknowledge the historical work of Ingrid de Zwarte whose careful work provided a setting for my characters.

Friends and neighbors generously provided sustenance, without which this book would never have been completed. I trust you know who you are and how much it has meant.

Finally, my thanks to Renata, Andrew, Jonas, and Trude—for both inspiration and joy.

PART I

Fall 1944

1.

LINA

S ITTING cross-legged on her unmade bed, with her back against the wall, Lina hunched over a homemade pennant with letters spelling out birthday greetings.

Earlier that afternoon, after finding some fabric remnants in her late mother's sewing room, Lina had made an impulsive decision to create a birthday banner. Unlike her sister who was good at this kind of thing, Lina had always rejected female arts such as needlework and had underestimated the degree of difficulty involved. Procrastination had once again twisted her good intentions into knots. Wartime scarcity made it impossible to bring cake or flowers to a birthday.

"*Verdomme*," she cursed, as she pricked her finger and blood spurted onto the fabric. She ran to the bathroom to rinse her finger and the material in cold water. Lina sighed as she looked at the stained fabric and then returned to her bedroom to try to finish the job. Fortunately, the stain was on the back—no one would see it.

The party for Jacques would be held at Maarten's house. Although they had been at the same school, she hadn't known these fellows well, but when she started dating Jos, his best friends were part of the package. Although she suspected they only tolerated her because of him, she tried to be a good sport when they got together.

There had to be a faster way to attach fabric letters onto each flag to spell out "Happy Birthday." She was running out of time—she had promised Maarten that she would arrive an hour early to help him set up for the party. He had turned the family home into a party destination while his parents were staying with his grandmother in the south. Since their usual places of entertainment had been shut down by the occupiers, everyone was happy to hang out there.

Maybe Ada could help her finish this project.

Lina jumped off the rumpled bed, grabbed the bunting, and ran downstairs to the kitchen where Ada was cooking. Even though the windows were covered with condensation, it was evident that dark was falling quickly. The smell of onions made Lina's stomach contract with hunger.

"That smells delicious," she said, hoping that flattery would soften up her older sister. "Ada, I know you're busy, but could you please help me? I'm trying to finish this before Maarten's party."

A strand of Ada's dark, curly hair escaped from a bun. She used the back of her hand to push her hair out of the way so she could see. Covering a dark green dress of Mother's, Ada wore a floral apron that had faded over the years. Of medium height, her curves had melted away as the war continued, leaving her looking gaunt. Her previously ample breasts sagged in her knitted bra. "What?" she asked with obvious irritation, blinking away the onion tears so that she could see whatever Lina was pushing into her face.

"I need to fasten these letters to the pennant, but I don't have time to stitch them all the way around. Would it work to tack the letters at critical points along the way or just pin them in place?"

"Where did you get the fabric?" Ada asked, ignoring her question and touching the cotton with reverence.

Lina shrugged. "In the sewing room," she replied. "There was a pile of fabric remnants there."

"That happens to be a very special piece of Liberty cotton that Father brought back from London. Mother was going to show me how to make a blouse from it."

Lina looked at her sad face in alarm—this would not help her case. "Oops, sorry. Well, Mother won't be sewing anymore." Their mother had died four years before in 1940, at the beginning of the war. Lina wondered if she'd ducked out to avoid the misery of the occupation—her mother would have had little patience with the deprivations they'd been forced to accept.

She should have recalled that Ada did not like anyone making light of Mother's passing. "Can't you see I'm busy?" she asked as she waved her hand towards the braising pan. Ada's wrists were covered with a reddish rash, and her fingernails were cut short.

Lina pointed to her wrist. "You should put some cream on that eczema," she said.

"I'm sure the store will have it in the morning," Ada said with sarcasm.

Lina realized another mistake—she should not have drawn attention to Ada's skin. "This will just take a minute." Lina glanced at the pan. "What are you making?"

"Have you forgotten? It's Father's birthday dinner tonight."

"I remember. But I asked Father if he would mind if I left early because I need to help decorate for the surprise birthday party for Jacques at Maarten's house."

Ada frowned. "Who is Jacques? Did Father give you permission?"

"He's one of Jos' friends. I asked Father, and he told me to go have fun."

"Did you at least make a card for Father?"

"I've been working on it," Lina lied, hoping that Ada would not ask to see it since she hadn't started working on it. Now she would have to complete the bunting, make a card, and stay for dinner. She'd be lucky to get to Maarten's house in time to yell "surprise," and Maarten would not be happy that she was late.

Ada reduced the heat under the pan to a simmer and took the banner over to the kitchen table. "You want to fix these letters to the flags?" she asked as she pointed to the floral letters, which Lina had pinned onto each flag.

"Yes," Lina said impatiently as she shifted her weight from one foot to another. This was taking too long, but Ada would not be rushed. That was exactly what drove Lina crazy about doing embroidery and knitting.

"I would tack each point separately and that should hold them in place. If you don't look too closely, that will work."

"Can you do one at least, so I can see it?"

Ada exhaled. "Give me the needle. Don't cut the thread so long, it will just get knotted." Ada sat on the kitchen chair, her back straight and her mouth set in a straight line.

Lina watched from across her at the table. "You sure dressed this place up," she commented as she looked around the room. The rectangular farm table was decorated with a damask cloth—one that Lina hadn't yet bartered in exchange for food because it had a wine stain in the middle. A large arrangement of dried weeds and lavender was positioned to cover the stain. Mother's good dinnerware and cloth napkins finished the table. Lina traced the gold border on the ivory plate with her index finger. "Haven't seen these since before the war."

Ada looked up from the sewing task. "I thought I should use them for our dinner before you sell them to some farmer for a few eggs."

Lina resisted the urge to roll her eyes. If Ada had her way, everything would stay exactly as it was. Didn't she realize their mother would never return to use those plates and silver? Their old life was over, and now they needed to do whatever it took to survive. There were no dinner parties these days. She had searched through cupboards in the house to find things that the farmers would be willing to exchange for food. Ada needed to face reality—stores had little to sell, the rationing system had fallen apart, and people were traveling further to find food. At the beginning of the war, Ada had packed up some of the brass, copper, and paintings in the attic in the hopes that any Nazis looking for loot would miss her stash, and so far Lina had left that untouched. Smaller objects were easier to transport on her bike when she traveled to local farms.

"Are you watching?" Ada asked as she created a knot that kept one corner of the fabric letter in place.

"I am," Lina replied as she leaned forward with her elbows on the table, holding her chin in her hands. "And I am very impressed."

Ada glanced at her to see if she was being sarcastic, but Lina smiled sweetly at her.

"Now you finish it," Ada said as she handed the cloth to Lina, keeping her fingers on the needle until Lina took it from her. "Remember the curfew when you bike home."

"I know the back roads. Plus, I can bike faster than those *moffen* anytime."

Ada raised her eyebrows with unspoken skepticism. "We'll eat in about half an hour, so get this done and come down." Ada got up from the chair and returned to the stove.

"What are we having?" Lina asked, looking at the stove with longing.

"Lentil stew," Ada said as she stirred the pot with a wooden spoon.

"Oh," Lina said with disappointment. Holding the pennant and the needle, Lina prepared to dash upstairs. "Thanks," she said. "You always were so much better than me at all this stuff."

Ada looked over her shoulder. "It's not that I am better at it, it's just that you can't be bothered to try."

Lina laughed. She was pretty sure Ada was not trying to be funny, but it struck her that way. "You might be right about that. I'll be down in a while."

"Half an hour. And we will sing to Father and light a birthday candle."

"Yes, sir," Lina said with a mock salute before she left the kitchen to climb the stairs. As she passed the living room on the right and Father's study on the left, she noticed that the door was still firmly closed, and the front hallway smelled of the pipe tobacco that had wafted under the door.

Father had not been out of his study all day—he was working on something and didn't want to be disturbed. *What a lousy way to spend a birthday*, Lina thought, but he had been working obsessively for months now. It seemed crazy to her, especially since the Nazis had closed the university in the fall of 1940, meaning he had no classes to prepare and no papers to critique. The subject of history, which Father loved, had never appealed to her—she was much more interested in the future. Her ideal future scenario would have the war end soon so that she could move to Paris.

She paused outside his door, tempted to see if he wanted to go on a photo expedition in the morning like they used to do on many Saturdays in the past, but she knew without asking that he would turn her down. Whatever he was working on was far was more important than anything else, even her.

The last time they'd biked through the country to a nearby village, he'd taken time to explain how to adjust her camera to accommodate low light. When they developed the photos, she was stunned to see how well the prints captured the mood. The silvery light on the canal provided a perfect backdrop for the barge that was tied up there. A makeshift clothesline sagged with the weight of trousers and shirts. A man's bicycle leaned against the deck railing. In the corner of the photo, she'd even caught a solitary duck creating ripples in the otherwise calm water.

She decided to leave Father alone. There was no time to delay—she had less than a half hour to finish this project, make a birthday card, and get dressed for the party. Lina ran up the stairs, holding the banner up high with her right hand to see if it would take flight in the air behind her shoulder. When the flags stubbornly refused to take flight, she laughed to see the banner bouncing up the stairs behind her. Maybe it would be enough to sew the letters to spell "Happy" on the flags. *Life was all about adapting.* The guys wouldn't notice the difference. By the time she arrived, they'd probably be well on their way to inebriation.

2.

ADA

THE afternoon light had retreated from the kitchen. Ada had watched as the slanted rays reached across the yard and then disappeared beyond the back gate. Darkness fell quickly, accompanied by cold, damp air that crept around the windows. The stew didn't require constant stirring, but it was the warmest place she could find.

The fall days were noticeably shorter now, and the darkness only increased Ada's sense of foreboding as another winter of war waited on their doorstep. The sights and sounds of planes, sirens, and antiaircraft guns had become even more intense, suggesting that the conflict was far from over.

She would never become accustomed to the dull thud, the engine vibrations, the roar, and then the crashes that punctuated day and night, but she was training herself to tune it out so that her stomach didn't churn at every sound. It was simply too exhausting to be constantly on alert. There was nothing she could do to save this house or its inhabitants from a misplaced bomb, or worse, an intentional attack. Sometimes she wondered if she'd been given too much responsibility at too young an age—it had become her habit to feel responsible for everyone. She heard Father close the study door and shuffle towards her in his worn slippers.

He sat at the table and stroked his silver goatee as he studied the table decorations. Was he so preoccupied with his work that he had forgotten that it was his birthday? Ada intended to talk to him after dinner about how they might encourage Lina to take some responsibility for the household chores. Father preferred to leave all the domestic details to her, but he didn't seem to realize that she didn't have the authority to force Lina to participate. Father might be a brilliant historian, but he was far too lax in disciplining her sister.

Although his hair was almost completely gray, he retained one patch of his original brown color across the top of his scalp. Ada regularly trimmed the sides and the back, but he was proud of the wave on top, so she left that longer. Sometimes he seemed almost otherworldly in his focus on writing; she was surprised that he had room for vanity about his hair.

He smoothed the damask napkin. His gold wedding band hung loosely on his fingers. "Ada, you have outdone yourself tonight." He pulled at his tie as if it had suddenly become too tight for him.

"Thank you, Father," she said, grateful that he noticed. He still dressed as if he were heading to the university to teach classes, but everything had become worn and shabby.

Lina bounded down the stairs, pushing the table decoration to one side in irritation before she sat.

"Girls, sit down, please. I want to talk to you." Father waited for them to settle in their seats, and then he looked at them through his rimless spectacles. He paused to polish the glasses with his cloth handkerchief before folding the cloth and placing it in his pocket.

Ada remembered practicing ironing those handkerchiefs as a young girl. Later she advanced to shirts and table linens, which took much longer to complete.

Uncomfortable with the silence, Lina broke in. "Guess what?" Lina asked Father. "The Allies are getting close, and the Germans are on the run."

"Lina," Father said, putting his hand over hers to quiet her. "I need to speak now." His blue eyes were serious and held her attention.

His tone startled them. Lina glanced at Ada, who looked confused as well. This didn't feel like a birthday celebration.

"I want you both to know that I have arranged with the bank to provide for you if anything happens to me. The house is debt-free, and an allowance will cover expenses and upkeep. There is also a fund for your education. If you are very careful, this fund will support you for the next ten years. I hope that you will both finish your education and eventually find meaningful work to do. When the war ends, there will be a shift in the currency, but you can talk to my bank about that. The house deed and other financial papers are kept in the metal box in my study cupboard. Do you have any questions?"

"But Father, it's your birthday," Ada said. "Do we need to discuss this now?"

"You need to know what to do if anything happens. You will be on your own, and you will have to work together. That won't always be easy," he paused to look at each one, "but it will be necessary. Difficult times will continue, and you will have to find ways to survive."

Ada watched Lina shift in her seat.

"Ada's just too bossy to work with." Lina smiled to soften her words.

Father looked at her carefully without changing his serious expression. "Lina, you are old enough to help without being asked to share in the work that needs to be done."

Ada's face betrayed how startled she was by Father's tone. Her eyes flicked to the stew, which grew cold as their tense discussion carried on. Father had not yet said grace.

"Let us pray," Father said, bowing his head and folding his hands. Lina put her hands in her lap, and Ada interlaced her fingers and rested her forehead on them.

"Deliver us from evil," Father intoned as he drew to the end of his usual table prayer.

After another silence that was too much for Lina, she looked at Father. "As I was saying," Lina said, "the Allies are getting closer." Her elbows rested on the table as she leaned forward, trying to engage Father in the kind of discussion he usually enjoyed.

When Father did not reply, Ada jumped in. "Where did you hear that?" Ada asked as she dipped the large serving spoon into the red pot filled with lentil stew to fill a soup plate. She passed it to Father, whose hands showed a slight tremor as he accepted the stew and placed it carefully in front of him. The steam curled slowly upwards and fogged his spectacles.

"I heard that in the café. They're planning a parade for Tuesday. It's going to be great fun!"

When Ada passed a plate to Lina, she set it down without looking at it. "Can you believe it? This whole stupid war might be done by next week." When no one responded, Lina sighed loudly. "Is anybody listening?"

Ada served herself and then brought the pan back to the stove. She wished Lina would stop talking.

Lina tapped her spoon on the table. "Ada, people are waiting for me. Can you speed it up?"

Ada sat down and stared at Lina in disbelief. "Don't be rude. It's Father's birthday."

Lina's blue eyes glittered with irritation. "I've told you several times that we're decorating for a surprise party. Don't you ever listen? Father said he didn't mind." Lina looked at her father for confirmation, and he nodded.

They ate in a tense silence. Even Lina busied herself with eating and did not speak.

Lina finished her soup and pushed it away. "I need to get ready. May I be excused?" She couldn't wait to get away. Standing up, she put her soup plate in the sink and then paused to give Father a kiss on his cheek. "I'll have your card ready tomorrow. It took a little longer."

"Thank you, Lina," he said. "Good art takes time," he said with a smile.

Ada watched the interaction with distaste. The planned celebration had fallen far short of her expectations, largely sabotaged by Lina's self-centered plans. Why did Father not see through her? Just when she thought he would be irritated by Lina, he smiled and encouraged her.

How did Lina get to enjoy an endless parade of fun while she had to keep everything running smoothly without complaint?

3.

LINA

Upstairs, Lina hurried to get ready. Every day was the same—Father worked all day and most of the evening in his study while Ada sighed and complained about the housework. Meanwhile, her life was being ruined by this endless war, and no one seemed to care. She was young and deserved to have fun—why didn't they understand that? Father didn't seem concerned about his birthday, so why was Ada making a fuss about it?

At Maarten's house there would be music in the form of well-played records and, if they were lucky, some alcohol to loosen things up. Dancing was so liberating sometimes—especially after a few drinks. Father and Ada could sit and ponder the state of the war, but as far as she was concerned, ignoring it was much better. No one was going to give her back the years that had been stolen from her by this endless war, so she might as well have a good time.

Pulling a well-worn oversize black sweater over her head, Lina added some dark pants. She checked her appearance in the mirror on the back of her closet door. In the past, she'd often been teased about her boyish figure and lack of curves; the weight loss of the past months made her look emaciated with her hip bones protruding and her collarbones exposed. Lina pulled the belt a bit tighter and used a new notch to fasten the buckle. There was not much she could do about it when there was little food to be had.

Lina ran her fingers through her blonde hair that Ada had recently cut into a chin-length bob, shorter in the back but with long bangs that she usually tucked behind each ear, unless she made a side part and swooped the whole thing over to the other side.

Although she'd urged Ada to cut it even shorter, Ada was afraid she would no longer look like a girl. Lina didn't care—being female in this war was a disadvantage. She preferred to be unnoticed as she biked past soldiers and angry mobs.

There had been times in the past when she enjoyed dressing up for dances or parties, but these days it wasn't possible because neither makeup nor clothing were available to anyone unless they had a special relationship with a soldier. *That was not something to flaunt*, Lina thought, thinking of when she had seen former school chums fraternize in dangerous ways with their captors.

She remembered how the other night, when they said good night to Father, he had looked at them fondly. "You," he said to Ada, "are the image of your mother, and you," he said to Lina, "have the perhaps unfortunate challenge of resembling me." She'd looked at Ada and then at Father and knew he was right. "You are both beautiful in your own right," he concluded. He had given each of them a good-night kiss on the cheek and returned to his study. Ada had looked at her with surprise when Father left, but Lina had shrugged. "Sometimes he remembers he has daughters," Lina said with a smile.

Lina pulled open the top drawer of an oak armoire that had come from her *Opa's* farm. Searching for a pair of socks that were still intact, Lina chose a knitted pair that had survived because they were a strange shade of purple. She grabbed her birthday banner that spelled out a minimal but multipurpose greeting of "Happy."

She looked around at the mess in her room and decided to leave it. As she scanned the piles of laundry and papers, she noted the wind pushing falling leaves around the backyard. One tree was already completely bare and exposed to the elements as winter moved forward in lockstep. She closed the blind.

Tucking her hands into her sleeves for warmth, she left the room, banner in hand.

Before she'd even put a foot on the top step to descend, she heard a loud knock on the front door. Some instinct caused her to pause and then take a few steps back. If it was the pesky neighbor Nel, she'd rather not be seen. Nel wouldn't hesitate to lecture her about the dangers of young women going out at night, and if Father heard that he might change his mind about letting her go. The woman thought she had a right to tell them what to do, and Lina resented it tremendously. Not that Father listened to Nel's opinions—it was clear that he didn't care for her.

It was not Nel, however, who was making a racket on the front porch. A loud male voice ordered them in German to open the door. She leaned forward so she could see better while remaining invisible to anyone standing in the foyer. Lina had plenty of childhood practice hiding in that very spot while she eavesdropped on her parents' company long past her bedtime.

Nighttime raids were commonplace—a disgruntled neighbor could make an accusation that would have the Nazis beating down doors and taking captives. So far, they had not been troubled by such incidents. What did they want on this night? She'd heard stories of people evicted from their home to provide the soldiers with rooms. Where would they go if they were evicted? What would she grab if she had a chance to take something with her?

Father and Ada stood in the downstairs hallway filled with obvious hesitation. When Father tipped his head to tell Ada to go upstairs, Ada scurried up the steps to join Lina and gave her sister a wary glance before scuttling next to her. Ada was close enough that Lina could smell the onions she'd cooked for dinner on her clothes.

When Father opened the door, a German officer in uniform and leather boots, accompanied by two soldiers, stepped boldly into the house.

"Herr Van Dijk, you have papers that are of interest to us. Surrender them now," the officer said.

"*Nein,*" Father said quietly. "I have no such papers," he replied in German.

The officer glanced at Father's study to his right. "Search that room," he ordered.

Father stood quietly while the two soldiers turned his study upside down. His arms were folded across his chest—he didn't even flinch when the soldiers threw books and ceramics to the floor.

The crashing sounds of pottery made Ada shudder. Father loved his books, and the vases he had carried in his hand luggage from Turkey.

Lina couldn't believe that they would be so disrespectful of Father's things. He was a harmless professor who kept himself out of the political fray. Several of his colleagues had been arrested for expressing their opposition to the occupation, but he had always remained quiet. What on earth were they looking for? Lina put her hand on Ada's shoulder to reassure her.

Ada's hand was clamped tight over mouth so she wouldn't give them away. Sometimes she had bursts of sneezing. Would they search the rest of the house? Ada looked at Lina in alarm and glanced at the open doors behind her. Where could they hide? Her bedroom door was open, as was Lina's, but Father's was closed. None of those rooms would hide them for long.

"Tip the desk over," ordered the Captain.

The old oak desk groaned and then landed with a thud on its side.

They tossed papers and threw books on the ground.

"We found something," the soldier said as he handed a folder to the Captain who was standing in the doorway of the study. "It says 'Hitler papers.'"

Lina and Ada looked at each other, but they had no idea what that folder might contain. Father had never mentioned such a folder.

The Captain glanced at the contents of the folder and then tucked it under his arm. He looked satisfied that he had the evidence he needed. "We will take you to headquarters for questioning," he told Father. "Take him," he ordered as he turned to the door, and the two soldiers seized Father. Even though he didn't resist, they still held him firmly, one on each arm. He looked frail between the two hulking soldiers.

Father did not look back or give the soldiers any hint that there were others in the house.

When they heard the front door slam, Ada and Lina were still too petrified to move. Lina grabbed Ada's arm and pulled her along to the master bedroom that provided a view of the street. They stood on either side of the window and peered into the darkness below, hoping that no one would spot them and come back to take them as well.

The soldiers walked Father to a black car parked in front of the house and pushed him into the back seat. One soldier got in beside him, and the other one climbed into the driver's seat with the Captain seated to his right.

Father still didn't look back or show any agitation; he seemed resigned to what was happening.

When the car drove away, the street fell silent. Without streetlights or lights from the houses, the darkness was complete.

Lina saw the banner lying on the floor where she had crouched. She scooped it up and put it in her pocket, racing down the stairs with Ada right behind her. When Lina opened the front door, she saw the taillights of the car that was headed towards town. "He's gone," she said, as Ada stood silently beside her.

Although they shivered in the cold, the prospect of the empty house seemed colder.

Lina noticed a blackout curtain pulled slightly to one side across the street where their neighbor Nel lived.

"Nosy bitch," Lina muttered.

"Watch your language, Lina."

Lina glared at her. How could Ada defend that woman? She didn't know what Nel's game was, but she was after something, and Lina didn't trust her. For all she knew, Nel might have been the informer that brought this trouble to their door. People did that all the time to gain favors from the occupiers. These days, loyalty was out of fashion.

Once they could no longer bear the cold, they went inside, Lina first, with Ada following behind. Ada locked the door and checked that the blackout curtains were closed in the living room and in the study.

The study was a mess with books and papers littering the floor. Father's Turkish pottery was shattered, and the frames of photographs were broken.

"Look at this," Ada said, on the verge of tears.

"Just leave it," Lina suggested. "Close the door. Maybe he'll be back in the morning, and he can help us put it back together."

Ada began to cry, holding her head in her hands. "I can't do that. It's a mess. It's an insult to Father to leave it like this."

"I'll take this end," Lina relented with a sigh as she pointed to the desk. There was no point in arguing with Ada.

They grunted as they turned the heavy desk upright.

Lina picked up one of the drawers and inserted it into the desk. "Do you think they'll come back to arrest us?"

"Hopefully they found what they wanted, whatever it was, and they will leave us alone."

"Why did they want that folder?" Lina asked. "Do you know what was in it?"

"Not really—something about Hitler, but I don't know the details."

Lina tried to arrange the books on the bookshelf while Ada swept up the shards of pottery. She then turned to arranging books on Father's shelf—the party was probably starting at Maarten's house right now, and he would be angry that she hadn't kept her promise to help him prepare for the surprise party.

Lina sighed as she tried to arrange the spines of the books to line up against the far edge of the shelf. She felt a heaviness in her body—Father might never return. No matter how carefully they cleaned up his office, he might never again sit at his desk, hunched over a paper, writing with his fountain pen and black ink.

When they finished straightening up the study, the girls returned to the kitchen.

"We have to do the dishes," Ada said. "This is a mess." She stood with her hand on her hip, taking the disorder as a personal insult.

Lina sighed loudly. This was not how she had expected to spend the evening. Lina looked at the table set for a celebration and the empty soup plates that had held Ada's stew. Father's napkin was carefully folded and placed beside his bowl. *Did he know this was coming?* she thought. *What secrets was he keeping?*

Ada's hope that the whole thing was a mistake might comfort her tonight, but Lina had a terrible feeling this would not end well.

She dried the dishes while Ada washed, neither one in the mood for conversation. Lina took the red and white checked tea towel, now faded from laundering, and hung it on the rack by the stove. "Sleep well," she said to Ada as she walked to the stairway.

The jute runner on the stairs was worn by years of feet ascending and descending. She'd always disliked the way the rough rug felt through her socks or bare feet, but these days it was worn smooth. To Lina, the staircase was merely a place of transit in and out of the house, but she had a feeling that for Ada, the banister and staircase were an essential symbol of belonging and order. A stairway to nowhere, Lina thought, unless it was away from here.

4.

LINA

Lina climbed out of bed and dragged the top blanket with her to guard against the morning chill. An early cold snap had brought an abrupt end to the lingering September warmth. She winced as her feet hit the frigid wooden boards.

Five days had passed since Father's arrest; they still hadn't heard a word. Ada was on high alert, startled by every sound, but Lina felt like every day that passed without any communication was a confirmation that Father was gone forever.

Ribbons of fog drifted aimlessly over the yard, obscuring her view of the back fence. How were they supposed to stay hopeful when there was no evidence that things would improve? If anything, conditions kept getting worse, with restrictions on everything from food to fuel. All that excitement about the war ending had been nonsense—she needed to learn to not be so naive the next time she heard that kind of rumor.

The constant rain in the past week permeated every corner of the house with damp and cold. Lina felt her joints aching and wished Ada would fire up the woodstove, but Ada said she was worried about having enough fuel to get through the winter. Ada worried about everything—it was so annoying.

Ada had asked her friend Lucas if he could make some discrete inquiries, but there was no trace—Father had simply disappeared into the Nazi system. What Lucas did know, he might be reluctant to share with them, perhaps afraid that any knowledge of their father's business would put them both in danger. He told them that the soldiers probably had what they wanted and would not return. If that was meant to reassure them, it was not successful.

A few days after the arrest, Ada told Lina that she felt burdened by the care of the household. "Why didn't you just say so?" Lina had asked. "We can make a list of chores and share the work." Ada especially dreaded the food hunts because she felt guilty trading Mother's beloved treasures for a few carrots or potatoes. "Don't you think Mother would want us to do whatever it took to stay alive?" Lina had asked. For her, practical necessity was more important than nostalgia.

That afternoon, Ada prepared dinner. "I'm afraid they will come back to arrest us."

"It has almost been a week, so maybe they have moved on. But if they decide to pick us up, there isn't anything we can do about it." Lina said as she watched Ada chop some carrots. "Do you need help?" Lina asked.

Ada looked at her skeptically and then handed her the knife.

"Don't expect those carrots to be perfect," Lina said as she pointed the knife towards the tiny squares that Ada had made. She was relieved to see a fleeting smile pass over Ada's face.

"We have to help ourselves," Lina said. "Or starve. However long this war takes, I intend for us to be there at the end of it." Perhaps it was a bit too enthusiastic, but it seemed that Ada needed to hear something encouraging. Ever since Father's arrest, she had seemed listless and depressed. Neither of them could afford to give up now, and it was clear that it would take a combined effort to survive the winter. "Father expects us to do our best."

Ada agreed. "That's true. We can't let them win. Whatever you find I will cook, and hopefully it will keep us going. We are heading into winter, and I am afraid of what will happen if we can't find food to eat." Ada turned to watch the liquid in the pot begin to bubble.

"You have done your best to preserve food and to cook in new ways. We will just keep going and do our best."

"I am sorry I have been so pitiful. It's just so hard not to know where Father is kept and how he is managing." Ada leaned against the kitchen counter and looked at the floor.

"I understand, but we can't linger on what we don't know. I'll bike to some farms," Lina said. She would be glad to get out of the house. Jos was busy with the farm and with his side business repairing Nazi vehicles. Since the only thing he wanted to do during his free time was hang out with the guys and mix up bootleg alcohol, Lina didn't really feel like spending all her time with him. She was certain there was more to life than that—but none of it was available to her.

She had to be careful not to express her frustration around Jos and his friends, or they would mock her endlessly for her ambitions. If they were satisfied with their little black-market schemes and deals, she wished them well, but she didn't intend to stick around once things finally returned to normal, hopefully because their side declared victory. The alternative was unthinkable. She just hoped she wouldn't be too old to start over whenever that day came.

The house felt empty without Father. Even though he had spent long days in his study, the house had felt anchored by his presence. Now, however, they were adrift in this large house that no longer felt tethered. At least, for Lina, it felt like a ghost ship that was heading nowhere.

Neither of them wanted to admit how worried they were—it became more real when one of them said it aloud. Lina needed action to counter the feeling of helplessness, and she hoped that she might spur Ada to do the same. They had to put themselves in charge of their situation and focus on survival.

Lina regretted all the bickering she'd engaged in with Ada over curfews and chores. Ada also felt frustrated by the constraints imposed by war in different ways, primarily because she longed to return to her studies. Although Lina didn't share her desire for formal learning, she could sympathize with the frustration of not moving forward with one's goals.

These days the challenges of procuring food took most of her energy—the irregular food intake reduced her energy precisely when she needed it to bike further to locate farms that still had food supplies. The change in season left them vulnerable to colds and coughs. Ada brewed teas and herbal concoctions with rose hips and parsley and cloves to try to boost their immunity, but Lina didn't feel much improvement. What they needed was a large portion of the goulash their housekeeper used to make, filled with chunks of meat and potatoes, simmered for hours in the orange enamel braising pan that had been part of the kitchen since her childhood. She closed her eyes and remembered the taste and texture of meat that had been simmered for hours in onions and beef stock.

She needed to convince Ada to fight the hopelessness that was as pervasive as the autumn chill. Ada was usually ready to take on whatever chores or volunteer work that required her attention. But then, the war had changed them all; how could anyone live through such misery and not be changed?

Lina relied on Ada to take the lead on the domestic front. If she gave up, they wouldn't stand a chance. Ada was a fighter in her own way, and she intended to encourage her.

How she missed Father—if he were here, he would have talked to Ada and praised her efforts. But now it was up to her to encourage Ada and keep her engaged in the struggle. Father had once commented that she was childish for criticizing Ada to make herself feel better. She had to find a different way of doing things.

Lina picked up her pants and sweater from the floor where she had dropped them the night before. Usually quite skilled at ignoring the mess, this morning the clutter irritated her. The bookshelves contained a miscellaneous collection of school texts that reminded her of claustrophobic classrooms and disappointing grades on her assignments. Perhaps she needed to clear this out before she could start a new life.

She pulled down an armful of old textbooks and made a pile on the floor. Maybe Ada could use them to light the woodstove, although she'd never consent to destroying a book. Lina never wanted to see them again. That life was over—she wasn't going to go back to the rules and restrictions of formal schooling. She wanted to learn on the job from someone who would be a mentor and see her potential; sitting at a desk was a waste of time.

Clearing layers of pictures, postcards, and messages from her bulletin board, she filled the garbage pail beside the desk. She set aside the photographs she'd taken for the last school fashion show. Birthday cards, notes from friends, a few sketches she'd made for a fashion show—none of that mattered anymore. That life was finished, and she intended to burn the remnants.

A travel poster of the Eiffel Tower remained in place over her bed— it would serve as a beacon to guide her journey. Even though the edges had curled up and the colors had faded, the poster was a map to realizing her dreams.

As the piles of books and trash spilled over the floor, there wasn't time to finish what she had started. She was due to work her shift at the café in half an hour, and she didn't dare to be late. Her boss, Lars, was looking for an excuse to fire her—she had no intention of making it easy for him. He had a reputation for being a demanding employer who liked to replace his staff frequently with newer and younger female faces, who were willing to tolerate his roving hands. It was clear that she was not interested, and if that job ended, she'd be relieved to never see him again.

5.

LINA

THE next morning, Lina spooned porridge into her mouth and sat hunched over the bowl hoping it might provide warmth on this cold September morning.

Ada had made a chart and pinned it to the cupboard, marking the days that had passed since Father's arrest—six days so far. Lina had no intention of participating in that sad enumeration of Father's absence; she continued to hope that Father was surviving wherever he was.

While Ada chopped nuts on a wooden cutting board, the kitchen filled with a rhythmic sound reminiscent of days when Lydia, their former housekeeper, would prepare and chop ingredients.

A knock on the back door interrupted the rhythm. They looked at each other in alarm but simultaneously realized that soldiers would not use the back door.

Lina leaned her chair back to see who it was but did not bother to get up. "It's Lucas," she said with an obvious lack of enthusiasm. She hadn't even washed her face yet, and she was wearing one of Father's bulky wool sweaters over her pajamas. Why should she care what she looked like if he was there for Ada and was only being polite to her? He seemed to show up regularly—maybe he had promised their father to look after them in case he was arrested.

"Come in," Ada said as she opened the door. "Would you like some tea?"

"That would be nice. Morning, Lina," Lucas said as he entered the kitchen and pulled out the chair across from her. He was taller than Ada and lean with big shoulders.

Lina grunted hello and slid her legs off the chair so that Lucas could sit on it. The chair seemed small for him, but he managed to make himself fit.

While Ada poured the tea into three cups, the scent of lavender and mint rose from the pot.

In the old days, as a graduate student of Father's, Lucas had been a regular visitor to their house. Since then, many students had been sent to work camps in Germany, but Lucas had secured an exemption due to a previous bout of tuberculosis.

He was apparently deeply involved in the local resistance although he preferred not to talk about it. Ada explained that he took seriously the safety of the network's members and knew that one slip could result in many arrests and deaths. Despite the weight of his responsibilities, he brought them any food he could find, and those donations were welcome.

Lina was annoyed at herself for being curious about him. He was such a contrast to her boyfriend Jos—Lucas didn't seem to mind helping with dishes or carrying a serving tray. Was he attracted to Ada?

Ada seemed to come alive in his presence, especially when they talked about ideas and books. Lina felt quite excluded by their discussions. Although Ada intended to study science, she had a solid understanding of history as well. Perhaps the editing she had done for Father had broadened her education. While Lucas discussed a book he'd recently read with Ada, Lina continued to work on a pencil sketch of a pitcher filled with dried milkweed pods. *Boring, boring,* she remarked to herself.

"I'm sorry about your father," Lucas said, "but I haven't been able to find out where he is being held."

Ada nodded slowly. "Please keep trying. If we could write him or send him a parcel, I would feel so much better."

Lucas nodded. "I will keep asking. Tell me once more how that evening's events unfolded."

Lina looked up from her sketch to listen to this part of the conversation.

"They turned his office upside down, quite literally; they turned the desk over and threw things on the floor that had been on the shelves. The desk apparently had a secret drawer where he had hidden a folder that they referred to as the Hitler papers. The soldiers were quite satisfied to have located it, so they seemed to know what they were looking for. Then the Captain said they had to take him for further questioning. Father did not resist or offer any explanation—he simply went with them and didn't look back."

Lucas looked at Lina, and she nodded to confirm the account.

"Do you know anything about why they arrested him?" Lina asked.

Lucas hesitated. "I can tell you this much," he said. "A few months ago, your father received an envelope from a Professor Dieter Krauss, a colleague in Germany who feared he was about to be arrested. The envelope contained a folder."

"What was in it?" Lina asked.

"Apparently, the folder contained evidence that Hitler was mentally unstable and unfit to lead, which gave those who wanted to get rid of him a good excuse for a coup. There's some dissension in the ranks as different groups anticipate a change in leadership. They are scrambling to get ready for whatever is next because any vacuum in leadership will create an unstable situation. This file was intended to help depose Hitler."

"Why didn't Father just tell that professor to send his papers somewhere else? Why get arrested for someone else's secrets?" Lina asked.

"He felt obliged to help his colleague. Years ago, this fellow spent his sabbatical here for a year, during which they became close friends."

"I think I remember meeting him," Ada said.

"I don't," Lina replied.

Lucas continued with the story. "After his sabbatical they corresponded regularly to discuss history, the changes in Germany, and their personal lives. When your Father started to work on an edited volume critical of Nazi ideology, this professor helped locate other German academics who might want to contribute. Your Father felt indebted to him and agreed to keep the file until he received further instructions."

"Why didn't Father just burn that folder? He was putting all of us at risk. Everybody knows Hitler is crazy, so that would not be worth getting killed for." Lina paused. "How are we supposed to survive without Father?" Lina asked. "Is that what he was talking about that last night at dinner?"

"I guess so," Ada said.

Lina still had questions. "How did those soldiers know Father was keeping that folder?"

"We don't know. It is possible that the German professor was captured and forced to reveal the location of the document."

Ada turned to Lucas. "Thanks for letting us know. If you get the sense that we are in imminent danger as a result, I hope you will give us warning."

Lucas nodded. "I will do my best to help you stay safe." To further reassure them, he continued, "I will tell you if I find anything out about his arrest. In the meantime, let me know if you notice anything strange. If you are being followed, or if anyone turns up to search the house, please tell me."

"We were hoping they had lost interest in this place," Lina said, "and in us."

"Let's hope so, but never let down your guard."

Ada and Lina watched him carefully to see if he would reveal anything else, but he looked down at his teacup and said nothing more.

Lina darted glances from her sketchbook to study Lucas from across the table—he'd probably told them all that he knew. Still, it was annoying that he was more informed about Father's activities than they were. Maybe Father had only wanted to share secrets with another man. That thought made her resent Lucas even more.

"Why are there so many delays in the Allied advance?" Lina asked him.

"I don't know what's going to happen, but look at *Reichskomissar* Seyss-Inquart—he sent his wife, Gertrude, back to Austria three days ago even though he forbade others to leave," Lucas said. "Thousands of National Socialist collaborators are defying that order; they are fleeing, leaving everything behind. They are calling it 'Mad Tuesday.'"

"Good riddance," Lina said. "Does that mean Police Chief Vriend and his wife have left?" Lina disliked their neighbors who lived at the end of the street and would be happy to see them go.

Lucas shook his head. "Vriend anticipates promotion to regional superintendent, so he's not leaving. He and his friends hope to have prominent places in the administration when the anticipated Nazi victory happens. What they don't understand is that there will be no Nazi victory and thus no promotion."

"But why haven't the Allies been able to get here by now?" Ada asked.

Lucas sighed. "There are problems with supplies and rivers and bridges. Winter is coming, and it will make everything more difficult. Perhaps the generals don't agree on the plan. We just don't know what's happening on the ground, and information is terribly scarce, but it's important to remain hopeful. You must be cautious in believing any information you receive because not only are the reports outdated but they are often meant to mislead."

"Are you saying that it'll be spring before they liberate us?" Lina asked. "Do you consider that hopeful?"

Lucas didn't react to her challenge. "That's what I suspect. Even though many Germans are starting to realize that they ultimately will be defeated, they'll try to destroy everything on their way out," Lucas said.

"Thanks for that. I feel so much better," Lina said sarcastically. *Why did he bother to drop by just to bring bad news?*

"We have to hope for the best," Ada said, looking at Lucas for agreement.

Lina couldn't see why Ada bothered with Lucas; in fact, watching them interact made her feel even grimmer. *Another year of my life wasted.* It was fine for Ada, she loved this house and had Lucas to entertain her, but the thought of enduring another year before moving to Paris was intolerable. She wanted the distraction of a romantic interest, something different from the predictable times with Jos, but that was not going to happen.

Lucas finished his tea and stood up. "Thanks for the tea. I have some notes for the newsletter if you have time." He pulled some papers out of his canvas bag.

"I'll get to it as soon as I can," Ada said as she glanced at the handwritten notes, squinting to try to read the writing. Typing was the easy part—the challenge was understanding the handwritten pages.

Lucas took his coat from the hook by the door and put it on. "Thanks for doing this," he replied.

Lina watched them with curiosity. *Why did Ada type and edit a newsletter for Lucas? Did he pay her?* It was annoying to watch them sending meaningful looks to each other, thinking she wouldn't notice. If Ada was involved with him, why did it have to be a big secret?

But it wasn't only Lucas that annoyed her, she was also jealous of Ada, who was doing something to contribute to the war effort. That newsletter she put together was circulated to many people who relied on it for crucial information about the war. What did she have to contribute other than washing glasses in a café and serving undrinkable coffee?

"Thanks for the good news," Lina said.

Lucas ignored her sarcasm, said his goodbyes, and left.

"You could be nicer to him," Ada said, gathering up the teacups. "The war is not his fault."

"If I have to blame somebody, why not him?" Lina took out her frustration on her sketch, moving the pencil heavily across the page, ruining the lines of the drawing.

Ada glanced at the sketch and sighed. She washed the teacups in the sink and let them drain on a tray. "What are you doing today?"

"It's my day off. Maybe I'll sleep all day."

Ada looked anxious. "But you will try to find food? We have very little left."

Lina looked at her and sighed. "I'll see what I can find." She closed the sketch book and stood up. "Maybe I'll steal some food," Lina said. "That way you can keep your plates and spoons."

"*Nee toch*," replied Ada in disapproval. She wiped her wet hands on the apron.

"Just kidding," Lina said as she gathered up her pencils and sketchbook. Ada sometimes had no sense of humor—it was hard to believe that they were sisters, they were just so different. It would have been so nice to live with someone who knew how to have fun. "I'll go on the food hunt this morning, and then you can figure out what to make for dinner." She knew it wasn't going to be easy—her recent attempts had involved biking much further into the countryside, hunting for farmers who still had some food and who were interested in the objects with which she wanted to barter.

Things were getting steadily worse—even the black-market vendors had trouble getting enough to sell. Food theft was common as children stole from bakery carts and vendors, going out in pairs to create a distraction. As people grew more desperate, their tactics became more aggressive. If she didn't step up, they'd have nothing to eat. Lina knew that Ada expected her to play by the rules, but unfortunately she didn't seem to realize that those rules were no longer in effect. Fear and desperation turned people into animals struggling for their own survival. Lina didn't intend to play nice—she always carried a knife in her sock and kept her wits about her. Some of her friends had been reckless at the beginning of the war, and they had paid a heavy price.

"Don't do anything crazy," Ada warned when she saw the defiant look on Lina's face.

"I never do," Lina said, "unless I'm really hungry." And she was hungry. She planned to do whatever it took to find food and pay with any material objects a farmer would accept. That was the big difference between her and Ada. Her sister wanted to keep everything intact so that she could eventually recreate life exactly the way it had been before the war. By contrast, Lina planned to escape the minute the war ended, and she wouldn't miss any of Mother's precious things. Instead, she planned to hunt for mismatched plates and glasses in the French flea markets.

She unlocked her bike in the shed and promised herself that the minute the war ended, she would find transportation to Paris. Those soldiers would be so full of their victory, they'd happily supply her with cigarettes. What a grand way to enter Paris, escorted by a truckful of American soldiers and flashing her silk stockings and red lipstick. This was the dream she had to keep alive, puffing on those embers and adding fuel to keep the fire burning. Without a dream, she would fall into a very dark cavern from which there was no escape.

6.

LINA

IN the past weeks, hundreds of planes from England had flown overhead. In the café, Lina heard someone explain that the activity was due to a ten-day campaign titled Operation Market Garden. Although she was glad to know that the Allies were mounting campaigns, Lina wasn't going to risk thinking the war was over. It was dangerous to want something as much as she wanted this war to end—and if Lucas was correct, they might still face a long winter.

When the Canadians, British, and Americans finally marched into town and chased out every Nazi, then she might accept that they'd been liberated, but she hoped that when they finally arrived, they wouldn't find the remnants of bombed out buildings filled with starved skeletons.

There seemed to be no limit to the evil the occupiers were willing to perpetrate. Lucas had heard stories about death camps throughout Germany and Poland and elsewhere—it made no sense that one group of people would try to extinguish another just because they had different beliefs or rituals or physical characteristics. Hatred prowled on the streets of their town, ready to attack anything that was seen as a threat. Lucas had warned them to trust no one, and that had become her guiding principle. She could only conclude that someone must have betrayed Father.

When Lina arrived home, Lucas was already there for dinner and was busy setting the table. Lina's first thought was that they looked like any comfortable couple making their evening supper. "You must have a short work day," she said to him. "Weren't you just here?"

"Lina," Ada reprimanded her, "Lucas is our guest."

As usual, he ignored Lina's comments intended to provoke him. He never said much about his personal life, but according to Ada he lived in one of the student houses on the *Oude Rijn*. Did he have roommates, or had they all left the city? Lina didn't want to be curious about his life, but what else did she have to think about?

"Have you heard anything more about the railroad strike? Someone at the community kitchen told me that maybe thirty thousand people will participate," Ada said as she stood at the kitchen counter and peeled the potatoes Lucas had brought. Lina sat at the table to cut up apples into quarters, leaving the peel on as Ada had instructed. She had foraged the windfall apples in a farm field, and even though bruised and rotten in places, Ada planned to make applesauce from them.

Ada sautéed some kale greens to mix with the potatoes once they were cooked and mashed.

"The government-in-exile thinks that shutting down the Dutch rail lines will delay German troop and supply transports," Lucas said.

"I don't think it's a good strategy," Lina said, but no one was listening to her. Lucas only listened to Ada. She wasn't university educated like the other two, but they could at least invite her to join the discussion. Were her opinions so juvenile that no one wanted to hear them?

"The *Reichskommisar* will interpret the strike as a blow to Nazi prestige and control," Lucas continued. "He will initiate measures to further punish our people."

All this talk was useless, Lina thought. Anyone could see what was happening and how it affected the lives of her friends. The Germans were desperate for workers, probably because most of their workers were already killed or stuck in Russia somewhere. They were rounding up men to send to Germany.

To avoid that, some of her friends had gone into hiding. She didn't blame them—there was little chance they'd return from work camps. Despite all that, Jos was confident that nothing would happen to him—as an unofficial mechanic and seller of homemade cigarettes, the occupiers had an interest in keeping him around. All the farm fellows felt confident that their role in food production would keep them safe from German labor camps. Lina was shocked that they spoke about the occupiers as if they were friendly acquaintances. "Ah, Lina, relax! They are just farm lads like us, who were conscripted to fight a rotten war." Lina didn't think that was accurate, but she decided not to argue with him.

That confidence could be his undoing—no one was safe from the arbitrary killings and violence. She had once found his cockiness attractive, but recently his attitude seemed foolhardy.

Ada had given Lucas a small screwdriver and a few pieces of jewelry that needed repairs while she cooked. He didn't mind fixing things. While Lucas tinkered, he and Ada exchanged news about people they knew from the university, and Lina studied the photographs that hung on the wall beside the table.

Lina wished she had taken her camera with her to photograph the apple orchard that she had visited earlier, showing the windfall apples that had created a carpet on the ground below. She remembered playing tag years ago in between the apple trees at her grandfather's orchard when they visited while Father helped with the harvest. They ran around the buckets filled with apples and dodged the ladders perched against the trees.

A few months ago, when she had started spending more time Jos and his friends, they all assumed she was his girlfriend. She wasn't so sure about that, but she hadn't corrected anyone either. He was entertaining at times, but sometimes she became weary of the same old jokes and stories. She wanted to ask him if he had any curiosity about the world outside of their town, but that would only irritate him.

Lately Jos had been very busy with the farm as well as his other businesses. His father's death from a heart attack meant the family depended on him to keep things going. In a way, she didn't mind. He was fun, but she didn't need to see him every day.

The four black-and-white photographs on the wall were taken one summer when she and Father had biked through the nearby lakes area, where the tulip farms stretched like colored ribbons across the fields. He'd framed her pictures as a birthday surprise, and she'd been pleased that he thought they were good enough to frame. Father had never been effusive with his praise, but when he said something was good, he meant it.

One of her favorite photos displayed a farmer who smoked his pipe on a bench outside a café, where he had a view of the farm fields. All his years of outdoor work were etched in his face—along with an expression of deep sadness. Perhaps he missed the rhythm of farm life.

Lina wished she had that kind of passion for some kind of work. She seemed to be adept at gliding over things, like a speed skater on a frozen canal, jumping over the cracks and bumps and feeling the wind on her face. It was fine for her to criticize Jos, but perhaps she was the one who was superficial.

Someday she'd find a job that grabbed her interest and gave her direction—she intended to do more than waitress. To figure that out, she knew she needed to get away from this town and the people she knew to make a new start.

Although she talked about Paris as the ideal place to start her real life, she realized she had neither the skills nor the language ability to make that happen. Still, it was important to have a goal—and be willing to adapt if it were unattainable.

Ada probably thought she was a fool, talking about Paris as if anyone there would welcome her. Ada had sailed through school at the top of her class and made an effortless transition to university. Having identified science as her field of study, it all fell into place for her.

How did people manage to choose lives of adventure? She knew no one who managed that, but there had to be something more to life than warworn clothes and drab landscapes. Lucas probably thought he was some great adventurer, but he didn't seem to do much more than look after that newsletter that Ada typed and visit them for tea.

Even this house felt suffocating in its drabness. When Lina looked around the kitchen, the paint had started to peel on the ceiling, and plate-sized portions threatened to land on the table; the tablecloth was so worn and faded that she wished she could just get rid of it.

Lina glanced up from her sketch as Lucas helped Ada dry the teacups in advance of dinner. Perhaps he had grown up doing chores, but most of the fellows she knew would never help like that. Lucas seemed to feel at home—maybe they were like sisters to him, and he could relax in their presence. Ada and Lucas were so busy talking, they didn't even seem to notice that she had not offered to help. What if she interrupted their conversation and said, "Lucas, give me a job. I can be trusted, and I have a camera. What can I do for your network?"

Lina knew that Ada would look surprised, and Lucas might laugh in her face. That would be hard to take. He probably saw her as Ada's little sister, unable to carry out any risky mission. Because she still had the café job and the challenge of food hunting, she didn't have a lot of free time. She had to think about it some more and give him some examples of how she might fit into the war effort. Maybe he didn't believe women should work for their country—it would be horrible to find that he had such archaic ideas.

Lina continued to sketch the tree in the backyard while her thoughts wandered. Ada and Lucas discussed a novel written before the war by a Russian author. The potatoes rocked in the boiling water, and the steam clouded the kitchen windows. The simmering applesauce filled the room with a fragrance that reminded her of the apple pies their housekeeper had baked on Saturdays. She finished her sketch and started another when Ada asked her to clear her things because they were ready to eat.

Although they tried to eat slowly, they were famished. Their simple supper was finished too quickly—they ate every speck of the mashed potatoes with kale, apple sauce, and the small tin of smoked fish that Lucas had contributed.

"I guess there are no leftovers," Lucas joked.

Ada invited him to stay and play cards, but he had another obligation. Ada handed him his coat, and he shrugged into it. He arranged to pick up the typing he had given to Ada. Lina tuned them out as they chatted by the door—Ada's story about the incompetent supervisor at the soup kitchen was something she'd heard several times before.

The color had leached out of daily life and left them holding faded dreams in a dingy world. There was another party at Maarten's this evening—she wished she felt excited, but it was little more than an excuse to get out of the house. Sometimes she felt like she was sitting in the waiting room of a cold and drafty station waiting for a train that never appeared.

7.

ADA

"Lina, wake up. You asked me to get you up early." From the doorway, Ada surveyed the chaos in Lina's room and frowned. Since Father's arrest eight days before, she hadn't been in Lina's room to see what a mess she had made.

Fast asleep, Lina lay sprawled on her back and snored lightly. Although her ivory wool blanket had shifted to the floor along with her pillow, she slept, oblivious to the morning chill in the unheated room.

Over the bed hung a poster of the Eiffel Tower. Her oak desk was covered with old magazines, sketchbooks, and pencils. There were piles of textbooks and clothes on the floor. On the top of the bookshelf stood a Leica camera.

Lina moaned and rolled towards the wall, felt around for the blanket without opening her eyes.

Ada crossed the room and shook her shoulder. "You're going to be late." She had to get her up—she would lose her job if she didn't show up on time. The last thing Ada wanted was a grumpy Lina who was home all day because she had nowhere to go.

Lina rolled onto her back and rubbed her eyes. "What time is it?" she asked in a hoarse voice.

"It's eleven."

"Thanks. I'll get up." She rolled to her side and yawned as she sat on the side of the bed.

When Ada opened the curtains, Lina covered her eyes and groaned.

Ada returned to the doorway of the room, making sure that Lina didn't crawl back into bed. "Have you been doing some cleaning?" she asked.

Lina glanced at the pile of books. "Just throwing away my text books. I won't ever need them again."

"But you might want to review them when the war ends. You will have forgotten so much."

"I'm not going back to school. Ever." Lina had one arm in her shirt as she glared at her sister.

"I see." Ada walked away. She returned to the kitchen where their neighbor, Nel, was testing new recipes for the Food Council. Because many people didn't know how to adapt to the scarcity of staples and other foods, the pamphlet was intended to encourage them to try new ingredients.

Although she didn't admit it to Nel, Ada had lost faith in the project—she had tasted some of the dishes, and they were inedible. Even when she tried to add flavors that would make the food palatable, nothing helped. If only she had some grains to grind into the mix or supplemental nuts or dates to add flavor, she might be able to produce something acceptable, but there was nothing to work with. Why wasn't the government better prepared to deal with a food crisis? Without the community agencies and local networks running soup kitchens, people would already be starving, but without some more supplies, even those options would fall away.

In August when Nel saw Ada's notes on new recipes, she wanted to show them immediately to the Food Council. She was eager to impress people, insisting that her name appear on any final publication. Ada was uninterested in such accolades, seeking only to help, so she didn't complain when Nel took most of the credit.

Ada was willing to overlook Nel's self-interest—if Nel thought she could build a career based on a rudimentary pamphlet with a few recipes, then Ada wished her well. Her ambitions seemed to be out of step with her abilities. Ada told herself not to be so critical, but Nel seemed to have few ideas of her own and showed no shame at taking Ada's work.

Although Lina had been suspicious of Nel's intentions from the beginning, Ada realized that she had initially been flattered by Nel's interest in her work. Since then, it had become apparent that Nel's ambitions were not matched by her ability. After only one year at the university,

Ada's eyes had been opened to the depth of learning required to become an expert in any field.

Last summer, Nel had shared that she wanted a job in any governmental department that dealt with food and agriculture. When her husband died five years ago, Nel had unfulfilled vocational ambitions. Her husband had been dependent on her, especially when his diabetes resulted in double amputation. After he passed, the war interrupted her plans to apply for ministry jobs. She felt the time had finally come to obtain a good government job. Ada could understand her frustration at having her dream deferred for so long, but she wasn't convinced Nel had the necessary skills. In any case, this was not the time to look for a job in any government department.

Nel's political ambitions were tied to the National Socialist movement. Nel had invited her to a meeting, and Ada had politely declined. If she was trying to recruit her, she had picked the wrong person. Lucas had warned her to be careful around Nel and her friends. Ada was very careful, but she also wanted to foster some trust because Nel had promised to ask her friends if anyone knew where Father was being held. As long as Nel had that potential, Ada knew she had to keep cordial relations with her.

Lina barely disguised her dislike for Nel whenever she visited their house. Ada was reluctant to admit to Lina that she was using Nel as much as the woman was using her—it made her seem manipulative, and she didn't like to think of herself as that kind of person. Mother used to talk about some of her friends in terms of what they could do for her, and those conversations had always made her wince. Mother had kept track of which friends owed her favors, and she fretted over that list endlessly.

The times were different now; war had stripped away the veneer of polite care, leaving people to fend for themselves. She was no better than anyone else, and that was humbling.

While upstairs, Ada quickly straightened her bedroom and the bathroom—even though there was no good reason for Nel to come upstairs, Ada still imagined Mother's voice admonishing her for leaving a mess.

When she returned to the kitchen, she was surprised to see that Nel was not there, so she tiptoed down the hall to see where she was. Maybe she'd gone home to get something.

After checking the small washroom in the hall and the living room, Ada started to return to the kitchen when she noticed that Father's study door was ajar. She paused nearby and waited. Her suspicion was confirmed by the sound of a drawer closing. Ada covered her mouth with her hand, the ugliness of Nel's self-interest now so obvious it stung. How did Nel think she could get away with this, knowing that both girls were home and could appear at any moment?

Ada hurried back to the kitchen and focused on writing a recipe. She would pretend she hadn't noticed, but she intended to keep an eye on her nosy neighbor. A few minutes later, Nel tiptoed into the small washroom to run the water and flush the toilet.

When she returned to the kitchen, Ada looked up in surprise from her notebook. "Everything all right?" she asked.

Nel shook her head. "Some of the sugar beets didn't agree with my stomach."

Ada nodded with false sympathy, but she wondered what Nel had been looking for. Was she following someone's orders or her own curiosity? What would anyone hope to find in Father's study since the soldiers had searched and tossed almost every inch of it? She'd cleaned the room from top to bottom and rearranged his books and files. If there had been anything interesting, Ada would have noticed. She hoped that the soldiers had lost interest and moved on to other targets, but perhaps that was just wishful thinking.

Yesterday, Lucas told Ada about an incident in the building where Father's office was located. The faculty secretary frequently entered the building through a back door for which she still retained a key. She duplicated the newsletter for Lucas in the basement. When she heard boots in the hall, she hid in a supply closet. Once the soldiers left, she saw that Father's office had been left in chaos. She didn't dare clean up after their search lest they realize that someone had access to the building, but the utter disregard for his books and papers shocked her. The lack of respect no longer surprised Ada, but she couldn't imagine what else they wanted. The prospect of soldiers turning up at their house again made her anxious.

Why hadn't Father trusted her more? Now she was left with a gnawing sense of dread, preparing for something she could neither see nor control. The days were markedly shorter, and the damp penetrated every corner of the house. Her internal furnace fought to generate the necessary warmth. The chill made it more difficult to resist the sense of hopelessness that had grown deep roots into her spirit.

She thought back to the days after Mother's death when Father had asked her to take over responsibility for the household. Their housekeeper had already returned home when war was imminent. That day, Father sat with Ada at the table and cleaned his glasses, revealing dark circles beneath his eyes.

"Ada," he said, "we will have to move forward without your mother. I am hoping that you can take responsibility for the house and for your sister. I know you have already done so much these past months."

Ada looked at him with dread. "But Father, I don't know how to run a household. How will I know when to clean and cook and how to manage Lina? It's too much."

He had put his hand over hers. "I am not an expert in these matters, but I remember that my mother organized the housework by doing a chore on each day of the week and resting on Sunday. On Mondays she did the laundry, and on Tuesday she cleaned the floors. And so on. Maybe you can make a schedule that fits with your classes and other activities, and that will help you to organize things."

"But Father . . . ," she protested.

He gave her an encouraging smile and patted her hand. "Your mother and I agreed that you are more than able to take care of things. I trust you, and I know you will do your best."

Ada looked at him, and he seemed utterly sincere. She wished she could share his certainty. He had always been patient with her, providing encouragement, sometimes in opposition to her Mother. He looked so vulnerable that she knew she had no choice but to agree. He gave her a hug and returned to his study, leaving her to draw up a chart to guide her amateur housecleaning efforts. It wasn't as if Mother would return to inspect things. She immediately felt ashamed of that thought and concentrated on the weekly chart of duties. The biggest challenge, she thought, was to keep Lina out of trouble.

8.

ADA

THAT same morning, Ada picked up her notebook and showed Nel what she had written for the recipe. She glanced at the kitchen clock, worried that Lina had fallen back asleep, but she relaxed when she heard footsteps upstairs. Worries ran through her mind constantly—Father, Lina, and food were the main ones.

"How much liquid was used?" Nel asked. When Ada didn't answer, she repeated the question. "Are you listening?"

"Sorry, I was thinking of something else," Ada replied. She was distracted—all she could think about was Father—where was he being kept, what were they asking him to do? Did he have more secrets? She glanced at the chart she had made to track Father's days away from them—eight days so far. Maintaining a friendly attitude in the face of Nel's snooping took a lot of energy.

In addition, she knew that this project with Nel was a waste of time. The shortages had rendered her previous recipes obsolete. She had mistakenly assumed that certain staples would remain available to them, but that was not the case. No one predicted that things would deteriorate to this point. Everyone suffered—the aged and infirm, pregnant women, and children of all ages. People didn't want to learn new ways to prepare food—they just needed enough to survive.

At the beginning of the war, the rationing system had supplied some of the basics—including bread, butter, and skimmed milk. Now that those were unavailable, despair was written on faces.

To make up for the lack of vegetables, the Food Council recommended the consumption of tulip bulbs. Ada had never been in favor of using bulbs as a food source—evidence suggested that the inner core was poisonous. Sugar beets were even more unappetizing in her opinion, but people needed something to cook. Bulbs and beets required a long cooking process to make them digestible; fuel shortages or restrictions made that impossible. She was already tired of scrubbing and grating beets for soup in the community kitchen. Boiled brown peas were equally unappetizing.

Ada felt let down by the government-in-exile in London. They celebrated the successful train strike while ignoring the fact that shutting down the rail transport of food had devastating effects on the population. Ada didn't understand their strategy—ordinary people paid a hefty price for the strike action. The military leaders were out of touch with the daily suffering of the people, and that was inexcusable. Her faith that governments and leaders would do the right thing and care for the needy had been challenged by their inaction.

"Next time we could roast the tulip bulbs and make flour out of them."

Ada sighed. Nel just didn't give up. "I guess we could try. Someone told me you could substitute tulip bulbs for potatoes and make fritters."

"That sounds interesting, but you'd need some oil." Nel peeled some beets and hummed to herself. "What do you know about the strike?" she asked.

"I heard that the Germans are blocking food transport to the western part of our country. They're flooding farm fields or turning others into airfields and recruiting men for the potato harvest with bribes, such as extra ration coupons or housing. The government-in-exile warned citizens not to cooperate with the harvest because they believe it could undermine the effectiveness of the railroad strike—things are a bit stalled."

"That's a problem," Nel observed, but she didn't seem too concerned.

Ada gazed out the window. "That will leave us without food with winter coming." That thought terrified her.

"Exactly," Nel said.

Would they really let people starve just to make a political point? If neither side backed down, ordinary people would be caught in the middle.

"When the southern part of Limburg was liberated in mid-September, it meant that no coal would be shipped, and that would affect the transport of supplies as well as the fuel for heating and for all kinds of other things," Nel continued.

Ada nodded but decided not to comment. When Ada finished washing some of the bowls and utensils, she used the dish towel to wipe condensation from the windows. The garden looked as dejected as she felt—it seemed they were on a downward spiral that could not be reversed.

With acres of arable land flooded by the occupiers and farms turned into landing strips, the possibilities for growing their own food in the spring were extremely limited. This past harvest had been a disaster—it was no wonder that food stocks could not be replenished. To top it off, most of the available food continued to be diverted to the German people and the troops. How did Nel feel about that? Ada did not want to know.

Lucas told her that farms in the north and east of the country still had supplies; many people traveled long distances away from populated areas to try to acquire food from those farms. Some generous farmers provided barns where food travelers could sleep for a night and eat a bowl of soup, but others were already fed up with the constant barrage of visitors who knocked on their doors to demand food. Would it be worth the risk for one of them to travel north to see what food they could find? Lina would probably view such a trip as a personal challenge, whereas Ada would find it a hardship. Still, she was the eldest. How could she ask Lina to undertake such a dangerous mission?

"Are you listening?" Nel asked.

Ada realized her attention had drifted away. "What did you say?"

"What's the matter with you today? I just asked you if Lina got up," Nel said. She used the back of her hand to push her silver hair back from her forehead. Wearing a faded floral apron, she deftly peeled a sugar beet and then cut it into slices to boil.

Ada glanced at the clock and then shrugged as if it was of no concern. She worked to excise the green heart of the tulip bulb before boiling it. "She'll be down in a minute."

Nel stood with her hand on her hip. "That girl will have to learn things the hard way. At her age, I was married and expecting my first. I didn't have the luxury of staying in bed and ignoring the work. Your parents spoiled her," she said, looking down her nose.

Ada suppressed the irritation that made her shoulders tighten. What right did Nel have to criticize her parents?

Nel continued. "In the old days, your parents had household help, but now it is up to you to do all the work. That is not fair."

Ada shrugged. "Lina does a lot of searching for food and bartering, and I cook whatever she brings. That is the way we divide the labor." When they discussed how to cope with the food shortage, she had been surprised when Lina volunteered to find food. She had always assumed that Lina did not want to help, but either Lina had changed or she had been wrong about her all along. Seemed like she was wrong about a lot of things, such as trusting Nel and not trusting Lina. She had believed that Father had no secrets, but it felt like there were things she didn't know. With the world turned upside down and her judgement of people unreliable, it was increasingly challenging to know who she could trust.

Lina came downstairs in her usual work clothes and grabbed her coat from the hook. Placing her black beret on her head at an angle, she pulled her canvas bag crossways over her chest.

"I wondered if you were up," Ada said.

"I fell back asleep. Now I must run," Lina said, but then she paused and turned back to look at the counter. "What are you making?" she asked as she scrutinized the piles of chopped bulbs and beets, winding her knitted scarf twice around her neck. "That smells awful."

Ada looked up. "We're testing some recipes for a pamphlet. Remember you promised to take photographs for the project?" Ada asked.

Lina looked confused. "Did I?"

Ada was annoyed because she had reminded her just a few days ago. She tried to be patient because she really needed the photographs. "Are you free on Saturday morning? We need to get the photos done. It's already late in the season to teach people how to forage."

"Seems to me they're doing well enough on their own. People are searching everywhere for anything edible. Anyway, I am due to work at noon that day," Lina said. She checked herself in the mirror that hung beside the coat rack.

"If we get up early, we can be back by eleven," Ada persisted.

"I guess so," Lina agreed with some reluctance as she glanced at the kitchen counter. "Maybe you should teach them survival of the fittest, you know, as in adapt or die."

"We'll only survive if we help each other," Nel said with a sniff.

Lina shrugged. "Somebody will win, somebody will lose, and then we can get on with life."

"Sounds like you have plans for the future," Nel said, skepticism written on her face.

"My only plan is to find fortune and fame," Lina said.

"Maybe you should finish school first," Nel replied as she chopped walnuts.

Ada watched them go back and forth. There was no love lost between Nel and Lina. She couldn't blame Lina for being annoyed; Nel made no attempt to hide her dislike for Lina. Maybe it was because Lina stood up to her and dared to disagree with her.

"Sometimes talent is enough. *Au revoir*," Lina said with an affected wave. She pulled the door behind her, walked through the sunporch, and headed for the shed.

Nel shook her head and muttered, "Talent for what?"

"She wants to work in fashion in Paris, but she has no training or experience." As soon as she said it, Ada realized that she was mocking Lina's plan. She hoped Lina hadn't heard her—she did not intend to be disloyal, but there was something about being in Nel's presence that made her want to lash out at things.

"If I were her mother, I'd change her ideas," Nel continued. "She's the image of your father, whereas you remind me of your mother."

Ada smiled. "Be my guest. You're welcome to take over. It's not a job I ever asked for."

Nel held up her palm. "Thank you very much, but I've done my share of child-rearing. Life can be her teacher; she will learn, but it will be painful."

Wasn't life painful for all of them? Although when she watched Nel standing at the counter, it seemed that she hadn't lost any weight, whereas she and Lina had to adjust their belts and alter clothes to keep them from sliding off. Nel might have all kinds of motives for her searches and intrusions in their lives—maybe she had never forgiven Father for rejecting her advances all those years ago. She had wanted so badly to be the professor's wife and move into their bigger house.

Ada told herself that Nel regularly received food from her son's farm, so she was entitled to look better nourished than most people. The fact that she sometimes shared eggs and potatoes with them was a powerful incentive to stay on good terms. But Ada also didn't want to depend on her, especially since Nel would assume that Ada owed her something in return.

As she chopped mushrooms, Ada wondered what kind of government food policies might ensure that this kind of scarcity would never happen again. Because food was perishable, it would be impossible to store surplus in case of war or famine. An emergency food plan also had to adapt to the specific needs of different age-groups and food prefer-ences along with dietary restrictions, such as allergies.

Somehow food needed to be available the instant a crisis began because the longer a food crisis endured, the greater the damage to the population's health. Slow and steady starvation would have consequenc-es—especially for children and the elderly, but over time it would affect everyone.

The questions were urgent, but there was nothing she could do about trying to find answers until the university resumed classes. Most of her classes in the first year had been required courses in science, but she had chosen one that focused on global issues.

In the latter, her professor had experience working with churches and volunteer organizations that encouraged responsible agricultural practices in Africa and Asia. He advised her about courses that would be useful in future. Father had been pleased that his colleague had taken the time to encourage her. Mother had pushed Ada to attend a domestic science school to prepare to be a good cook and wife. Luckily, Father supported her university aspirations and refused to let Mother influence her choices.

Father encouraged her volunteer work with community networks that helped the hungry. Hunger, he told her, was a worldwide challenge that had landed on their doorstep. Lucas was helpful in connecting her to organizations looking for help. He understood what she wanted to do and helped make it happen.

The British had developed a vitamin-laced formula that most peo-ple rejected because they found it inedible. If starving people couldn't tolerate the taste, the laboratories had to find a way to improve the flavor while maintaining the nutritional value.

"What are you thinking about?" Nel asked.

Ada was not planning to share her thoughts with Nel, who would be threatened by Ada's plans. "Just trying to think up new recipes with the ingredients that we have on hand."

Nel held up a sugar beet. "This is the ugliest vegetable ever made. People can bake cakes or make cream from the syrup or boil it till it falls apart, but there is nothing we can do to make it edible."

Ada looked at the beet that she was holding up. "What about curry powder?"

Nel groaned.

Maybe Nel wasn't hungry enough. Most of the housebound elderly Ada visited were grateful for any food she delivered. But the thought of further shortages frightened her. How would they survive?

Hunger was like a wild animal, gnawing and chewing to free its leg from a trap. It wasn't the animal's fault—it was the fault of the hunter that had set the cruel trap. Still, rage and despair were triggered by hunger. People were already stealing and fighting for anything available, and who could blame them? No one wanted to face their hungry children to tell them there was no supper.

Nel didn't seem concerned about Father's arrest—she assumed that the occupiers would send him home whenever they were done with their questions. It wasn't quite that simple—if Father had been sent to a camp, his health would be severely challenged by physical labor and harsh living conditions. There had been a finality to his goodbye that made her worry.

The folder they had found in his study showed he was keeping secrets. Although the information had once been of great interest to some of the Nazis, Lucas had heard that a group of generals in Berlin already had a copy of the same document and consulted it to plan to topple Hitler. It was discouraging to think that the document was no longer worth much since there was another copy in Berlin. Why had Father risked everything for it?

But the news that they were already searching for Hitler's successor was encouraging—perhaps the war might wind down. If the occupiers were defeated, the National Socialists would have to follow them or risk punishment for their crimes in their home country. She looked at Nel and listened to her chatter and wondered if she had considered her possible fate.

9.

LINA

PEDALING hard to get to work that morning, the wind felt like a hand pushing against Lina's chest to keep her in place—it was like running a race that had no finish line. As the days shortened, she felt the cold. Having lost so much weight, it was impossible to stay warm, and the lack of sunlight was depressing. As the wind blew in her face, she felt her skin tighten and her eyes water profusely.

Despite boasting to Nel about her future, she knew her dreams lacked substance—trains weren't running, cars had been appropriated by the Germans, and she was stuck. Although Paris had been liberated in August, it would take time to rebuild. If the fashion industry survived, they wouldn't hire someone with no work experience; there would be plenty of experienced people desperate for work who had appropriate qualifications.

Even the thought of presenting herself for a job interview was overwhelming—she had no decent clothes, her French was inadequate, and her portfolio nonexistent. What she needed was someone to help her plot the steps towards that goal, but Lina didn't know who to ask. Requesting assistance seemed like a sign of weakness—she hated the thought of being that vulnerable.

Before the war, someone had told her about a photography program at the Royal Academy. That kind of training was impossible now—she had to educate herself, but did she have the discipline? Nel's attitude irritated her to no end—what did she know about dreams? As annoying as the woman was, Nel was right that she needed a better plan.

She biked past shuttered houses with blackout curtains in place even in daytime. At one time, these streets were filled with people walking dogs and children running across yards, but these days people stayed out of sight as much as possible.

Where was Father? The uncertainty continued to make her anxious. Why had he hidden papers in his desk that would turn the Nazis into angry hornets? Why didn't he consider giving them to someone else—especially if he thought that the occupiers were on to him?

But she knew how principled he was. She had always admired that about him—he was a man of his word. It seemed a rather old-fashioned way to live amidst war and hunger, but she was proud that he stuck to his principles. She just wasn't sure those principles were worth dying for, especially if the Nazis already had a copy of the document he had been so carefully guarding; but he must have had his reasons.

Father's students admired him and appreciated his classes—at least that's what she had heard. When he invited students over once a month for dinner, Mother had enjoyed the evenings as well. It was a bit embarrassing that she felt the need to explain to the gathering that instead of attending university, she was a graduate from a prestigious cooking school in The Hague. Students didn't care what kind of education she had—they were there for the food and for some personal attention from their professor.

During the dinners one student, Willy, stayed close to Ada. Her face glowed when she was around him, even though they pretended not to know each other very well. Lucas had told her that since then, Willy and hundreds of others had been arrested and deported to German camps. Ada never mentioned any of it to Lina, and it was clear that the subject was off-limits. Did Ada intend to spend the rest of her life being faithful to his memory? Maybe she would be better off joining a convent and living a nun's life—although most days it seemed she was already doing that. Sometimes Lina wanted to tell her not to give up, but why would she listen to her younger sister?

The fact that Ada was friendly with Nel was unsettling. Lina couldn't figure out what Nel wanted, but it didn't feel right. Even Lucas had warned them about her. Lina planned to keep an eye on Nel, and if it seemed she was influencing Ada in unhelpful ways, Lina would say something to her.

After Mother's passing, Lina had been afraid that Nel would convince her newly widowed Father to marry her. Nel had tried to make herself indispensable, helping with the housework and cooking Father's favorite foods. To Lina's relief, Father had politely thanked her and told her that Ada would take over. He didn't like having an outsider in his house, and he was completely uninterested in a relationship with her. Although he never said anything, Lina had the feeling that he didn't care for Nel.

Did Nel intend to create a wedge between them? As sisters, they'd always had their differences, but having a stranger meddle in their affairs was disturbing. She and Ada had made some progress working together on the challenges of finding food, but Nel's influence could ruin things.

She didn't trust Nel's political opinions, and she hoped that Ada would see through her. Nel's work with community groups might seem admirable, but it also gave her an excellent chance to watch people and report them to the Nazis. Ada would admonish her for being paranoid and uncharitable, but Lina did not trust her.

While biking to the café, Lina rehearsed her excuse for being late, knowing that her boss would not be amused. At the beginning, he'd been so charming to her, but then he had grown increasingly critical of everything she did. Perhaps her lack of interest in him meant that he would soon find an excuse to terminate her employment and to find someone more willing to put up with his wandering hands. She shuddered to think of it.

The café was a depressing place—people only went there because they were desperate to get out of their homes for a while and to see friends. They certainly didn't come for the food, which was barely edible on good days, or the coffee, which had been replaced by some powdered ersatz blend containing barley, chicory, green peas, and tulip bulbs. Lina refused to drink it—she even told Lars that it tasted like cat urine, and he had not been pleased.

Customers needed a place to tell their stories and jokes—it had always been part of their daily lives. In much of the city, silence and suspicion undermined the fellowship that used to take place around markets or churches. Lina was sure that some of the café clients were members of the resistance—they huddled in the corners and dropped their voices when she approached.

When the war ended, she'd make her move. Paris, fashion, and a small room somewhere. She could picture it so clearly. Every item of her wardrobe would need replacement, including her worn shoes, ill-fitting pants, and knitted cotton bra that had turned gray a long time ago.

What she missed the most were the entertainments—the concerts, dances, and movies. This was her time to be young and to make mischief that turned into good stories later. At parties alcohol was difficult to find, so her friends mixed up a homemade brew that resulted in impossible hangovers—like the one she'd had recently.

Even though she was grateful for the occasional parties that broke up the monotony, she was bored with their predictability. They repeated the same jokes over and over and responded with loud laughter. Tolerated only because she was Jos' girlfriend, it was obvious to her that they didn't like her much. They were a ragtag bunch of people—acquaintances from school or church or from farms near town. They were all marking time and remembering the past, which in retrospect looked much more glamorous than the present.

While they played various records on an old record player, everyone pretended they hadn't heard the music a hundred times before. Romantically inclined couples carried on in dark corners or in the basement.

Jos was always at the center of things as he leaned against the kitchen counter, poured drinks, and told jokes. As her irritation grew, Lina wandered through the house looking for a quiet corner. Jos was in his glory among his family and his friends, whereas she just wanted to meet new people and see the world. She knew that this was all he wanted, and she knew it would never be enough for her.

His friends looked down on her and saw her as a city snob. New friends, or even potential boyfriends, were impossible to find these days. Being with Jos guaranteed belonging to a group—she didn't have to like them, but without them she'd be just as alone as Ada was.

Maybe compromise was what made life possible, whether in relationships or in jobs. She disliked her café job but knew she needed to keep it until she found the next thing. Maybe Jos was also just a stop along the road. If Ada heard her say this, she would criticize her for using him, but then Ada had such impossibly high standards.

She reminded Jos frequently about her plans to move to Paris when the war ended, but he chose not to believe her. When she did go, he would have no trouble finding another girlfriend—she'd seen how girls at parties wound themselves around him whenever they could. He was an attractive fellow who would not only inherit his family farm but also acquire his own automobile garage. He was not entirely without ambition, she had to admit, but their ambitions were a world apart.

Was it her fault that her dreams were bigger? Paris seemed to be a place where dreams blossomed, unlike this place where people were stunted by their own low expectations.

When she began hanging out with Jos, they'd had a few rocky moments. One evening, Jos drank too much and disappeared from a party. The next day, he confessed that he had slept with Maria. If there was one person she couldn't stand, it was Maria. Why had Jos picked her for a drunken fling? He apologized and promised to behave, but after that she'd never trusted him fully.

Lina shook that memory away as she locked her bike and walked into the café, waving to the regulars who always sat at the same table by the window.

Lars glared at her from behind the bar. "What's your excuse this time?" he asked as he ran the dishcloth over the counter.

"I'm really sorry," she explained, trying to look appropriately penitential. "I'm not sure what happened. I slept late, but I'll stay longer tonight to make up for it."

"If you're late once more, consider yourself fired. I need reliable employees. In case you haven't noticed, people are hungry for jobs. Get to work. All those dishes need washing and putting away. It's a mess here."

Shortly after chastising Lina, he seemed to have plenty of time to pull up a chair and join the two men by the window.

"These young people don't know what work means," he complained loudly enough that she could hear him.

"You just have to break them in," the bald one replied. "Every horse farmer knows that."

"You're a horse expert now?" asked his companion.

"I've bet on a few in my day," he answered, "and lost."

"I think I'm losing as well," Lars said as he tipped his head towards Lina.

The men laughed together.

She turned her back to them while she sorted and polished the utensils. "You're all nothing but a horse's ass," she muttered. There had to be something better than this job—whatever it was, she was going to find it because Lars was intolerable. Not even the food she gleaned from discards could make up for his stupidity.

Lars probably planned to fire her soon no matter what she did. She dreaded telling Ada that she had been fired. How would she ever find another job? If only Father would return and advise her. Things always went smoothly for Ada, whereas Lina regularly messed things up. Was it a flaw in her character or just endless bad luck? Somehow, she had to do something to turn her luck around.

She polished rows of drinking glasses with her back to the men—she was depressed enough without listening to their conversation. They considered themselves experts on the progress of the war, but she was convinced they knew nothing. To distract herself, she imagined climbing the steps at Montmartre to photograph the locals and the street vendors, as well as the couples kissing on bridges and parks. Romance, not war, would be in the air as the warm springtime allowed love to blossom. Where did people find hope? Did it stay hidden somewhere, waiting for the right conditions? Trying to motivate herself by feeding the same fantasies was no longer enough, especially because a life in Paris seemed like a mirage that never got any closer.

Admiring the neat row of polished glasses on the shelf over the bar, she saw Lars and his two customers reflected in the mirror. She refused to be limited by their low expectations of life—it was up to her to prove them wrong. She turned her back to them and proceeded to polish the surface of the bar, humming a French song to herself.

10.

ADA

O N Saturday morning, Ada woke Lina up and made some oatmeal while ignoring her complaints.

"Why do I have to get up so early?" Lina asked. "Can't you just take my camera and go take pictures?"

"I cannot because you are the expert, and I want to see excellent prints."

"Why do you want this?"

"The end of September is almost here, and this is probably the last week we can take pictures of mushrooms and things people can forage. I need them for this pamphlet. The editors are not sure they can print the information with the photographs, but that's up to them."

"Why do you care what they think?" Lina said.

"I want to be reliable. I hope to have good relationships with people in the community and in food issues because that's what I am interested in doing."

"Why do you care about all that? It may never happen if we lose the war."

"Try to think positive sometimes, Lina; it might make your day better."

"I'm so glad we are going for an expedition in the forest. I am so glad you woke me up early on a Saturday." She looked at Ada with a grin. "How's that?"

"Some sincerity would help. You need to be back by eleven, so we need to hurry."

They biked to the woods and leaned their bicycles against the trees. There was a stillness in the forest. Pine needles crunched underfoot as they walked. Birds flew from branch to branch, disturbed by their footsteps.

"Too bad you can't cook something with these pine cones," Lina said. "There's hundreds of them."

Ada didn't reply. She was busy scouring the ground for mushrooms and anything else that could be foraged. "Here, look at these," she said as she pointed to a cluster of white mushrooms in the ground. "Can you get some shots of these?"

Lina took off the lens cap and crouched on the ground to get some close-up shots of the mushrooms. "Are you sure these aren't poison?"

"These are fine, but the ones over there by the maple tree are not."

Lina continued to shoot wherever Ada directed and then helped her gather mushrooms in the cloth bag she had brought.

"I'll make some mushroom soup tonight," Ada said. "And dry the rest for the winter."

"If we had tomatoes, you could make a sauce and put it over pasta."

"Topped with cheese," Ada said.

"Followed by gelato and espresso," Lina said.

They laughed at the impossibility of it, but they stopped laughing when they heard a twig crack and the sound of heavy footsteps crunching the pine needles.

Ada and Lina stood up and brushed the leaves from their clothes. Lina swung the camera to her side. They hardly dared breathe, especially when they saw the uniforms. Both reached for their identity cards before being asked.

"What are you doing here?" the older soldier asked while he studied their cards and then returned them.

"We are collecting mushrooms for our dinner," Ada said.

"And what are you doing with the camera?" the younger one asked.

"Taking pictures of nature," Lina replied. She put her hand over the camera in a protective gesture.

"Give it to me," the soldier commanded as he held out his hand.

Lina was reluctant to let it go. She looked at Ada who gave her a slight nod—she reluctantly handed it to the soldier.

Opening the back of the camera, he pulled out the film and threw it to the ground and then stomped on it with his boot.

Lina inhaled sharply, but Ada put her hand on Lina's arm, cautioning her against speaking.

"Here, take your stupid pictures. Let's go," the soldier said.

The girls stood under the pine trees, afraid to move, while they listened to the sounds of their bikes grow more distant.

Lina picked up the film. "I'm sorry for your photos, Ada."

"Don't worry. At least you still have your camera. Let's go home. The Food Council can manage without photographs. It's a good thing we were photographing nature. Imagine if they had caught you taking pictures of military camps or ammunition depots."

"Good idea," Lina said, "Maybe that's how I can be useful to Lucas."

"Stop it," Ada said, eyeing her carefully. "Don't get any crazy ideas. Let's go home and have some tea before you go to work. I will have a pot of soup waiting when you finish your shift." She held up the bag triumphantly.

11.

LINA

A FEW days later, Lina entered the house through the sunporch and uttered a few curses as the belt of her raincoat got stuck in the door.

She kicked her shoes off in the corner and threw her wet coat over a kitchen chair with another curse. "Ridiculous weather," she said. "Sorry I'm late." She ran her fingers through her short, blonde hair. "It really feels like October now."

"Hang that up, please?" Ada said as she tipped her head towards the coat while holding a potato in one hand and a paring knife in the other. "And mind your language."

Did Ada have eyes in the back of her head? Lina sighed and hung the coat on the rack beside the back door. She dropped her cloth bag on the table. "Guess what I have?"

Ada looked over her shoulder at the bag but didn't move towards it.

Lina grinned at her. "Go ahead. Open it up."

Inside the bag was a half loaf of bread, a piece of chicken, and a small slice of hard cheese wrapped in wax paper. As Ada slowly unwrapped the cheese, she sniffed it and smiled. "Where did you get this?" she asked. "I can't remember when I last tasted cheese."

Lina shrugged. "I went to the farms. One farmer knew Father from church and had pity on me."

Ada continued to look at the cheese, her face lit with happiness.

"Either we wait, or we eat some now," Lina suggested. It was worth everything to see the look on Ada's face. She didn't need to tell Ada that she'd traded a pure damask tablecloth from Belgium and a silver bracelet Father had brought her from Turkey. Lately, she'd found that many farm women already had cupboards full of people's dinnerware, silverware, and linens, and they were reluctant to accept more unless they were of excellent quality.

"Thank you," Ada said as she quickly pulled two plates from the cupboard and put the kettle on. "Do you think Father gets enough to eat wherever he is?" Ada asked with tears in her eyes.

Lina stared at her plate in silence. It was too painful to imagine Father trying to survive the harsh conditions in those camps, but it was even worse to think he might already be gone. She didn't want to say anything to Ada, but she had a horrible feeling that father's chair would remain empty. The occupiers had more than a week to question him, so if they were going to return him, he should have come home by now. "Let's not think the worst," she suggested, "and send him good thoughts."

Biking to the farms that morning, she'd been turned down by the first three farmers, until one woman was willing to look at the goods she hoped to barter for food. Eventually, Lina knew, she'd have to bike further north to find supplies. In the old days she could have done it without too much effort, but she'd been better nourished then. If she waited much longer, the cold and rain would make the trip more difficult, especially if the rain turned to ice. Still, she knew she was the one to make the trip—she was in better shape than Ada, who looked very peaked these days and had a chronic cough.

"I'll cook the chicken, and we still have some carrots from the garden. Give me half an hour."

"I'm going upstairs to take a nap. Call me when you're ready. I'll do the dishes and set the table, but right now I need to sleep."

Lina climbed the long staircase slowly, using the banister to support herself because she was so tired. She'd biked to farm after farm only to be turned away by most of them—it was so discouraging to see that the farmers had nothing to share.

The people she'd seen hunting for food and fuel reeked of desperation—unwashed ragged remnants of their former selves. When Lina photographed them, they barely noticed her as they shuffled along the country roads. Some part of what defined them as human had been lost, leaving them with a hard outer shell. Despite that hardening, the drive for survival pushed them onward to feed themselves and their loved ones at any cost. Whatever hardship she and Ada had suffered until now was nothing compared to those food travelers. She knew she'd been guilty of complaining about the simple meals Ada prepared, but they'd been lucky to have that sustenance.

Ada's careful preserving and cooking, combined with the donations Lucas made to their table, helped them maintain a minimal level of nutrition. They were still hungry and suffered from colds and coughs and skin problems, but so far they'd avoided more serious infectious diseases. Lina had heard of people suffering from cholera, diphtheria, and tuberculosis. She hoped they could avoid those.

As she climbed the stairs, she paused in front of a series of family photographs that hung on the wall. She had walked past them hundreds of times, but today she looked more closely. In one, her mother stood beside a friend, wearing the starched white aprons that were required at the School of Domestic Science. Their faces exuded a joy and anticipation that Lina never remembered seeing on her mother's adult face. Although Lina regarded household science training as utterly boring, she realized that her mother had found some measure of freedom in attending that school and in sharing that experience with a friend.

The next photograph showed her parents standing side by side in the apple orchard at her grandparents' farm. They looked so young. As Mother gazed directly at the camera, her posture was defiant, seeming to resist any definition of herself in this family photograph. Father, by contrast, gazed with love at baby Ada in his arms. What happened to Mother between her time as a student at the domestic science school and the wife and mother depicted in the orchard?

Lina continued to trudge up the remaining stairs, wondering how anyone could read a photograph with accuracy since each picture revealed some things and hid others. Sometimes the photographer controlled the story by framing a photograph to exclude certain things, but in other cases the subject of the photograph stared at the camera, determined to keep their secrets private.

Lina climbed into bed fully dressed and wished with all her heart that Father would return to help them sort out the challenges they faced. She pulled the blankets up to her chin and hoped the bed would warm up quickly. How were they going to survive this winter with no food and little fuel? Ada depended on Lina to find something, but supplies were almost nonexistent. She wanted to spare Ada the worry of a famine that was getting worse, but Lina knew that was impossible—Ada would see soon enough that Lina returned with an empty bag. Her community projects had already shown her that food was scarce.

As the scents of rosemary and thyme wafted from the kitchen, Lina smiled in anticipation of the dinner ahead and fell into a deep sleep.

When she heard Ada calling her for supper, Lina felt like she'd traveled far in her dreams. The memories of her *Opa's* farm and the apple harvest lingered. She remembered the juice of the apples running down her chin and the smell of fresh *applegebak* emanating from *Oma's* kitchen. Those happy memories felt like they belonged to someone else's life.

Lina ran down the stairs, glancing at the family photographs on her way. She had to accept that there were parts of the past that she would never fully understand. Maybe every generation carried an imaginary satchel filled with untold stories and well-kept secrets that were better left alone.

If Father never returned, his untold stories would go with him. She regretted her lack of curiosity; she should have asked him to tell her about his youth. Perhaps it was that way with every generation—by the time they were old enough to be curious, their elders were gone, and stories were buried with them. What was worth preserving, she wondered, and what would endure from her own life, other than the misery of this hungry winter and endless war? No matter what, she was entitled to her own adventures and fun, and one way or another she planned to find them.

12.

ADA

A FEW days later, Ada diced the carrots that Nel had dropped off, along with a small bag of potatoes. She felt conflicted about accepting food donations from Nel—but she was far too hungry to refuse. She glanced at the chart that marked the days since Father's arrest—fifteen days, she noticed—and sighed.

"I'm so hungry," Lina said as she entered the kitchen to see what Ada was preparing. "Why was Nel here again?" Lina asked.

Ada felt defensive. "We're working on the second pamphlet for the Food Council. You know, we're lucky that Nel shares food with us from her son's farm. I hope that the partial lifting of the embargo might help us get some food. In a week or two, they will begin the potato harvest in Drenthe. Hopefully some of those potatoes will make their way here."

Lina lifted the lid of a pot that was filled with boiling water and some potato peels. She groaned quietly and sat at the kitchen table. She tried unsuccessfully to control her irritation at Ada's overly optimistic outlook and her defence of Nel. "How are they going to get here? The occupiers aren't going to deliver potatoes door to door. They're not known for sharing."

Ada sighed. "Why are you always so pessimistic? When I try to cheer us up, you always pull us back down."

"I didn't ask you to cheer me," Lina replied. "Sometimes being miserable is the best way to survive."

"That's ridiculous," Ada replied. When she turned her back to Lina, her shoulders were elevated near her ears and her back was rigid.

There was silence in the kitchen. "Is there something I can chop?" Lina asked.

Ada rinsed a dish at the sink, but she was clearly annoyed. "Maybe you could set the table, please."

"Ada, I know how to peel a carrot. Pass me the knife."

Ada looked at her and attempted to lighten the mood. "You've been hiding your talents under a bushel."

"Just give me that carrot," Lina said. "I hate watching you act like a kitchen martyr."

"I do not act like a martyr," Ada replied. She handed Lina a bowl to hold the peels that she planned to add to the broth—nothing would go to waste in her kitchen.

"When do you think the war will end?" Lina asked as she peeled a large gnarly carrot.

Ada turned and leaned against the counter. "I don't know. I can't stop wondering if we'll ever hear anything from Father, but the days keep passing."

"Maybe he's not allowed to write," Lina said.

"They promised that the Allied troops would break through by Christmas. Why do they make promises like that?" Ada asked. "The disappointment makes things worse."

"They underestimated the German army's strength before," Lina said, "and they keep making that same mistake."

"Those mistakes make us look weak—the occupiers take advantage of that."

Lina retrieved part of a newspaper from her raincoat pocket. "Listen to this: *In September weeks, we saw the operation called 'Market Garden,' which was a combined land and air attack intended to end the war by cutting the German positions in half. The Germans, however, mounted strong resistance, and as a result, the plan failed.*"

Lina put the paper on the table. "It would help if the Allied soldiers learned how to fight," Lina continued. "Look at the Germans—they're more disciplined, and they know how to hit targets and drop bombs. They've got that new rocket, the V2, that can wipe out half of cities like London, especially if they're launched from our beaches. Maybe the Allied soldiers don't know how to read a map—they bombed a town in the south by mistake, and many people lost their homes. They weren't even close to the factory they'd hoped to hit." Lina gestured with the paring knife to underline her point.

"I think they're doing their best," Ada said. "At night, the conditions are so bad that they can't identify their coordinates through the fog and rain."

Lina shook her head in disagreement and tapped the paring knife on the article. "According to this, General Montgomery messed up Market Garden. In addition to his unfortunate choices, the weather was bad, communications failed, and the Allied troops underestimated the German opposition."

"How many things can go wrong?" Ada asked as she shook her head slowly.

Lina put down the paper. "Too many to count. The war is not finished with us yet. We're like a mouse in that cat's mouth, getting thrown around for fun."

Ada added the carrot peels to the potato peel broth. When the water reached boiling, the broth created a curtain of steam that shrouded the kitchen window. She turned the pot to simmer and sat at the table across from Lina.

Ada turned the newspaper on the table so that she could look at it. A headline in bold type declared the destruction of an entire village in the south. The survivors found themselves homeless. She felt sad for them but couldn't afford to imagine their devastation—she was just trying to endure her own. Human compassion had its limits when losses piled up like fallen leaves.

13.

LINA

WITH no word from Father after two weeks, Lina felt certain that he was no longer alive. She had overheard enough horror stories about the camps from customers in the café to realize that this silence was not a good sign, but she refrained from sharing that with Ada.

Lucas dropped by to see if they had any news. He sat at the table and picked up Lina's sketchbook. "May I look?" he asked.

Lina nodded—she watched him carefully as he studied each page before turning to the next one.

Ada brought the bread to the table followed by the tea pot and cups.

Lina shrugged when she saw the surprise on her sister's face. Lina didn't like to share her art with anyone else, but she wanted to know what Lucas thought.

When he finished, he handed the book back to her. "Lina, you have a very good eye. I can see why your photographs are strong because you have a good sense of composition." He looked up at the framed photos above the table and then turned his eyes back to her. "What do you plan to do with your talent?"

Lina was startled by the unexpected praise. "I don't know. It's impossible to get any training now."

"There will be many opportunities when the war ends. The government will have to create new or accelerated programs for all the people who will need training. But there's nothing wrong with practicing on your own in the meanwhile and pushing yourself to improve your craft as best you can."

Lina shrugged. "Lots of people have talent, but only a few can turn that into a career. I'm not sure that I have enough."

"Your sketches are excellent, your photos stunning. It's not too soon to imagine a career."

Lina looked at Lucas to see if he was kidding. "But the war drags on."

"You must believe that the end is in sight. We all need to find a way to rescue our plans from the places where they are buried like hidden treasure."

"What plans have you buried?" Lina asked.

"I intend to finish my graduate degree and get a job. It won't be easy to pick up where I left off, but I intend to work on it when this is over."

"Didn't the war change your motivation? Maybe a thesis isn't worth the trouble anymore."

"Not at all. We have adjusted to the current situation; but I loved history before the war, and I intend to pick up my research and writing as soon as possible. The war has taught us how important it is to remember the past and to learn from it, and I believe historians will be an important part of that effort."

"Well, if you really want me to work on my photography, I have an idea. Why don't you let me work for you? I can take pictures of army camps, storage depots, train shipments. I can take pictures of people for identity cards." She held her breath. What would he say?

It was quiet while Lucas considered her proposal. Ada looked at him and then continued washing the dishes.

"That's an interesting idea, Lina, I'll need to think about it," Lucas replied.

"Don't think too long. I have other offers on the table."

Lucas looked at her in surprise and then burst into laughter. "Making identity cards is not only dangerous, but it involves a great deal of skill. When they change the requirements, it becomes even more complicated. One mistake puts a lot of people in jeopardy. I will think about it and get back to you."

Lina nodded and decided to rest her case.

While Lina sipped her tea, Ada joined them at the table. Lucas discussed with her a group of students who had been arrested.

Lina didn't know the people they mentioned, so she tuned out the conversation and studied her framed photos on the wall. If she didn't find something worthwhile to do, she might lose her mind. She could learn to take portraits for the identity cards, and she could bike around the countryside taking pictures of important locations—Lucas would be crazy to turn it down. She was hungry to do something real instead of fantasizing about starting life in a new country. Did she flatter herself and her ability? Probably, she concluded, but a balloon would never rise without some hot air.

"What are you smiling about?" asked Lucas as his conversation with Ada ended and he noticed Lina's distracted presence.

Lina pointed to the photograph. "I was just remembering the day that Father and I went on a bike tour and took those pictures."

Lucas looked at the picture and nodded. "These are very good, but perhaps you know that?"

"Of course," she said with a smile. Hopefully her confidence would convince him to give her a chance to work for him.

That Saturday, Lina helped Ada tidy the house and do some of the backyard cleanup. Ada had decided she couldn't leave it till the spring, so Lina offered to help. They worked for two hours and cleaned up the rest of the vegetable bed and pruned some of the bushes. After carrying the leaves to a corner of the garden behind the shed, they covered it with a tarp and secured it with bricks in the corners.

Both were tired when they went inside. Lina sat down heavily on a kitchen chair.

"I'll make tea," Ada said. "Manual labor is a challenge."

"I'll say," Lina replied. "Tea would be welcome. Don't you wish we had some almond cakes or *speculaas* to go with it?"

They were startled by a knock on the front door. "I'll get it," Lina said as she hoisted herself to her feet with a grunt and walked to the door. She sensed Ada watching from the kitchen, afraid of who might be there. Had the soldiers returned for another search?

The man at the door greeted her and handed her a telegram. He turned and departed on his bike without looking back, as if in a hurry to leave the scene.

What a miserable job, Lina thought as she watched him bike away as fast as he could. She returned to the kitchen, handed Ada the telegram, and sat down heavily.

Ada shook her head vigorously. "No," she protested as she pushed it back to Lina.

Lina opened it up. She stared at the page and held her breath as she reread it again. She looked up at Ada who looked at her with wild eyes.

"Read it," she ordered.

Lina read it quietly and slowly: "We deeply regret to advise you that according to information received through the International Red Cross, Albert Van Dijk lost his life at Sachsenhausen on September 30, 1944. Please contact the local branch of our office for further details. Our sincere condolences. ICC."

Lina handed it to Ada.

Ada looked as pale as a sheet. She read and reread the text. "On September 30—and it took these weeks to notify us?"

"I am sure it is no easy matter for the Red Cross to keep track of what goes on in those camps." Lina fell silent, studying her hands to avoid seeing the pain in Ada's eyes. Ever since his arrest, she had a terrible feeling they would send Father to a camp. Sometimes people were taken to Westerbork, the transit camp, and then by train to other camps further away in other countries.

Lina retrieved a shawl from the coat hook by the door and wrapped it around Ada's shoulders. "Drink some tea," Lina suggested. "Do you want to lie down for a while?"

"No," Ada said with a stone face.

Lina wished Ada would cry, but she was completely rigid.

Ada circled the teacup with her fingers but didn't seem to have the strength to lift it to her lips.

Lina wanted to hug her, but she seemed brittle like a dried twig—if Lina touched her, she was afraid she would snap.

Just then, she heard Lucas call out from the back door. He came to the kitchen whistling a tune and stopped when he saw Ada's face.

"What's wrong? What has happened?"

Lina picked up the telegram and handed it to him.

After he read it, Lucas sat heavily on a chair beside Lina and exhaled as if he had been punched in the abdomen. "I am so sorry," he said quietly. He covered his face with his hands. No one spoke as the grandfather clock in the hall continued to tick loudly.

ADA

The next day, after spending most of the day and night in bed, Ada got up and made soup with some carrot tops, a potato, and an onion. Lina worked quietly at the table, studying some of the photo prints she'd recently processed. They both jumped when they heard a knock on the front door.

"What now?" Lina asked, fear on her face.

"I'll go see," Ada said as Lina followed close behind her.

"Reverend, please come in." He was wearing a lined raincoat and a hat, which Ada took and put in the hall cupboard. The minister was the same age as Father, but his hair was had turned completely gray. His eyes were a deep blue, and they focused on each girl as he shook their hands formally.

"Hello, Ada and Lina. I heard the news. I want to give you my condolences on your Father's passing. I ran into Lucas who told me. I would have come sooner, but I only just found out."

"Thank you. Would you like some tea?"

"That would be nice," he said, taking out his white handkerchief and polishing his tortoiseshell spectacles. He had dressed up for this pastoral visit—even though his shirt was worn at the collar and cuffs, and his pants were shiny at the knees.

He followed Ada into the kitchen. In the old days, she would have given him the best chair in the living room, but that room was too cold and uncomfortable. She also would have addressed him as *Oom*; his frequent visits had made him an honorary uncle. This occasion, however, was so solemn that a formal address seemed more appropriate.

Because Ada had hidden valuable items in the attic, the living room was bare and unwelcoming. Even the harmonium stood unused with the cover securely closed. Ada couldn't bear to play it anymore. When mother was sick, she had often asked Ada to play her favorite hymns, and sometimes she heard her mother's thin vibrato singing along. These days no one requested music, and she had stuffed the organ books inside the bench.

"Tell me how you heard this terrible news," he asked when he was settled in the kitchen.

"A fellow brought a telegram, but it doesn't give any information or details." She handed it to him and then turned to prepare tea.

"I hope the Red Cross will eventually be able to give you a fuller picture. Your father and I worked on many projects together. He was a fine man with a deep faith. We will all miss him very much."

"It's so hard to believe that he won't be coming back. His clothes are in the cupboard, his coat is in the hall closet, and his books and writings are in his study," Lina said.

The minister nodded sympathetically. "Your father once talked to me about what kind of funeral service he wanted. He asked me to wait until after the war ended. I made some notes on his preferences for the text and hymns. I just want to make sure that you agree to delay the service."

Ada nodded but couldn't speak.

The girls sat quietly as they digested the information that Father had made plans for his funeral. How much had he known?

"Just before his arrest, he told us that he had made arrangements for us so that we could maintain the house and continue our education eventually."

"That doesn't surprise me. He was very organized," he said. "If it's agreeable to you, I would like to read one of the psalms that your father loved." The minister looked at the girls, and each nodded her agreement.

Ada looked at her hands as he read the familiar words. She remembered a family vacation years ago in Switzerland. Father had read to them the same psalm about lifting their eyes to the hills from where their help was derived. She had listened differently that day, surrounded as they were by the grand peaks of the Alps. Father had been so happy at that small inn in the mountains. That was what she had to remember—not these years of war and struggle but Father hiking in the mountains he loved.

When the minister concluded with a prayer, they all sat together in silence. The house shook and windows rattled after a bomb strike happened on the far side of town. Not even this house would protect them if one of those planes decided to drop one on them, whether by intention or by mistake. If everything was random, then fear was irrelevant.

Ada stood up and poured some more tea.

The minister studied the photographs on the wall. "These are your work, correct?"

Lina nodded. "Father and I used to go on photo tours on Saturdays."

"He told me that he thought you might become a gifted photographer. I can see why he said that."

Lina was surprised. She glanced at the photos and then at the minister, checking to see if he was kidding her, but he looked very serious.

"Sometimes we can turn our grief into a memorial by continuing those things and by honoring their memory in our work."

"But what if your work doesn't end up being good enough? Won't that be a half-baked honor to someone's memory?"

Reverend Arie smiled. "You are not afraid to speak truth. I think we continue to choose life as a tribute to those who have left us."

He turned to Ada. "What about you, Ada? Do you have plans to continue with your studies?"

"I hope so," she said. "The war has taught me a great deal about the importance of food. I would like to work on the science that might make us better prepared."

Reverend Arie nodded. "That is a perfect example of taking an evil situation and trying to work for the good. Your father would be very proud of both of you. Please come to see me if you have any concerns in the days ahead."

He finished his tea and stood up. "I should get home before curfew. It sounds like another active night in the sky over us. Someday these planes will be gone, and the night sky will be reserved for stars and planets."

The girls stood up and walked him to the front door. Ada retrieved his coat and hat and waited as he put them on. He stood in front of Father's study door and bowed his head briefly before turning to go. They stood on the porch together and waved as he unlocked his bike and cycled away.

14.

ADA

WHEN Ada returned from town, she slammed the door behind her with sufficient force that it knocked a framed photograph sideways. Stopping to straighten it, she muttered to herself. After standing in line with her ration card for two hours, she had been told that there was no margarine, butter, or cooking oil. Ada missed Father's voice—he would have calmed her and told her not to lose heart, but he was gone. It was so difficult to accept. Soaked from the late October rain, she hung her coat on a hanger to dry and trudged up the stairs to change her clothes.

Everyone was cold and hungry, and the long, dark days didn't improve anyone's mood.

Searching through the kitchen cupboards for pasta or lentils, all she found was oatmeal. In despair, she decided to take a nap. An hour later, she awoke when she heard Lina's feet on the stairs. She pulled herself up to sitting on the side of the bed, but it was impossible to hide that she had been sleeping in the middle of the day. At one time she would have felt ashamed to be caught wasting time that way, but she no longer cared.

"I got fired today," Lina confessed as she stood in the doorway of Ada's room. She didn't comment on Ada being in bed.

Ada smoothed her hair into a bun that shifted sideways. She pulled her cardigan close and wrapped her arms across her chest. "You hated that job."

Lina was startled by Ada's lack of criticism. "I'm not sure what I'll do next," Lina said.

Ada shrugged. "Something will come up. Talk to Lucas again. You will have more time now to do other things."

"Are you feeling all right?" Lina asked, looking at her closely. She was certain that she was about to get a lecture.

"I'm fine. Were you able to find any food?"

"Not much. I have a small bag of lentils."

Ada stood up slowly and paused at the bedside. "I'll make dinner with that." She would add some spices, and hopefully it would fill them adequately. There was nothing worse than lying awake with hunger pangs in a cold and dark house, wrestling with frightening night thoughts.

Ada smoothed the sheets and the blankets and stepped into her slippers.

The girls went downstairs, and Ada made tea for them.

While they drank their tea, Lina showed Ada the prints she'd developed of some local settings.

Ada studied them carefully. "These photos are good. Father thought you had natural talent."

Lina was surprised by the praise. "How can I learn to get better? There's a war on."

Ada shrugged. "Take pictures of the war—but not those predictable photos of soldiers carrying guns. Show how women and children cope at home while men wage war. Your pictures might bring people's attention to the food crisis as well."

Lina laughed. "There are war correspondents who do that for a living. People would never take me seriously, especially since I am not a man."

Ada shrugged. "You will make your place among them."

"But I have no technical training."

Ada was surprised by how little confidence Lina seemed to have. She had always assumed Lina had endless amounts of courage. "If you become a photographer, someday you can either open a studio or travel the world. You'll have plenty of options."

Lina looked confused. "Father never suggested that to me as a career," Lina said. Was that what he'd been telling her all along, but she'd been too stubborn to realize it? Maybe he had been waiting for her to show some initiative.

"He took the time to teach you because he believed you had talent. He also gave you one of his best cameras. But he didn't want to impose expectations on you—probably because he knew how stubborn you could be. But he gave you the materials you needed so that you could choose for yourself."

Lina groaned. "Why didn't he say something?"

Ada shrugged. "That wasn't his way. But at least it's something you can do right away instead of waiting till the war ends. Don't wait for Lucas to decide if he wants your work—just take pictures."

"Everything looks bad; trees have been destroyed, buildings are piles of rubble, and people are starved and filthy. Who wants to see those photos?"

"Although we see that every day, there are many people who have no idea."

"Why should they care?" Lina asked.

"You will make them care by telling the story in ways that move them."

Lina looked at Ada. "First you told me to finish school; now you're telling me to travel the world with my camera. You are full of surprises."

Ada liked being full of surprises for a change. "That's nice to hear. I realized the idea of finishing schooling is not for you, but you still need a plan," Ada said as she stood and paused for a moment to get her balance. "I should cook those lentils."

Lina watched her struggle. "I hope you feel better. By the way, there's one more thing. I talked a farmer into giving me an onion. It's on the kitchen table."

"Now we are in business," Ada said. "That will add some flavor. Thank you."

Lina went to freshen up from her long day on the bike. When she returned to the kitchen, Ada was busy chopping the onion and occasionally wiping her eyes. Lina knew she wasn't feeling well but didn't want any attention.

Ada turned towards Lina. "I've been thinking about this war— sometimes I think it's a mistake to wait for the Allies to set us free. Maybe every person who is strong enough should do whatever it takes to end the war."

Lina looked at Ada in surprise. "Maybe you should put the knife down first," she said with a smile. "Have you become a radical? What's happened to you?"

Ada shrugged. "Too many people are dying. Maybe it's wrong to expect someone else to liberate us. There are plenty of women who are both brave and willing to fight."

"I couldn't agree more," Lina said. "But what are you suggesting?"

"We could do more, instead of waiting to be rescued."

"With all their guns and planes, the Allies still can't make their way here. What do you expect a bunch of starving women to do?"

"I'm not sure, but we have to continue to fight," Ada said.

"Don't you think that all the volunteering you do is part of that fight?" Lina asked.

"Sometimes it doesn't seem like enough," Ada said. "Nothing seems enough," she said as she rinsed the lentils.

Lina was quiet—she wasn't sure what she could say to encourage Ada. But before she could say something nice, Ada turned around with a frown on her face.

"By the way, your room is a mess. I'd like you to straighten it up today, please, before you leave the house."

Lina glared at her. "There's one way to fix that—close the door, and stop looking in my room." Lina stomped down to the basement darkroom to process a film.

Ada sighed and realized she should have kept quiet. It was harder than she had realized to stop acting like she was Lina's parent. When she was a girl, she had been expected to take care of her sister. Either their mother had been away at one of her rest cures in a private hospital, or she was in bed with a migraine. Ada had to change her ways, or she would drive Lina away.

They often did a dance, composed of two steps forward and three back. Their approaches to life were very different, but Father had often reminded her that difference could be a source of strength. "There's always more than one way to look at things," he had told her.

Ada believed that Lina would leave the country at her first opportunity, leaving her alone in this house. She probably couldn't wait to go.

Ada could not afford to give in to this bleak mood—it was important to keep busy, and sooner or later she would feel better. These days, the gray mood didn't seem to lift. Even the smallest things required enormous effort.

Ada pulled the broom out of the narrow closet and began to sweep the kitchen floor that was overdue for a good cleaning. The smell of onions reminded her to keep an eye on the pot and add the lentils—burning food was unacceptable when supplies were so scarce. Lina would never forgive her if she ruined the food for which she'd biked for hours. The dish would benefit from a few of the tomatoes she had dried in the summer, along with some dried chili peppers. Mother would have turned up her nose at this culinary experiment, but then she wasn't around to taste it. Maybe if she made a spicy stew, Lina would be happy again and forgive her for being bossy. Food was love, after all, and even when food was scarce, she could still try to practice being generous.

15.

ADA

In the following week, Ada decided her idea of a establishing a women's army would solve nothing; in fact, it would leave numerous children and aging adults without care.

"Have you heard any more war news?" Lina asked. Sometimes Ada learned things while typing the newsletter for Lucas.

"Not much. There are so many rumors out there I just tune them out."

Sitting at the table, Lina used a pencil to outline and then shade a drawing of a pewter urn. "When I worked at the café, it was easier to get information. Yesterday, I heard someone say that west and central Brabant were liberated. I'm glad somebody is liberated—all we do is sit and wait. Tonight I am not waiting; I am going to a gathering at Maarten's house."

"Another party? What's the occasion this time?" Ada asked. "After all, Father just—"

Lina interrupted her. "I can't change what happened to Father, but I also cannot sit here and do nothing. Father would have told me to go out, just like he did that night."

Ada didn't look up from the sweater on her lap as she undid the yarn and rolled it into a ball. "Don't come home too late," she warned. She had unraveled some of Father's sweaters to provide wool for her knitting—the thick Irish wool promised extra warmth for the cold days; Father would have approved of using his things to keep them warm. It made little sense to keep them in his cupboard when the winter promised to be long and cold. "Lucas told me about the Battle of the Scheldt, and he said they hope to get access to that port to supply Allied troops."

"Where does Lucas get all his information?" Lina asked. When did he and Ada talk about these things? Did he come around when she wasn't home? She knew it was none of her business, but everything irritated her these days. The hunger gave her a constant headache, and the smoke and noise on the street only aggravated her mood. Because her skin was so dry, she felt a constant need to scratch her arms, but that caused angry welts to appear, making her look like she'd been in a fight with a wild cat.

Ada ignored the question. "When they liberated Breda, a lot of Allied soldiers were killed or captured. There is always a terrible cost, whether the result is a victory or defeat. Can't people see that war is not the way to accomplish things?"

Lina looked unimpressed. "There's no way to reach the end without losing people. The troops are spending so much time in the south, I wonder when it will be our turn?" Lina asked.

Ada shrugged. "The Germans are blocking their advance."

Lina closed her sketchbook. "I'd love to continue this discussion of military strategy, but I must get ready for my party."

LINA

When Lina arrived at the party at Maarten's family home, the guys were busy mixing drinks. Jos gave her a kiss and returned to his mixing duties. She had no desire to sample their experiments—the hangover wasn't worth it.

As the evening went on, she became aware of a note of desperation underlying their party talk and games—probably because she was the only sober person at the party. If the parties had once been a good distraction, they bored her now. The drunken laughter, the card games, and rowdy fights happened in the same order every time.

Sensing her disengagement, Maria approached her. "Let's go outside and have a smoke."

Lina didn't feel like spending time with Maria. She had never trusted her, and she couldn't understand why the guys invited her to this party.

Everyone had heard the rumors of her socializing with the occupiers. Her clothes and makeup suggested that she had found a sponsor.

But she didn't have the heart to refuse with Maria standing by the door there looking like a puppy wanting to be taken out for a walk. What did it cost to be nice to people? Lina followed her to the back porch where Maria offered her a cigarette. Who was supplying her with cigarettes? Was Jos sharing his homemade ones with her, or was she getting them from the soldiers?

"Sorry about your father," Maria said.

Lina resisted the impulse to tell her that it was her new friends that had killed her father, but what was the point? Maria had chosen her side, or perhaps she thought that she could benefit from being on both sides. That would only last so long, but she wouldn't want to hear that. "Thanks," Lina replied.

"Ever get bored of these guys?" Maria asked as she tossed her hair back with the hand that held the cigarette.

Lina wondered if she had practiced that in front of the mirror—it was a movie star kind of move, which could end up singeing eyebrows if done improperly.

Lina took a long drag on the cigarette and blew out the smoke, watching it waft away on the cold night air. She didn't owe Maria any explanation for her choices. "Better than nothing."

"If you ever want a change, let me know. I get invited to parties where there's lots of food and real booze."

Lina looked at her. She clasped her arms around herself to try and stay warm. "You mean with *moffen*?"

Maria shrugged. "Some of them aren't bad."

Lina shook her head slowly. "Have you seen how they terrorize innocent people and children? Maria, this is not a good idea. I should have known—cigarettes, lipstick, and nice stockings."

"Just gifts from admirers," she said, preening in front of Lina.

Lina felt she had to try harder to convince Maria that this was too dangerous. "You need to be careful," Lina warned, "people don't like girls who hang around with the enemy. When the war ends, they'll run you out of town."

"And if they win? I'll get my pick of the litter."

Lina sighed. "Maria, I can't tell you what to do, but those *moffen* kill our people and steal our food. If you get on the wrong side of this, there'll be an awful price to pay."

"I don't care. They're a lot more interesting than those losers." Maria swept her hand to the living room of the house where the loud laughter of the men filled the air.

Lina wasn't sure what to say. The fact that Jos was one of the group Maria referred to as "losers" made her feel defensive. The fact that she was bored with the fellows and the parties was a compromise she made with the current situation. But sooner or later, Maria would realize she couldn't be with the soldiers and keep her old friends from school—something had to give.

Lina was disgusted by the whole evening. She leaned against the porch railing and finished her cigarette. Jos' loud laughter was a sure sign that he was getting drunk. If he didn't show some intention of leaving soon, she'd go home on her own. It was getting late, and Ada would worry.

She flicked the cigarette butt into the yard. "I gotta go, Maria. Thanks for the smoke. Be careful."

Lina found a corner of the sofa where she could wait while the guys played cards at the table. Despite their loud conversation, she slept for a little while. When she checked the time, she realized that another hour had passed. "We must go now, Jos. If you're not ready, I'll leave by myself."

As they biked home from the party, the night was cold and silent. There would be frost on the rooftops and the fields in the morning. Lina looked up at the night sky—the cold, clear night was splashed with stars.

"Jos, be quiet. It's after curfew," she told him as he continued to sing loudly.

Someone at the party had managed to find a bottle of whiskey. Although Jos was a large man who could handle a lot of liquor, he'd clearly passed his limit. As they biked along the silent road, Jos weaved back and forth unaware of how unsteady he was. She hoped he wouldn't create a ruckus when he got home—his mother would not appreciate being awoken by her drunken son stumbling through the house.

They biked to the crossroads and then paused. Normally, Jos would take a right turn towards his farm, whereas Lina continued north towards town. She leaned over to him to give him a good-night kiss, but he grabbed her handlebars and told her to get off the bike.

Lina's teeth chattered—she couldn't wait to get home to bed. "Come on, Jos, I really need to get home. We are past curfew."

"Let's just take a moment. I need a smoke. And my bladder is bursting."

She was annoyed that he refused to take no for an answer. "I'm freezing. If Ada wakes up and sees I'm not there, she'll be furious."

"Ada's probably fast asleep. Come on, just for a minute."

She followed with a sigh. He was so stubborn.

After parking the bikes, Jos took her hand and led her deeper into the woods. He stood behind a tree and rid himself of a torrent of urine before finding his way back to her. "Here," he said as he gently pushed her into a tree with a broad trunk and pressed against her. "We're alone now."

Lina looked up through the tree branches and saw a swath of stars in every direction. Although it was beautiful, she just wanted to be home in bed.

She wound her hands around his neck as he kissed her. The taste of whiskey hung on his lips, and his scarf smelled of tobacco. He was a good kisser even when he was drunk. His lips were cold as they huddled together to create some warmth. He pulled back and looked at her. It was so dark she could only discern the outlines of his face.

"Listen, Lina," he said, "I've been thinking—we should get married."

"What?" Lina asked. "Are you crazy?" She pushed lightly on his chest to get him to move back a bit and give her space.

He took a step back. "I'm serious. You can't expect a man to wait forever."

She tried again to push him away, but he moved in to press himself against her. She had to be careful. He was an even-tempered fellow unless he'd had too much to drink, and then he turned mean like his father. He had never directed that towards her, at least not till now.

"You could live on the farm until we get our own place."

Lina groaned. "What am I supposed to do if they send you to Germany?"

"You can wait for me. When the war is over, I plan to open my own garage."

"Good for you. And what do you think I'll be doing?"

"We'll start a family. You'll have lots to keep you busy." He laughed loudly.

That made her even more irritated. How could she make it clear to him? "That is not part of my plan. I told you that I'm going to Paris when this is over. Don't you ever listen?"

Jos stepped back and lit a cigarette. He took a drag and then looked at her. "I listen all the time to your complaints about living with your sister and about your boring job at the café. I'm offering you a way out. And, by the way, I love you."

Lina shook her head. It was suddenly so clear. "I think we want very different things."

Jos became agitated and grabbed her arm. She shook off his grip. But he pleaded, "Come on Lina. We're good together."

"Shh, keep your voice down. We've had fun, but I'm not ready to get married. I want to have a career and see the world. I'm not going to let this war steal my dreams. Jos, you're a great guy, but I can't do this. I'm sorry."

"To hell with you," he said. "I don't understand—"

"*Halt!*" a man's voice ordered. Jos shifted his focus slowly to face a soldier, who had crept through the woods from the other side while they argued.

16.

LINA

Lina was so startled she leaned back into the tree trunk and felt the edges of the bark dig into her back through her jacket. She realized that Jos was blocking her from the soldier's sight. Glancing up at the starry sky, she wished that she could disappear into its vast darkness.

"What are you doing here?" the soldier asked. He appeared to be alone, but he was armed.

"I was just having a cigarette. It's a nice evening," Jos said as he turned slowly towards him. "Cigarette?" he asked as he pulled one out of his pocket. As he leaned to offer the cigarette, the soldier shouted again.

"Don't move." The soldier's voice was high and shaky.

Jos held up his hands to show he meant no harm, with the cigarette stuck between his index and middle finger. "I am on my way home. I was helping a neighbor with a sick cow, but nothing could be done. Just having a cigarette to recover. So sad to lose a fine animal. Are you from a farm or from the city?" He kept his tone even and conversational.

The soldier, who was a foot shorter than Jos, looked at him. "Farm," he replied somewhat reluctantly, wondering whether he should have this conversation.

"Then you understand how it is. It's a huge loss for everyone. And there is no medicine available if they get an infection."

"I . . . I don't know about that. We didn't have animals."

"That must have made things easier for your father," Jos observed. "Having cows means you are tied to the schedule of milking."

The German soldier took a step closer. "You have been drinking," he said.

"I had a drink or two with the farmer. He was so miserable at his loss. He had five children who needed to have the milk from that cow."

Lina knew she needed to stop holding her breath or she would pass out. She felt the warmth of Jos' back through his jacket, and she tried to breathe along with him. His deep voice resonated through his chest.

Jos tried to keep the conversation moving to seem less of a threat. Would it be better, she wondered, if the soldier had a comrade with him? He was much smaller than Jos and likely felt threatened facing him alone.

As the conversation went through fits and starts, she was impressed with Jos' command of German. Doing business with the *moffen* must have been good for his language ability. She'd have to tease him about that when this was over.

As Lina hid behind Jos, she was grateful for his huge shoulders. She hoped that Jos wasn't too drunk to talk his way out of this. Her rejection of his proposal was still fresh—between that and the alcohol, Jos wouldn't be receptive to taking orders from a young soldier. Jos pointed out the Big Dipper to the fellow.

As the soldier looked up at the sky to see where Jos was pointing, Lina peeked around Jos and noticed that the soldier's eyes were large with fear. He was young and had very short, clipped blonde hair. Who gave this lad a gun and sent him to war? She wondered who was more afraid. She decided that the soldier was most afraid because he felt like he had a duty to behave like a soldier, but he was unsure what that duty might involve. His face was calculating whether to leave Jos to the woods and his cigarette or to intervene in more aggressive ways. There was no way he could manage to take him captive because he was too large. Lina interpreted his silence to mean that he couldn't make up his mind.

Jos was standing on uneven ground made bumpy by the exposed tree roots. He overbalanced to one side probably due to the drinks he had at the party. The soldier reacted immediately and aimed his gun at him.

Jos reached behind himself and pushed Lina hard. She fell to the ground and lay gasping as the air was knocked out of her. She clamped her hand to her mouth to keep from making a sound.

In a flash, a second later, two shots broke the silence, and Jos fell backwards on top of her. Winded by his weight, she felt crushed. Not daring to move, she waited to see what would happen. She heard feet tramping the undergrowth and then another crash as her bike fell and the bicycle bell hit a rock. After that everything was quiet.

"Jos, is he gone? Can you see him? Are you OK?" Her heart was beating so loudly she felt like she couldn't hear properly. Had anyone heard the shots? There were a few farms down the road, but the inhabitants were probably sleeping—even if they were awake, they wouldn't risk interfering. She shoved him again, but his heavy weight didn't move. By wriggling and pushing, she finally rolled free of his weight.

"Jos, are you all right?" She shook his shoulder, but his eyes didn't blink. She felt something warm and sticky on her hands. Feeling for a pulse in his wrist and then in his neck, Lina realized that he was dead. He had pushed her to safety just before he died.

Lina sank back against the tree in shock. One moment, they were having a stupid argument, and seconds later he was dead. How could a strong man like Jos be killed so easily? Remembering their argument about his proposal made her feel worse. Without hesitation, he'd saved her life; he had more courage than she would ever have. The soldier had pulled the trigger out of fear and then fled.

A wave of inertia overwhelmed her, and she couldn't imagine how she could get her legs to move. If she froze to death on the spot, at least no one would question her loyalty to Jos. Had she been loyal to Jos?

She would never have married Jos—his family didn't like her, and she had no interest in farm life. She wanted the city, the bright lights, and a job that meant something. After wasting most of her teenage years in a war, she wasn't ready to be anyone's wife. Jos had more ambition than most of his friends. His work on the vehicles driven by the occupiers had given him a training that cost him nothing. He was willing to work hard and to help his family on the farm. She was the one who thought she deserved better. She felt nauseated and overwhelmed by this situation. How had things changed so quickly?

The earth almost creaked in the silence, and out of the night sky fluttered tiny snowflakes that she brushed off her coat like dead skin. She rolled her feet and wiggled her toes to restore some circulation and then got on her hands and knees to push herself up.

Too numb to cry, she felt like she was waiting for something to happen, someone to help, but the night remained dark and unmoving. Lina had never felt so alone in her life—she felt almost smothered by the silence. She knew it was up to her to summon the strength to move.

As she struggled to stand, she brushed the leaves from her pants and swung her arms to get some feeling back. Even in the dark, she could see the outlines of his inert body. It was hard to reconcile the thoughts of the fun-loving Jos with violent and unexpected death.

Would his mother and sisters wash his body and lay him out in the formal living room? These days, all the old rituals had been suspended—without wood for coffins, bodies were wrapped in sheets and brought to churches to be placed on the floor until a mass grave could be dug. Why was she thinking about this? She had to get moving. Ada would be so worried.

Dead, she thought, trying to connect that word with the inert heap that was Jos. The only other dead person she'd seen was Mother when Father had invited them into the guest room to say their goodbyes. Her hair had been combed, and her bed jacket was neatly tied over her washed body. In Mother's case, death had crept towards her in slow steps. Even at the end, Lina had been surprised how her body clung to life. After Mother's death, she felt guilty for not loving her more. And now again, it was her fault that she hadn't loved Jos enough. Maybe there was something wrong with her—was she incapable of deep love?

What should she do? The soldier might return to look for her. She was relieved to see her bike on the ground by the tree.

Think, she told herself. She had to tell someone about Jos' body. She couldn't leave him in the woods for the animals to find.

If she biked back to Maarten's house, she could ask him to help retrieve the body. He'd probably gone to bed already, so he wouldn't be happy about getting up to answer the door.

After straightening the wheel and the handlebars, she was relieved that the bike still worked.

At Maarten's house, she pounded on the front door for a few minutes. When he finally opened the door, he rubbed his eyes and looked disoriented. He was wearing a pair of pajamas that might have been his father's, and he was unaware that his hair was standing straight up at the front.

"I'm so sorry to wake you," Lina said. She wrapped her arms over her chest—she was shaking from fright and cold.

He looked at her dumbfounded. "What the hell? You just left. What's wrong? Where's Jos? Come inside." He looked up and down the street to make sure no one was watching the house. "What do you have on your hands?" He looked at her in shock and horror. "Blood? Whose blood?"

Lina couldn't stand up any longer. She sank to the first step of the staircase and wrapped her arms around her knees. "He's been shot. We must get the body. He's in the woods at the crossroads."

"Come on, get up, it's too cold to sit there." He reached for her arm to help her to her feet and led her inside. "Start from the beginning because I can't quite believe this. Jos is dead?" He shook his head in disbelief. "But . . ."

Lina nodded. "A German soldier shot him. He panicked when he saw how big Jos was, and he pulled the trigger. We were at the crossroads in the woods, and we didn't hear him." She didn't add that they were too busy arguing to hear the soldier's arrival—fighting about a marriage proposal. Had Jos told any of them his plans? They would never forgive her if they knew she'd rejected him—they'd always thought that he was too good for her. His mother thought that Lina wasn't religious enough to be part of their family.

"Stay right there. I'll wake my brother up, and we'll use the bicycle cart to take him to the farm. You can show us where he is and then go home. His parents don't need to know that you were with him. In fact, tell no one that you were there."

Lina nodded her agreement. If Jos' mother knew that he'd been with her in the woods, she would be furious. The blame would fall squarely on Lina, not on some stupid soldier who pulled the trigger.

While she stood in the hallway waiting for the fellows to get dressed, Lina couldn't control her shaking. She leaned against the wall and hoped there was no blood on her that might stain the floral wallpaper.

Maarten and his brother retrieved their bikes from the shed and told her to come along. Together they biked silently to the crossroads: Maarten in the lead, Lina in the middle, and his brother taking up the rear. None of them spoke. And they were silent when Lina showed them the body.

Then Maarten cursed quietly and waved his hand at her to tell her to go away. "Go home. I'll tell his parents something about Germans firing without cause."

"Thanks." She touched Jos' forehead with her fingers and then turned to go. She could hear them struggle to lift Jos into the cart. Feeling a desperate need to escape those woods, she pedaled hard to get home and hoped that no one would try to stop her. This night would haunt her forever—she would never forgive herself for this terrible night. If only she had gone home earlier without him. He deserved so much better than dying in the woods; in fact, he also deserved someone much better than her. But none of that mattered now.

17.

LINA

A T the house, Lina did not bother putting the bike in the shed but activated the wheel lock and left it leaning against the exterior of the shed. She would take care of it in the morning, but at this moment, she needed to get warm because she was shaking so hard she could hardly move her fingers. Creeping inside, Lina hoped that Ada would not come downstairs and see her blood-spattered state.

Lina shut the door quietly behind her and entered the kitchen. Leaning against the kitchen counter, she tried to move her fingers and then rubbed her hands together vigorously. She longed for a cup of hot chocolate and a hot water bottle to warm her bed. As far as she could tell, her coat didn't have any blood on it, but her hands were covered with blood. Carefully washing her hands and her face at the kitchen sink, she knew that she would never be able to wash away the memory of this terrible night.

A rising sense of panic made her chest tighten. Jos was dead. How could everything go so wrong? How could she have this much death in her life? First it was Father just over a month ago, and now Jos. It was too much.

She had been bored at the party and anxious to get home, but Jos had lingered and refused to leave. That he might propose to her had never crossed her mind—she couldn't imagine a less romantic setting or a worse outcome.

Why had he pushed that issue when she'd been so clear about not being interested in marriage? It almost felt like he was daring her to turn him down. She felt guilty being angry with him, but the whole scene could have been avoided. He had too much to drink and tried to push her into making a commitment.

Remembering his face as it went from disappointment to hurt to anger was her final memory of Jos, and it was hard not to feel responsible. She hadn't fired the gun, but she had disappointed him deeply in his last moments alive. And yet, his instinct had been to protect her. He was a much better person than she was.

She crept up the stairs, avoiding the steps that had loud creaks.

Bundling her soiled clothes on the floor of her closet, she made a mental note to wash her pants in the morning. She wished she could just get rid of them, but it would be impossible to find replacements.

Lina slipped into her pajamas. Despite her exhaustion, sleep eluded her. The sheets refused to warm up as she shivered under the blankets.

She tried to remember happy moments from the past, but she felt guilty that Jos would never realize his dreams—he would not open a garage, become a mechanic, or raise a houseful of children. Lina wouldn't have the chance to tell him she was sorry or to thank him for saving her life. His inherent goodness only magnified her essential selfishness. She really was as self-centered as Ada had always claimed. But she knew that Ada would not have supported the idea of marriage because she understood that Lina was not ready to settle down.

The finality of it tore at her heart—she cried quietly in the dark. Jos had deserved better than this; he certainly deserved better than her. Nothing would be the same—his group of friends would never welcome her again. They would hold her responsible for his death almost as if she had pointed the gun. It all came down to that fact—he was gone, whereas she still had her life ahead of her. The consecutive deaths had a cumulative effect pulling her downward into a well of grief.

When she'd finally generated some warmth in the bed, she felt herself on the verge of falling asleep but then would be startled awake as she relived the sound of those shots. That soldier had stolen Jos' life, and his family was going to have to carry on without him. She would miss him—they had been friends since their school days and shared many fun times together. Although she never would have married him, she had hoped they would remain friends even as they went their separate ways. The finality was the hardest thing to accept. On the cusp of their adult lives, he would never experience the possibilities that peacetime might someday offer.

When Lina awoke the next morning, she was exhausted by the terrifying dreams she'd had. What right did the *moffen* have to terrorize innocent people, steal their food, bomb their homes, and send people to prison camps? Why had that soldier pulled the trigger when the whole incident could have been resolved with words?

Although war had surrounded them on every side for years, she had chosen to keep part of herself detached as much as possible. She refused to let the war define who she was, even though it had stolen most of her teenage years. Participating in the social rituals of youth felt like an act of resistance, but recently it left her feeling empty. After Father's death, those parties no longer held much appeal.

The war had become deeply personal. Jos' family would struggle to manage without him, but they would not want her help. His mother was probably distraught—in her eyes, he could do no wrong. From the start, his mother had warned Jos that Lina was a town girl who would never adapt to farm life. After his father died, Jos and his three sisters did all the work. Lina knew she would have been useless on the farm and incapable of the kind of hard work that was expected. But now, what was she to do? She had to convince Lucas to give her work.

As she got dressed, she spotted the bundle of clothes she'd worn the night before. Taking the stained pants downstairs, she scrubbed them in the basement sink. After washing, she hung them outside on the line. They would freeze into stiff boards until she brought them back inside.

She paced around the kitchen with nervous energy. How was she going to spend her days? If she sat around doing nothing, she'd lose her mind. Searching for food took a big part of the day, but she also wanted to do something for the war effort.

Perhaps as a temporary solution, she could convince Lars to take her back. Convincing Lucas to let her work for him might take some time. She'd try to talk to her former boss—by now, he might realize he still needed her. Although it was a stupid job, it helped to pass the day, and she often picked up important information by eavesdropping on the customers. In a practical way, the leftovers and snacks in the café had supplemented her diet more than she realized—these days she was hungry all the time. She couldn't hang around the house all day, replaying Jos' death over and over in her mind and feeling guilty.

Determined to think about something else, she glanced at the Leica camera that she'd left on the table. She picked it up, feeling its familiar weight in her hand. Maybe Ada was right to suggest that she could improve her skills. Father had frequently recommended reading his photography books to learn about technique. It was not enough to have good instincts—she needed to be able to shift settings to adjust to changing conditions. If only she'd taken the opportunity to learn from Father—she wasn't sure she could teach herself.

She searched the bookshelves in Father's study for the photography books he had recommended. "Lina," he had told her, "photography is an art, but the art is built on technique that provides a framework for all you want to do. You need to practice and practice some more. Your hand controls the camera, but your eye judges the shot and evaluates the result. When all those aspects work together, it's like a well-rehearsed and superbly conducted symphony."

If only she could apologize for being so resistant to his teaching. She could at least try to make up for it by teaching herself some technique. From now on, she would carry her camera with her. Maybe she would still have the chance to honor his memory through her pictures. She owed it to Jos to do something useful with her life. She vowed to be a better person and attempt to become more disciplined.

18.

ADA

"ARE you home?" Ada called from the back door.

"Where have you been?" Lina asked.

"I was trying to find some food," Ada said as she hung her coat on the hook by the door. "I just heard about Jos. Lucas told me. I'm so sorry."

Lina nodded.

"Do you know anything more?" Ada asked. She leaned against the kitchen counter and waited for Lina to answer.

Lina paused, unsure of how much to tell. "Please don't tell anyone. Promise?"

Ada sunk into one of the chairs and nodded. She watched Lina struggle to control her emotions. Her hands trembled, and she swallowed several times. Ada got up to get her a glass of water.

"I was there," Lina stated in a flat tone, trying to keep her emotions in control.

Ada inhaled sharply. "What do you mean?"

"We were on our way home from Maarten's house. Jos wanted to stop at the crossroads and have a cigarette before we went our separate ways. We were standing by a tree just off the road when a *mof* heard us, but we didn't hear him. He came through the woods silently and then suddenly pointed a gun at us. Jos tried talking to him to calm him down and show him that we were not a threat. Jos did his best to reassure the fellow that we were just normal people. He talked about the farm and cows and asked him about his family background, but he still didn't trust us. When Jos offered him a cigarette, it seemed like he might warm up to him. But . . . Jos was drunk and lost his balance on the uneven ground thanks to the tree roots. The soldier jumped for his gun and fired twice."

Ada put her hand on Lina's arm. "I am so sorry," she said.

"Jos protected me, and I hid behind him. Just before the soldier fired his gun, Jos pushed me out of the way so I lost my balance and fell to the ground." Lina paused, taking a shuddering breath, "I didn't know he was dead until I tried to get out from under him."

Ada removed her hand from Lina's arm and sat in silence with her hands folded. She didn't know how to comfort Lina, who was struggling to keep her composure. Ada tried to picture how this horrible thing could have happened. It was an unprovoked incident on a cold winter's night. A young couple took a moment to be alone in the woods. It reminded her that no one was ever safe—neither in their homes nor on the streets. Lina was lucky she survived unhurt. "I am so sorry. That's terrible. What did you do then?"

Lina gulped a few times as she suppressed her tears. "The soldier panicked and ran. I'm lucky he did because otherwise he might have wanted to finish me off as well. Maybe this was the first time he shot anyone at close range." She paused to get control as some ragged sighs escaped from her throat. "He grabbed Jos' bike and left. I waited till he was gone, and then I biked to Maarten's house. I showed them where the body had fallen, and they used the cart to bring the body to the farm. He told me to stay out of it because Jos' mother doesn't like me, and she'd never forgive me if she knew I was there." Lina put her face in her hands. Her shoulders were slumped in despair.

"I can't believe you were there. I am so sorry. What a terrible thing to see." She paused. "But I am glad you are safe. Jos had the presence of mind to push you out of harm's way." She looked around the kitchen and tried to imagine living there alone without Lina's company. "I don't know what I'd do without you, Lina." She almost started to cry. Looking down at her hands on the table, she wished with all her heart that Father could be there to comfort them. He would know what to say, whereas she felt completely inadequate in this moment. As sisters they had ways of being together, but none of those involved reaching deeply into each other's pain. All their old habits of bickering and arguing now seemed so childish. Would Lina suffer long-lasting effects from witnessing this violence? How could she help her through this?

Was this what Father had meant? Could they find new ways of getting along instead of relying on well-rehearsed strategies of refusing to be vulnerable to each other? Before this, she would have said it was impossible, but perhaps tragedy broke apart their routines. Lina would need her in the months ahead. She would receive no support from the friends and family of Jos, and that isolation would hurt her. It had never been quite so clear to Ada—the war had to end. Lina would probably carry this night and these losses with her the rest of her life.

As Lina continued to sit with her head in her hands, lost in sadness, Ada knew she had to do something to ease Lina's pain. "You've had quite a shock. Let me make you some tea." Ada started to stand.

Lina reached for Ada's wrist. She cleared her throat. "The worst thing was . . . just before it happened, he proposed to me."

"What?" Ada sat back down.

"I told him that I wanted to have a career. He thought I could live and help on his family farm. That was his idea of a career."

"How did he take your refusal?"

"He was angry. I had told him so many times that I wanted to go to Paris, but apparently he never believed it."

"I'm so sorry," Ada said. Lina looked genuinely distressed. "What are you doing?"

Lina held up the photography book. "Father told me to study these books. I need to think about something else."

"Have you talked to Jos' mother?"

Lina shook her head. "The guys told me to stay away. I won't be invited to the funeral, whenever they are able to have one. Maybe they will bury him on the farm." Lina stared at the floor.

Ada touched her shoulder lightly. "I am so sorry. Someday if you want to do something to remember him, we can have our own memorial."

Lina looked as if her very spirit had collapsed inside her. Ada's heart was moved by her sister's pain; she wanted to take it from her but knew that was impossible. She turned to make the tea, putting a spoonful of the last of the honey in Lina's cup and stirring it until the thick substance had melted.

19.

ADA

SEVERAL days after the death of Jos, Ada entered the house and stopped short at the entryway. Almost every utility service had been reduced or stopped. Fortunately, in anticipation of such a service interruption, Lucas had rigged up a battery unit to her illegal radio; without it, she would have felt cut off from the world. But it was November, and they couldn't possibly manage without services.

Ada grabbed the broom and swept the floor. She needed to do something to redirect her anxiety. If only Father was there—she missed him so much.

She didn't need the radio to tell her that the situation was deteriorating in their city. Her work in the community gave her a firsthand view of the scarcity of food; no amount of goodwill on the part of the volunteers could compensate for the lack of food supplies. When there were so few ingredients available to make soup, people became frustrated and took it out on the volunteers. The nastiness and name-calling were fierce, but she realized it was an expression of the intense frustration and hunger that governed their daily lives. When she brought food to elderly people in their apartments, she felt sad for the isolated lives they led.

Lucas told her how six hundred men in the village of Putten were sent to Germany as punishment for a resistance plan that failed. Retribution was so severe that the death of even one Gestapo could result in the murder of hundreds of innocent people.

She washed the floor on her knees using a heavy cotton cloth. After thinking about her proposal to employ more women in direct warfare, it no longer seemed like a good idea. Without the women in communities, things would really fall apart. Their families would starve, and children would be abandoned. Women kept everything going while men were conscripted or killed. Perhaps that was the unspoken formula for war—men fought each other to the death, and women remained at home caring for the vulnerable. If some women were fit and ready for combat, however, they deserved to have a chance at service. And although Lucas never revealed the identities of people who worked for him, she was certain that women played a role in the resistance. She respected the need for secrecy about such matters but wished sometimes she could know more about those brave people and the things they did to push back against the occupiers.

What would be left when the war ended? Families broken, men buried in unmarked graves, and children perished through starvation or illness. Didn't God just want to strike them all down with fire or flood and start over with a new creation? This world, after all, seemed broken beyond repair.

Ada stood up, took the bucket to the backyard, and pitched the gray water.

Lina didn't seem to bother herself with those kinds of thoughts; in fact, Ada envied Lina's cool demeanor under pressure. Ada watched her carefully in the days after Jos' death, and she could see Lina's sadness but also her determination. She wanted that for herself and knew she couldn't let herself sink into despair.

Ada had always hoped she would be brave enough for combat if required, but in fact she preferred administrative tasks, such as the work she did for Lucas. Somehow, she had to trust that when each person contributed something, together they would create a force of good that would overcome evil. It was important to keep believing that evil could be overcome, but it took an act of will when despair was the easier choice.

Ada gathered up a pile of used tea towels and put them carefully into a pot of water she had brought to boiling for the purpose of washing them. The lack of soap was making all these household tasks ineffective, but Ada planned to go through the motions anyway. It was important to stick to the routines of a proper household—some order in the chaos was essential. Mother had always insisted on that even though she had created her own kind of chaos within their family life.

It was difficult to see the long lines of displaced people who carried their belongings in wagons or prams, forced to find new homes in other towns because their own had been destroyed. Executions in plain sight and bodies on the streets were common. Trying without success to avert her eyes when she biked past bodies sprawled on the streets, Ada wondered how anyone could see so much suffering and not be destroyed by it.

All her attempts to keep their lives normal seemed futile—the only normal now was the suffering of the people. *Give us our daily bread,* she recited to herself over and over, wondering who would put bread into all those unwashed and outstretched hands? She remembered the communion services in their church. They had often complained at the prospect of extra-long services with the communion tables, but there was a dignity to the act of remembrance and the sharing of bread. She wiped the kitchen table and thought about the slender offerings Lucas and Lina brought to this table. There was a choice—she could either keep worrying about the future when there might be nothing to share, or she could face each day with hope.

When Lucas expressed optimism about the future, she wondered if he really believed what he said or if he was trying to encourage them. Sometimes she had heard people arguing about whether the country should surrender rather than continue the fight. How many more people in her country would die from starvation or execution while the Allied soldiers slowly crawled north through mud and cold, hoping to rescue whoever was left?

The next day when Ada arrived home, she sensed that someone had been in the house. She hung her coat carefully on the hook and looked around the kitchen. With her heart beating loudly, she removed her shoes and tiptoed down the hall. Pausing to listen, the only sound she heard was the howling wind rattling the storm windows. A storm had rolled in bringing wind gusts and freezing rain that pelted against the windowpanes.

A faint smell of *eau de cologne* hung in the hallway—something that reminded her of Mother, who had often patted her forehead with lacy handkerchiefs doused in the scent. Without any soaps or lotions available these days, the fragrance was more noticeable. Whoever was there must have left shortly before Ada arrived. If she had encountered someone in the house, she didn't know what she would have done. What exactly was she capable of doing if pushed to an extreme by an external threat?

When she checked Father's study, she noticed that the closet door was open even though she'd closed it tightly yesterday. She looked around the room. Because she dusted those shelves every week, Ada knew exactly where things should be, and she took pride in keeping things the way Father had left them. Whoever had searched had not covered her tracks very well. One of the desk drawers was left open; the books were rearranged. When she opened the cupboard door, nothing was out of place, and the lack of light might have discouraged anyone from searching further. Lucas had warned her that people might prey on them now that Father was gone.

Nothing was disturbed in the rest of the house. Ada sat at the kitchen table and tried to calm herself. Mrs. Vriend was the only person she knew who doused herself with *eau de cologne*. Such luxuries were impossible to obtain these days, but she'd be able to get it on the black market or through her husband for astronomical prices. Ada stood up and opened the kitchen window and the door that led to the sunporch to clear out the scent.

If the Nazis had searched the place, they would have left it in a shambles, but someone like Mrs. Vriend would be more careful. Maybe she'd been searching for the deed to the house or details concerning Father's financial accounts. Ada went to the closet, but the metal box appeared to be undisturbed, and the papers concerning the house were in order.

It was unsettling to think that neighbors might be breaking in and searching their house. If Mrs. Vriend planned to move into their home, she had a surprise coming because Ada planned to defend this house. Maybe she thought young people could be intimidated into handing over their home, but this home was their legacy. Memories lived here—this was where they had celebrated holidays and birthdays, and no one had the right to take that from them.

20.

LINA

THAT morning, Lina was on her way to the café to talk to Lars and see if she could get her job back—even if it was temporary, it would give her some time to convince Lucas that she might be helpful to the resistance.

The familiar smell of the place hit her when she entered. Food fried in cheap cooking oil mingled easily with the scent of stale cigarette smoke. The patrons didn't seem to mind—there was nowhere else to go. There were tables around the perimeter of the café with a large bar in the center. The walls were painted a dark green that made the interior feel dim. The table positioned in front of the window was usually occupied as customers desired some light. Lina had told her boss several times that he should repaint the walls and add some art to make the place more attractive, but Lars was uninterested.

"Hey, Lars, how are you?" she asked as she entered the café. She nodded to the regulars who sat at the window table.

"Well, look who's here. Are you planning to sit and order? I'll have my new waitress serve you."

Lars waved to someone who was busy wiping the tables. As the young woman turned, Lina caught a flash of red lipstick framed by jet-black hair. The woman walked towards her with confidence.

"Maria, what are you doing here?" Lina asked when she realized who it was. As far as she knew, Jos had never gone back to Maria, but she still didn't like her. There were some things that were hard to forgive. She could bet that Maria's bright red lips were a gift from the soldiers, and they kept her fed because she didn't look half-starved like the rest of them. Her dark hair fell into movie-star waves. With blue eyes, her face had a startling effect that made men look twice. She had admitted to hanging out with the *moffen*, and that was all Lina needed to know. The fact that Lars hired her made her wonder about his Nazi sympathies. Perhaps they deserved each other, and she should be relieved to be gone.

"Lars hired me last week," Maria said with a small shrug.

"A farm girl knows how to work," Lars said as he smiled at Maria and then looked pointedly at Lina. He put his arm around her waist as if he were boasting of his newest possession. Maria didn't look at him and held herself perfectly still.

Lina felt a flash of sympathy for her. She had heard that Maria's mother was sick, and Maria had to support her and her four siblings. It was no surprise that Lars took advantage of her situation. They all had to find ways to survive, but it was disheartening to realize that a fellow countryman might take advantage of a vulnerable young woman.

Lina stared at him. How dare he suggest that she didn't work hard? After she had washed countless glasses and wiped tables, he had a lot of nerve insulting her. She felt her temper rise, so she took a few breaths to remind herself why she was there. That plan needed revision on the spot. She was not going to beg him for anything. As she stumbled to find the right words, he looked at her with impatience.

"Did you want something?" he asked rudely.

Lina looked at him and remembered clearly how much she disliked him. "I was just passing by and thought I'd say hello. See you around." *In truth, I hope to never see him again.*

As Lina moved away from the bar towards the door, Maria followed her.

"I heard what happened to Jos," she whispered. "That was awful."

Lina nodded. "It certainly was. I must go. Take care of yourself." She thought about warning her about Lars, but she knew Maria would make her own choices.

Maria walked towards the regulars who had called her over. They had already forgotten Lina and were joking with her replacement. It made her furious that people had so little loyalty—she had no doubt that if that soldier had shot her instead of Jos, Maria would have been knocking at his door the next day, offering him solace in his time of grief.

Lina buttoned her coat and fastened her scarf around her neck. She put a smile on her face, waved to her former customers, and left the café.

Although the sun was shining, it was cold. A thin layer of ice created a shiny mirror on the canal. No ducks feasted at the edges where the water wasn't completely frozen. No skaters were on the ice. Lina leaned against the railing on the bridge and stared at the almost frozen canal. She tucked her hands in her armpits to warm them.

Life felt desolate—no job, no friends, no boyfriend. It felt like one of those V2 rockets had fallen out of the sky and demolished every piece of her old life. Even if this war ended tomorrow, she could never get her life back. There was no going back to her old job or her old friends.

She tried to remember what it was like before the war when the streets around the café were filled with people who exchanged greetings. After locking their bikes in the long rows of bicycle racks, they shopped in the stores and market stalls. Filling their panniers with a fresh baguette and wedges of cheese, they headed home for lunch at the dining room table. She remembered birthday parties with pastries and gift tulips.

If she'd ever been miserable or grumpy in the past, she had no excuse. They never went hungry, they always had a new dress for church on special Sundays, and they had all the school supplies and textbooks they needed.

Ada had been extra kind to her after Jos' death—maybe that was a sign of a change. Someday, she might look back at this moment and realize that her adult life had begun not with a birthday banner but with an experience so stark and horrible it had changed everything.

21.

ADA

THE next day, Lucas sat at the table while Ada served tea. "Lina will be home soon. She went to see if she could get anything from the farms on the road to Oegstgeest."

"Has she been finding any food lately?" Lucas asked.

"Not much. Before Lina arrives, there's something I want to ask you. She has been despondent ever since Jos died, and with Father's death as well, she is having a hard time. Without work to distract her, I think she has lost a sense of purpose. She spends time trying to locate food, but she needs something more. Is there any way you could use her in the network? When Lina asked, you said you would consider it."

"She's young," Lucas said.

"There are ten-year-old children running messages and scrounging for food."

"You've often described her as immature and unreliable," Lucas said.

"I was wrong," Ada admitted.

"It's dangerous just to walk on the streets these days. They're rounding up young men to help build German defenses. Pretty soon they'll take young women too."

"Are you trying to protect her?" Ada asked.

Lucas was silent. He was clearly uncomfortable with that question.

She wanted to ask him what his feelings were for her sister, but she decided to respect his privacy on that. "What about you? Aren't you at risk?" she asked.

"I carry my medical exemption with me, but if they get desperate, they'll even take tuberculosis patients."

"Is it true that the *Reichskommisar* lifted the embargo?"

Lucas sighed. "That's true, but the food shortage is still acute. As you know, community kitchens are keeping people alive, but there's just not enough food to distribute. In the north they have potatoes, beets, and rye, but there's no way to transport it. People are traveling further for food, but the more people do that, the less food there will be up there. So far, the occupiers have let food travelers pass without a problem, but they could change their minds at any time."

"I think that the community kitchens are like putting a small dressing on a bleeding wound."

"I wouldn't minimize the benefits of the community kitchens," Lucas said. "Many communities have done an amazing job, working together with different denominations, to help the citizens. It gives me hope to see that kind of cooperation."

"Perhaps you should look again—what we're offering is not solving anyone's hunger problem. Maybe it helps the government-in-exile feel less guilty so they can concentrate on the military action and forget about the ordinary people."

Lucas looked at her. "I think the government in England must work with the military authorities, but I want to believe they have our best interests in mind. It is important to remember that even some of the occupiers have shown a willingness to cooperate with food relief."

"I just think people need to do more. I should do more."

"You are making an important contribution by typing the newsletter and by working with the Food Council."

"Never mind," she said with irritation. "I'm not looking for you to give me an assignment. I would be terrible at that kind of thing."

"It is dangerous out there," Lucas warned.

Ada felt irritated, and she knew it wasn't his fault. The lack of food made her feel faint and jittery. Against her better judgement, she pursued the argument. "Of course, I know it is dangerous out there, but someone like Lina is quite capable of taking care of herself. Sometimes I wonder if you underestimate what women can accomplish. You say that you don't have enough members in your network, but you exclude women and choose men who pretend they can handle guns. I've been shooting since I was ten, and I'm pretty sure I could outshoot any of your men."

Lucas put his cup down carefully. "I don't mean to underestimate anyone's contribution. We all have important work to do."

Ada wanted to quit the discussion. She wasn't being fair to Lucas and was just venting her frustration on him. She waved her hand to push that discussion aside. "Never mind all that. We need to search Father's study again and figure out why someone might have been snooping around. I cannot imagine that we missed anything in the cleanup we did."

"I am happy to help."

"Why would there be renewed interest in his office here and at the university? I don't want to assume everyone is looking for the same thing, but one of the searchers wears perfume."

Lucas nodded. "You think it was a woman? And perhaps someone you know?"

"Exactly." Ada looked at the back door when she heard the door open. "Ah, there's Lina now."

22.

LINA

Lina entered the kitchen and hung her coat on the hook by the door. "I didn't find much food. Hello, Lucas." She was surprised to feel happy to see him. That made no sense. He was there to talk to Ada, not her, and whatever tricks her mind was playing needed to stop.

"What did you find?" Ada asked as she took the small bag that Lina handed her.

"All I could get were some split peas and an onion. Maybe enough for a soup." She sat at the table across from Lucas. "Tell me some good news, Lucas."

"There was a successful raid on an ammunition depot at the edge of town. Those arms will be distributed to various groups who will be battle ready. The sentries were not expecting any kind of raid at that time of the night, and it was easy to tie them up and put them in a storage room."

Lina listened with interest. "Why not kill them?"

Lucas looked startled. "I think we must do our work but still maintain some ethical and moral perspective. These fellows were merely guards and didn't deserve to be murdered."

"But they kill our people even when they are innocent," Lina argued.

"That is true, but we have to do our best to not become like them."

Ada and Lucas changed the subject and began to discuss a book by an author Lina didn't know. It was difficult to be around such learned people—she often felt like a fool. Lucas and Ada had so much in common. *How could it be that I had not felt at home with Jos' friends nor with Ada and Lucas? Where do I belong?*

"Lina, are you listening?" Ada asked.

Lina was startled to hear her name as she'd been so lost in thought. "I can't figure out what is going on," Lina replied. "Why did they arrest Father and take those Hitler papers but are still searching through his stuff? What else could there be?"

Lucas hesitated and cleared his throat. "It's true they took that folder."

"We know that; and besides, everyone knows Hitler is a bad guy, so they don't need a file to prove that."

"They arrested your father because he hid the papers containing information that a small group of generals intended to use to depose Hitler. The fact that your father hid those papers gave them an excuse to arrest him. But the Nazis are not as unified as people assume. At the same time that the Captain and his friends in this region were hoping to reinsert themselves into the power structure in Germany, another group in Berlin was already making moves and had obtained a copy of that file to help them get rid of Hitler. The thing that I have learned since then is that the generals realize they are losing the war. Time is running out to put a new regime in place. The infighting between these groups is creating chaos and weakening the movement. The Captain is watching his chances fade as things fall apart around him. That means he is desperate, so we need to be very careful because he will become increasingly dangerous and willing to risk everything."

"What difference does it make whether this Nazi or another is in charge? If we don't win the war, the new Nazis won't be any kinder than the last ones."

Lucas nodded sadly. "From our perspective, that is true. Their ideology of supremacy and domination will be unchanged; only the players will change. That's why we must win this war."

Ada joined them at the table, picking up her knitting and listening to Lucas as he answered Lina's questions. *It still made little sense why the occupiers would be searching and turning offices upside down. What more could there be?*

"Why didn't Father just hand that file over to them? In the end it was worthless because a copy already existed. Perhaps the Captain might have thanked him and made him a hero."

"Your father promised his colleague in Germany that he would keep that information safe. Handing it over might have compromised an entire network of people. As you know, your father had a very strong moral sense. We think that perhaps the German professor was taken captive and forced to reveal the location of that file."

"I thought someone around here had betrayed him," Lina said.

"I don't think so, but we can never know for sure," Lucas said.

"You are suggesting that we prepare ourselves," Lina said, "even though we don't know what they are looking for."

Lucas paused and studied his hands that were folded on the table, his long fingers intertwined tightly. "It's very complicated, but I think you deserve to know more about your father's work. Your father wasn't just holding the papers for his friend; he was a main guardian and caretaker of a repository of information. The papers they found the night of his arrest, the Hitler papers, were just a decoy. Hitler was already losing control of his people in Berlin, and various attempts to assassinate him were being discussed. But the Captain did not know about the other papers yet."

"I don't understand. If those papers were a decoy, what are they looking for now?"

"This other file has greater potential to damage the Captain and his friends."

"What file? I am confused," Ada said, refusing to believe that Father had kept such a secret from her.

Both Ada and Lina stared at Lucas. What on earth had Father been doing?

Lucas took a breath and dropped his voice. "Your father was compiling a list of war crimes and criminals, based on evidence sent to him from various sources. This is a top secret document that provides information on individual names, types of evidence such as documents, films, or photographs, and location of the evidence—all this information will make it possible to prosecute war crimes when the war ends. Many people have risked their lives to get this information to your father, so he was very motivated to keep it safe."

Ada looked at him in disbelief. "That's what Father was doing?"

"It's hard to imagine Father being involved in such things," Lina said. "He was just an ordinary history professor." Lina looked uncertain even as she said the words.

"That was a clever cover for his other work. Your Father was far from ordinary," Lucas said. "Even in his writing, he provided a critical analysis of current events. His forthcoming manuscript explores the failure of Nazi propaganda that will be essential to our understanding of fascism for years to come. He had a strong bond with scholars in Germany who were opposed to the Nazi movement. Many of them perished because of their work and beliefs, but your Father helped compile their work in an edited volume. We hope that it will be published when the war ends."

Lina and Ada looked at him in surprise. "Father did all that?" Ada asked.

Lucas nodded.

"Let me get this straight," Lina asked. "Not only was he was editing a book about Nazi failures, but he maintained documentation of war crimes? No wonder they wanted to put him away. That also explains why he worked day and night."

Lucas looked at them and paused. "Your father was a remarkable person."

"And what about the war crimes file?" Ada asked. "Tell me again what it contains?"

"It provides evidence and testimony that will be used to hold people responsible for their crimes."

"Who will hold them responsible?" Ada asked.

"An international tribunal will be assembled to hear the evidence and to decide on the punishment. The Captain knows he will be judged, and he is becoming increasingly agitated as reports of the Allied advance reach him. His attempts to interrogate government leaders to find out about the war crimes document have yielded little because no one knows where this file is kept. The searches at the university and at this house may indicate they are getting closer, but they may also be searching for professors as possible organizers. We need to be very careful."

"How did you get involved in this?" Lina asked.

"Your father trusted me. I had more freedom to travel to collect testimony in ways that he could not. There are transcripts of interviews, photographs, and maps in the file."

"What was your excuse for visiting us so regularly? Surely people notice something like that?"

Lucas blushed and looked down at his teacup. "I might have hinted that I was romantically involved with the professor's elder daughter."

Lina studied him carefully. She was intrigued by the blush and thought it was quite attractive.

"But that's not true," Ada exclaimed. "You lied!"

"Sometimes a lie is necessary for the greater good."

"Maybe it was good for your reputation," Lina joked. If Lucas was not interested in Ada, with whom was he involved? If the answer to that was no one, then he was available. She tried not to smile at the thought, but it made her curious about him. He never spoke about his personal life. Perhaps he was so involved in his underground work that he had no time for relationships.

"Stop it," Ada said, covering her own embarrassment. "Can we get back to the important stuff?" She pulled a strand of hair out of her face and tucked it back into the bun at the nape of her neck.

"We can't just sit here waiting for someone to come skulking. If you think there's any chance that the war crimes file is in this house, we need to search everywhere and bring it to a safe location," Lina said.

Ada nodded agreement. "The fewer people who know about this, the better. I can imagine that those who submitted information live in fear that their cooperation will be discovered. I can also guess that those implicated would do anything to keep their names out of this document."

"That is true on both accounts. But those who gave testimony trusted your father to keep it safe. They are probably very worried that the information will fall into the wrong hands. For them, there will be no rest until the perpetrators are arrested."

"When Father asked you to collect information, didn't he tell you where it was going to be kept?"

"He was very careful about that in case any of us were captured and forced to talk."

"Should we assume that the occupiers have not located the source or managed to get this information from Father? Otherwise, they wouldn't be scrambling around the way they are now."

"When your father was arrested, the occupiers in this area were not yet aware of this file. Your father may have been questioned about the Hitler file, but once satisfied they sent him on to a camp, not knowing that there was more information hidden. We must remember that desperate people are dangerous, so we need to be very careful."

Ada and Lina looked at him in alarm. How could they protect themselves?

"We should eliminate the most obvious hiding places. I suggest we give his study a thorough search before we look elsewhere."

Lina began to protest. "But Lucas, we cleaned that room thoroughly after the soldiers tossed it. And they turned it upside down."

"It's worth a try," Ada sighed. "Maybe together we will see something we missed the first time."

"What do you think happened to Father?" Lina asked.

Lucas shook his head. "Conditions in those camps are very rough, and your Father had health issues."

"What health issues?" Lina and Ada asked simultaneously.

They sat in silence as the clock in the hall clicked loudly.

"There was a problem with his lungs. He didn't like to talk about it, so I don't know the details," Lucas said.

"He did have a cough but said it was an allergic reaction to dust," Ada said.

Lucas nodded.

"We need to fight to protect his work," Lina said. "I think he would have wanted that."

Ada agreed. "If anything is hidden in this house, I would rather know about it and find a safe place for it than wait for the Gestapo to find it. Let's get started."

23.

***

LINA

THEY stood in front of Father's desk wondering where to begin. The oak surface, now completely tidy, had recently been polished. Father's fountain pen and ink were the only objects on the surface of the desk. Ada made sure that the room was tidy and dusted it every week.

"Where do we begin?" asked Ada. "Lina and I went through most of this the last time," she said pointing at the desk and bookshelves. "If anything was here, we would have found it."

"Let's not repeat what you've done, but let's try to imagine what might have been missed," Lucas suggested.

"We didn't roll up the area rug last time," Lina offered.

"We didn't check the cupboard," Ada said.

Lucas looked up at the ceiling, but there was nothing irregular there. "Why don't we start with the cupboard? I will pass you the contents."

"You mean unpack everything?" Lina asked in disbelief.

"This will be thorough. If something is there, we will find it."

Lucas took the academic robes that were on a hanger on the inside hook of the door and handed them to Ada. "You might want to store this properly somehow," he suggested.

Ada found a cloth storage bag in the hall closet and put the robes inside, taking a moment to sniff the woolen fabric that still carried the scent of pipe tobacco. She smoothed the collar with her hands and closed the bag. When the war ended, she would find a home for these robes, but till then she would store them in the closet. They served as a tangible reminder of her father, and she wasn't prepared to surrender that yet.

Perhaps someday Lucas would help her find someone who needed these robes, or he might wear them himself.

Lucas piled journals into Lina's open arms. "I think that's enough," Lucas said with a warm smile.

Lina caught her breath—his eyes regarded her with such warmth and affection. Was she imagining it? Perhaps she was losing her mind. She placed them carefully on the top of the desk.

Returning to the entrance of the closet, she held out her arms for the next load. When they finished with the books and journals, he handed her a metal document box, which she put on the desk.

Ada opened it and quickly looked through the contents. "I've looked inside this before, and this is where Father stored legal and financial papers."

"Anything interesting?" Lucas asked.

"Just family documents," she said as she closed the box. "That's too obvious a hiding place."

They continued until the closet was completely empty.

Lucas looked at a pile of student exams and essays. "There might be some of my brilliant grading in this pile. Do you think we can burn them in the woodstove?"

"What are they?" Lina asked as she peered at the pile of paper in his hands.

"When the university closed, these tests and papers were never returned. We can get rid of them."

"Let's not destroy anything today. I can do that some other time," Ada advised.

"Let's keep going," Lina said. "We don't want to miss anything."

They all froze when they heard a voice call out.

"Did you lock the back door?" Ada asked.

"I'm not sure," Lina said.

Ada hurried out of the study.

Lina and Lucas listened as she greeted Nel.

"What should we do?"

"Let's see if Ada can get rid of her. We'll keep quiet, or she'll want to know what we are doing."

"That nosy witch. Where did you put your bike?" Lina asked.

"I pulled it behind the shed. I don't think she can see it unless she went looking around the backyard."

"I don't know why Ada bothers to be friends with her," Lina said as she sat in the chair opposite the desk. She remembered how Mother sat there while having tea with Father.

"I think she's after something," Lucas said. "And Ada knows it."

"Are you saying that Ada is just pretending to be her friend?" Lina asked. She watched Lucas pick up more term papers and read them.

"Maybe," Lucas said.

"Are you checking for more of your brilliant comments?" she asked.

Lucas laughed. "No, there's not much evidence of that. But I was thinking how innocent we were then, how little we knew about what was coming."

"Would knowing have made a difference?"

Lucas thought about that for a moment and shook his head slowly. "Probably not." Lucas said as he put the essays on the desk and turned towards the closet.

Lina was still sitting in the chair, trying to imagine Father seated at his desk, leaning back with his pipe, and listening to her. It was so hard to imagine that he would never be with them again. She was overcome with a sadness so profound she sat immobilized in the chair, wishing the pain would end.

Lucas looked at her. "Lina, are you all right?"

She looked at him blankly, lost in her pain.

He walked over to her chair and crouched on the floor in front of her.

Startled by his proximity and his concern, her cheeks grew warm as she looked into his eyes and then shifted her glance to the floor. He did not move away. She saw the pilling on his handknit sweater around the arms and shoulders where a moth hole revealed a black T-shirt underneath. She wanted to raise her hand to touch his cheek and to feel the bristles of a few days' growth on his skin. It was overwhelming—his nearness, his attention, his physical presence.

He wiped away a solitary tear from her cheek. "Lina, remember you are not alone."

Lina attempted a weak smile, wanting to mask her vulnerability, trying to shrug off his concern just in case she was misreading the situation. "Thank you," she whispered, the intimacy of the moment causing her heartbeat to accelerate. Because she had assumed he was interested in Ada, she couldn't quite trust herself to interpret his concern. And yet, the caring appeared genuine, and to her surprise she welcomed it.

She might have reached out to hug him, but she heard Ada's steps in the hall and sat back in the chair as Lucas quickly stood up and moved back to the desk.

"Any progress?" Ada asked as she glanced at them, trying to interpret the silence in the room.

"We wanted to wait until you returned," Lucas said. "How was your visitor?"

"I got rid of her. Told her I had a problem with the downstairs toilet and asked her if she wanted to help. Turned out she had some urgent errands."

Lina chuckled and avoided looking at Lucas. "I hope you locked the back door," she said.

"I did. Have we finished emptying the closet?"

Lucas waved his hand at the empty closet. "I need a light to check the walls and the floors."

"I'll get one," Lina offered. She ran to get the tool kit in the hall closet that contained their emergency supplies, relieved to escape the study for a few moments to collect herself. Could it be that Lucas was there not just out of loyalty to his teacher or to Ada as a fellow student, but for her? After Jos' death, she swore she would never get involved in a relationship again, but Lucas was of a different order, and he already proved his commitment to them. She grabbed the light and returned to the study. She avoided his eyes and kept her hands busy straightening the piles of books and papers on Father's desk.

"I'm going to need both hands, so if you hold the light and move it slowly over the surface of the wall, I will feel the walls for any irregularities." He rapped on the wall with his knuckles and ran his hands from ceiling to floor. "Nothing there. It all seems quite normal. Now shine towards the back."

Lina did as he asked. Ada was right behind her, peering over her shoulder. The steps ran upwards and away from them, and the closet was built to include the underside of the stairs.

Lucas ran his hands over the wood that covered the steps and then rapped his knuckles on them as well.

He looked again at the steps and felt the edges of the each one. He instructed Lina to shine the light on a step at eye level. She could see the rough wood that comprised the backside of the steps. A tiny hook and eye closure on each side held a wood panel in place. Lucas lifted the left and then the right hooks and then peeled back the board carefully before handing it to Lina.

"What is it?" Ada asked as she tried to see over Lina's head.

They backed out of the closet so that Lucas could carry out the contents of the hiding place inside the stair step. Placing a stack of papers on Father's desk, they looked at them, hesitant to uncover whatever secrets had been placed there. On top of the papers was a gun.

"What are we waiting for?" Lina asked.

Lucas lifted the gun from the pile and moved it aside. He handed Ada the bundle of papers. "You look first." Ada sat in Father's desk chair and quickly leafed through the pages. Lina returned to the wing chair opposite the desk while Lucas closed the closet door and leaned against it with his arms across his chest.

Lina felt a sense of pride. Some may have underestimated him, but Father had been a hero, and he had done his work with great courage. This only confirmed what she had been thinking about her possible contribution. Realizing how heroic her father had been, she knew it was long overdue for her to commit to the war effort in any way possible. If Lucas doubted her capability, she would find someone else who would let her help. Father had given her the key to how she might contribute, but it had taken her a long time to understand. Her camera and her bicycle were weapons against the *moffen*.

Lucas had moved over to stand behind Ada and read over her shoulder. "This chart provides a coded list of names, types of evidence, and locations of documents, films, and photographs."

"Meaning what?" Lina asked.

"This is a master document that contains proof of the acts committed by the occupiers in this country. We must keep this safe at any cost. Do not doubt they would kill to get their hands on this."

"Why didn't he tell me about this?" Ada asked. "I typed so much of his other work and even his correspondence. Why not this?"

"He was protecting you."

Ada looked up at Lucas and then at Lina. Her heart was beating so quickly, she felt a bit dizzy and short of breath. The document she was holding would guarantee a death sentence. She was still stunned that Father had kept such enormous secrets from them. All the work she'd done for him never included any hint that he was collating this information.

"We should have searched more carefully. How did we miss this?" Ada asked.

"Never mind that. We should figure out what to do," Lina said quietly.

"We have to find a very secure place to hide this until the war is over," Lucas said.

"Do you think the occupiers know that this file exists?" Ada asked.

Lucas looked at the papers. "We can't be certain, but the fact that they are searching at the university makes me think they know something. With rumors of an imminent military defeat growing louder, those in charge are planning their exits and hoping to avoid years in jail or even death. One can assume there is a certain amount of panic among the leaders."

Ada and Lina sat quietly, trying to absorb what Lucas was telling them.

Ada was lost in thought. Why had Father not trusted her with his secrets? She had been so proud to work for him by typing, editing, and taking care of all the domestic details so that he could finish his book. She had often felt privileged by his attention and secretly gloated that she had a closer relationship than Lina. But now it seemed that she had a different relationship but not necessarily a deeper one, and in the end he had not trusted either of them with his secret work.

Why had she felt the need to compete with Lina for his attention and approval? Father had been generous in seeing them as individuals with different strengths. She had foolishly believed that her school prizes and grades gave her more value in his eyes. He had loved them both without hesitation. Father had shown them fatherly love; it made her sad to realize how complicated things must have been for him. She felt embarrassed that she had bothered him by complaining about Lina and chores.

Lina seemed to absorb the news in a different way—her face showed a level of resolve that made her blue eyes turn fierce. Ada wanted to ask her what she was thinking, but Lina would not appreciate being asked to reveal her thoughts in front of Lucas.

Lucas paced back and forth in the space beside the desk. He looked out the window to make sure no one was watching the house. "We need to be careful," he said. He began to replace the papers and books to their rightful places.

"I agree. We need to find a safe place for this. But before we think about that, there's an introduction written by Father. He wrote: *This is a list of war crimes and criminals with the location of the evidence and the type of evidence, whether a written transcript, film, photograph, or other documentation. We trust that a military court or an international tribunal composed of judges will convene when the war ends. May this information, gathered by many brave hands, be used by those who will judge and sentence them for their deeds."*

They sat in silence, imagining Father writing those words. He was firm in his commitment, and his courage was a model to them.

Lina looked at Ada. "He was very brave."

Ada nodded her agreement. "What should we do?"

Lucas cleared his throat. "We all agree that we must keep this safe. In that regard, where could this be stored until the end of the war?"

Ada nodded, but she was still troubled by the process. "How did Father receive all this information? No one ever came to the house when I was here. Did you collect and transport it to him?"

"This involved many ordinary people, including clerks, bookkeepers, and housewives. Some of them may have been forced to work for the Nazis in offices and workplaces. Others may have had a good cover to transport information from one place to another. Sometimes your father sent me to meet someone, but I didn't ask for details."

Lina and Ada stared at him. Could he not have known anything about the information he was collecting?

Lucas continued, "They may have used children or women on bicycles to courier information to agreed-upon sites. We can assume that they risked everything to collect the information, duplicate it, and send it to a location or to a person that they didn't know. We may never know the details, but your father edited the information and perhaps even confirmed some of the details and then organized it in this way. He depended on a network that operated in secrecy to protect the individuals."

"He was a very careful scholar. I imagine that's why they picked him," Ada said.

"He also avoided notice because he wasn't overtly political," Lucas said.

Lina nodded agreement. "That's true. Even we had no idea. We will protect this for Father. He risked everything for this and so must we."

"Are we in agreement that we will do whatever it takes to preserve these papers?"

"I agree," Ada said.

"So do I," said Lina.

"Me too," said Lucas. "I will put them back in the stair step, which is the safest place for now. Ada can transport them to a future location of her choice."

"It's so hard to trust anyone," Ada said.

"Think of somebody your Father trusted."

Ada nodded. "I'll give it some thought. Just having it in the house makes me anxious, but I don't want to put someone else in danger."

"What about the gun?" Lina asked. She got up from the chair and picked up the gun.

"Maybe he thought you might need to defend yourselves. You mentioned that your Father had trained you to handle a gun."

The girls both nodded.

"We learned at my *Opa's* farm," Ada said.

"In any case, it's not going to be useful hidden in the stair step. Where could you hide it and still have easy access?"

Ada and Lina looked at each other.

"I know exactly where to put it," Lina said, "but let's put away the papers first. There's too much risk in having them out in the open."

After Lucas made sure the papers were replaced in the stair step, Lina led them to the kitchen and pulled out a porcelain canister labeled *Suiker*. "We haven't had sugar for a long time. No one will look here." She wrapped the gun in a tea towel with the ammunition and replaced the top. Lina put the canister in its usual place on the counter. "Now is there anything to eat?" Lina said. "Searches make me so hungry."

"I have something," Lucas said. He pulled a tin of herring out of his bag and a few slices of bread wrapped in some waxed paper. "Do you think you can do something with this?" he asked.

Ada accepted his gift. "It'll just take a few minutes. Have a seat, and I'll make something. I am still trying to take all this in—I feel like I underestimated Father."

Lucas chuckled. "I think that was his intention. He wanted to be almost invisible so that he could do what he needed to do."

"We have to keep this stuff safe no matter what it takes," Lina said.

"I just hope it doesn't take our lives," Ada said.

"We must be prepared for anything," Lina said in a somber tone.

24.

ADA

THE next morning, Ada biked to Reverend Arie's church office behind the church. She'd been awake till the wee hours trying to think of a place to hide the secret file. The only person she could think of who had both the courage and the commitment to hide the papers was their minister.

Although her family had attended his church since she was a child, she had never visited him in his study, and she was anxious because it felt so official. People probably came to him with all kinds of problems, but she was here to ask a favor—a very big favor. He had been so kind to visit them after Father's death.

Both sides of his study were lined with theological books from floor to ceiling. Ada could see that the titles represented both modern and classical languages.

As she stood in front of a large desk covered with books and papers, Reverend Arie stood up to shake her hand. Light filtered in from the window behind his head and covered the papers on his desk. He smiled at her, but he seemed exhausted, with dark circles under his eyes.

"How are you?" he asked.

Ada sat in the chair that he had indicated. "I'm fine. Thank you for visiting us after Father . . ." Her voice broke, and she paused to collect herself. "Today I am here to ask you for some help. Father told me that we could trust you."

He leaned forward with his elbows on the desk. When he stretched his arms, she saw that the elbow of his dress shirt had split. His gray wool vest was worn thin along the shoulders. "Of course. What can I do?"

"Father collected information in a file that must be kept safe until the war ends. The information is so important that it must be delivered to the proper authorities the moment the war is over. Father knew how dangerous possession of this would be, so he made certain we didn't know about it. The Nazis have been searching everywhere, and we think this is what they are looking for."

"I see," he said as he took off his glasses to clean them. "This is not the folder for which he was arrested?"

"We think that the first one might have been intended to mislead them from locating this most important information."

He nodded. "Your father was such a brave man."

"There is a tremendous risk in having anything to do with this, so you have every reason to refuse this request. Three of us know about this, and we are sworn to secrecy. We believe we have had intruders searching our house while we were out, so we are eager to find a new place for this."

Reverend Arie listened carefully and nodded. "What exactly do you need from me?" he inquired.

"Could you find a place to keep them safe until the war ends? Our house is no longer secure."

Reverend Arie did not hesitate. "I will hide it, and I will not look at the contents."

Ada held up her hand. "Please do not tell me where you plan to hide this—it's safer if I do not know."

"I'll leave a clue for you. Ada, your father would be very proud of you."

"Thank you," she said, blinking away her tears. Ada held the envelope for a few seconds longer and then stood up to hand it to him. Although it was hard to release it, she felt like she had found the right person to guard it. Father and Reverend Arie had been friends since their student days, and he had always been a part of their family. She hoped that this would not put him in danger. Her hands felt empty after handing him the envelope.

Reverend Arie rested his hand on the envelope. "How is your volunteer work going?" he asked.

"It is very challenging. Clients get angry and blame us for the lack of food, but it's not our fault. We have so little with which to work."

"That makes things very difficult. We have tried to take care of people in the congregation who are housebound or unable to visit the community kitchens, but that has become challenging."

Ada crossed and uncrossed her legs. She wasn't sure how much to confide in the minister, not wanting him to think she didn't have enough faith to find her own answers. She had come here today because she trusted him, but she wasn't sure how to begin.

While she deliberated, Ada stood up and pretended to read the book titles on his shelf, running her fingers over the gold letters on the spines. She turned back and sat in the wing chair.

"What is it, Ada?" he asked. "You look perplexed."

"I know you are busy," she replied as she twisted her ring but didn't look him in the eyes, "and I hate to bother you further."

"Don't worry. Ask whatever you want to ask. You have trusted me with your father's work. I hope you can trust me with whatever is on your heart today."

Ada cleared her throat nervously. "I've been wondering about something . . . do you think Christians should fight wars?"

He paused. "War is an abomination. But there are times we are called to speak out and fight against injustice," he replied, "and sometimes that might involve warfare. When an aggressor like Hitler kills and appropriates land from people for his own evil purposes, I believe we have a duty to oppose him with all our might. In my opinion, war is never good, but in some cases it might be necessary to defend the rights of innocent people."

Ada studied his face and tried to understand. "But what if they arrest you for your work as a minister? Wouldn't it be better to submit to an evil regime than to be murdered for one's beliefs—like Father was."

"Your Father had so much integrity. If he believed in a cause, he would not turn his back on it no matter what the cost. In my case, I need to defend my congregation and my beliefs. That may demand a price, but that is part of the commitment I have made to my calling, so I will continue to preach and to serve the people until they stop me."

"Do you think that Father was afraid?" Ada blinked back tears as she imagined Father's final moments.

"I am sure he faced his adversary with calm and conviction. When we act in accordance with our deepest beliefs, we can trust that courage will arrive when we need it."

Ada tried to imagine an infusion of courage. "But don't you worry anyway? What if courage comes too late, or you don't have enough to do the right thing?"

"None of us can claim perfect courage, but we can trust in the choices we make if we are guided by our personal beliefs. That doesn't mean we won't struggle. In these dark times, I worry about the safety of my wife and children, and I worry about the congregation. There is no end to the worries one can have. Will there be food? How will we stay warm? How can the children get an education when the schools are closed?

"But I try to remember that, even in this horrible war, there are moments for which I am grateful. We had a full church at Christmas, and the singing was marvelous. There is a spirit of cooperation between various churches. Unfortunately, that show of solidarity has angered the occupiers. The cooperation between some denominations threatens the enemy. I suspect that there will be repercussions if some of the churches and church leaders continue to speak with one voice against the occupiers."

Ada nodded. "Would you choose it again? To be a minister?"

"It's my calling, and I feel very fortunate. What about you? Do you have a sense of a calling?"

"I'm not sure about 'calling,' but I hope to finish my studies. Working for the Food Council has helped me see how important food issues are."

"We have seen how important that work is for all our people. What other fears do you have?"

"I am afraid that the soldiers will return to arrest us. I fear that Lina will be arrested as she tries to find food. I am afraid a bomb will land on our house while we sleep."

The minister nodded. "These are very real fears."

Ada nodded. "After the news of Father's death, I lost my belief that the future would be any better than the present."

"I understand. You need to take the time to grieve your Father, while being patient with yourself. A great responsibility has been placed on your young shoulders, and that can feel too heavy at times. Know that you are not alone, and take comfort that we can support each other in various ways. This is probably one of the hardest times you will ever face, but even in this you are learning and becoming stronger. You will do good things with your life, and your parents would be very proud. The questions that are too big for us to answer can be given over to God, who has promised to be with us both in the depths and on the mountain tops."

"Do you ever try to picture what life will be like when this war ends?"

"There will be a lot of work to do. Healing will take years because there were so many losses. We will need people to rebuild the country when this war ends—teachers, nurses, doctors, engineers—every hand will be required. There will be demand for people like you."

Ada couldn't so easily adopt such a positive outlook. "How will we recover from the physical and emotional devastation? There are so many things that never will come to pass—young lives lost, families broken apart, houses destroyed by bombs, farmland flooded, bridges bombed."

"We will mourn our losses, and then we will get to work doing all we can to honor those we lost to make sure that this never happens again."

Ada sat forward on the edge of the chair. "There's one thing that bothers me. Where is God in all this? I have trouble finding God these days."

"That's a very good question. I met a German theologian at a conference before we were banned from travel. He explained that Jesus stands with us through his own weakness and suffering, not through omnipotence. The suffering God is not one who will smash the German army for us, but instead will nurture and comfort us and give us strength to fight for justice."

"But I feel like God is absent," Ada said quietly, "and we have been forgotten." She looked at her hands, afraid to meet his eyes. Mother would have been furious if Ada had ever expressed such doubts.

"I understand why you might feel that way. I can't always see God in these dark times, but that doesn't mean we can't hear the still, small voice that calls us to listen and to see. We can't let evil define God—we must actively seek beauty and light and hang on to the belief that God is with us."

Ada leaned forward in her chair. "But does God want us to meet violence with violence and to fight the enemy to the death? If all are God's children, how can we justify killing even one of them?"

"I believe we must be willing to sacrifice all that we are and all that we have in the fight to defeat evil. There are others who believe strongly that war is never justified, and I respect their opinion. Many of them find other ways to care for people that do not require carrying guns or engaging in violence. We all contribute in different ways and together will hope to see victory."

Ada had forgotten her previous lack of confidence and courageously engaged in the conversation. "But if you are preaching that people should actively resist or fight, doesn't that put you in danger?"

He nodded. "The theologian I mentioned has been jailed for two years now. We pray that he will survive. His teaching and writings are a powerful witness from prison."

Ada shook her head slowly. "I can't imagine having that kind of courage."

"There are many forms of courage whether we feed and clothe the needy or wage war on the front lines. The war will not be won by one person but by the cooperation of all."

Ada thought about the ordinary courage of people who had contributed to Father's file on war crimes. They knew that the consequences of their actions might lead to death, and yet they chose to act. "Are you saying that when people act together, they can make each other braver than they could be on their own?"

"I think so," he said with a sad smile. "We tend to think of the lone hero, defying all odds, but these are ordinary people—farmers and housewives, old and young—who want to preserve the life they know in their town and in their country."

Ada pictured grandmothers and grandfathers as well as young women and men defying the evil that surrounded them, using ingenuity and imagination to undermine the iron grip of the occupiers.

"Trust that you have all that you need. Ada, you are doing such good work. Don't doubt yourself."

Ada wiped her eyes. She was annoyed with herself; she did not want to cry in front of the minister.

"We live in hard times, Ada, that challenge our most deeply held beliefs. Just remember, you are not alone. Our faith will be changed by all that we experience, and we will have to work together to refresh our beliefs. We will be changed by the things we have seen and done in these past years, and I cannot predict exactly what peace will look like. The damage to our country and our spirits will be immense, but I believe that we can rebuild. Faith is, after all, trust in things unseen."

Ada gave him a sad smile to reassure him that she heard what he said and was trying hard to absorb it. She watched as one ray of sunlight fell across Reverend Arie's shoulders. The years had aged him, but wisdom shone out of his eyes. He must have been a good friend to her father.

He picked up his spectacles and carefully placed the ear wires around his ears.

"We are both following Jesus' command. Do you know which one?"

Ada shook her head.

"When Jesus said, 'Feed my sheep,' I think that included the various ways that people are fed, whether through food or care of the spirit, which means we are both in the same business—responding to variations on human hunger."

Ada smiled. "I never thought of it that way."

"I must excuse myself as I need to visit someone who is sick, but please come back any time you wish. Shall we pray together before we leave? We will remember your father in our prayers."

Ada nodded and bowed her head. When he was finished, she turned to pick up her coat so he wouldn't see the tears in her eyes. "Thank you," she mumbled, deeply moved.

"Be proud of your father," he added, "he believed in what he did."

She carried those words with her as she biked along the path, for once not feeling the penetrating cold or the icy wind. It would take her some time to sort through his words, but he had given her encouragement that she hoped would help her move forward. If Reverend Arie had weighed the costs and still believed in the fight, that was worth considering. She had never been prepared for any of this to go on for years, and the fatigue she felt undermined her belief that any of it was worth doing. It was time to recommit to the fight and keep going.

PART II

Winter 1944–45

25.

LINA

Novemer delivered a layer of fine snow. As the sun crept higher in the morning sky, the backyard reflected the light. It was such a change from the dark fall days. Lina smiled when she saw the snow. The first snowfall was always a surprise, even when it was just a sugar coating on the rooftops.

Ada shivered as the cold air leaked around the windows and under the door. "You might want to get dressed," Ada advised. "Lucas will be here soon to drop off some typing. I need to tell him about my visit with Lykke."

"Who is that?" Lina asked.

"Lykke runs an orphanage in town. She needs help because the occupiers want the building for their soldiers. She needs to find homes for the children and get rid of the furnishings."

"You've always been good with children," Lina observed. "You used to enjoy teaching those classes at church with all those snotty-nosed kids."

"They were cute. Where are they all now?" she wondered.

"Who knows? How much work will this involve?" Lina asked.

"The work is mostly in the mornings. I'll be home to cook supper, in case you were worried," Ada said with a smile.

"Not worried about that," Lina said, "I just hope I can find food."

Ada glanced at the cupboard that was now filled with empty cannisters and unused serving dishes.

Lina went to her room and put on the same clothes she'd worn the day before, making sure she combed her hair. She added a pair of the gold earrings that Father had given her many birthdays ago. Hopefully

Ada would not notice the extra attention she had given to her outfit, as drab as it was. Why was she even thinking she needed to try to look better for him?

Lina returned to the kitchen table to sketch a copper bowl she had found in the attic. There was an annoying sameness to the days—same clothes, same war, same hunger. Sketching gave her comfort and made her feel like she'd accomplished something creative in the day. Maybe that's why she was being silly trying to dress up for Lucas.

A few moments later, Lucas knocked and entered the kitchen.

Lina felt her face warm when he hung up his coat and smiled at her. For a moment it felt like time stopped. *Was it my imagination? Did he feel it too?*

"Tea would be nice—it's cold out there," Lucas said. "How are you both doing? I brought a few slices of bread." Lucas reached into his cloth bag and pulled out some bread wrapped in waxed paper and handed it to Ada.

"You can drop by anytime," Lina said. "I don't suppose you have any chocolate sprinkles to put on that bread?"

"I regret that those aren't available at the moment," he said with a smile, "and you really need butter to make them stick. Someday there will be apple butter and chocolate paste and fresh cheese to put on your bread."

"Stop! You're making me even hungrier," Lina said. She watched Ada unwrap the bread.

"How are you both doing?" Lucas asked as he cradled the teacup in his hands. "Ada, did you have any luck finding a hiding place?"

"I did," she said. "The file is safe."

"What else is going on?" Lucas said with apparent relief that the issue of the secret papers had been taken care of.

"As you know, it's difficult to find food now that the ration cards are meaningless. Things keep getting worse. Do they mean to starve us to death?" She poured some more tea in his cup and placed small plates on the table for bread. Although there was no butter, she brought over a jar of jam that she'd made last summer from currant bushes in the garden.

Lucas nodded. "The hunger is severe, and people are suffering while politicians and generals debate their next moves."

"Thank you for suggesting that I meet Lykke," Ada said. "I had no idea she had so much experience working as an advocate for children. The orphanage seems well run."

"I hope that works out. She might be an important person to know in future," Lucas said.

Ada nodded. "By the way, Lina has volunteered to travel north to find food since little is available around here. The farmers no longer have anything to give or are unwilling to barter, so more people are traveling to farms in the north where they apparently still have supplies."

Lucas glanced at Lina, who worked hard to not look at him. She felt exposed and was afraid that anyone might read her interest in her face. She picked up her pencil and continued to work on a sketch.

"Many women are traveling for food, so you won't be alone. You've probably seen them pushing prams and carts in the hopes of bringing home supplies. Some farmers are very hospitable and provide soup and sleeping space in their barn for a night, but others will chase you away. It will be a long journey with no guarantees that you will find food—or that someone won't steal it from you."

"There's no guarantee of anything, but I can't sit here while we starve," Lina said looking up from her sketch. "I plan to leave on Friday." The only way they'd survive was by going further to access supplies. They needed more food, and there was no magic that would bring it to their doorstep. She knew it would be dangerous, but so far the occupiers had allowed the food travelers to pass.

Her growing feelings for Lucas left her feeling confused and vulnerable. His concern made her feel cared for, but she told herself it didn't mean anything more than that. She told herself to be irritated by his concern as it showed he underestimated her, but that didn't work.

"Let's hope you return with your panniers filled with food," Lucas said. He lightly tapped her hand.

She looked up at him, startled by his touch and pleased that he believed she could do the trip. *Surely, I am imagining it.* She had to get out of there and collect herself—she was acting like a fool. The complex feelings and confused thoughts made her feel uncertain. Did he realize how he was affecting her?

Why would he bother with her? Ada was so much better educated and able to engage in discussion with him. They seemed to talk for hours about books and people that she had never even heard of. She appreciated that he was concerned about the upcoming trip, but he didn't try to tell her not to go. Jos would have tried to forbid it, which she would have ignored. Lucas also took her photography seriously and encouraged her to continue, whereas Jos had believed it was a waste of time.

He sat at the table and concentrated on repairing a whisk that had come apart. As he leaned over the project, she saw his fine eyelashes and the way he held his mouth as he concentrated. She would love to photograph him while he worked, using the light from the window to illuminate at least one side of his face.

Lucas looked up and caught her studying his face. He smiled, and she looked away, her cheeks warm with embarrassment. Was he amused by her attention? She would never ask him. She returned to her drawing and focused all her attention on perfecting the shadows in the sketch. She had to unlearn this crush she'd developed on him and keep her focus on her goals. Lucas would never be interested in her. It was time to smarten up and move on.

26.

ADA

THE next day, while Ada folded laundry on the upstairs bed, she wondered how anyone made plans during uncertain times. November's darkness signaled that winter was on their doorstep, which, combined with another season of war, was a depressing prospect. She'd always disliked it when the golden days of autumn turned into the dark and rainy days of November. But these days, the combination of hunger, darkness, and cold invaded every cell of her body, making hope an impossible goal.

There was an unpredictability to life—Allied bombs dropped on people's houses while they slept, and the German V2 rockets fell short of their targets, killing people in the street. In The Hague, the navigational error made by an Allied bomber had destroyed an entire neighborhood. Random events and timing could put one in mortal danger no matter what precautions one took.

If death was inevitable, perhaps it would be better to die while fully engaged in the fight. Playing it safe didn't guarantee anything. When Father was arrested, he seemed reconciled to his fate; perhaps because he'd done what he could. She hoped that he had been at peace when he passed in that camp. When she tried to imagine that her own life might end by a random shooting or a misplaced bomb, she hoped that she could face it bravely. She was trying so hard to remember her conversation with Reverend Arie.

When she had promised her mother that she would take care of things, she'd had no idea she'd carry that responsibility for years. She remembered the night Mother had called her into the room they used as a sick room on the main floor. "Ada," she'd said, "you know how proud I am of this house. You are the eldest, and you are responsible for keeping it in excellent shape." Then she'd continued, perhaps in order of importance to her, "Your father and Lina will need looking after. I trust you to do this to the best of your ability. Do you promise?" Ada agreed because she had no choice, but lately she resented the burden her mother had placed on her.

None of her diligent housekeeping had prevented Father's arrest and death. She placed the folded laundry in two piles on the bed: one for her and one for Lina.

As she did up the buttons on one of Lina's shirts, she wondered how they would face this next chapter of war. They needed to take back their country from the evil powers that were destroying it. Hitler had managed to sow hatred and fear, turning people against each other. Did good have the same power to inspire such devotion? It was fortunate that people like Lucas, Reverend Arie, and her father had continued to risk everything for what they believed was good.

Perhaps she had played it safe doing work for Lucas that didn't take her into the danger zones. She enjoyed helping him with the newsletter that he distributed to resistance workers in the field, highlighting the latest war news, but could she do more? She continued to fear for Lucas, for Lina, and for their home. Danger lurked everywhere. How could she control her fear and not surrender to its control?

She watched the sun send rays into the windows and yards of the houses on the street. Could light overcome darkness?

Lucas was a lifeline. When he was able, he brought news and food and companionship. There was something in the way he looked at Lina that sometimes made her think that he was interested in her. Not that war was any time to be falling in love—life was too precarious for that. Ada wondered how Lina felt about him, but she knew it was better not to ask. Still, the possibility of their attachment gave her hope. Lina had been so sad after Jos' death.

Lucas was a good man, and Lina would be lucky to have him. She knew it was selfish, but if Lina took up with Lucas, maybe she would choose to stay close to home instead of escaping to Paris. Lucas had once explained that he lived a solitary life because he did not want to put someone in danger by association with him, but he still managed to visit their house regularly. The newsletter was a good excuse for some of those visits, but Ada had wondered for a while if there was more involved. His work left him alone with many secrets and responsibilities. Perhaps being with them provided solace and companionship.

Ada didn't want to live in the past, but it was a challenge to figure out how to inhabit the present. But it was difficult to resist the downward pull of despair when confronted with so much suffering. After talking with Reverend Arie, she worked hard to find reasons to be grateful. The work in the orphanage had been a wonderful change from the conflict in the community kitchen. The orphanage workers were dedicated to the children, and Lykke's leadership made them work harder to create a home for them.

She tried to imagine what peace might look like after years of war. It required such a shift in thinking. Peace had to be more than the cessation of war—it would require a rethinking of relationships and a rebuilding of all that had been destroyed. They couldn't just go back to who they were before the war because they were no longer those people, and they had been through more than they could ever describe. Who would articulate that new way of being? Maybe people such as Lina would be able to do that using her art, or Reverend Arie using his faith.

Science was the framework in which she felt at home; she longed to reengage with her studies. Since that wasn't possible now, she would continue to be practical and keep house to the best of her ability. Her job for that day was to wax the wood floors in the hallway and living room to make them shine. Like a pilgrim she would inch forward on her knees, hoping that some insight would be gained in the road to peace.

27.

ADA

T'HAT Thursday evening, before Lina left to travel north to find food, she and Ada went to the basement to read a novel together to distract themselves from the relentless sounds of guns and planes. Although neither wanted to admit it, anxiety about Lina's trip had filled the day.

Before Father's arrest, they often read books in the basement so that the house would be quiet while he was writing. But after his arrest, they had stopped the ritual. On this night, Ada sensed that Lina needed distraction from thoughts about the trip ahead.

"Will you be all right while I am gone?" Lina asked.

"Don't worry about me. The neighbors will keep watch, and of course there's always Nel. And I'll be starting work at the orphanage too."

Lina made a dismissive sound and pulled the blanket over her. "Do you have the book?" Lina asked.

"Right here," Ada indicated, pointing her chin to the book tucked in her armpit. She placed the tea tray on the heavy oak coffee table. She pulled a blanket over her legs and poured the tea. She knew the doors upstairs were locked, and the lights were off.

As they sipped their tea, several planes passed overhead and shook the windows of the house.

"Stupid planes," Lina muttered.

When Ada began to read, Lina dug deeper under the blanket, absorbed in the drama of Cathy and Heathcliff in *Wuthering Heights*.

"It's so romantic," Lina said at a pause in the reading.

"And brooding and ominous, don't you think?"

"I'd like to have a romance like that. Lots of drama and shadows with crashing waves and powerful moments of forgiveness. Have you ever been in love?" Lina asked.

Ada was quiet for a few moments. She wasn't sure she wanted to discuss that subject with Lina, who would tell her how ridiculous it was to be loyal to someone who had passed years ago. She couldn't explain it, but she was sure she would never feel that way about anyone else. Reluctantly Ada explained, "I met someone during my first year at the university."

"Who?" Lina asked.

Ada pulled at her hair and smoothed the errant strands into a bun. "I met him in one of my classes. He was an assistant and one of Father's students."

Lina smiled with confirmation of something she had suspected. "I know who you mean. He came here for some of those student dinners, but you were trying to keep it secret."

"I was not," Ada replied. "When the university closed, he returned to Amsterdam to live with his parents. After a big demonstration, the Nazis rounded up students, so he went underground. Father helped him stay at *Opa's* farm for a while. One of the neighbors informed the police of his presence, so he was arrested and sent to a camp. He apparently died there several months later. He had an older brother who studied medicine, but I don't know what happened to him." Ada leaned forward to pour tea into the two cups. She handed one to Lina who breathed in the steam and fragrance from one of Ada's homemade herbal teas.

"Father would never have let you get serious with a Jewish fellow," Lina said.

"Father was more open-minded than you think," Ada said curtly. She was irritated by Lina's presumption. Father had never voiced any objection; in fact, he'd sometimes carried her letters to the farm when he went there to help his parents.

Lina put the cup down. "Mother never would have approved."

Ada felt a growing irritation—Lina was such a know-it-all. "What difference does that make now?" Standing up abruptly, Ada gathered the cups and picked up the tray. She left the book on the couch—Lina could read it herself if she wanted, but Ada didn't feel like it anymore. She knew she was overreacting to Lina's questions, but she couldn't stop herself.

She went to bed and thought about Willy. Although she wanted to be loyal to his memory, what purpose did that serve? Even now, it was hard to remember the sound of his voice. Whenever she couldn't quite remember his face, she felt guilty.

Was Lina correct that it never would have worked if Willy had lived? There was no way to know, and it was useless to speculate. That was what frustrated her—the pointless discussion of something that could never be, not because they hadn't cared enough but because life had not given them the chance.

Most of the time, she believed that she would never love again. Did people get second chances to find love and to expand their circle of friends and family? Father had lived that kind of expansive life, making room for strangers. He would have welcomed Willy—she was sure of it.

She still remembered every detail about the first time they met at the university. She pulled out her diary from its hiding place and held it in her hand. Was she ready to revisit that time in her life that seemed so full of promise? In those days, she had been willing to do her homework late at night and care for Mother with exemplary patience if it gained her some time to spend with Willy during the day, between classes, or whenever they could meet.

ADA, OCTOBER 1939

I have not taken the time to write in my diary lately, so now I must try catch up on the fall semester. So much has happened I do not know where to begin. My days have been so full attending school, caring for Mother, and finding time to spend with Willy. I remember every minute of how we met. I want to record it here so that I have it forever. It was such a surprise that someone like him would notice me.

It was a warm September day. I was so happy to attend the university and to bike to class for the first time. Leaving behind the confines of the house was a relief. Mother relied on me heavily for entertainment and care as she was confined to her bed. She had been opposed to my attending university, but Father persuaded her that I was a good student who deserved to study. When Mother became even more demanding and needy of my attention, it was a challenge to balance my schoolwork with her demands. I wondered if she was jealous that I was permitted to go to university. If she had her way, I would have been sent to a household cookery school to prepare myself for being a wife. Awful!

Lina didn't want to be home, and Mother didn't want her there, so I did what I could to meet her needs. If I thought Mother's illness would soften the edges of their relationship, I was wrong. Perhaps Mother wanted me to be the one who took care of her because she knew I would do everything she ordered, whereas Lina would simply refuse. Maybe her confinement made her eager to exercise control over someone who would do what she asked.

At the university I felt some freedom from those demands, as if I was finally on my way to becoming an adult. I'd taken a variety of science courses and one philosophy class to see if I could manage the studies. Being at the top of my class didn't mean much when many students were clever. But I quickly adapted to the university system and even received praise from my professors.

I met Willy in a general philosophy elective. He was studying philosophy and history, and I was surprised to find that Father was his advisor. He was an assistant in my class.

Earlier that day, on my way to the university, I noticed that the flower sellers had filled their stands with bouquets of mums in rust and yellow and purple. It was such an explosion of color; I wanted to stop to take a closer look, but I was already late for class.

Although I usually arrived at class a half an hour early to find a good place to review the notes I'd made about the readings, that day I arrived late, just as class was about to begin. Mother had wanted her hair fixed in a certain way, and I apparently did not have the right touch. The classroom was already full—only one seat was left. The student beside that empty seat was deeply engaged in his reading and didn't notice that I was waiting for his reply.

"Excuse me," I repeated, "is this seat available?"

The fellow, with dark, curly hair that spilled over his forehead, looked at me through wire-rimmed glasses. With a serious face he replied, "I've heard that the queen will be visiting class today. I saved this place for her because I have a few things to discuss."

I stared at him. The queen? In their class? I looked around, but all the other chairs were occupied, and people were chattering as usual and paying no attention to me. There was no sign of any preparations for a royal visit. The professor strode into the room smartly dressed in a tweed blazer with a shirt and tie and a briefcase in hand. He would soon begin his lecture and wonder why I was still standing.

As the fellow watched my confusion, his face broke into a lovely smile. "Now that you're here," he said, "you might as well stay." He stood up and pulled the chair out for me.

He extended his hand to shake mine. "Willy," he said.

"Ada," I replied as I shook his hand. I was somewhat embarrassed that he'd fooled me so easily, but his smile and personable manner soon made me forget that.

"What do you study?" he asked.

"Science," I replied. "And you?"

"History," he said, "but they offered me an assistantship in this class, so I took it."

"What do you do?"

"Whatever the professor wants me to do. I mark papers and meet with students to give them help with the readings or their assignments."

The professor draped his coat over an empty chair and opened his worn leather briefcase to take out his lecture notes. He ran his fingers through his hair and blew his nose loudly into a handkerchief. His face was ruddy from the bike ride. He looked at the class, cleared his throat, and began his lecture.

Willy leaned over and whispered, "If you have time, we can talk more after class."

I wanted to meet other students, but it was difficult because I lived at home and could not attend social activities. I envied students who were free to socialize. They enjoyed freedoms that I couldn't imagine, as I tried to balance my conflicting roles as student and Mother's nursemaid.

The professor reminded us that by the next class we would be expected to submit a short essay that identified themes in the assigned reading. I noted the assignment in my agenda. This would be a challenge. We were expected to identify a global issue and then write a proposal on how to address it. I was more comfortable with scientific observation and conclusions that with argumentation and logic.

After class Willy left the room with me. We stood in the hall as the rest of the students passed, chattering loudly. He seemed genuinely interested in continuing the conversation. In school, I had never had a boyfriend. I knew I wasn't perceived to be fun, and I wasn't interested in listening to superficial chatter, but I longed to have at least one person with whom I could talk freely.

I confessed my fear about the assignment, and he helped me to identify an issue for the paper. I made notes and worked on it over the weekend.

I studied drought resistant crops that could thrive in the world's desert regions and suggested that a food bank offer those countries weather resistant seeds through a food bank. It was a rudimentary proposal, but I enjoyed working on it.

That day started a tradition where Willy and I went for coffee after class and took walks around town. He took me to working-class neighborhoods and past factories that I'd never seen before. My life had been very sheltered.

On Thursdays, because my second class wasn't till two, no one expected me home until the end of the day, so we spent the afternoon in each other's company. I worked harder on Wednesday evenings to make up for the time spent with him. Looking forward to those occasions helped me through the weeks.

Some days I felt like nothing Mother might say would affect me because I had this inner source of happiness that she didn't know about it. If she had known about Willy, she would have done everything possible to undermine our relationship.

That was the thing about Willy, he made me want to pay attention to every detail—so many things I had never noticed about my own city. Although he lived in Amsterdam, he managed to find the best cafés and cheap restaurants as well as quiet gardens in the small courtyards that were hidden behind gates. He taught me to be curious about places and people that were outside my usual travels. He kidded me that I had my nose in a book so much that I missed out on life. Perhaps it was true, but I knew that he was also proud of my dedication to learning. There was an ease between us that was a new experience for me.

There were so many shadows, so much fear; Mother was getting weaker, and the doctor didn't offer much hope. Father was preoccupied and had little time for conversation. He was worried about the threat of war and how it would affect the university, but he never discussed that with us. I overheard him a few times when colleagues came to drink coffee in his study. Willy assured me that his fears were justified and that everything would soon change.

TUESDAY, OCTOBER 3, 1940

I sat across from Willy at a small table in the student café down the street from our class.

On that day he was very serious, and he talked to me about the impending war and what it would mean for them, especially for his family. Even though I had tried to keep up with the news, I felt alarmed when he shared his thoughts about war. Suddenly the threat was close to home, even though Father didn't talk about that in front of me or Lina. Willy was convinced that we were heading for the darkest time in history, and he wasn't sure his family would survive. I had heard rumors but there was still so much I didn't know. I tried to comfort him, but I had the feeling he knew things he didn't want to tell me because things were much worse than I could imagine. It felt like he had already left that small corner of life that we had shared, not as lovers but as close friends. I could wait for him—I would wait for him.

Most people would never believe that a first love could be that significant, but I never doubted that Willy and I had forged a deep connection in a short amount of time. Perhaps the shadow of war lent an urgency to our friendship and pushed it to grow into something deeper. We talked about our respective faiths and appreciated that we both believed that faith was important. It made me want to learn more about the practices that were part of his family life.

I knew I wasn't as attractive as Lina nor was I adept at games involving flirtation. I'd always been shy and somewhat awkward, especially around my male classmates. Willy had taken the time to win my trust by listening carefully to my ideas and encouraging me to have opinions. His kindness and care for living things made me feel safe. But we were not safe, as I would soon learn.

ADA

Ada closed the diary. It had been impossible to record the events as war crept closer. Mother grew sicker, and Willy missed classes to stay close to home. The closure of the university, the riots, and the arrests were terrifying. One day Ada saw Father in his study holding his head after hearing the news of the arrest of one of his colleagues. They didn't talk about all these things, but the atmosphere in the house grew heavy. A nurse came to wash mother, and the doctor made occasional visits, but it was clear that nothing could be done but keep her comfortable. I read to her and played the harmonium, but nothing seemed to make much difference; she was sleeping more and more. I am not sure where Lina was most of the time, but she didn't like being in the house. Without the weekly visits with Willy, there was nothing to look forward to. She remembered the oppressive sense of hopelessness that became the norm.

Memories of those precious times with Willy filled her with sadness. She had to accept that their brief time together had been a gift. Holding the diary to her chest, she closed her eyes and tried to remember how safe she felt in his arms. She put the diary away in its secret place and prepared for bed.

Lina was probably still in the basement—maybe she'd fallen asleep there. What did Lina know about how a great love could transform everything? Jos had been her boyfriend, but she had never imagined a future with him. Whatever might grow between Lucas and Lina was still a long way off. Perhaps they would they have a chance to explore that in the future. Ada knew that Lina also had her own struggles and challenges, and Ada regretted being angry with her. She resolved to do better but had a feeling that her patience had limits.

28.

LINA

THAT Friday, as Lina biked north, she was grateful for the heavy sweater that Ada had refashioned from Father's wool sweater. Her jacket alone wasn't warm enough to resist the cold wind. Lina was nervous about the journey, but Ada was even more anxious. Lina had spent their last moments before departure trying to reassure her and to hide her own anxiety.

Lina biked hard to generate heat, but she couldn't keep up that pace all day. Biking past clumps of two or three women walking together, who pushed prams and pulled carts, made her grateful for her bike. Hopefully the tires would last, and the chain would not fall off or break. There was no point in worrying about what might happen—she just had to do her best to complete the journey. Father had given her this bike for her birthday before the war began, and she was grateful he'd chosen a quality bike that could survive harsh conditions. With any luck, the panniers would be filled with potatoes and vegetables on the way back.

Ada had prepared a lunch for the road, but Lina was saving it for later. Biking made her hungry, and she could feel her legs and arms become shaky. She followed the crowd of travelers north—they were all on this journey together, with no guarantee that they could bring home food to their families.

At some point, maybe tomorrow, she hoped to break away from the crowds by taking secondary roads to find farms that had less traffic and more food. She might have to bike all the way back to the main road if the search proved fruitless, but it was worth a try. She wasn't sure how many hours she could bike in a day since that depended on the direction of the wind and the rain as well as on how much food she could find to eat.

Lucas had told her about a farm that was about ten kilometers from this place where the farmer offered soup and a hay loft for sleeping. She hoped that he would still have room and food by the time she arrived.

At the farm, she rested her bike against the barn where she could keep an eye on it while she knocked on the back door of the house. A stocky woman wearing a dress covered with an apron answered the door. Lina nearly fainted when she smelled the pea soup simmering.

Lina introduced herself and explained that she was traveling north for food.

The woman nodded. She'd heard the same story hundreds of times and wasn't particularly interested. Pointing to the barn where Lina could sleep, she handed her a bowl of soup and a crust of bread. Lina sat on the back step and tried to eat the soup slowly, chewing any peas that hadn't been cooked to pulp. Strangers helping strangers—it was quite humbling to see that spirit in action and to be a recipient of their generosity.

Lina trudged up the ladder in the barn, hoping that her bike would be safe with the wheel lock enabled. The occupiers were stealing every bike they could find, but maybe they wouldn't come near this place. Other travelers on foot might see her bike and realize they could cover more ground with it. She had tucked it into a corner behind a bush and hoped it would still be there later.

She found a far corner in the hay where she had some privacy from the dozen or so travelers, who were mostly women.

With no need to make friends, Lina was quite happy to rest her legs and watch the light retreat through the gaps in the barn boards. A few barn swallows flew about but then settled as night fell. Lina had used the pit toilet outside and hoped she didn't need to go again in the night. She had no desire to find her way down that ladder and into the dark yard, but having had so little to drink all day, it was unlikely.

In the morning, she was one of the first to awaken. She gathered her things and made her way down to the barn where the farmer was busy milking the one cow that he had left. He waved her over and filled an enamel cup with warm milk. After drinking it eagerly, she thanked him for his hospitality. He nodded and returned to his work.

Lina biked for hours on secondary roads that were rough and filled with potholes. As she hustled along on her bike, she felt her jaw and shoulders, even her teeth, absorbing the bumps in the road. She couldn't afford to daydream—if her bike got caught in one of the potholes, she'd be thrown over the handlebars. Few people passed by there, so she'd be on her own with an injured body or destroyed bicycle.

There was less evidence of the occupation here—buildings and farmhouses stood intact and farms were tended. That night she slept in a barn with a small group of people that again included mostly women but also with some boys too young to be conscripted. The farmer's wife handed out some dry bread and said it was all she could give them. Lina climbed wearily into the loft and found a corner where she hoped she would sleep.

At some point in the night, she felt someone climb on top of her and fumble with her clothes. Her eyes snapped open. First, she saw the outline of his shoulders, and then she felt his stale breath on her.

His hands fumbled around her chest and then grabbed her breast. Trying not to gasp, she kept her body still, waiting a moment longer to ready herself. When he tried to pull her sweater up, she slid her right hand towards the knife that she always kept beside her. The familiar feeling of the knife in her hand kept her calm.

Lucas showed her how they trained women who worked for the resistance to defend themselves. He warned her that it was dangerous to keep a weapon close at hand because it could be taken and turned against her. On this occasion, she was grateful to have it. Lucas warned her that she had to commit completely and show no hesitation, or the opponent would sense it and overwhelm her. Even if the enemy was larger, Lucas said he would likely underestimate her speed and courage, so he showed her how to use that to her advantage.

Lina breathed evenly and with one smooth movement, she stuck it with some force in his side, not quite deep enough to puncture his skin. He was caught off guard, focused as he was on undoing his pant buttons.

She didn't want to create a commotion with a boy requiring medical attention for a stab wound—she merely wanted to teach him a lesson to get rid of him.

He cursed under his breath, not wanting to wake the women sleeping in the loft around her and scrambled away from her as fast as he could. It was almost comical to watch him scuttle away from her like a sand crab.

Two of his friends who had been watching whispered and quickly gathered up their things and raced down the ladder. They didn't look back because they were afraid that she would raise the alarm and get them in trouble. She was tempted to do so, but it was not worth it. Her goal was to obtain food, and she didn't want to be distracted by anything else.

Sleep was impossible for the rest of that night. She had experienced her share of groping by soldiers, and she knew how to handle herself. Because Ada didn't seem to have those kinds of experiences, it was hard to confide in her, as her sister would worry even more than she already did. Lina had decided long ago that such behavior would not constrain her freedom. Rage was a helpful companion to keep her from doubting herself—she placed the blame on the aggressors. Like that little piece of garbage who was trying to impress his friends. How many times did they make a game out of the hunt for food while molesting women in the barns and fields along the way?

As soon as the morning light became visible, Lina packed her things and slipped out of the loft. Her muscles ached, and her brain felt foggy from the sleepless night and the biking marathon. She dreamed of a hot bath to wash away the unwelcome touch of that teenager and the barnyard smell that clung to her skin and clothes.

That day, she visited three farms along the secondary route she'd chosen and was turned away from all of them. The road was in poor condition, and her neck and shoulders were tight from holding on to the handlebars as she bounced along.

As she biked up to fourth house while fighting the downward pull of despair, she saw a woman struggling to take the clothes off her line while the wind whipped everything about. One of her towels blew off the line and tumbled around in the wind. Lina let her bike slide to the ground and ran to fetch the towel, as well as the washcloths and socks that had joined the rebellion. The women laughed as they chased the items around the yard, while the woman's dog barked at them.

Lina handed the woman the items she had retrieved.

She scrutinized Lina and made up her mind. "Would you like some tea?" she asked.

Lina sighed at the thought. "I would love some tea."

"Put your bike over there," she said, pointing to the side of the house beside the shed.

When they walked into the kitchen, the woman introduced herself as Femke. "You can wash your hands and face in the sink," she instructed as she handed Lina a bar of soap and a towel. "I think it's been a while."

"I'm sorry, I've been sleeping in barns. If this is Sunday, I have biked two full days."

Femke smiled. "I understand. Why don't you sit here while I boil some water? Would you like some apple cake?"

"Please," Lina said. She stifled a yawn as a deep relaxation made her limbs feel heavy. Handing responsibility to Femke took a weight from her shoulders. Watching her complete simple domestic routines such as boiling water and making tea was so reassuring. While the tea leaves infused in the pot, Femke placed cups and dessert plates on the table and cut slices of apple cake.

"Tell me about the place where you live," the woman said. Lina felt comfortable with her. She was a bit older, with red cheeks from outdoor work and strong hands. Her kitchen was simple and cozy with a set of porcelain cannisters on the counter and a bright orange braising pan on the stove.

Lina told her about their town and how she and her sister shared the family house. "My father's mother was from up here somewhere. I remember he used to talk about it."

"What was her name?" she asked.

"Her name was Steenstra. Her family had a farm up here."

Femke pulled out some plates and a knife and cut the cake. "I have heard of the family. I went to school with some of them. When the farm was sold, I don't know where they went. The war has made it harder to keep track of people."

"Here you go," Femke said as she handed her the cake plate. "Knowing your mother's family makes you family. You better stay here tonight and have a good supper so you can build up your strength to bike home. How brave you are to go on such a journey. The water is heating for your bath. Tomorrow Jan will send you home with some food."

Lina had just taken a huge bite of the cake, so she let the cinnamon hit her tongue as she purred with joy. "This cake is the best thing I have ever tasted. I would be so grateful for any food you have. I can pay you something. My sister, Ada, can make a meal out of very little, and she is waiting for me to bring anything I can find."

"I will not accept payment. Just promise me if you or your sister are ever up here again that you'll call on us. We don't get many visitors anymore."

"I promise," Lina said. "As long as you bake this cake, I would bike up here just to taste it again."

Femke laughed and cut her another piece. "If you keep purring like that, all the barn cats will run into the house to see what's going on."

"Thank you. This is so good."

"Tell me more about yourself."

As they talked, Lina helped her get dinner ready, peeling potatoes and scraping carrots. Femke fried some sausage and saved the drippings. Lina's stomach growled again as the scents of cooking filled the kitchen.

"*Hutspot*," Lina declared, the familiar dish of cooked carrots and potatoes that was a staple at home in the old days.

Femke nodded and brought a pot of hot water into the room off the kitchen. She handed Lina a towel and soap and closed the screen.

Lina was moved by her generosity and kindness as she sank into the steel tub, her knees almost to her chin as she made herself fit. Her skin reddened and tingled in the hot water, but Lina breathed the steam and relaxed into it. Once she had soaped herself and scrubbed her skin with the washcloth, she stayed in the tub until the water cooled. She heard Femke singing while she worked in the kitchen.

Lina dried herself with the towel and got dressed. Even though she'd worn those clothes for days, she felt cleaner than she'd been for ages. Someday, Lina thought, she'd have a tub and hot water and fine soaps from France, and she would take long baths daily and dry herself with enormous towels that smelled of summer sun and lavender fields. But for now, this was the best experience she'd had in a long time. The apple cake was a close second.

29.

ADA

A DA had trouble concentrating on anything after Lina's departure north. She wondered when she would return. It was Sunday, so by the end of the day, she would have biked three full days. What if she couldn't find any food? She hoped Lina was safe, but she still spent the day doing unnecessary cleaning to distract herself from worrying.

When the cleaning was finished, she took apart Mother's former sewing room and sorted the fabric and embroidery threads to store in the basement. Although she had put off the task for a long time, there was some satisfaction in seeing the room cleared out. With new drapes and a coat of fresh paint, it would make a cozy room someday. Maybe she would turn it into a study, because working in Father's study did not feel right.

Days later, Lina finally returned. She had been away more than a week and was dusty and exhausted. "What day is it?" she asked as she collapsed on a kitchen chair. Ada picked up her two panniers filled with vegetables.

"Tuesday. Oh, Lina, this is great. You were so brave," Ada said.

"It was nothing. I could do it again tomorrow," Lina replied with a smile. "Or maybe the next day."

"I'll make some tea," Ada said, "and then you probably need to sleep."

"I slept in a barn that had been full of pigs before the occupiers took them all away for butchering. It was very smelly. It rained so hard I had to stay an extra night."

As Ada prepared tea, she heard a rap on the back door.

Lina was surprised to see Lucas holding a glass jar.

"Welcome home," he said with a smile. "You have made quite a journey. I hope you found some food."

"Have you been doing surveillance? Because I just returned. And I smell like all the barns I slept in."

"No surveillance, just good timing. And everything went well?"

"The wind pushed me home, so that made up for my heavy panniers."

"I'm glad you arrived home safely. I made some pea soup last night." He put the jar of soup on the table.

"Thanks so much, Lucas," Ada said. "I was trying to figure out what to cook. I hope you'll stay and eat with us."

"That would be great. We need to celebrate Lina's epic journey. And I have just the thing." He reached into his coat pocket and pulled out a small bottle. "French brandy," he explained, "it can serve as dessert, or it can help you sleep."

"How wonderful! I look forward to sleeping in my own bed. Thanks for this."

Ada smiled. "Don't tell us how and where you got it. We don't need to know."

Lucas laughed. "It was completely legitimate as a gift. But feel free to refuse it if it pricks your conscience."

"Not a chance," Ada said. "I'll get some glasses. This is a celebration."

30.

LINA

Lina was tired of coughing and being sick. Two weeks had passed since her return from the marathon bike ride to obtain food up north, and she had barely left her bed. Although Lucas visited regularly, he refused to give her an assignment until she had recovered. She protested that she was fine and needed to do something, but he refused. He brought any food he could find, and Ada made soups from his offerings. Lucas found four books somewhere, and Ada read them to her every evening. It was wonderful to laugh aloud to the fictional stories of teenage Joop's misdeeds.

"She sounds a bit like me," Lina noted.

"I agree," Ada replied with a smile.

Ada fed her broth and herbal teas. Their neighbor, Mrs. Groen, sat with Lina and read to her on the days when Ada had volunteer commitments.

Gradually Lina stopped coughing and had more energy. She was excited when Lucas finally gave her an assignment to accompany a downed airman to a safe house. Lucas instructed her to head to the farm to meet the airman in the late afternoon.

Lina shook hands with Oliver, the British airman, who had landed into a tree in a farmer's field the night before. Already looking ill at ease in the barn, his face fell when she told him that she would take him to a safe house since the farmer was eager to get rid of him.

She didn't care what Oliver thought—she was going to complete her mission without a hitch if she had to knock this fellow over the head to do it. She was in no mood to deal with anyone who questioned her authority or ability.

Lucas warned her that some of the airmen might be reluctant to take orders from a woman. Lina did not care—Oliver would soon discover that she wasn't planning to coddle him. His safe escape depended on following her orders, or he might find himself stranded in a foreign country.

Lina was ready to take as many assignments as Lucas could give her. She desperately needed to keep busy and to feel that she was contributing to the war effort. Lina wasn't afraid—it was easy to be brave when there was so little left to lose. Her bicycle trip north had boosted her confidence. Both Ada and Lucas had been proud of her persistence on that journey.

Despite the overalls they'd given him to wear, Oliver looked completely out of place. If there had been any cows left in the barn, Lina would have enjoyed seeing if he knew how to milk a cow. She knew she shouldn't let herself be irritated by him, but there was something about his attitude that annoyed her. Maybe he had enjoyed a posh life back home, but now he was a downed pilot who didn't have a chance of seeing his homeland again without her assistance.

His hands were covered with several cuts, and he had an abrasion on the left side of his face. She pulled a small first aid kit from her bag and cleaned the abrasion. He winced when she applied some ointment on it, but he didn't say a word. Lina treated him with quiet efficiency and didn't waste time on sympathy.

She gave him the money that Lucas had arranged. When she had asked Lucas about the source of that money, he explained that a secret organization raised money to support the resistance to assist with rescues and to help those who were in hiding. Lina couldn't convince Lucas to tell her more, but it was heartening to think that people worked to support the resistance. That alone made her part of a bigger movement, even if she would never make friends with her comrades. She wished Lucas would give her more responsibility—just a week ago another group blew up train tracks that were used to deliver food to Germany. How she would have loved to be part of that.

Her motivations were complicated—she wanted to avenge the deaths of Jos and Father, and to help end the war. Recognizing that those were very different reasons to do the work, Lina preferred not to think about it too much but instead to plunge headfirst into the action.

As Oliver limped towards the bike, Lina studied his gait. "I hope you can bike with that knee."

"It's fine," he said. "Hard landing."

"You got rid of your parachute?"

"I buried it."

She looked at him critically. Would he pass for a farmer if they were stopped? His appearance was still too British—his overalls would fool no one. And the story about being mute seemed a bit contrived and might serve as a red flag to any soldier that stopped them.

"You know how to ride a bike?" she asked.

"Of course," he replied with a sniff, somewhat offended by the question.

He was probably more accustomed to being chauffeured. Lina put her hand on her hip and glared at him. "If you have a problem following my instructions, you can find your own way home. The Germans would love to get their hands on someone like you."

He was startled but reacted by being flippant. "Maybe we could roll around in the hay first," he said laughing loudly as he looked her up and down.

Lina kept her face blank and her temper under control. "You're quite hilarious. But listen carefully, I'm not risking my life for some jackass who can't keep his mouth shut. Many people are risking their lives for you, so try to show some gratitude by following orders."

He dropped his smile and stood up a little straighter.

"Here are the rules. You're supposed to be deaf and mute, so pretend you know sign language. Don't talk at all. And don't look like you can hear. If you break the rules, I'll dump you in a second without hesitation."

He nodded.

"Let me handle the conversation if we're stopped. Here's your identity card. Don't try to be a hero because it doesn't look like luck is on your side. Let's get going. Is that bicycle seat at the right height for you?"

"I think so."

"All right. I'll go first. We won't be using lights, so pay attention and don't crash into me if I stop."

She biked slowly at first and glanced back a few times. Luckily, he seemed steady on the bike, favoring one leg to shield his injured knee, so she picked up speed because she did not want to be out on this road any longer than necessary.

After half an hour, he came up beside her and whispered that he needed to stop. She sighed and pulled off the road where there were some large oak trees.

"Hurry up," she said as she turned away from the trees.

While he rustled around in the leaves, Lina looked up to see if there were any stars visible. Suddenly she heard the click of a gun and turned to look at the source. *Stay calm*, she told herself, *and don't be a threat to this guy.* It was another cold and starry night just like that other one that had ended so tragically. She remembered the chill of that cold winter night in the forest. This time, without a hulking body guard, the night might end differently.

A German soldier stood beside her pointing a gun in her face. "What are you doing here?" he asked.

She answered him in German. "Just waiting for my man to get finished there." She tossed her head towards the trees casually. "He's got some kind of bladder problem," she said.

"You better hope the rest of his plumbing works," the German replied as he laughed loudly.

Lina obliged him with a laugh.

"You better get to where you're going. I'll overlook it this time, but the next fellow will arrest you."

"I'll tell him to keep it zipped."

The soldier laughed and walked away. Lina took a breath and hoped Oliver would stay in the woods till the soldier was far enough away.

She waited a few minutes and then whispered, "Where are you? We must get going!"

He stepped out from behind a tree. "You told me not to talk, so I was being obedient."

"Well, hurry up. I still need to bike home tonight after I drop you off."

When they arrived at the house, Lina told Oliver to stay with the bikes while she went to the house to check with the farmer.

Mr. Smits showed Oliver where to place his bike in the barn and instructed him in broken English to climb up the ladder to sleep in the loft. He handed him a sandwich and some drinking water in a jar and told him not to leave the loft until they came to get him in the morning.

Lina watched him limp towards the ladder and then climb up. He didn't thank her or say goodbye. She was glad to get rid of him.

Farmer Smits handed her a bag with several potatoes and some kale. She thanked him and biked away from the farm. If the airman broke any rules now, it wouldn't be her responsibility.

As she biked, she reminded herself to stay alert. With the job finished, the adrenaline drained away leaving her exhausted.

When she turned onto their darkened street, she was relieved to see the house and know that she would soon be in bed. She really hoped that when she next saw Lucas, he would be pleased with the mission and praise her for a job well done.

So far, the resistance work was disappointing. She hadn't expected to bike around to deliver papers to various addresses—she hoped that he would give her something more challenging soon.

When she was on a mission, Lina tried not to imagine all the things that could go wrong because it took her attention away from the task at hand. She could only imagine how much responsibility Lucas carried as he sent people into dangerous situations and hoped that they would return safely. Maybe his visits to their house provided him with some moments to relax and enjoy company. Being responsible had to be a burden, but he never complained about it.

She put her bike in the shed and walked towards the back door. After her recovery from the flu, she still tired more easily than before but was grateful to have completed this mission.

31.

LINA

ALTHOUGH the transport of the British airman had gone well, Lina had not been given any more assignments since that time. According to Ada, Lucas was working on something that required travel to the south. Lina resented the constant reminders that she wasn't really on the inside of anything. If he didn't trust her, he should just tell her. If he shared secrets with Ada, that was even more infuriating.

After Ada returned from volunteering, she invited Lina to have tea. "Have you heard about the Battle of the Bulge?" Ada asked.

"No," Lina replied. "How would I hear about that?"

"Apparently the Germans tried to stop the Allies from using the port of Antwerp and attempted to split the Allied lines. Casualties were horrendous—about seventy-five thousand Allied soldiers and a hundred and twenty thousand Axis soldiers died."

"Sounds like another disaster," Lina commented. "The numbers are too difficult to understand—and whether it's ten people or ten thousand, it is all a big tragedy, and it makes me feel numb."

"It could have been much worse," Ada said. "And I fear that it will get worse. How will we survive all this?"

"How do you get all this information?"

Ada shrugged. "I listen to the radio and Lucas tells me some things."

Lina sighed. *When did he share information with her? And why only with her?* She wondered if Lucas still saw her as a child and Ada as his equal. *Although in his defense, he did send me to pick up that British airman. Perhaps I am confusing his professional role with my personal hopes for something more between us.*

"Could you go to the bakery later and see if there's anything to eat? I have a meeting of the Food Council," Ada said.

"I thought the bakery was closed."

"Someone told me this morning that he opened for one day only."

Lina would have preferred to have a nap, but she had promised to do her part to keep them fed. "I'll go in a little while," she said.

As she bundled up in two sweaters, she wondered again why Lucas hadn't given her more assignments. He had told her to wait until he contacted her, but she heard nothing. If he was so short on comrades, he needed to give her more chances. Perhaps he was not happy with her work, but he had never said that. He drove her crazy sometimes—he never gave anything away. She was tired of thinking about him—it was time to redirect her attention to something else. Maybe it was time to study Father's books on photography. She had tried a few times, but it was difficult.

Learning from a book was a challenge, but if she tried to practice the techniques described in the book, maybe the ideas would stick. The technical decisions had to become automatic so that in any situation she could maximize all the factors and still choose an interesting composition. Father had made it seem effortless, and she wished she had paid more attention.

Taking exceptional photographs demanded both technical competence and an instinct for framing the shot. Instinct was mysterious, but it was something she knew could be honed with regular practice. Technical competence would require hard work to master, and she was fighting her usual tendency to give up too quickly.

After locking her bike to a post near the bakery, Lina went to the back of the line. Her camera was draped across her body—her scarf concealed it. She doubted there would be anything worth photographing on a dreary day like this, but sometimes the low light on rainy days yielded surprising results.

With kerchiefs over their heads, the women in the queue wore oversized and mended jackets with a variety of weathered shoes or men's boots. They were a ragged but determined bunch. Their scuffed shoes were firmly planted on the cobblestones; nothing would distract them from their mission because they knew that children were waiting at home for their return with bread fresh from the oven.

Lina looked around the gray square that had once been the heart of the town. She missed the crowds that pushed through narrow streets on market day with their bicycle panniers and baskets stuffed with leeks, potatoes, lettuce, and carrots along with bunches of yellow freesias or purple chrysanthemums. She missed the glorious cacophony of sounds that characterized market days in the past—church bells, shouts of vendors, women calling out to friends, men laughing as they sampled the raw herring with onions, accompanied by the staccato burst of bicycle bells. It wasn't just the laughter and fun that had disappeared from daily life, it was the color and the textures that were also absent.

A movie theater, now shuttered, had featured foreign films. In the past, she had loved going to movies, and she didn't care if they were German propaganda films or American romances—she simply wanted to be transported to other worlds. When they first started dating, she and Jos made out in the back row accompanied by the sounds of German actors flying planes and firing guns. Afterwards, when neither one of them could recall one detail of the movie's plot, they had laughed so hard.

Could she have done something to prevent his death on that cold night? Perhaps if she had tried to stop him from drinking at the party or made him leave earlier, he might still be alive. But he would not have listened to her. There was nothing she could do to change the outcome, and that made her very sad.

When Lina stepped to the back of the line, a few women glanced at her briefly and looked away. Tired of standing in the cold, they were desperately hungry and couldn't be bothered with social interaction. There had been a time when women would gossip in the shops and in the street on market days, but now their silent desperation drowned out any conversation. They were competitors for the same scarce goods, and they couldn't afford to let down their guard.

Although the women shared the same hardships, their suffering kept them isolated and distrustful. She had always assumed that people would band together in their fight to survive. But she and Ada lived under the same roof and never seemed to become much closer. Maybe the truce they had forged was enough, but she sometimes longed for a closer relationship. Conversation with Ada tended to stick to predictable topics.

"Why hasn't that bakery opened yet?" demanded one woman in a shrill voice that echoed over the square. "He is supposed to open at nine, and we have been waiting for two hours. You know what I think? I think he doesn't have any bread." Silence met her observation as she voiced their fears—no one wanted to hear that. What if there was no bread?

Some shoving and pushing ensued as their frustration found expression in physical aggression. Something wild and ugly was bubbling over while their patience ran out.

In the jostling of bodies, an elderly woman lost her balance, fell to the ground, and hit her head with a terrible *crack*. The woman who'd been in front of her in line squatted down beside her and checked her pulse. "There is no pulse," she said to the women who had gathered round her. The crowd was silent as they waited for some sign.

Heads craned to see, but no one risked moving their feet and losing their place in the line.

"Should we call an ambulance?" someone asked.

"The police will collect the body eventually," another voice stated in a matter-of-fact way.

A few women nodded to show agreement with the decision and support for the idea that it was not their problem. They studiously ignored the woman's body sprawled on the cobblestones.

Lina gave the woman a last look and then walked back to her place in line. She wanted to get far away from the troubling sight of the old woman. Who had been responsible, if anyone, for the stumble that led to her fatal fall? Were they all responsible due to their impatience with the line? How had they turned into hungry animals fighting for themselves and their families but lacking all compassion for others? War had done this to them, and Lina wasn't sure what would undo it.

When the door of the store opened, the line fell silent, and all eyes focused on the baker who stood in front of them in his white apron. He swallowed once or twice, and cleared his throat, intimidated by the silent stares of the women.

They began shoving towards the open door, but he held up his hand. "I'm very sorry ladies, but there's no bread today. I hoped we would receive some flour this morning, but we haven't, and I'm not sure when supplies will reach us."

Women waved their coupons at him and yelled that they were entitled to bread.

He held up both his hands with palms open and then gave a little bow. "I'm very sorry." He stepped back inside, locked the door, and pulled down the blind.

Fueled by their collective anger, the line continued to push forward, requiring them to step over the inert body of the old woman. Those in front of the line were forced to choose to turn away from the door by either moving to the right or to the left and then returning home.

Lina wanted to get away. This was an angry mob. There would be many disappointed children waiting for their mothers to return with bread. How could an occupying force starve people like this?

The dead woman's wool coat was bunched up above her knees, and her wool stockings had been darned in various spots. One shoe had fallen off, and her big toenail, turned brown and crusty from a toe fungus, stuck out through the stocking. Lina turned her face from it but then remembered her camera. She kept it at her side and took pictures of the women in the mob and the dead woman on the ground, hoping that the settings were appropriate because it was impossible to change them now. Her brief hesitation at filming such a disturbing scene was replaced by a need to capture the misery of the moment.

Lina felt the women behind her pushing against her back. She stepped out of the line before she had to make a choice to step over the body or to go around it. He'd already told them there was no bread—there was no point in pushing towards the locked door of the bakery. The crowd was irrational. She wouldn't be surprised if they started pelting the bakery with stones.

The frustration had boiled over, and heavy disappointment hung like ground fog over the cobblestones. They had nothing to feed their hungry families. Having failed to obtain supplies, they realized their ration coupons were meaningless. Lina watched as the fight went out of them—it was like watching a tent collapse once the supporting poles were removed.

The women drifted away, humiliated by their failure. As the square emptied, they ignored the body on the ground—collateral damage of a fight they'd never wanted.

The rain began to fall slowly at first but then turned into a deluge. Tiny insistent rivers ran down her neck. She wrapped the camera in her scarf and placed it in her empty bicycle pannier.

Would anyone miss the woman who had died—would someone sit by a window until dark wondering why she hadn't come home? Her camera had recorded the woman's death, but what difference would such a photograph make? It wouldn't bring her back to life. Either no one was responsible, or they were all responsible. Neither of those seemed to be good choices, but it hurt her head to think about it.

32.

LINA

LINA gathered up every blanket she could find, but Ada was still shivering. Lina had never seen her sister so sick, and she was afraid.

When Ada said her throat felt like it was closing, Lina knew she had to find a doctor. People were dying of typhoid and diphtheria—Lina could not let that happen. Medicine was scarce, so she didn't want to wait until it was too late.

Lina tried to give Ada sips of water, but she was too weak to sit up. During the night she'd been confused, calling for their mother and rolling restlessly in the bed. She was hot with fever and at times didn't recognize Lina. Her skin felt like it was burning up.

Earlier that evening, Nel had arrived at the door with some soup. She told Lina she'd been visiting her son to help with the children. When she asked if she could sit with Ada, Lina told her Ada was resting and couldn't have visitors.

Lina sat with her that night and talked to her quietly, reassuring her that all was well. In the middle of the night, when Ada had soaked through her nightclothes, Lina washed her and changed her nightgown. They had always been very private about their bodies, and Lina could not remember seeing Ada naked, but there was no one else to do it.

Lina was shocked by how thin Ada was. Under her ribs, her belly sunk into a concave gap. They'd worn multiple sweaters these past weeks, so she hadn't noticed her weight loss. Had she eaten any of the food Lina had found or was she giving it all to her? Ada had said once or twice she was worried that Lina wouldn't have enough energy to bike around looking for food. If Ada wasn't eating, that was unacceptable. Lina had never expected such a sacrifice from her; she planned to be more vigilant in future.

Ada's collarbones protruded, and her ribs were visible, one by one. Even her breasts had shrunken. Lina washed her carefully and dried her with a towel. She wished she had some lotion to apply to her dry skin. She had never washed another person, not even Mother when she was sick because the nurse had done that. Lina was certain that Ada would not remember any of it and hoped that she would not be embarrassed.

Lina knew she would never be able to manage on her own if Ada didn't survive this illness. They were sisters—if sickness or the war took one of them away, the world would never be the same.

Lina pulled a clean nightgown over her elder sister's head and gently combed her hair before putting her head back on the pillow.

When Ada whispered something, Lina leaned close to listen. "Thank you," she said. Lina ran her hand across her forehead, which felt cooler.

"Try to sleep. I will be right here."

As she watched Ada sleep, she wondered if there was something more she should do. What if Ada died on her watch? Although she was not qualified to make nursing decisions, she found herself in charge of her very ill sister. Lina tried to get comfortable lying on a blanket on the floor beside her bed. She dozed and woke herself frequently to make sure Ada's condition hadn't worsened.

The next morning, Lucas brought a doctor who examined Ada. She diagnosed Ada with a serious case of influenza and gave Lina some medicine to administer every four hours. Lucas offered to stay for a while so that Lina could catch up on sleep. She was surprised by the profound relief she experienced at his offer. She had reached her limit and needed to sleep.

As she climbed into bed, she thought about Lucas and his loyalty to them. Lucas could be trusted to keep watch. She sank into her bed and pulled the woolen blankets up to her nose, falling asleep in just a few minutes.

When she checked on Ada later, she was sleeping quietly and seemed to be without a fever.

"Thank you, Lucas, Ada looks a lot better. And I slept like a rock."

"Let me know if you need my help. You don't want to get completely run down, or you will be sick too; and then I will have to nurse both of you."

"I hope that doesn't happen," Lina said, hiding the blush that crept into her face at the thought of his cool hand on her fevered brow.

After Lucas left, Lina sat at the kitchen table holding a cup of hot water in her cold hands. The kitchen windows were covered with frost—although the patterns looked like lace, Lina would happily exchange their artistry for some heat. There never seemed to be enough food or heat to sustain their bodies. She sat at the table and studied the garden, now frozen solid. It was a bleak sight—the morning light was a flat gray that showed no sign of brightening.

Suddenly, she sat up and listened carefully—someone jiggled the lock on the back door. Not sure whether to run away or stay where she was, Lina concealed herself behind the door to the basement.

"That was easy," a man's voice said. "That lock is ancient. We'll have to replace that. Are you sure no one is home?"

"They are always out during the day," Mrs. Vriend said.

"Well, aren't you clever?" Chief Vriend replied. "And how do you know that?"

"I have my ways. Let's take a quick look. This house will be perfect for us—we'll have more rooms for the grandchildren and for guests," said the woman. "Look at this sunporch. We could put some wicker furniture and plants in here."

They walked into the kitchen. "It's a nice-sized kitchen, but it will need to be updated," Mrs. Vriend declared. "Definitely not up to my standards. When you are promoted to inspector general, you'll need a good house like this for entertaining."

Lina stepped out from behind the door and stood directly in front of them. "Good morning. Can I help you?"

Mrs. Vriend jumped and held her hand to her chest. "Oh, you frightened me."

Lina stood her ground. "You startled me too. I'm not used to people entering my house uninvited."

Chief Vriend pulled himself up to his full height and smoothed the front of his uniform jacket, trying to look important. "We saw someone lurking around your house and thought we should investigate," he said in his loud voice.

Lina almost laughed in his face at his excuse, but there was no point in angering him. "Whatever it was, things seem to be under control."

"Are you sure you don't want me to check the house?" he asked.

"Quite sure," Lina replied firmly.

"It's certainly a large house for two young girls," Mrs. Vriend said with a sniff.

Her husband shot her a look to keep quiet. "All right then. Good day," he said as he turned and escorted his wife out the back door.

Lina locked the door behind them. How dare they! With Ada sick upstairs, they were trying to steal the house from them.

As she stirred the oatmeal that she planned to bring to Ada, she thought about the Vriends. How could they justify stealing their neighbor's property? They were committing crimes against their own people. Someday they'd be judged harshly by the townspeople, who would never forget the things they had done.

"Who were you talking to?" Ada asked as Lina entered her room with the breakfast tray.

"The Vriends assumed we were out for the day, so they broke in to have a look at the house and make plans to decorate it."

"I don't believe them," she said.

"I can't stand that guy." Lina helped Ada sit up and put the tray in front of her. "Do you want me to feed you, or can you do it yourself?"

"I can do it," Ada insisted.

Lina nodded but stayed nearby in case Ada needed help. It was a relief to see her looking so much better—she had to thank Lucas for bringing the doctor. She'd never pictured Ada as someone who needed looking after, but it was clear that her health was increasingly fragile. Lina remembered how Father had urged them to look after each other.

Enduring the constant reminders of war was bad enough, but adding a food crisis made survival feel almost impossible. Lucas reminded them that the end was in sight, so there was no question of giving up now. She would search the closets and cupboards to find something she could barter for food. Ada needed some eggs or some milk to regain her strength, and if there were any available, Lina would pay whatever price they demanded. Mother's silver and gold would of little value if they didn't survive the winter.

33.

ADA

A FEW days later, Ada sat in the kitchen and had a cup of tea. She felt very weak but was grateful to be out of bed. Her memory of being sick was quite vague—the fevers had gone on for several days, and crazy dreams had filled those nights. Lina still seemed unusually solicitous, so she must have been very ill. It was very much out of character to see her fuss like that, but she was grateful that Lina had done her best to nurse her.

Lucas brought some typing for Ada. He usually had sheets of notes that various people sent him from locations around the countryside. Ada edited and typed those notes to generate a coherent copy. Whenever she finished typing and editing the newsletter, Lucas took the copy to her father's former departmental secretary who used the machines in the basement of the faculty building to duplicate the paper.

After the newsletter was duplicated, women couriers transported them in market bags or prams. Some couriers wore special vests under their coats that held copies of the newsletter. For many, this was their only source of information about the war.

"I hope you're feeling better. Don't bother with this typing until you feel well enough," Lucas said.

"Thanks for bringing the doctor when I was sick. It's time I start getting up and doing things. I'd welcome some work," Ada replied. "It's not good to sit around."

"I forgot to ask you when I was here before, but how is your volunteer work going with the new interchurch food bureau?" he asked.

"I have missed some shifts, but they do good work. For me it's only a short-term assignment. I also work in a clinic where they evaluate children's nutritional status for possible evacuation to the north. The staff separate those who need immediate nutritional support or are unable to travel from those who are fit enough to make the trip."

Lucas nodded. "The big obstacle is transportation. Apparently, a barge left Amsterdam last week with children heading north. I hope that they can find places for the children and that their hosts will be good to them. Some Red Cross relief was finally approved, and a food relief ship is due in Delfzijl in a few days. People should start feeling some easing of the famine."

"I don't understand why it's taking so long to distribute the promised food aid," Ada said.

"It will still take some negotiating, but at least the Germans are not opposed."

"The fact that the government-in-exile wants the rail strike to continue doesn't help the food situation."

"Churchill doesn't want food relief to interrupt the military strategy, but among the leaders, none of them can apparently agree whether military strategy or food relief should come first. If they saw for themselves how dire things are, maybe they would move a little faster to distribute food."

"While they play politics people are starving, and children and the elderly are suffering terribly."

"I agree, but there's not much I can do until the commanders agree on a good strategy."

"Lucas, I need some advice on something else," Ada said. "The Vriends seem determined to take the house from us, and now that Father has passed, I think they will become bolder. Lina was in the kitchen the other day when they broke in. It sounds like they are keeping track of our movements. I'm almost afraid to leave the house because they might change the locks on us."

Lucas shook his head slowly. "Be careful not to antagonize him, or he'll put you both in jail and take your house while you're gone. He has no legal right to do that, but he is well-connected to the occupiers. Also, be careful about leaving any information lying about."

"I usually burn my notes for the newsletter in the woodstove so there's no trace."

"Good. Continue to be cautious and trust no one."

The next day Nel stopped by while Ada was in the kitchen. She wanted to gossip about some of the women volunteers. Ada nodded as she listened, but she really wasn't interested. Although it might make Nel feel important, Ada wanted to plug her ears and yell, "Stop!"

Ada rubbed her forehead as she felt the beginning of a headache. Taking a few breaths to calm herself and keep her voice steady, she said, "War doesn't seem proper either, and yet nations throw their young and their resources into battles that lead nowhere. Women and children are left to fend for themselves or starve. This needs to end," Ada replied.

Nel seemed briefly taken aback by Ada's statement, but then she moved on to her next complaint about a neighbor who, she believed, engaged in suspicious activities. Nel wondered if she should report the woman to someone.

"I think you should leave her alone," Ada said.

"You just don't know who to trust these days," Nel said.

"That might be true, but we've known Marijke for years, and she can be trusted." Ada took a breath and changed the subject. "Now what are we working on today?" Ada tried very hard to stay calm—it wasn't Nel's business to police the neighborhood. Lina was right that the woman was insufferable. How had she ever fallen under her influence? She was clever and knew how to manipulate people's weakness. Ada felt like a fool for believing that Nel was genuinely concerned about her well-being, but she still wasn't sure what Nel wanted from them.

"Where is Lina anyway?" Nel asked.

Ada wanted to tell her it was none of her business. "She's doing some photography. Father always thought she had potential."

"Could you tell her that there is a part-time cleaning job at the Captain's house? Might be good for her to learn a useful skill if her big plans don't work out. If she's interested, she should go to his house at ten on Friday and talk to the housekeeper, Berthe."

"Thanks. I'll pass it on," Ada said. She planned to ask Lucas whether he thought Lina would be safe working in the Captain's house. "Now let's get to work. You want to outline a new pamphlet for the council?"

The next day while Ada washed some of their shirts in the kitchen sink, Lina studied prints of her most recent photographs, choosing her favorites to add to her portfolio.

Lina watched Ada wring out the shirts in the sink. She'd offered to do the laundry, but Ada had insisted. She said it helped clear her mind, so Lina returned to sorting out prints and negatives.

"How about this one?" Lina asked as she held up a black-and-white photograph of a canal in the center of the city. There was an eerie silence to the photo—the water was still and there was no evidence of human or animal presence. The row of trees that lined the canal were all broken. Limbs had either been torn or chopped to use for firewood, leaving rows of dismembered tree trunks.

Ada wiped her hands on her apron and walked over to study the picture. "When the war ends, they're going to have to replant trees all over the country. This picture shows the scars left by war. Sometimes we only think about human suffering, but nature suffers as well. When you think of the unexploded ordnance on our beaches, the inundated farmlands, and bombed fields, our country will be visibly wounded for years to come." Ada shook her head slowly. "Lina, you have a remarkable sense of composition, and you are not afraid to show the truth."

"How about this?" Lina held up the photograph of the elderly woman who'd been knocked down in the bread line. Her posture was so awkward that it was immediately clear that she was dead.

Ada inhaled sharply when she saw it. She held her hand over her mouth.

"Ada, are you all right?"

"I can't believe that picture. That poor woman. How did that happen? How did you manage to take that picture?"

Lina was startled by Ada's strong reaction to the photo. "I shot it from my hip, and luckily no one noticed the camera."

"That was when you went to get bread?"

Lina nodded. "When the baker said he had no bread, the women became angry and started to push and shove. That woman tripped and fell and hit her head."

"That is a very powerful picture." Ada wiped her eyes and continued to hold the print and stare at it. "And very sad because no one seems to care."

Lina looked at her with surprise. "Thanks Ada." She was touched by Ada's heartfelt response to the photograph. Maybe Ada was right, she had to keep going with this. Father had left her supplies including film, paper, and chemicals, as well as a darkroom and a very good camera. Maybe he hoped that she would take up photography, but he hadn't wanted to impose it on her. He knew how stubborn she was when anyone tried to give her advice. She wished she could tell him that she was learning to be a better person. He would pat her hand affectionately, and his eyes would twinkle with amusement at her attempt at humility.

Ada sat at the table and sorted a bowl of lentils, checking to see that there were no small stones in the pile. "Lucas asked me if I wanted a short-term job."

Lina looked up at her. "A job? Are you sure? You are already working a lot, and you are still recovering. What does he want you to do?"

"Some Allied soldiers are here to do advanced planning. I think they are Canadian. It's all very quiet because they don't want to alarm the Germans. The soldiers need a translator and a secretary to help with communications. I think I should do it."

Lina looked out the window. "What would Father say?"

Ada thought for a few moments. "I think he'd tell us to do everything we could to help the Allies because our people can't survive much longer this way."

Lina turned to look at her. "I agree. You should do it. But you'll have to be very careful because if you're biking regularly along the same route, you might get noticed. You don't want to lead the occupiers to wherever these fellows are hiding out."

"I'll make sure I have a carrot or a potato in my bag, even if it's all shriveled, so I can say I was traveling for food," Ada explained. "I have a few in the root cellar that might work as decoys."

"Tell those Canadians to pay you with food," Lina quipped.

"Maybe they don't have any," Ada said.

"They feed their soldiers something, even if it's prepared army rations," Lina said. "Things are so bad now even the farmers have almost nothing to eat. Those lentils are all I could find, and I spent the whole day looking."

"Everyone is suffering and some more than others. This war must end because people can't hang on indefinitely. Starvation might be a slower form of death, but it is inevitable. For those who are already vulnerable, death will come even more quickly."

"Lucas keeps saying the war will end soon, but how does he know? I think it's a good sign that those Canadian soldiers have arrived. You should help them in any way you can," Lina said. "They may be the ones who will finally liberate us. And that can't come a moment too soon. We must make sure we survive till they do."

"You're right. I'll accept the job and see what I can learn from it. I almost forgot, Nel told me about a job for you. The Captain needs a house cleaner. If you are interested, you might want to check with Lucas and see how he feels about you being in that house. You need to go to there on Friday and talk to Berthe, the housekeeper."

Lina looked skeptical. "You know I am a lousy cleaner. And work for that creep? He is the one who sent Father to a camp."

"It is a chance to get inside his house and keep your ears open for any information. Anyway, if you want the job, you need to talk to the housekeeper. I think you can manage to clean that place—after a while you will develop a routine."

Lina looked at her with skepticism. "I'll think about it."

34.

LINA

On Friday, Lina went to the Captain's house to ask about the cleaning job. Although she hated housework, she was going to lose her mind if she didn't do something besides try to find food.

The interview was brief—the housekeeper, Berthe, asked a few questions and seemed satisfied, mostly because Lina's German was fluent. She was a solid woman with generous hips who moved slowly. Her thinning gray hair was held in a twist by a clip. She wore no jewelry except a small gold watch on her thick wrist. As the person in charge of the domestic side of the Captain's life, she made it clear that Lina would report to her, and she was not to address the Captain.

"Start Monday," Berthe said, "at nine o'clock sharp. And then on Friday the same. You might be asked to work extra during the holiday time when the Captain has some parties here."

"That's fine," Lina said and thanked her.

Berthe didn't reply, and she turned to the sink to wash some potatoes—she was obviously a woman of few words who ruled the house with efficiency.

Lina knew she needed to do her work without expecting any polite conversation from the woman. She biked home feeling elated that she had landed a job without too much effort. She hoped she could manage to clean the place well enough that Berthe didn't fire her after her first shift.

When she asked Lucas for his advice about the job, he had expressed concern about her safety, but he was also pleased to have a source inside the Captain's house. "Your job is to clean that house and observe. Don't be caught snooping around. I've heard rumors about the Captain and his entertainments. Keep quiet about anything you see."

"Do you think they'll give me anything to eat?" Lina asked. "It's hard to work on an empty stomach."

Ada shook her head. "I wouldn't count on that. Just show them that you're willing to work hard, and don't get defensive if the housekeeper corrects you. You need to have her on your side, or she'll have you fired."

"You're already picturing me getting fired! Thanks a lot for your confidence."

"You know what I mean. I've heard from Nel that the housekeeper has control over the household. It would be wise to get along with her, or at least stay out of her way if you can."

The day after her interview at the Captain's house, Lucas sent her on an assignment. Lina didn't think she could go on a food search and do the job for Lucas, so she warned Ada they would have to make do with what they had for dinner.

Lina biked to a farm to the north of town where she met the other men Lucas had assigned. They glanced at her but ignored her and continued to converse among themselves. She could sense their skepticism, but two of them looked about eighty and the third fellow looked fourteen. Lucas must be having difficulty finding able recruits for the work. Wearing a cap over her hair and her usual men's clothes, she kept to herself and waited for a sign that they were going to move to the site of the air drop.

They did not exchange names but followed the leader to a field a few kilometers away where an Allied plane was scheduled to drop crates of weapons and ammunition.

With their bikes resting against the trees at the edge of the field, the older man shared cigarettes with the other two. Lina didn't care that he didn't offer her one—he was making a point that she was not one of them. If she had hoped for a sense of comradeship, she'd given that up; and besides, Lucas had warned her against fraternizing with the others.

They listened carefully for the airplane's engines. The leader warned them to stay out of the way until the bundles were dropped. Being hit with a crate of guns or ammunition was not in her plan, so Lina was happy to wait until the drop was finished and the plane had left.

It was a cold and overcast night; snow was expected by morning. The soil crunched when they walked—it sounded loud in her ears. Without a moon the darkness was complete, but the leader had placed a few flashlights on sticks at the edges of the field to help guide the pilot. She was glad the men were not talkers, because sounds carried far on these cold nights. Lina tucked her hands in her coat pockets and moved her fingers to restore circulation.

The leader held up his hand as they heard the airplane come closer. It dipped over the field as if planning to land, released the cargo, and then pulled up again. The sounds of the engine faded into the night. They were all temporarily stunned by the quick drop, but when the men ran into the field, Lina followed.

The wooden crates had rope handles, so Lina took turns holding one end while one of the men took the other. They carried the crates until they'd retrieved all of them. The farmer came out to check and instructed them to distribute the crates into the various animal pens that carried a strong scent of previous occupants. The barns that housed the dairy herd still contained piles of straw, so they took handfuls of it to cover the crates. One man shone a flashlight to see if anything was left exposed. Since the farmer no longer tended a herd, they doubted that the occupiers would be back to inspect the pens—it was a risk the farmer was willing to take.

"Glad that's done," the leader said after the farmer left the barn and returned to his house.

"Come on, let's relax a bit," the younger one said. "I've got something." He held up a flask that Lina presumed was filled with whiskey. She tried to tell them she needed to go home to rest, but they wouldn't hear of it. First, they wanted her to know she wasn't considered part of them, and now they wouldn't let her leave. She had mostly given up late nights and partying after Jos died; she wasn't sure this was a good idea.

They built a fire in a stone pit behind the barn and sat on some logs that had been hidden on the side of the barn. One of the older fellows told stories of outwitting the Germans in various ways—stealing their bikes or taking food out of delivery trucks. They laughed hysterically.

Lina was amazed that these fellows who'd been so taciturn had such a capacity for fun. When they finished the whiskey, Lina stood up and told them she had to get home. She felt a bit unsteady at first. The alcohol had gone straight to her head because she had only eaten a piece of bread all day. She was exhausted by the physical work of hauling heavy crates, but she didn't want to appear weak.

Lina biked home using the back roads and paths as much as she could. She felt a bit shaky on the bike, but she took big breaths of the cold air. When she approached the outskirts of town, she biked quickly through the town center. Nobody was around, and the shops were boarded up. Would they ever return to sell ordinary things to the people?

Her legs ached from the effort of biking. What a relief it would be to put her head on the pillow and pull up the blankets.

"*Halte!*" a voice cried out.

She groaned and briefly considered biking away as fast as she could, but she knew that would be futile. The soldier grabbed her by the arm and pulled her off the bike and slammed her into a stone wall. The bike clattered to the cobblestones. She glanced at it and hoped it wasn't damaged.

"What are you doing here?" he asked. "It's long past curfew."

"A friend was in labor, and I had to help deliver the baby."

"That's an interesting story. Do you always drink whiskey when you work? Where was this delivery?" he asked.

"At a farm on the road to Oestgeest. The father insisted we toast the new baby."

"You're a midwife?"

"I hope to take my nurses' training soon. I'm planning to be a midwife, but the war . . ."

The soldier released his grip on her collar to light a cigarette. "My wife has four." He seemed bored, so Lina tried to humor him.

"Boys or girls?" she asked, not that she cared, but she had to act interested.

"Two of each. When she said that was enough, I had to listen."

"You wanted more?" Lina asked in mock surprise.

"I wanted at least ten, but my wife has the final say."

"I'm sure she knows what is best. I hope you'll soon be able to go home to see how much they've grown."

"Can't be soon enough. Now get out of here and go home."

"I will. Good night." Lina biked away as fast as she could. She'd been spared and hoped whoever was keeping watch over the night sky would forgive all her lies.

The rhythmic squeal of her bike wheel carried through the night, but she could fix that. Once she unlocked the back door, she felt overcome with fatigue. Lina climbed the stairs slowly, feeling every muscle in her back and legs and wishing she could sink into a hot bath.

35.

LINA

WHEN Lina arrived at the Captain's house on Monday morning, there had been a party the night before, and the place was a mess. Berthe muttered her disapproval as she peeled potatoes, clearly unhappy about the chaos but making no attempt to address it. The living room reeked of stale smoke and wine, but it was too cold outside to open the windows.

While she was polishing the enormous mahogany dining room table, the Captain's aide, Raoul, came into the room. He leaned against the door frame and watched her work, arms crossed against his chest. The housekeeper had finally gone home for the day, and Lina was trying to get everything done. She hoped he wasn't there to check her work—everything felt like it was taking longer because things were such a mess.

She tried not to stare, but he was the best-looking man she'd ever seen. Tall and lean, he moved like a dancer. His olive skin set off his impossible greenish-gray eyes with long lashes. He wore a uniform without any markings to signify rank.

His scrutiny made her nervous, and she dropped the polishing cloth twice. Was he inspecting her work or planning to ask her questions? "Did you want to ask me something?" she said in German.

He replied in accented German. "You better do a good job, or she'll have you fired," he said with a smile.

"Don't worry, I'm Dutch. I know how to clean."

A chuckle escaped his lips.

Lina was relieved to see he had a sense of humor. After all, having an ally in the house would be very helpful. Berthe ignored her completely except when Lina dared stray into her kitchen while she was cooking.

"What other languages do you speak?" she asked.

"Spanish, French, English."

"No Dutch?" she said with a smile.

He chuckled. "Not yet. Have you survived the terror?"

"What do you mean?"

"Frau Berthe," he said in a mock whisper.

Lina snickered.

"She's all right if you stay out of her way. Are you hungry?" he asked.

Lina looked at him and tried not to look too eager. "I'm always hungry."

"I know where there's some cake."

"But . . ."

"He won't be home till later tonight."

Lina followed Raoul into the kitchen where he made tea and cut two enormous slices of a chocolate cake. She watched as he moved around the kitchen, displaying both a natural grace and a sense of ownership of the space—something that she was certain he would never do in Berthe's presence and perhaps not in the Captain's presence either.

When he pointed to the table, she reluctantly took her seat hoping that no one would come home early and see her making herself at home there. She'd be fired on the spot, but she wanted that cake so badly it seemed to be worth the risk.

"Have you ever done any fashion work?" she asked him.

He looked startled. "Some. How did you guess?"

"You walk like a model."

He laughed. "I grew up in Argentina. My father is from there and my mother is German. I learned to dance as a young boy, and I did some modeling in Berlin. What about you?"

"I like fashion photography, but I still have a lot to learn."

"Have you done any photo shoots?"

"Only in high school. We put on an annual fashion show, and I took the photos. It was great fun."

"I've done modeling, but I would really prefer to design."

Lina nodded. "We need the war to end so we can chase some dreams."

He nodded, but a shadow moved across his face. "I should get back to work," he said.

Lina took the last bite of the cake and stood up. "I'll take care of the dishes. Thank you for the cake." As she washed and dried the plates and cups, she heard his feet moving around upstairs. She didn't understand what his role was, but if he was stuck in this house with only Berthe and the Captain for company, it had to be an isolated existence.

Lina finished cleaning downstairs and then put away the dust cloths and mop. She looked around to make sure she hadn't forgotten anything. Standing at the bottom of the stairs, she thought about calling out to tell Raoul that she was leaving, but that seemed too familiar; so she went out the back door and closed it firmly behind her. Fueled by chocolate cake, Lina felt she could bike all day. Next time she would ask Raoul if she could take home a piece for Ada.

36.

LINA

WHEN Lina returned from her cleaning job later Monday afternoon, she was surprised to see Lucas waiting for her.

"What did you think you were doing on that job?" he asked.

"What do you mean?" she asked, her heart sinking at the tone of his voice. Was he talking about her cleaning shift at the Captain's house?

"You had strict orders."

"You mean the airfield. What is the problem? We did the job and hid the stuff. It all went well."

"It seems like you don't know how to take orders, and I can't afford to have you improvising."

"What are you talking about?" Lina was perplexed. Why was he so angry?

"You were supposed to retrieve and hide the boxes. I didn't tell you to enjoy a cozy campfire while drinking whiskey."

"I just stayed for a while. We didn't exchange names or locations if that's what's worrying you."

"The farmer whose property you used for your party told me. And he wasn't happy. A fire can attract attention, to say nothing of the noise. You stole his wood, and you were drinking and fraternizing. As I told you, it's very important to keep your distance and not socialize with the others. That precaution is for your safety and for theirs."

"We weren't making noise. We were just having a drink."

Lucas groaned. "And then what?"

Lina took a breath. "I was stopped on the way home by a *mof* who wanted to know where I'd been."

Lucas glared at her. "What did you tell him?"

"I said I had attended a birth at a farm, and it went very late. I told him I was hoping to be a nurse midwife someday."

Lucas sighed loudly. "And the next time he sees you, will you have more lies ready for him? Do you think you can fool him twice?"

"What are the chances I will run into that guy again?"

Lucas didn't answer that. "At the moment, I am having a hard time accepting that you can do this work."

His eyes were cold. She didn't think he'd react like this—it was just an innocent drink. If he didn't think she could do the work, he should tell her. She felt she was at the edge of her patience. The least he could do was thank her for her efforts. Hopefully those guns would land where they were most needed, and it would be thanks to her and the others who did their work on a freezing cold December night.

They sat in silence for a few minutes. Lina bit her lip to keep from reacting in anger. He appeared to be silently fuming across the table. Was he going to dismiss her?

"How did it go at the Captain's house?" he asked at last.

She was startled by the change in topic. "He's not around much. Mostly I deal with the housekeeper and Raoul, who is an aide to the Captain. Although he wears a uniform, I have a feeling he's a companion rather than a soldier."

"Keep your ears open. You never know what kind of information you might glean from being there. Just observe the tone in the house, any increased activity, house guests, or meetings. If you get the feeling that they are working on something or an attack might be imminent, just tell me, but don't try to get more details. They'll be watching you, so don't run any risks. I mean it."

"He's having a party next weekend with some military people, and the housekeeper asked if I would help serve."

"You should do it if you can. Be very careful not to appear interested in anything they say. You are there as a servant who is completely uninvolved in the event and uninterested in the conversation. They might assume you don't understand German. As for the assignment last night, I'm giving you a warning. If you improvise on my orders or socialize with the others, you will no longer be working with us. Is that clear?"

She nodded. She still couldn't see why it was such a big deal, but she didn't want to give up the job. He certainly was clear about his expectations. She had to admit, he was a good leader—the others had learned to trust his judgment.

"I promised Ada that you would be safe, but if you are going to take risks, I can't keep you safe. Please follow the instructions closely and don't improvise unless it is necessary."

No matter what he thought, she wasn't going to give up until he fired her, and if that happened, she'd find another group to work with. It might not seem like much, but if everyone did their share in opposing the occupiers, the war would eventually end. Even Ada was biking out to a hidden camp to help the Canadian soldiers. This was no time to retreat—all hands were needed to end this war.

37.

ADA

A FEW days later when Ada came in through the back door, Lina looked up from her sketch pad. Ada placed her cloth bag on the table with a thud.

"What's that?" Lina asked.

"Dinner for tonight," Ada said.

"That's good. Because I biked all over and found nothing. How was work?"

"It was good. The Canadians are preparing for something big. This could be the end."

Lina felt her envy increase. It sounded like Ada had landed in the middle of the camp that would be central to the battle. "What exactly do you do?"

"I work as a translator so they can coordinate with local units and the resistance. Sometimes I type or edit memos and letters. They're so friendly, it's nice to work for them. And look at this." Ada showed her the cans in her cloth bag. "Owen, one of the soldiers, sent this along so we can have a good dinner tonight. What do you think of spaghetti?" Ada pulled out some pasta from her bag.

Lina exhaled. "I was afraid we were going to be very hungry tonight. Make sure you keep this job."

Ada smiled. "Should I start cooking?"

"Please! What can I do?"

"If you open this can of tomatoes, I'll boil some water and see if we have any dried mushrooms left from the fall. You could set the table too, please."

Lina got up and did as Ada asked. "Tell me about this Owen soldier. He sounds like a romantic hero."

"He's a tall guy who comes from Nova Scotia in Canada. He has twelve brothers and sisters. He has red hair and freckles with green eyes. He told me that his father has a photography studio in town, and his sister has followed him into that business as well."

"What kind of photography?" Lina asked.

"Portraits, family occasions, some weddings."

Lina nodded. "And what does this soldier do?"

"He's trained as an engineer, and he does a lot of advanced work in planning. I don't know the details, but he's an interesting fellow."

"Is he single?"

"He has a wife and family back home, and he misses them terribly. He hasn't been in any homes here or met people outside his work, so I invited him to come for Sunday dinner."

"Here? For dinner?" Lina couldn't believe her ears. They hadn't had company, other than Lucas, in years. "What can we cook? We have nothing."

"He's going to bring eggs and whatever else he can find so we can make crepes. I thought about inviting Lucas too, if that's all right with you?"

"Lucas? The more the merrier, especially if there's going to be food."

"And wine," Ada added with a smile.

"I like this soldier, and I haven't even met him."

"He's going to ask you about your photography, so be prepared. Maybe we should get the shuffleboard ready too. We haven't played *sjoelbak* for a long time. It's in the front corner of the basement if you want to get it ready and dust it off."

Ada stirred some of her dried herbs and spices into the pot of tomatoes and then added the dried mushrooms. The water in the pasta pot started to bubble and steam.

"What's the first thing you're going to do when the war ends?" Lina asked.

Ada turned towards Lina. "I'm not sure that I ever believed it would end, but I would hang out the flag if it did."

"I plan to go to town where they will have a parade. In other places, the soldiers handed out chocolate and stockings and cigarettes."

"What do you need stockings for? You only ever wear those black pants."

181

"I plan to burn them. It's time for a new look."

"Can you imagine what it will be like when the stores open again, and we can buy things?"

Lina smiled. "And a bakery. And cheese."

"Lucas says it will take a while to restore life to normal, but just imagine biking to the market and eating frites and drinking real coffee." Ada had a wistful look as she imagined that life.

"Do a good job for those soldiers. Those Canadians might just be the ones to help finish this war."

38.

ADA

WHEN Ada started working for the Canadian soldiers, she was unprepared for their friendliness and generosity towards her. Her work involved correspondence and creating charts with detailed map locations as well as other charts of supplies and locations. Working for Father had prepared her to deal with detail. Her boss was always grateful for the work she did and thanked her with food rations. Much of the work she could do at home, so she moved things around in Father's study to accommodate the things she needed to do.

She thought about painting Mother's former sewing room and finding a proper work table, but for now Father's study would have to do. It still felt uncomfortable using his space, so she always worked on the opposite side of his desk to avoid sitting in his chair. Sometimes the faint scent of smoke would emanate from the walls, and she would put down her pen and take a moment to think about him.

Ada and Lina took turns making crepes while Owen told them stories about his life in Nova Scotia as a young man. His green eyes twinkled with mischief. He had a soft baritone voice that made everyone stop and listen. As a storyteller, he was exceptional. Lina was pretty sure he'd embroidered the details quite a bit and exaggerated his role, but he was so engaging that she didn't care. Lucas took care of the wine that Owen had brought and made sure their glasses were filled. Ada put several bowls on the table filled with toppings for the crepes. Lucas had brought a can of crab meat, so Ada prepared that with some herbs, and she'd put out some of her red berry jam so they had a choice of savory or sweet flavors.

They ate dinner by the light of a beeswax candle that Ada had made in the summer. The candlelight disguised the peeling paint and faded color of the walls and made the kitchen feel festive. The light moved across their faces, sometimes illuminating them and sometimes casting shadows.

While listening to Owen's fishing adventures from back home, they ate the food and drank the red wine. Owen knew how to stretch out the tension of a story until he released the punch line to howls of laughter. Ada hoped the neighbors didn't hear them. She especially hoped that Nel would not show up with some excuse to see who was visiting them. Nel had been scarce lately because she had been asked to work with the socialist group that was organizing child evacuations. She was relieved that Nel seemed to have lost interest in producing another pamphlet for the Food Council.

For once, there was neither fear nor hunger in the kitchen. Instead, they managed to push the war out of their minds for a few hours. It was encouraging to share food together with a group of adults, drink wine, and hear about their life experiences before the war. Was this a taste of the future? The idea of a happier tomorrow was difficult to picture, but it was important to try to imagine it.

39.

LINA

DRESSED in the black pants and white shirt that had previously served as her uniform in the café, Lina studied her reflection in the mirror. The Captain was always immaculately groomed and uniformed—he would not tolerate a wrinkled server at one of his parties.

His house had a generous living room that could easily accommodate a large group. As far as she knew, only Raoul and the Captain lived there full-time—the housekeeper rented an apartment a block away.

Lina wondered what happened to the original occupants of the house. Had they been arrested on some phony charge, or perhaps deported? The Captain was proud of his art collection—she'd heard him boasting to someone about it, but when she dusted the heavy frames, she wondered how each piece had been acquired. At the beginning of the war, many Jewish gallery owners sold masterpieces in desperation to raise funds to escape the country. Perhaps he had bought these paintings from dealers, or maybe he'd stolen them.

After cleaning a few times, Lina realized that if there were secrets there, she wasn't going to uncover them. The Captain was fastidious and didn't leave things lying about. He was rarely home when she cleaned, but in his absence she had a feeling that Berthe monitored her progress through the house.

She'd wondered if he had some motive in hiring her or if he even knew who her father was, but it seemed that she had been the first person to show up. Somehow Nel received advanced notice of the job through some of her friends and had passed it on to Ada. Why Nel would do her any favors was not clear, but she tried to be grateful. Maybe Nel wanted her out of the house at predictable times so she could continue to influence Ada.

On Saturday, she arrived at the house in the early afternoon to help Berthe with the New Year's Eve party preparation. She saw plates of chocolate and festive cookies that she had not tasted in years. Her mouth watered at the sight of them. With Raoul's help, she moved chairs and side tables into a large circle that left plenty of room for guests to circulate.

While she was dusting the living room, she heard Berthe greet someone with a familiar voice. Lina peeked into the kitchen and saw Nel carrying a tray of pastries into the kitchen that she had baked. She appeared to be a friend of Berthe's; they chattered in fluent German together. When she got home, Lina knew she had to warn Ada that Nel was friendly with one of the Captain's employees.

Lina ducked back into the living room, pretending to dust around the doorway so she could listen to the conversation.

Raoul set up a bar on the buffet with a generous selection of liquor and crystal glasses. While he did that, Lina helped Berthe arrange platters of meats and cheese with sliced baguette and a selection of crackers. Her stomach grumbled as she saw the abundant food arranged on huge platters. Because Berthe seemed to have eyes in the back of her head, Lina didn't attempt to sneak a slice while her back was turned. One word from Berthe and she'd be fired—that was not a risk she was prepared to take. With any luck, Raoul would give her some food later.

When everything was arranged to Berthe's satisfaction, she ordered Lina to clean the bathrooms and polish the mirrors. On the second floor, she noticed that the door to the Captain's study was open. The top of his desk was empty. It was such an opportunity, but this was exactly what Lucas had warned against. She couldn't afford to stand here and consider it because Bertha would soon call out to see what she was doing. Unlike Father's desk that had always been covered with piles of papers and books, this desk seemed purely ornamental and unwilling to yield any secrets. She had to walk away.

Lina hurried out of the study to polish the bathroom as ordered. Although Berthe claimed to be deaf in one ear, the other one functioned very well. Although it seemed like an opportunity, she didn't dare pursue it further. Berthe was more short-tempered than usual due to the extra work.

Lina was grateful that her father had insisted they learn German, but there were still times when she had trouble understanding Berthe's dialect, especially when she was agitated. Normally, Berthe did not believe in wasting time on idle chatter—there were no stories about the Captain in her kitchen. Lina decided to refrain from showing any interest in the secrets the house held. She'd been lucky to get away with the brief look into his office.

As the guests began to arrive, they were mostly military men dressed in uniform. The Captain greeted each person as they entered the house, kissing the cheeks of the women and shaking hands with the men. Lina shuddered at all the Nazi uniforms and salutes, but she concentrated on serving, keeping her eyes downcast, and moving quietly through the growing crowd.

The Captain was skilled at putting people at ease—Lina hadn't seen him operate in this kind of social situation. In fact, he'd hardly been around at all since she took the job. He exuded charm and confidence, complimenting women on their clothes or jewelry. Their eyes followed him as he moved around the room. He enjoyed being the host and the center of attention.

While people competed for the Captain's attention, he circulated through the room, keeping his eye on Raoul. As far as Lina could see, Raoul was expected to serve drinks, replenish food dishes, and only interact minimally with the guests. He was very polite to the partygoers, but he didn't ask any questions or initiate conversation. The Captain seemed to control Raoul from the opposite end of the room.

Last week, Raoul had told her that the Captain had originally been sent there from Berlin by one of Hitler's generals who saw him as a threat. Because the Captain's wife had no desire to move to another country, she chose to take her children to stay with her parents in Germany. Perhaps she was relieved to stay behind, Lina thought, and live her life far away from him. He was an ambitious man who imagined a bigger future for himself.

The guests helped themselves to generous portions of cheese and meat washed down with whiskey or wine. The noise in the room increased as people continued to consume copious amounts of alcohol. No one paid attention to her as she floated through the crowd, listening to the German but hearing little of consequence. Lina kept her eyes averted and moved constantly with trays of food, bringing them to the kitchen to be replenished as needed. As a server, she was invisible to most of them, except some of the older soldiers who gave her speculative looks but then lost interest when she ignored them.

Some of the men were accompanied by women who were their wives, she assumed, whereas others brought local women as their dates. The wives gathered in their own small groups and turned their backs on the "escorts." Lina was relieved she didn't recognize any of the younger women—it would have been awkward to run into girls from her school who were involved with the occupiers.

No sooner had that thought crossed her mind when Maria walked in wearing a very tight black dress and a lot of makeup. Lina groaned inwardly when she saw her. Why did she turn up on every occasion? Maria was clearly taking advantage of every invitation to a social life, but in this case she did not realize what kind of trouble she was bringing upon herself.

"What are you doing here?" Lina asked.

Maria put her finger to her lips. "Water?" she whispered.

Lina filled a glass from the kitchen tap. As she turned to hand it to Maria, a man in uniform with his chest covered in medals entered the kitchen.

"Where did you go? I was looking for you." His tone was annoyed—Maria was clearly on a very short leash with this man.

"Just needed some water to take my headache medicine," she said sweetly, with a warning glance to Lina.

Lina quickly assumed that she did not want that man to realize that they knew each other. "I hope that helps," she said to Maria, "but come back if you need anything else."

Maria nodded and left the kitchen with her Nazi following right behind, his hand firmly in the small of her back.

Lina wondered if she thought it was worth it, but perhaps Maria wasn't ready to realize the full cost of her choices. Attempting to be charitable, Lina considered that Maria might be helping to feed her family and thus had no other choice, but she knew from their past conversations that Maria also loved the attention and the presents.

Still, she didn't know Maria's whole story, and she tried not to judge her. She had been hungry enough recently to consider any way to get food—but she knew she could never cross that line. It hurt her to see Maria and other girls being used by the occupiers, who in most cases had wives somewhere and just wanted to be entertained. They would not hesitate to dispose of their girlfriends if they were inconvenient, or worse, pregnant.

While she worked in the kitchen to replenish the platters, Lina tried to suppress her hunger by drinking several glasses of water. But all that water only meant she needed to empty her bladder. Could she slip upstairs to use that washroom, since most guests used the main floor toilet? She glanced at the clock—there was still an hour until midnight, when she hoped the party would wind down so they could clean up. But she needed to use the toilet before then. She waited until she could no longer bear it then slipped away.

When she was finished in the bathroom, she found one of the older soldiers standing right outside the door.

"Excuse me," she said in German as she tried to pass through the narrow space that he had left for her.

In one smooth move, he pushed her into the wall. She had underestimated him, and when she felt his strong fingers pressing into her arms, she knew she'd have bruises in the morning. His breath reeked of whiskey and of the liverwurst appetizers Berthe had made. It was so disgusting that Lina swore she'd never eat or drink either again.

"I must go," Lina said, trying to push against his chest with both hands. She wanted to yell at him, but she was in her employer's house, and this man was his guest.

When he persisted, Lina became very angry. "*Nein!*" she told him.

Suddenly Raoul appeared at the top of the back stairway that came up from the kitchen. "The Captain requests your help immediately," he said. He didn't look at the soldier.

The man took a step back and glared at Lina. He turned abruptly and descended the main stairway to the front room, the sound of his boots eventually swallowed up in the noise of the party.

Lina followed Raoul down the small back staircase.

"You owe me," he whispered.

"Are you kidding? I am indebted for life. Thank you."

During the rest of the party, Lina did her best to stay far away from the man and was relieved when he didn't approach her again.

Gradually, after midnight and many toasts, the guests departed with the women's drunken laughter following their over-perfumed bodies into another cold night. While all the guests had eaten their fill, the townspeople were huddled in unheated houses, worried about feeding their children.

The room, blue with smoke, irritated Lina's throat. Since most of the guests had left, Lina began to clear ashtrays and plates from the room.

189

She was tired from being on her feet all evening. While she collected the dirty glasses on a large tray, two uniformed men lingered to talk to the Captain in the foyer. Moving slowly and quietly while she picked up glasses and plates, she tried to listen to the conversation without being obvious.

"I know," said the Captain. "Their attacks are becoming bolder, and we are losing ground. We must round up those troublemakers. Last month they hijacked an entire train filled with food for our soldiers."

The older man was not satisfied. "This file documenting alleged war crimes is a serious threat to all of us. This will be used to prosecute people when the war ends. That won't be a problem if we win, but . . ."

The Captain looked surprised. "I am not convinced such a document exists. It might be a rumor."

"Well, you should believe it because you and Seyss-Inquart are at the top of the list. If that file goes to court, you will be lucky to face life in prison instead of execution. I took the liberty of searching Van Dijk's university office just to make sure he wasn't involved in this, but there was nothing there."

"Nobody is sending me to prison," the Captain said. "That would never happen. Van Dijk has been taken care of."

The general leaned forward and said in a loud whisper. "Find that file."

"Someone might have destroyed it already," the third man said.

"Nonsense," said the older man. "Anyone would realize the value of such a file. Find it or else."

After that stern warning, the others left as the Captain saw them out. He stayed on the front porch to smoke a cigarette.

Lina hurried into the kitchen with the tray. "Are you ready for these?" she asked.

Raoul looked up from wrapping some cheese. "What took you so long? I thought you used to work in a café?"

Lina shrugged. "I actually got fired from that job."

Raoul laughed quietly. "Good thing you didn't tell me that earlier."

"You would have hired me anyway just for my charming personality. Now let me wash, and I'll show you how fast I can be."

"Your charming personality resembles a very bossy ten-year-old."
He used his hip to shove her aside. "I'll wash, and you can dry."

She sighed.

"I have sisters. You can't let them get their way," he said. "I don't suppose you're hungry?"

"Always," she admitted. She glanced at the kitchen table with platters of uneaten meat and bread.

"I'll pack some up so you can take it home."

"I'd be happy to take it home. You wouldn't happen to have a bottle of cognac to spare as well?"

"Don't push your luck," he replied with a smile.

"Can you speed it up? I don't want to be here all night."

"I forgot. A girl like you has places to go."

"Shut up," she said, snapping a wet tea towel against his arm.

She didn't hear the Captain enter the kitchen.

"Everything in order here?" he asked.

"Yes, sir," Raoul answered. "I told Berthe to go home, and we'll clean up."

"I'm going up to bed. Make sure she's paid from the household money and pay Berthe extra tomorrow too."

"Yes, sir," Raoul replied.

They worked quietly while they listened to his feet climb the stairs. When there was no more movement on the second floor, Raoul put his finger to his lips, and he went into the other room to pour two generous glasses of cognac. "It won't be missed," he said. "There's a few more boxes in the basement."

"Nice of the French to send along a box or two. Give them my address next time."

"Don't drop any glasses, or he'll be down here in a flash. He's a light sleeper."

Lina looked at him and was tempted to ask him how he knew that but decided it was none of her business. As unlikely as it might seem, she felt that she and Raoul were becoming friends, and she didn't want to jeopardize that.

They washed the dishes, wiped the counters, and organized the garbage. On an empty stomach, the cognac made her feel quite tipsy, but she was very careful not to make any noise.

"Where did you meet him?" she asked softly when they paused to sip their drinks.

"In a bar in Berlin. He came in with a bunch of soldiers, and I waited on them. We started talking, and he became a regular. He was lonely because his wife had moved to the country with the children. He thought he would be posted in Berlin, but then he was sent here, so he asked me to come along."

"Are you part of the army?"

Raoul shook his head. "He makes me wear this uniform and calls me his aide, but I am basically a houseboy and personal servant."

"Is that your choice?"

He shrugged and looked away. "I have to survive this war just like you do."

Lina didn't ask more. She hung the tea towel on the rack and looked around. They worked well together—the kitchen was spotless.

They moved into the living room and put the furniture back in place. Cigar and cigarette smoke pervaded every corner—Lina couldn't wait to breathe fresh air.

In the kitchen, she tossed back the last of the cognac and brought her glass to the sink to wash it.

They heard steps on the stairs. "What's taking so long?" the Captain asked as he leaned over the banister.

Lina looked at Raoul in alarm and pointed to the door. She grabbed her coat and the bag of food and slipped out.

"Be right there," Raoul replied as he turned out the kitchen light.

When she got home, she ate two sandwiches with meat and cheese and put the rest away. Ada would be so surprised when she saw the food in the morning. Raoul had also wrapped up a variety of cookies, so she ate one slowly, savoring each bite. Ada would never know if she ate them all, but the thought of her sister's joy in the morning kept her honest. She wrapped them up and put them away. She would report to Lucas any details she'd heard at the party, but so far it didn't amount to much.

40.

LINA

AFTER working at the Captain's party and then doing a job for Lucas on Sunday, Lina was exhausted on Monday as she biked to her cleaning job. Sometimes the assignments for Lucas were very physical, requiring many miles of biking or carrying heavy crates. Recently he had allowed her to be involved with a mission involving explosives. Watching the experts was inspiring as they planted the charge and blew up the building. There was a lot to learn, but she liked the intensity of it. If Ada knew, she would be horrified.

Although the work was exciting, she had hoped to feel some sense of belonging, but Lucas continued to be very strict about not socializing. Recently a resistance cell in Amsterdam had been compromised by one of their members who had been arrested and surrendered names of others under torture. Lucas warned her not to think that she could withstand interrogation as the stories of the occupiers' cruelty were not exaggerated. She hadn't repeated her mistake of socializing at the campfire that night after the weapons drop, but Lucas never commented on that. Lina hated that she still wanted him to notice and to praise her, but that was not his style.

Shortly after she arrived at the Captain's house, Raoul told her that Berthe was sick at home and that he had to do some errands. Because the Captain was working at home in his study, Raoul told her to concentrate on cleaning the downstairs so she wouldn't disturb him. He warned her that the Captain was under a great deal of pressure and was very irritable.

While washing the dishes, she heard his footsteps, but she continued with her task and didn't turn around. He stood at the entryway to the kitchen, and she felt his eyes on her back. Steadying her hands, she took her time washing each glass, hoping that one wouldn't slip out of her hands.

The Captain cleared his throat. "What do you know about your father's work?"

He was an intimidating figure in his uniform and leather boots. His skin was smooth and closely shaved, with a blond mustache. His hair was cropped very short in the sides. The thing that was most terrifying were his cold eyes.

Lina felt her shoulders tighten as she tried to think what to say. She looked at the Captain and said, "I have no interest in history, so he never talked to me about his work."

She could see the interest in his eyes fade when he realized she was useless as an information source. He suddenly changed the subject. "What will you do when we win the war?" he asked.

She shrugged and tried not to react to his presumption that the Nazis would win. "I hope to get a job or complete my education." She stood quietly and leaned against the counter with her hands folded in front of her, hoping to portray a subservient attitude.

"You don't need education. You should find a husband and have children. The new Germany will need workers for farms and factories."

While he lectured her on the new regime, she reminded herself to be still and appear to agree with him. But the thought that the occupiers might be victorious was nauseating. She would do anything to keep that from happening, even if it meant risking her life. He really was a fanatic, she thought, as she listened to him ramble about Nazi ideology. She nodded and said nothing.

"Get back to work," he ordered. Lina turned to finish the dishes, focusing on each glass and cup and trying to calm herself by taking deep breaths. She finally let her shoulders relax as she heard him go back upstairs. How did Raoul live with him?

41.

ADA

Ada was worried—Lina was on an assignment for Lucas, and it was getting late. Ada tried not to fuss over her absences, but she still worried. It was much more difficult to give up the habit of worrying than she had realized. Fear was a wild animal that had taken shelter in her mind, and she wasn't sure how to extricate it from its lair.

The cold snap had continued into the middle of January from its beginning in early December. She worried that Lina would get sick again from biking in the cold.

When Lina finally arrived home, it was late in the evening. Wearing a nurse's uniform with a pair of clogs, she carried a knapsack over one shoulder. Many nights she chose to go out as "Hans," but on this occasion she pretended to be a nurse returning from her shift—it gave her an excuse to be out late that was apparently acceptable to the soldiers.

Ada wasn't convinced that Lina's dressing as Hans made her any safer. Lina took pleasure in fooling people and was grateful that her voice and short hair made it possible, but Ada thought it might make someone angry to discover her deception.

Kicking off her shoes in the sunporch, Lina collapsed on one of the kitchen chairs and tossed her knapsack on the floor beside the chair. "It's bloody cold out," she said, rubbing her hands together to create some heat.

Ada studied Lina's uniform. "Did you get a new job?"

Lina cheeks were red from the cold, and her blue eyes sparkled. "Don't you think I make a good nurse? I had to bike to a house to make a delivery." She didn't bother to tell Ada that Lucas had asked her to deliver guns to a farmhouse.

"Are you being careful?" Ada asked. "It seems like a game with you."

"I'm just a simple messenger—they don't give me the big stuff. Most soldiers let nurses in uniform pass because they realize it might eventually be their turn to be in a hospital bed. Look what I got from the farm." From her knapsack, she pulled out two chicken legs wrapped in newspaper. "This is fresh," she proclaimed triumphantly, hopeful that Ada would forget her line of questioning.

Lucas had originally promised Ada that he would keep Lina safe and give her less dangerous assignments, but she knew he was short of volunteers and needed her help sometimes.

When she thought about Lina's fearless approach to most things, she wondered if her sister fully appreciated the risks she was taking. It was one thing to decide that she would no longer hover over Lina, but it was difficult to trust her to assess her own risk. On the evenings when she was on a mission, Ada watched the clock and waited until she knew that Lina had returned safely. She pretended to be busy with something so that Lina would not be upset with her vigilance, but it was hard to sit at home and imagine all the things that might go wrong.

One time when she was working on a translation at the base camp for the Canadians, Owen had a talk with her. She confessed that she lived in a state of anxiety trying to keep her sister out of harm's way. He reminded her that Lina was doing what she wanted to do, and she deserved to choose how to live her life. When he had asked her whether some of her fears were for herself, she had to admit that was correct. If something happened to Lina, she would be alone. And even though she and Lina had their share of disagreements, Ada would be inconsolable if she lost her sister. Owen was right—she had to trust Lina's survival instincts to get her through. If Lucas had feelings for Lina, as Ada suspected, then she hoped that he would be extra careful in assigning dangerous tasks to her.

The next morning, while Ada prepared porridge, someone knocked loudly on the front door.

She glanced up the staircase and hoped that Lina would stay in her room.

Ada unlocked the door, and two German soldiers in uniform flung the door open wide and stepped inside without invitation.

"How many people live here?" the one asked her.

Ada was startled. "Two."

She watched their backs as they headed into Father's study. Yesterday she had hidden her own notes for the job with the Canadians in the secret compartment under the stairs. She had closed the cupboard door and looked back at the desk to make sure there was no evidence left in the room.

She held her breath as the men began to search the study, taking books off the shelves and opening cupboards and drawers. They created a huge mess as they threw papers and books to the floor and walked over them. Ada was again horrified at their lack of respect for Father's study, but she kept quiet. Father's papers were now in the hands of the minister, and she trusted him to take care of them.

Reminding herself to look at ease, even bored, with the search, she could feel her heart pounding loudly. If they knew she had taken the papers to a safe place, she'd be arrested and killed. And the important evidence of crimes would be lost. She could imagine why the Captain and his soldiers wanted to get rid of the documented evidence before anyone could see it.

The soldier brushed past her with impatience, causing her to lose her balance. She grabbed the wall to steady herself. The man walked towards the kitchen checking the small downstairs washroom. When he opened the door of the main floor toilet, he gagged. They'd been unable to flush toilets for a few days. The restrictions on electricity had affected the pumps—the stench was powerful. He glanced around the kitchen and went to the basement.

The other fellow walked around upstairs, his boots clomping loudly on the wood floors.

Ada heard him pause at the doorway to Lina's room. "Who are you?" he asked when he saw Lina sitting on her bed reading a book.

"I'm Lina," she replied, sounding unconcerned.

He looked at her for a moment and then searched the rest of the rooms on the second floor.

Ada waited by the staircase trying to appear unconcerned. She could extract the gun from the cannister in the kitchen, but she'd never have a chance against the two of them. If they were lucky, the soldiers would give up the search and leave.

After they'd checked the basement and every other room, the two soldiers left without saying another word, slamming the heavy front door behind them.

Ada locked the door and returned to the kitchen. Her legs shook, and she held on to the counter until the wave of fear passed.

Lina ran into the kitchen, wearing her pajamas covered by an old housecoat with frayed cuffs that she'd had for years. "How bad is the mess?"

"We'll have to do another cleanup, but at least they didn't find anything."

"It's a good thing you took Father's file to a hiding place," she whispered.

"Yes," Ada replied. She decided not to tell Lina about the reports she was doing for the Canadians. Details of logistics and troop movements would not interest her anyway, but it was safer if she didn't know about that. "I hope you are being careful."

"I'm always careful. You need to trust me." Lina looked annoyed.

Ada knew she'd gone too far. "I'm sorry. You contribute so much to our household. I don't mean to doubt your judgement."

Lina had started to walk out of the kitchen, but she stopped and swung around, her eyes wide in surprise. "I don't think I heard that correctly. Could you repeat that?"

Ada threw the tea towel at her. "Don't make fun of me. I'm slow to learn new things."

"Keep working on it," Lina said. She chuckled as she left the kitchen.

42.

LINA

OWEN had become a regular Sunday night dinner guest. He and Lina often discussed photography and the challenges of getting good pictures. On that Sunday he mentioned that he had to take a truck to Amsterdam on Tuesday to pick up a Red Cross shipment and offered to take Lina along so she could photograph the city. She hoped it wouldn't be quite as cold as it had been in early January, or it would be difficult to walk around comfortably. The sun had gradually become just a bit stronger every day so that the thick ice on the canals had melted to a paper-thin layer.

That morning, she dressed in her usual pants and sweater with a knitted wool cap covering her hair. She'd left a note for Ada on the counter letting her know she'd be back later that day and not to worry because she was with Owen.

When Lina arrived at the meeting place in town, she found Owen waiting in the truck reading a Jane Austen novel she'd loaned him.

"How do you like the book?" she asked with a smile.

"Oh, Emma," he said in a fake English accent, "I'm so pleased to meet you."

"You like it, don't you?" Lina said with a triumphant smile.

"It's not my usual fare, but it has a certain charm."

He helped her into the back of the truck where, he explained, she'd be safer in case they were stopped for inspection. Owen showed her the tarp she could pull over herself if they were stopped. She hoped she wouldn't need to pull that dusty canvas over her head.

As Lina rolled around, she buffered her camera inside her jacket and patted her pocket to check that she had the extra rolls of film. By the time they got to the airfield, Lina had a headache from the jolting of the truck on bumpy roads. When Owen stopped the truck and helped her out of the back, she was unsteady and needed a few moments to catch her breath. He suggested that she sit in the front and keep a low profile while several soldiers helped him load boxes into the back. Lina was grateful for the chance to recover.

Heavy barriers restricted access to the city, and the barbed wire that cordoned off certain areas created a deeply inhospitable mood. With street signs displayed in German and Nazi propaganda posters attached to poles and walls and barriers, Lina felt like they were visiting a foreign country. The filthy streets, piles of rubbish, and garbage floating in the canals were shocking.

"Why does it look like this?" she asked.

"They've stopped cleaning the streets, and garbage is not collected. I've heard that rats are climbing out of the canals in the search for food, a sure sign that everyone is hungry."

"That is disgusting," Lina said as she studied the canal walls and shuddered.

Owen found a place to park the truck.

"Is this safe?" she asked as she climbed out and looked around.

He pointed to the police station across the street. "Should be OK," he replied.

"What if people knew there were boxes of food in the back?" she whispered.

"Then we would be in trouble, but we're not going to tell anyone. We won't be here for long."

"Won't your boss be angry if you don't get back?" Lina asked.

"I am the boss," he said with a laugh.

There was no way to tell if he was kidding. Owen didn't talk about his work, and even when she did ask, he politely deflected her questions. When he used words like logistics and advanced planning, she had no idea what he was talking about. Sometimes she overheard Lucas and Owen discussing some detail related to strategy as they studied maps, but when they were visiting for dinner, they wanted to forget about war. Not that forgetting was possible with planes flying day and night over their heads, but sometimes when they were playing cards after dinner in the kitchen, they pushed the war away for a short while.

When she asked Owen about the Captain's predictions of victory resulting in a new German regime, Owen shook his head. "Not bloody likely," was his response. Lina felt confident that Owen would figure out a way to defeat those occupiers, and he had hinted that the end was in sight.

They walked past a church. Lina pointed to a sign that advertised a one-hour afternoon concert. "It's amazing they're still performing," she said.

"Apparently one hour is all that the audience and the performers can stand in an unheated concert hall. Can you imagine trying to play with icy cold fingers?"

Walking with Owen through the inner streets of Amsterdam, she admired the canal houses that stood proudly. "I hope bombs never fall on them. Can you imagine living in one of these with those long windows looking over the canal?"

Owen looked up at the houses along the Herengracht. "Wouldn't it be fun to move a piano up to the top floor using that hook?"

Lina shook her head. "I wouldn't stand underneath, that's for sure."

Her senses were assaulted by the smell of unwashed bodies, wood smoke, and garbage. "I can't believe this—it's not like I remember at all. Can a city ever recover from this kind of neglect and destruction?"

"It will take a long time and a lot of work. Compared to other cities with extensive bomb damage, like Rotterdam, this city has held up well so far. Once the war ends, many hands will be willing to do that work."

"Are you going to help rebuild when the war ends?" she asked.

"I would love to be involved, but my family is waiting for me to return. There are other Canadians who will stay and help."

Together they walked along the *Waterlooplein* with Owen leading the way so that Lina could take pictures.

"When were you last here?" Owen asked.

"My parents took us here years ago, but it looked so different." On that day, she had fallen in love with the city, with its cafés and bistros filled with fashionable people. Flowers bloomed in pots on doorsteps and on barges. The sense of possibility was heady and made her long for opportunities that she couldn't quite name.

That evening with her parents and Ada, they had dined outside on the Leidseplein, where they watched street entertainers and musicians. People of every age rode their bicycles over the bridges and through the narrow streets, bicycle bells clanging. Pedestrians carrying a loaf of bread had stopped to chat with neighbors.

On that evening, Lina promised herself that someday she would live in a city and explore every corner of it, sampling cafés and shopping in markets. The next spring after her family's outing to Amsterdam, Father took them to Paris, and she fell in love with that city, too. Maybe she was just a city person. She loved the sense of anticipation that such places provided. There was freedom to try new things, to adopt a new persona, and to be accepted by others doing the same—it felt like unrehearsed pleasure.

But on this day, as Owen walked beside her through the center of the old city, the streets felt oppressive. The damage was greater than ruined buildings—the people themselves were wounded. There were no street entertainers; instead, people moved furtively across the streets and ducked into alleys hunting for food or fuel. Evading the watchful eyes of guards and security police took all the energy people had. They were also in competition with each other for scarce resources, and that made the atmosphere charged and dangerous.

Lina followed Owen through the cobblestone streets, shooting image after image. Owen walked beside her and occasionally took her elbow to guide her, but otherwise he remained unobtrusive as she documented the scene. He didn't try to tell her what to do or interfere with her shooting in any way. She appreciated how he trusted her to figure it out.

Lina stood on a corner where she had a view of the black-market vendors who sold goods for prohibitive amounts of money. Back home, she'd purchased clothes and necessities from black-market vendors to dress the downed airmen, but these people were charging prices much higher than what she'd paid.

She continued to frame the shot, check the light, and press the shutter release over and over. Until she returned home and developed the shots, she wouldn't know if she had captured anything worthwhile on this roll of film. People stared at the camera without protest and without blinking—lethargy, powerlessness, and deep hunger in their faces. Occasionally she tried to ask permission, but people were too miserable to respond.

"Don't ask," Owen advised, "just shoot."

Lina took pictures of mothers holding listless infants, begging for food or money. She saw people breaking branches for firewood or clambering into abandoned buildings to strip remaining wood from the structures. Some houses had completely collapsed when the structural beams were taken for firewood.

Malnourished children covered with skin sores and bites looked at her with sad eyes, holding out an empty palm or an enamel bowl hoping for some donation. She remembered the huge platters of meat and cheese at the Captain's party that would be discarded at the end of the evening.

Lina held her camera in her hand, wondering if she'd taken enough shots. While Owen was talking to one of the black-market vendors, two young boys raced past her. They were maybe ten or twelve and were dressed in dark blue ragged clothes. One had blond hair and the other was a redhead. That was all she noticed about them until one pushed her to the ground, and the other grabbed her camera before they both ran off. They were a well-practiced team, and they had run far from her before she could even get her breath back.

She looked up at Owen. His eyes were filled with intense anger, but he checked her and then took off.

Her heart raced as she watched him chase the young boys. She managed to get up first on her hands and knees. Her pants were ripped at the knees, and she lightly brushed the abrasions from her fall on the cobblestones. She managed to stand but was still feeling shaky as she watched Owen reach the boys. He grabbed them by the scruff of their necks like they were kittens, and they looked terrified as they took in his height and strength. They stopped struggling immediately and started to beg for mercy. She walked towards them and took the camera that the redheaded boy was holding.

Lina looked at the boy. "What were you planning to do with this?" she asked.

The boy, whose face was filthy, shrugged. "Sell it," he said. "What else?"

"Should we drop them at the police station?" she asked Owen.

"We could do that, or just hand them over to the occupiers."

"Maybe that's better," she replied.

"Please, sir, don't do that," the older boy begged. "We promise we'll never do this again."

Owen looked at them with a stern face. "I want to hear each of you say that."

They did as he asked, and then he let them go. They ran away as fast as they could. Lina checked her camera and was relieved that it was undamaged.

"Maybe it's time to head back," Owen said. "That was enough excitement for today."

Lina nodded agreement—she had taken plenty of pictures and was ready to go home. She felt depleted after trying to document both the places and the people and recover from the shock of having her camera stolen. She held it close to her. This was her legacy from Father—a connection to her future, and a link to her past.

On the way back to the truck, they walked past the Jewish quarter. Despite the fences, people were moving around and instructing children to creep into small spaces searching the vacated houses for anything of value. Owen explained that the synagogues on the square had been stripped of wood for fuel.

"Why do people do this to each other?" she asked.

"Do you believe in evil?" Owen asked.

Lina looked at him and shrugged. "I don't know. You mean things like the devil?"

"More like the devil within."

"I don't know, but I'm pretty sure I have one of those. If it exists, how do you get rid of it?"

"Cut it away. Get the people back to work to repair the bridges and roads. Give them pride in their country and safety when they sleep at night."

"That's a tall order. Is that what you came here to do?"

"We need to defeat the enemy first, and then rebuilding can begin."

Lina tried to absorb that. "But how will that happen? The country needs medical people, engineers, teachers, and construction workers. Families are broken, neighbors are gone, houses are destroyed. That's a lot of loss. Who will fix that?"

"The mourning will continue for as long as memory lasts. Think of what your photos can do to help motivate people to donate money or volunteer to rebuild."

"I think you are overestimating my ability."

"We'll see," he said. "I am quite confident in my ability to judge a good photograph."

Lina was quiet as they walked back to the truck. She climbed over the food boxes and found an open area where she could rest on the ride home. "Don't take any sharp corners or this stuff will roll over me."

"The load will not shift no matter how recklessly I drive," he said with a smile. "I know how to pack a truck."

"That is reassuring, I think." As she crawled into the space that he had made for her, she replayed in her mind some of the scenes she had shot that day.

She did not know what to make of Owen's confidence in her future; after all, her work history wasn't impressive. She had been fired from one waitress job and worked as a house cleaner for a Nazi Captain. When the war ended, hordes of people would be looking for jobs. Ada had urged her to think about it and plan, but she'd been too stubborn to listen. It had been easier to live day to day, putting off thinking in concrete terms about her goals.

For Ada, things seemed to fall into place without any effort—her volunteer work had already helped define her future direction. Ada had been strategic, whereas she had merely been lazy.

When the truck stopped, she listened for Owen to call out or open the back, but then she heard voices and realized they had been pulled over. A soldier loudly demanded to see Owen's identity card. Lina pulled the tarp over her and stretched out under it. The dust triggered her cough reflex that she fought to suppress. Then she felt an insistent scratch in her throat. Lina tried to swallow a few times, but her mouth was too dry. The scratch slowly grew to a rumble that started in her chest and worked up to her throat. She clamped her hands over her mouth and tried not to breathe.

When she heard the soldier demand to see the inside of the truck, she was grateful for the boxes of food that were between her concealed body and the truck's opening. Owen talked and joked with the soldier, making lots of noise as cover.

Owen opened the back slowly, giving her time to secure her hiding place. He explained to the man that this food was part of his work for the Red Cross. He offered the soldier a cigarette, and they chatted some more before Owen offered the soldier the rest of the pack. The German asked whether he could move to Canada after the war, and they laughed together when Owen described snow drifts as high as his head.

Once the guard cleared Owen, he didn't waste time driving away, in case the soldier changed his mind. Lina held her breath until they were far enough from the soldiers to be safe then sat up, throwing off the tarp to let out a series of violent coughs. Lina tried to wedge her feet against the boxes so she wouldn't roll around.

The next time they stopped, Owen helped her out of the truck. She looked around and was relieved to see her bike locked to a lamp post across the street.

"Thanks for taking me along. I'm glad the soldier didn't make trouble."

"I was worried he might ask me to unload all the food or just take the truck, in which case you would have had to go along with it. What a surprise you would have been!"

Lina shuddered at the thought.

"I look forward to seeing those photos when you develop them. I'll be away for a few days, but when I get back I hope to see your prints. By the way, after dinner on Sunday, I'd be happy to beat you in a game of shuffleboard."

"You could try," she said with a grin. "If you could possibly find more American beer, I play better with fuel." Lina waved as the truck drove away. She ached from bouncing around in the truck.

She hoped some of the pictures would turn out—it would be embarrassing if she had nothing to show Owen.

43.

LINA

WHEN Owen arrived the next Sunday, he offered to make some coffee. Lina didn't care if it kept her awake all night; she wanted to taste real coffee. "I would love some," she replied. "Ada is upstairs, but she'll be right down, and I know she would appreciate a cup as well."

"Did you develop the pictures?" he asked as he took a small bag of coffee from his pack.

Lina was surprised. She thought he might have forgotten—after all, he had more important things to do than worry about her photos. "I'll go get them." She retrieved the folder from her room and put it on the table. Lina sat across from him, sipped her coffee, and watched his face as he reviewed them slowly. Finally, he put them down.

"Lina," Owen said, "I don't know what to say."

Lina's face flushed in embarrassment. "I have a lot to learn," she said, holding her cup with both hands to warm her fingers.

"Wait, I'm not finished. These are amazing!" He tapped his finger on the edge of the print. "Look at this child with his skinny legs, sitting on that cold step begging for someone to fill that bowl. It's heartbreaking."

Lina put down her coffee cup with care, still not releasing her fingers from its lingering warmth. "Do you mean it?"

"You captured the desolate feeling of the city and its people. Anyone looking at this will see the cost of war. There's no glory—just hunger and fear."

Could it be true? Were they good? She didn't dare trust what she was hearing. There was something bittersweet about finding some success with pictures of starving children. Would any of it help those children or end the hunger for all of them? She wished she could ask Father whether there was any justification in documenting the suffering of children.

"I know someone who works for a press agency in New York. Years ago, I was his guide on a fishing expedition on the east coast of Canada. Because he had such a good time, he came back every year. I owe him a letter. If you give me several of these prints, I will send them to him, but make sure you keep the negatives in a safe place. There's no harm in trying."

Lina looked at him, hardly daring to breathe. She released her coffee cup and folded her fingers into a prayer-like stance. "Do you really think he'd bother to look?"

"I know he will, and he'll give an honest opinion. Many people across the ocean want to know what's happening here." He pointed to the little boy on the steps. "Europe will need a lot of help to rebuild after the war, and I think your photographs could motivate people to get involved."

"Do you think it is right to take pictures of children and others who are suffering? Will their publication make any difference?"

"Photographs can move people in ways that words never will. This is an important thing to figure out for yourself, especially if you choose to document the difficult and heartbreaking things that happen in the world. If you are sincere in your desire to show people difficult things and to move them to act, your photographs will be authentic, but if you are chasing fame and taking sensationalist pictures, people will see through that."

"I hope your friend knows I am a complete beginner."

"In the end, it's the product that counts. Let's see what happens. Hopefully the letter won't take too long to reach him. What do you think?"

"If you're willing to try, that's fine with me. I really appreciate your help. And by the way, this is the best coffee I've ever tasted. But it makes me wonder, what's for dinner?"

Owen laughed. "Don't worry, I have that covered. It's my turn to cook, and it's going to be good."

"Will it be a stew this time?"

"I have more than that in my repertoire. Today I'm planning to cook fish, and you've never tasted anything like it."

"Don't tell me anything else. I want to be surprised." Lina watched as Owen picked up the photos carefully, holding them by the edges and studying them. What if Owen overestimated her ability? If his friend thought the pictures were terrible, it would be one more disappointment. Hope was dangerous when it resulted in disappointment. She wrapped her fingers tightly around the empty cup.

"If the electricity gets cut any further, it's going to be impossible to work in my darkroom," Lina said.

Owen thought for a moment. "Give me any rolls of film you want developed. I know someone who can do it."

"Do you mean a military person?"

"Don't ask," Owen said with a serious face before he broke into a smile.

Lina was so grateful for his encouragement but also for his attitude, which met challenges head-on and saw them as something to be resolved. She could see why the army put him in charge of logistics. His faith in her made her determined to show him that she'd been worthy of his trust.

Light from the beeswax candle on the table danced against the walls of the kitchen. The few pieces of firewood Lina had collected had burned to ashes, but they still glowed crimson in the woodstove. Lina let the conversation swirl around her as Lucas and Owen talked about a variety of topics while Ada commented occasionally. She didn't hear the words so much as the tone of the voices; one taking the lead, then the other. Hearing Ada laugh after her illness and weeks of sadness was a relief.

Surrounded by friends and the feeling of food in her stomach also filled her with an overwhelming sense of contentment. But most of all, she felt an infusion of hope thanks to Owen's willingness to take her photography seriously. She had to admit she wanted this more than she had wanted anything till now. Something she couldn't explain took over when she held the camera in her hands and heard the click of the shutter. It was like a dance—seeing, responding, and documenting at the right balance of stillness and motion or darkness or light. It was a kind of magic when the film was developed, and the images came to life before her eyes.

At this moment, she felt optimistic that this war would end and allow them to repair the threads of their interrupted lives. In any case, she planned to hold on to the memory of this moment filled with stories and laughter. She watched Ada's face light up in the candle light as she laughed—she wished she could capture that moment in a portrait. Why had she never fully appreciated the beauty and strength in her sister's face? Her insecurities were like a wall that kept her from seeing things clearly. Father had told her this so many times, and she had stubbornly refused to hear it.

Around her the laughter continued while Lina studied the candle and wondered if it were possible for people to change some of the beliefs they had clung to since childhood. Owen must have sensed her withdrawal, as he put his arm briefly over the top of the chair and gave her a quick hug. Lina pulled her attention back to the conversation.

PART III

Spring 1945

44.

ADA

ADA looked up from her desk at Lykke, the director of the orphanage. "Would you come to my office for a moment? I need to ask you something."

Lykke was in her fifties, and she commanded an authority that was both loving and strict. Ada was impressed how smoothly the orphanage ran under her leadership.

Ada had volunteered at the orphanage for several weeks.

Housed in a modest brick house, the orphanage had recently been ordered to close by the occupiers, who planned to turn the building into a recreation hall for soldiers. Because the house sat on a generous lot, there was plenty of room in the backyard for sports.

Ada followed Lykke to her office where she closed the door behind her.

A large picture window overlooked the long garden enclosed by a fence. The grass was filled with tiny white and blue flowers—harbingers of spring. Near the fence, she saw a clump of snowdrops pushing through the soil and the tips of crocuses about to emerge. It was hard to believe, but spring was finally emerging after a long winter. There was something reassuring in the realization that nature would continue to move forward despite the war. The lilac bushes that lined the back of the yard would eventually fill the air with their scent. Several children played outside with one of the volunteers who threw a ball to them.

"Lucas told me I can trust you," Lykke said.

Ada turned her attention away from the garden. "What do you need?"

"Could you get in touch with him on your way home? I have meetings till late tonight and won't be able to talk to him."

"Certainly," Ada said, "I can stop at his place."

"I received information about a food shipment due by train tomorrow night. The train will arrive at midnight, but they won't unload until the German workers show up in the morning. The train will be parked at the east end just outside of town where there's a loading dock for the trucks."

"I will let him know," Ada said.

"Thank you," Lykke said. Wearing a worn navy-blue dress with heavy tights and sensible shoes, Lykke looked like a schoolteacher. Her hair was pulled into a bun at the nape of her neck. Her observant blue eyes were kind but missed nothing. Trained as a social worker, she was also known as a child welfare advocate. According to Lucas, Lykke had also served on several government commissions before the war. Ada was in awe of her and tried hard to tackle any job that Lykke assigned.

"Our plans to close by the required spring date are proceeding, but we need to find good homes for the remaining children. Displacing orphans to provide a place for soldier's entertainment is just cruel. If we can't find homes for the children, they have threatened to send them to Germany, so I am working very hard to get them settled."

"How is that going?" Ada asked.

"It's very challenging. Most people don't have enough food or clothes for their own children, so it is hard for them to accept even more responsibility. She leaned forward and dropped her voice. "Some of the children have false identity cards—their parents were sent to the camps."

Ada nodded but did not comment. According to Lucas, Lykke had helped locate and hide Jewish children, and in doing so took risks to travel to places where they'd been stranded or abandoned. Ada wished she could be that fearless.

"How can I help?" Ada asked.

"I could use some administrative help because the records must be updated. I will store them in a safe place, perhaps in my basement. We need volunteers to escort children to their new homes if the parents are not able to pick them up, and we must find foster families for the remaining ones. I will not allow any of these children to be sent to Germany."

"What would you like me to do today?" Ada said. "I can work until three o'clock."

Ada could see the steely determination in her eyes—she admired Lykke's commitment. She glanced at the Nazi propaganda poster that Lykke had been obliged to hang in her office. How did she manage to work fearlessly under that shadow?

Lykke smiled. "Maybe you could start updating records from these notes to make a revised master list. You can work at the desk outside the office." Lykke stood up and brushed her skirt to smooth it out.

"I'll get started," Ada said, as she stood up. Although it was only office work, Ada was eager to start. She loved organizing things and typing letters and anything that reminded her of her life as a student. "Thank you for this opportunity," she said politely.

Lykke laughed. "I need to thank you."

Ada smiled and walked a little taller when she left the office.

45.

ADA

ADA hesitated at the door to her parent's bedroom. She had procrastinated long enough about cleaning up the room—the finality of it was something she had wanted to delay. Even Father had been reluctant to let her clear Mother's things from the closet, but now it was time. With a day off from her various volunteer assignments, she could tackle the project and hope to complete it. There were so many people in town who desperately needed clothing and shoes—there was no reason to keep these things in a closet.

Ada had improved her skills in altering clothes and had reworked some of the dresses and skirts to be serviceable, if not stylish. Knitted dresses proved to be impossible to alter, but she had some success with the others. She was several sizes smaller than her mother, so the dresses required a great deal of alteration and sometimes still felt like a tent. Mother had kept everything—there were maternity dresses that she had worn during her pregnancy with Lina.

Mother's feet were also a few sizes bigger, and even though Ada had tried stuffing her shoes with newspaper, it was impossible to walk normally. When Ada had initially requested help with the cleanup, Lina had agreed, but she never seemed to be available when Ada was ready to start the task.

Ada finally realized that Lina was deeply averse to the task. She was surprised when Lina had told her why she didn't want to be involved. "Mother didn't want anything to do with me. She told me so often about how miserable her pregnancy was, and that misery continued once I was born. I am happy that you have good memories of her, but I would be grateful if you took care of her things."

Mother's lack of patience with Lina remained a mystery. Sometimes Ada wondered if she had used the distance between Mother and Lina to make more room for herself. She felt ashamed of how hungry she had been for Mother's approval. As she pulled the dresses from the hangers, a faint scent of her mother's French perfume filled the air.

After folding the dresses, Ada dumped the contents of the drawers onto the bed. Separating the items to donate to charity from the pile she wanted to keep for now, she wondered why she needed to keep any of it. They'd already taken what was useful. She felt guilty sending things that Mother had prized to some anonymous charity box, but it was time.

She made another pile of Father's clothes on the floor and then bundled them into a cloth laundry bag. He hadn't owned much, and his clothes were well worn.

When the closet was completely empty of shoes and belts, she noticed a small gray metal box pushed into the back corner. She retrieved the box and sat on the bed with it in her hands. Why had someone put it in the bottom of the closet behind the shoes?

Ada carefully opened the lid and stared at the pile of letters and photos. The return address on the envelopes revealed a street in The Hague.

She studied the small black-and-white glossy prints with a white border. Her hands trembled as she held the pictures, almost expecting Mother to appear and accuse her of snooping. She had always been very strict about keeping the girls away from her things and out of her room.

One photograph showed her mother and her friend, both dressed in the white starch aprons that were required at the domestic science school. Mother was taller and broad-shouldered with a generous bosom and a small waist, whereas her friend was a head shorter and slender.

Ada recognized it as a copy of the print that hung on the wall by the stairs—Gerda had been her best friend throughout school, though Mother seldom spoke of her. Another picture showed the two girls in long dark raincoats, standing with their bikes outside the entrance to the School of Domestic Science. Their smiles lit up the picture.

Printed on heavier-quality paper stock, embossed in one corner with the name of a studio, a large photo showed a handsome man wearing a formal suit. With dark hair, deep-set eyes, strong eyebrows, and well-defined lips, his demeanor was serious and dignified.

Another photo showed the same fellow in an informal pose with his arm around Mother's shoulders, sitting side by side in a café, seemingly basking in the attention as Mother looked at him with adoration.

Ada studied the man's face, but he did not look familiar. Who was he? Was he someone she'd known before she married Father? Ada clutched her cardigan closer with one hand as she continued to gaze at the photo, willing it to speak. She had never thought of her mother as someone with secrets—she had certainly never held back from expressing her opinions or emotions, but all of that might have been a cover for the things she held much closer to her heart.

It was hard to imagine another man in her mother's life, but this photograph showed her affection for him. His wavy dark hair, intelligent eyes, and chiseled chin were striking—his posture suggested he was at ease with his own authority. The fact that she'd kept these photographs for decades suggested that they were important to her. But why had she kept them even when she knew she was dying? Did she want them to be found?

A small diary with a red cover was buried under the letters and photos. Ada recognized her mother's handwriting. The diary began in the fall that her mother had started studies in domestic science. Ada pushed aside the remaining clothes on the bed and began to read her mother's diary.

JANNY'S DIARY, SEPTEMBER 1922

I had planned to write every day, but two weeks have already passed since school started. There is so much homework and reading to do, but I will try to catch up. Because Truus takes piano lessons, she always has an excuse to skip chores, claiming she needs to practice. My days are filled with classes, homework, and chores at home. I am also expected to do needlepoint and crocheting. Mother demands extra attention, and I do not want her to feel neglected by my school life, or she will complain to Father. The worst is sitting through tea visits at the houses of her friends when I know I have readings to do before my next class.

Gerda had already been accepted at the School of Domestic Science when I decided to join her. I fought hard for permission to attend, and finally the semester began in early September. All summer I was afraid that Father might change his mind about my attendance. Mother agreed to the plan because she thought it would be useful for my future as a housewife. I wasn't concerned about the rationale for my attendance; after all, the idea of being anyone's wife was hard to imagine, but I was willing to go along with whatever argument Mother used to persuade Father. I held my breath in fear that Father would overrule her at the last minute and forbid my attendance. It would be terrible if Gerda started school without me.

I often wish they had visions of a more exciting future for me than being a housewife, but they believe that their job as parents was to prepare us for a "good" marriage. They want me to be trained for the domestic realm, not as a house servant, of course, but as a bossy supervisor of servants in a wealthy (one hopes!) household.

Gerda finds this ridiculous because she has no intention of ever marrying, and the notion of bossing around servants is disgusting to her. My sister, Truus, is already hunting for a husband by attending all the events that would make such a meeting possible—Mother completely supports her quest. Gerda tells me to fight for what I want, but I don't even know what that might be. I only know what I do not want.

But back to the first day of school. I was so excited that I could hardly sleep. In the morning, I had to force myself to eat some porridge. I was glad that Gerda and I could bike together and then find our way to our classroom.

The school was so clean I almost felt sorry for the janitors who were required to keep it that way, but it wouldn't be a good sign if a domestic science school was left dirty! Gerda said we could probably eat off the floor—something that threw us into giggling fits that earned a disapproving look from our teacher. We cannot not sit together in class, or we will get into trouble. But the seating is assigned and strictly monitored, so we don't have any choice. Still, after class we often make fun of some of the students or teachers and the many rules we are expected to remember.

My head was swimming after the introductory lectures and discussions about our written work, including tests and assignments. Classes include housecleaning, cooking, etiquette, laundry, baking, and care of servants. Because we have a housekeeper at home, I never did much domestic work, but Mother believes that every woman can benefit from scientific training in those subjects.

My life has been so sheltered I have no idea if I could become a teacher or a nurse. How do people find out what they are meant to do? Most of mother's friends do not believe it is appropriate to have a job outside the home. They keep busy with charitable work, church matters, and the arts.

When I see Gerda's determination to find a career that will allow her to be self-supporting, I envy her—she will use her diploma as a stepping stone to become a teacher. Maybe I am not smart enough for that type of thing, or brave enough. After all, she already has her own place to live and seems fearless going to clubs and restaurants by herself, whereas I have never done anything like that. If I were caught in any of those places, Father would pull me out of school immediately.

JANNY'S DIARY, SEPTEMBER 1922

Another ten days have passed, and I haven't had time to write. The days are very full, and I am so tired in the evenings. I will try to catch up with these pages.

In late August, before classes began, I was given a stern lecture about not socializing outside of school. I agreed to their demands without hesitation. That seemed like an acceptable compromise, but Gerda thought it was ridiculous. I told her never to express her opinions in the presence of my parents, or they would never let me see her again. She is fearless and outspoken, and I know my parents would decide that she was a bad influence.

The only official extracurricular activity I am allowed to join is the Student Christian Club. I had been involved in this during school, so it was familiar to me. Gerda thinks that it will provide us with a good cover story to justify some outings. I told Mother about the good work that the club supported, and she agreed to let me attend an evening meeting.

Sometimes I wonder, dear diary, why I bother writing in this journal, but the fact is that I want to remember every moment of this important time of my life. This is the beginning of something very exciting, and for the first time I am hopeful that my real life is underway. Gerda tells me that I must become an independent woman, but I am not sure I know how. Wanting something is only one part of it—believing in it is much harder.

JANNY'S DIARY, OCTOBER 1922

I must record the events that led to meeting Frans. It was a warm September day when Gerda and I left our bikes locked at the school, and we walked to the café where the social was planned. We were dizzy with the freedom and laughed all the way there. My parents were out of town for the evening, so we took the opportunity to have some fun. Truus was involved in a piano recital that evening that I luckily was not asked to attend. I have heard her play that stupid piece a hundred times, and I am sick of it. She has a way of leaning over the piano keys and lifting her hands dramatically at the end of a phrase that I find completely phony. My parents always ask her to play when they have company, and she loves performing for them.

After class ended, we parked our bikes and entered the café, choosing a table that was in the back so no neighbors could spot us and report us to my parents.

I noticed him right away, sitting with his friends at a table near us. He was good-looking in a chiseled way, with a long face, prominent nose, expressive brows, and well-defined lips. He seemed quite serious, but when he laughed, his face was transformed. I could not take my eyes off him. I have never seen such a handsome and confident man. Gerda told me to stop staring. Although I tried, it felt like there was a magnetic force pulling me towards him. Never have I felt such a force.

Gerda found out from the waiter that they were medical students. They certainly noticed us, but we did our best to pretend to ignore them. I could not concentrate on what Gerda was saying. Instead, I listened to his rich voice explain a surgical procedure that he had observed that day. A surgeon! I watched his long fingers draw something in the air, and I could imagine him in an operating theater lecturing to other medical students. Judging by the response of the others at the table, he had a quality that made people want to listen to him.

I would never have approached him, but Gerda is much bolder and skilled in the art of flirtation. I felt breathless when they came over to talk to us and moved their chairs to sit at our table. Gerda asked questions and dispelled awkwardness, whereas I was silent and intimidated by their banter. I was jealous of her ease with them and wished I were less awkward.

Perhaps it was the effect of that glass of beer, something I normally don't drink, but he seemed to be paying attention exclusively to me. We talked about his studies and mine, and somehow the time passed so quickly that Gerda and I had to race home on our bikes so as not be late. I have been thinking of him ever since. Gerda told me that Frans is from one of the prominent Jewish families in town. His father is a lawyer, and his mother is a doctor. He has one sister who lives in France.

Two days after our first encounter, Frans sent me a message through Gerda. One of the medical students knew her and told Frans he could get a note to me. Anyway, it all worked out, and I met Frans after class. We talked about everything, and when I left he kissed me, just briefly, on the *lips. I biked home smiling all the way, but I made sure I looked very serious when I arrived home. I showed Mother the recipes we used in our pastry class, and she seemed pleased with that.*

ADA

Ada looked up from the diary and stared at the empty clothes closet without seeing it. Frans? Who was Frans? Her mother had a relationship before she married their father. It was almost impossible to imagine her sneaking out to spend time with a man, let alone kissing him on the street! This was quite astonishing—she'd never once mentioned him. What had happened to him?

Ada dragged several bags of clothes to the hallway—she would ask Owen if he could help her transport them to a local church that had set up a donation center. Studying the room, Ada was pleased with how tidy it looked. She'd dreaded this task for months but was proud she had completed it. She would return to her reading whenever she was assured that no one would interrupt, especially not Lina. If the layers of her understanding of the past were about to be peeled away, she needed privacy.

Reading the diary reminded her of stolen moments with Willy. Her Mother apparently had some experience with secrets, which might explain why she was so vigilant with Ada.

Ada hurried to hide the metal box in her room. She would have to tell Lina about this eventually, but she was not ready to do so yet. She returned to her parent's room to take another look before closing the door.

Was she ready to face Mother's secrets? She felt a wave of dizziness—what else would she discover? Father was not there to help her understand. There was no one with whom she could discuss such matters. She needed time to digest this new information before she could read another word.

Why had Mother not destroyed the diary and photos? Had she wanted them to be discovered at some point, perhaps after her death? She could have burned the letters and destroyed the evidence when she first became ill. Perhaps the diary was too precious to destroy. But that meant that the experience with Frans was also too precious to erase. Did any of this explain Mother's unpredictable impatience and irritation?

When Mother was confined to bed, one day she had grabbed Ada's hand and told her, "There are things you cannot understand, but I hope you'll forgive me someday." At the time, Ada assumed that Mother was confused. Towards the end, she had often muttered and spoken in sentences that made little sense. The doctor claimed it was the pain medication, and mother's illness had affected her mental state. But on that day, Mother was not confused. Why did she seek forgiveness?

Ada continued to think about it as she dusted downstairs and washed the floor. The air was cold as she beat an area rug with a rattan carpet beater on the back step. Her actions were automatic as her mind struggled to absorb the new information. The unfinished story made her feel anxious; her stomach churned with a combination of hunger and fear. Although she wanted to criticize Mother for keeping secrets, she had done the same thing. Meetings with Willy had been a carefully guarded secret.

If she showed the diary to Lina, she would tear through it and perhaps find it amusing. Before being subjected to that, Ada wanted to clarify her own feelings. If her mother had kept secrets, how much had her father known? Had they both agreed to keep things from their daughters? They might have realized that Ada would find out sooner or later, and their silence would feel like a betrayal.

46.

LINA

LINA had been working as a cleaner at the Captain's house for almost three months, and she felt like she'd established a routine. She was never going to be the best cleaner, but if she managed to keep her job, she'd be happy. The food that Raoul gave her was more than enough compensation for her hours of cleaning—to say nothing of the growing friendship between them. Without Jos and the regular parties with his friends, she'd been lonely. Raoul understood her desire to see new places, to develop her craft, and to be involved in the world beyond the street where she had grown up.

They encouraged each other to keep their dreams alive. Raoul showed her sketches he'd made for a men's clothing line that she thought they were very good. After the war, men would be eager to dress up and explore new fashions. After so much austerity, she was convinced that people would be longing for glamor, even though they might have few resources to pay. Raoul spoke of creating a minimalist collection with lasting quality for the postwar era. Lina dreamed of taking pictures of his work against the backdrop of great cities, showing people returning to life from the ashes.

Even in the stolen moments of studying sketches and discussing fashion, Lina knew that the Captain would be displeased to realize that they were becoming friends, or even worse that Lina was encouraging Raoul to dream about a separate future for himself.

Meanwhile, Lina had a job to do, and she tried to do it well but still leave time to talk with Raoul. Although Berthe had not complained about the quality of her cleaning, Lina realized that she didn't have the best eyesight. Because the Captain was often away, Lina didn't have to worry about running into him. Raoul told her that he had been very preoccupied and moody lately—was he anticipating a military defeat or having trouble locating a certain war crimes file? Raoul was anxious and jumped at any sounds that might indicate the Captain had arrived home early, which made Lina feel even more uneasy.

When she told Lucas that working at the Captain's house did not allow access to war information or military strategy, he advised her to be observant, but above all to do her cleaning job well. He didn't think the Captain would leave anything top secret lying about for her to find. Monitoring the mood of the household was enough information for him.

Lucas had also given her a few more jobs, including weapons transport. He preferred to use men for the complicated or risky jobs, something that Lina thought was ridiculous; but there was no point in arguing with him. She wanted to work and to keep busy so the time would pass.

She was willing to take whatever assignment he gave her. Her comrades commented that she was composed under fire—she joked that she was too stupid to know better. She wanted to prove to all of them that she could be trusted, but sometimes it felt like an uphill battle.

Luckily, Father had given her practical skills that she could apply to this type of work—she read maps and navigated unfamiliar roads without hesitation. Recently, Lucas had asked her to produce photographs and to work alongside forgers to create fake identity cards. A great deal of precision was required to produce a flawless document that would pass scrutiny—lives depended on it. Although she'd never been precise about anything, she was surprised to find the careful steps of the process both challenging and pleasing.

Lina regularly questioned Lucas and Owen about when the war might end. Owen told her about victories elsewhere. Troops were on the move—the city of Nijmegen had seen an influx of Canadian and British soldiers that winter. Lina could only imagine how difficult it was for them in such a cold, unrelenting season. How did they feed and house all those troops? And when would they come to their region? She was happy to hear they were on the move, but it was impossible to imagine how long the advance might take.

The noise of bombing flights and antiaircraft guns continued day and night. According to Lucas, the Americans bombed Germany during the day, whereas the British RAF continued at night. Unfortunately, it was not a straightforward march towards victory—some of the campaigns did not yield expected results. Lucas told her there were victories, such as Operation Veritable, when a force of three hundred thousand British, Canadian, and Polish soldiers managed to push the Axis forces back into Germany. Lina had limited patience for the details—she wanted a clear confirmation of Allied victory so life could return to normal. How exciting it would be when trains were filled with civilian passengers instead of soldiers.

"Lucas, some of us are not military historians—just let me know when Allies win. That's all I need," she said.

"It's really happening. They are moving forward," Lucas said.

Lina remained skeptical but kept that to herself. That fact that some of the Canadian soldiers were camped close to town was promising though, even if Owen didn't provide much information about their mission. He seemed to coordinate food relief efforts with the Red Cross and the army's distribution network, and he was also involved with logistics for a large incursion of troops into the area. Maybe both those things were related, but Lina knew enough not to ask because he did not want to discuss it.

Lina now had a routine for cleaning the Captain's house. She had found ways to clean more efficiently, performing some tasks every other week to save time. Berthe started her shift before Lina and then left an hour earlier. Every day Berthe prepared lunch and dinner for the Captain unless he was going to be away. Raoul received instructions about the menu and was expected to heat the food and serve it when he demanded.

Whenever Berthe left, Raoul made some espresso and fed her whatever he could find in the cupboards. Lina looked forward to these stolen moments with anticipation—it was such a light moment in an otherwise dark house. Although they chatted and laughed freely, both were on high alert. According to Raoul, the Captain would not appreciate their growing friendship; he warned her never to look at him or talk to him in the Captain's presence.

One afternoon, Raoul and Lina were sitting in the kitchen basking in the February sun that angled through the kitchen window. Lina sipped her coffee and ate the pastry Raoul had served. They were startled when the front door opened, and they heard the Captain's boots walk towards them on the hardwood floor.

Lina jumped up and washed the cups while Raoul hid his sketchbook in the pantry. He went to talk to the Captain, hanging up his coat and asking him about his day. The Captain was very curt and went upstairs without noticing Lina's presence. She slipped out of the house through the back door, where her bike leaned against the shed.

She needed to make sure her actions didn't get Raoul in trouble with the Captain—as a new friend, Raoul already meant a great deal to her. With Jos, the conversation had been about partying and about his big plans to run the best garage in town, but he had not cared about Lina's photography or her interest in design. She realized now that she had stopped talking about her dreams. Now that he was gone, it was clearly dangerous to bury one's dreams because once out of sight, they could easily disappear forever.

47.

ADA

As February rolled into March, Ada watched a few of the children leave the orphanage to go to their new homes—it was always a poignant moment when the remaining children and staff lined up to wave goodbye to a departing child. If a prospective foster parent was unable to make the trip, a member of the staff or a volunteer accompanied the child to their new home. Volunteers sewed drawstring bags from leftover fabric that held a card and a small toy for each departing child.

Ada understood why Lykke was concerned about the records at the orphanage. Once the institution closed, it would be very difficult to keep track of the children unless their files were preserved. When a new inter-denominational organization, the International Bureau for Emergency Nutrition, was formed in December 1944, they made it part of their mission to help track and coordinate the location of displaced or orphaned children. If parents were separated from their children or allowed to return home from deportation, there had to be a clear way to reunite the family. That missing parents were unlikely to return was something most of the staff did not admit—but they wanted to be prepared in case there would be inquiries from relatives in future. Lykke was determined that there would be no "lost" children, but in the chaos it was a challenge. Ada was happy to update files and add the new addresses for the orphans, silently wishing each one of them well with their new families.

Ada folded the small-sized clothes and restocked the bedside cubbies that held each child's pajamas. Their clothes needed constant mending—donations had dwindled to nothing because people no longer had surplus clothes. Volunteers helped a great deal—an elderly man who'd run a barber shop for years came every week to trim children's hair and to check them for lice. A former teacher taught reading and writing. Ada respected the work that Lykke and her staff did and was pleased to see how the community supported them. She had grown attached to both the staff and the children. While she continued to fold laundry, she noticed a little boy named Benji playing nearby. One of the staff had pointed out that he seemed to follow her around the building.

Ada asked Lykke what she knew about him.

"He's such a good lad. When she was about to be arrested, his mother asked a neighbor to keep him safe. Eventually that neighbor couldn't provide for him because she had her own children, and she brought him to us. Unfortunately, I haven't been able to find any relatives. Potential foster parents are hesitant to take him due to his inability to speak. He was examined by a doctor who explained that his mutism has been triggered by things he witnessed. He believes that with time and care, Benji will speak again."

They saw him in the hallway. "Hello, Benji. Say 'good morning' to Miss Ada," Lykke said.

Benji looked at Ada and shook his head. The dark curls danced as his brown eyes studied her. Ada was struck by his seriousness.

"That's all right, Benji," Ada said. "Let's make our own language. How can we say good morning with our hands?" she asked. She held out her hands and looked at them, willing them to speak for her.

He watched her carefully as he tried to figure out what she meant.

"Imagine that you're a bird, but for some reason you can't make bird sounds? How would you greet the other birds?" Benji looked out the window at the large forsythia bush where small birds often took shelter. He lifted both his arms, keeping them bent at the elbow, and he flapped them a few times. Afterwards, his arms fell back to his side, and he looked at Ada, waiting for her reaction.

Ada smiled. "That's perfect. Let me try. Make sure I do it right." As Ada lifted her arms to flap her wings, she watched his face.

Although he didn't smile, he nodded to show his approval. After that morning, it became their special silent greeting.

It was such a small moment, but it made Ada's heart hurt. Seeing his silent but determined face, she knew she would do anything to make his life better. It surprised her—she'd enjoyed being around children, but she wouldn't have predicted she would develop such strong feelings in such a short time. Being attached to anyone was such a risk—losing both

Willy and Father left her with the feeling that anyone she loved would be taken away. What if a relative showed up and wanted to take him? What if he found a foster family? Or the unthinkable, what if he was sent to Germany? Ada pushed away such thoughts, alarmed at how sad they made her feel.

Benji's inability to speak kept him isolated. Although he watched the other children play, he didn't approach their games, and they didn't invite him. She'd been an awkward outsider often enough to know exactly how he felt.

Although Ada wanted to help him, she was unsure of herself. The director didn't have any specific advice either, other than patience and care.

"I'm a bit old-fashioned," Lykke said, "but I believe that love can heal."

Ada took a piece of paper and a pencil from the office and sat at one of the children's tables that were scattered around the common room. Folding the paper into quarters, she began to draw. Benji moved closer and watched with great interest. She drew a circle and a triangle and then explained: "This is Fred, and this is Lizzie. They are best friends until one day, Lizzie doesn't want to share a cookie that her mother made. She goes home and feels sad for being so greedy. She asks her mother to help her bake more cookies, and then she brings them to Freddie in a tin with a card that says, 'I'm sorry.' They sit on the front step and eat cookies before going off to play."

Benji nodded his approval.

Ada took another piece of paper, divided it into quarters, and handed Benji the pencil. "Can you think of a story?"

He looked at the blank page and then drew a circle. He pointed to himself and then handed her back the paper.

Ada had to look away to hide the tears in her eyes.

Over the next days, Ada watched him carefully as more children left the home. He seemed to withdraw further into himself. Was he afraid he would be left behind because no one arrived to take him home?

"We won't leave you here by yourself," the supervisor reassured him, "but it takes a while to find the right home."

He looked at her without a smile. Wearing a faded shirt and pants that were at least two inches too short with holes in both knees, he needed some new clothes.

As more children were placed in homes, it became clear that Benji would not join them. The soldiers wanted them to clear out of the house by April, and March was well underway. The spring sunshine energized everyone to play outside and enjoy games in the backyard. It seemed like things might go on indefinitely, but one day Lykke had a visit from an officer who pushed them to vacate the building.

While Lykke worried about closing the orphanage, Ada tried to find an answer for Benji's situation. She wished she could ask Father's advice. Willy would have told her to fight for Benji, but it was hard to imagine taking on such a responsibility when so much was uncertain. What would Lina think? Ada was terrified to bring the topic up because if Lina refused, she did not know what she would do. Did Lina have the right to refuse if Ada was committed to this plan? Round and round she went, trying to find the right answer.

While she tried to figure out what to do about Benji, her mind was still busy trying to absorb what she had learned from Mother's diary. She could only handle small amounts of it at a time—it was confusing and upsetting. But she knew she had to face whatever was in the story—it was time.

When she arrived home, she took the box from under the bed. As she pulled out the journal, she tried to calm herself, but her hands shook as she opened the diary.

48.

JANNY'S DIARY, NOVEMBER 1922

*A*LTHOUGH *I started this diary with good intentions, I am now weeks behind in recording the events of the fall, and I believe it is important to have a record of that time. Frans and I did our best to find time to spend together. He managed to escape his hospital duties to meet me in cafés or in parks whenever he could. I even skipped classes to meet him, while Gerda covered for me and collected notes and handouts. Although tired from nights of being on the wards or in surgery, he sacrificed sleep to spend an hour with me.*

Gerda and I continued to participate in the school's branch of the Student Christian Club that organized camps and activities that even Father thought were worthwhile for our religious education. One of the activities included organizing fundraisers for students in other countries who needed support after natural disasters or war.

We became part of the executive committee of the club. Gerda was very good at planning events, but I preferred taking minutes and keeping track of the finances. We planned to attend an overnight camping retreat for students representing a variety of schools and colleges. We volunteered to help organize the food for the camp, for which we would be given extra credit at school.

Luckily it was a relatively mild October weekend. On the first night, the singing went late into the night. Although the night was cold, we gathered by a campfire to keep warm. When we finally climbed into our tents, we were completely exhausted, but we knew that we had to wake up early to prepare breakfast and lunch.

On the second night, I had arranged to meet Frans, who planned to set up a tent at a safe distance from our camp. I slipped away from the evening worship and retrieved my bike where it was parked out of sight of the main meeting area. Would he be there? What if I got caught? If Mother ever found out I had met a man without a chaperone, she would lock me in my room for the next ten years.

Frans was waiting for me at his campsite where he'd built a campfire. He passed me an enamel cup filled with wine. I've never cared for wine, but it seemed rude to refuse. We wrapped in a blanket and sipped our wine by the campfire. After a great deal of kissing, Frans helped me to my feet and guided me into the tent. Maybe I am naive, but I hadn't really considered that I would do anything more than kiss him and be close. He was so sure of himself that I followed him into the tent and hoped I would get back to the conference before daylight.

I will not share, even with my diary, the details of that night—that is private. I will never forget any of it, and I have never told anyone. Frans and I discovered each other in the dark, against the backdrop of night sounds. He was so tender and caring—I knew that he loved me, and that knowledge changed everything.

In the early morning, I woke up with a headache from the wine but was happy to see Frans beside me. I had never spent a night with a man before, and I loved watching him sleep in the early morning light. His face was relaxed in sleep, and the whisper of a beard made him look rugged.

I had to get back to camp before anyone noticed my absence, so I slid out of the tent, doing my best not to disturb him, and dressed myself outside. The morning was chilly, but I was lucky it was not raining. I had arranged for someone else to serve the breakfast, so I had some time to get myself together. The sun began to break through the fog and promised to turn it into a beautiful day. A few coals still glowed in the campfire, and two enamel cups contained remnants of wine.

I wanted to leave him a note but had nothing with which to write. I picked several wildflowers and placed them in one of the cups near the entrance to the tent where he couldn't help but notice them.

When I got back to the camp, Gerda looked at me with curiosity. "And?" she asked.

I smiled but was not ready to share the experience with her. She took note of my beard-scratched face and dark circles under my eyes without comment. When I think about it now, she knew exactly what had happened but refrained from asking questions. She had a much better knowledge of the ways of men. My parents might have thought it was good to keep me so innocent, but that only left me unprepared for the real world. I had been chaperoned and accompanied at every event where I might meet men. I was told that when it was time, I would be introduced to an appropriate match chosen for me by my parents. My only education on romance was gleaned from the plots of romance novels where I learned that a heroine could be swept away by emotion and find love in the process. Mother refused to talk about such things and told us not to be disgusting if we asked questions about normal bodily processes.

As we sat through the lectures and Bible study and singing, my mind was elsewhere. When would I see him again? How would we find a way to be together? As the hours passed, I began to doubt that he cared for me as much as I cared for him. Did he mean it when he said we were meant to be together?

The next weeks passed without any opportunity to spend time with Frans. He was doing a two-month surgical rotation during which he needed to prove his worth to his clinical supervisor. It was one of those times when I caught a glimpse of how ambitious he was. It was clear that he would do his best to make time for me, but his career would always come first.

We were busy as well—Gerda and I had numerous assignments and tests to pass, but that seemed insignificant compared to Frans' work of learning to become a surgeon. I realized I needed to get good grades so my parents could see that I was serious about my schooling.

Sometimes I wished I could talk with similar passion about what I was doing. Although I was grateful to attend the School of Domestic Science, it was never going to be my life's passion. According to Gerda, men are given a huge arena in which to work and move, whereas women are allotted a small space cluttered with domestic details that they are expected to manage without complaint. I have no doubt that Gerda will push her way into a larger arena to announce her presence, but that was unlikely in my case.

JANNY'S DIARY, DECEMBER 1922

As the weeks passed, I managed to ignore things, but then I started to need more sleep, almost dozing off in class. My appetite for sleep was bigger than anything else.

The trees were stripped bare now, and the days were dark. The canals and paths that had looked so radiant in the early fall with sun filtering through the golden leaves now looked dismal and deserted. December meant Sinterklaas festivities at home, for which I had little enthusiasm.

My breasts were very sore, and I couldn't bear to sleep on my stomach as I had always done. Cooking class was the worst, as the smells of food assaulted my senses and made me want to throw up. I was reprimanded sharply by our cooking teacher who thought I was daydreaming, but I was just trying to control my nausea.

When Gerda took me to a doctor, he confirmed what we both had guessed. The doctor asked me if I knew anything about preventing pregnancy, and I was embarrassed to say I did not. Gerda had more knowledge than I did, but she hadn't realized I was going to go that far with Frans that night. Neither did I; but it was just the perfect moment, and we took it. Gerda couldn't understand why Frans took that risk. "He's a doctor, and he should have taken care of this."

My parents were furious. Father ordered me to pack a suitcase and gave me a small amount of money. Mother stood beside him, clearly in agreement with everything he said. "You have shamed me," she told me, "and I will never forgive you. Whatever will I tell my friends?"

I looked at her, and at that moment I felt a deep loathing for her. "Tell them you're about to be a grandmother." When I walked away from them, I had no idea it would be the last time I saw them.

I had one more meeting with Frans, and it was to be our last. He was in a hurry as he had to lead a conference with other students. We met in a café near the medical school. The smell of coffee made my stomach queasy.

When I told him I was pregnant, I thought he would want to help me. After he told his parents, they sent him to Paris to complete his surgical training.

Gerda told me I had to forget him and move on with my life. It was not easy. I had fallen completely for Frans, and I couldn't imagine feeling the same about anyone else ever again. She accused me of being a romantic.

I didn't want to admit to her that I still longed for him and thought about him daily. She would have told me to smarten up. Maybe that's the thing with first love—it marks you forever and refuses to leave you, no matter how far you travel from it.

There was only one place I could go once I was thrown out of my parent's house. Before she started school, Gerda had purchased a fifth-floor walk-up apartment. Her father had been successful in business, and after her mother died he courted a much younger woman whom he planned to marry. Gerda threatened to reveal to his future wife how he had stolen her childhood by interfering with her. She demanded the exact sum she needed to buy the apartment, and once she had the money, she told him she never wanted to see him again. Gerda. called it "righteous blackmail." I don't know how she dared, but Gerda had learned courage a long time ago.

Gerda welcomed me into her apartment for as long as I needed a home. The smaller second bedroom was perfect. The long window gave a view of the street and allowed the afternoon light to dance across the floor. The apartment was conveniently located near the main shopping street. I was more than happy to help with the chores since I didn't have any money to contribute.

Without her generosity, I would have been on the street. As much as I appreciated her hospitality, it also changed our relationship. I depended on her and made sure to do things the way she wanted them to be done. I agreed with her opinions and approved of her friends because it was too risky to find myself on her wrong side.

In that process, I felt like I was less me and more of a shadow, like the shadow puppet that hung on my bedroom wall at home—a gift my father had brought from Indonesia. Made of leather painted in bright colors, a puppeteer controlled the puppet by the bamboo sticks attached to its limbs. I was that puppet now as the drama of my life was out of my control and fully in the shadows, manipulated by unknown forces. I wanted to cling to the shadows many days, as I heard my mother's voice in my head speaking to me of shame and guilt. I wanted to protest that we had loved each other, but where was that love now? He had disappeared into his professional training, avoiding a baby and a wife who would only hold him back.

Once I stopped having morning sickness, I dove into my schoolwork and did my best to improve my grades. If there was one thing I could try to do, it was to finish my diploma, unless they decided to expel me. I wanted to graduate even if the future looked murky.

I still spent too much time looking back. It took me much longer to surrender the dream of being with Frans. In my mind, I imagined his return, his eagerness to experience this pregnancy with me, and his commitment to be a father to his child.

But as the weeks passed without a word, I realized that he was gone forever. Something in my heart and soul turned to stone. This was his child too, and his parents' first grandchild, but it made no difference—both grandparents had erased us from their lives. If there was no forgiveness for me, then I would make sure that I never forgave them. All Mother's piety and proclamations of loving her neighbor meant nothing when her own daughter stood before her needing help.

49.

ADA

A DA stared at the page. Before reading this, she had always thought that motherhood was instinctual, but it seemed her mother was ill-prepared for any of it.

Perhaps this explained some of Mother's behavior especially when she veered between energy and despair, trying to find some sense of importance among the church women and their projects. Her mother had complained loudly about the women's society work but still threw herself into it with complete abandon. She had at times expressed jealousy about both her sister's life and Truus' opportunities.

It was evident that she wanted to have meaning beyond the requirements of caring for her household, but she had never resolved the issue of what she wanted to do. Perhaps that had motivated Father to push for his daughters' education.

After reading the diary and the letters between Gerda and her mother, Ada studied the return address on the envelope. Owen sometimes went to The Hague for meetings; maybe he would be willing to deliver a letter if Gerda still lived at that address.

When Owen returned from The Hague a few days later, he carried a response from Gerda, who had apparently been so pleased to hear from Ada that she asked him to wait while she wrote a reply. Ada thanked Owen and put it in the pocket of her apron for later reading. She appreciated that he didn't ask any questions.

After dinner was finished and the dishes were washed, Lina said she was going to bed early. Ada planned to continue reading her mother's journal, but there was one thing she needed to know before she read any further.

As soon as Lina went upstairs, Ada retrieved the document box from Father's study and checked through his papers. There were deeds, financial papers, and documents related to his father's farm. Sitting at Father's desk, she leafed through papers from the university detailing Father's employment contract and promotion. Ada ripped open a sealed envelope that contained her birth certificate. On the page, she read her biological father's name in a whisper: Frans Josef. She stared at it, wanting the paper to speak. *Why had they kept this secret from me? Wasn't it my right to know?*

Her mother must have been devastated when Frans disappeared from her life. After falling in love with him, he left her pregnant and never contacted her again. Why couldn't he have written to her secretly or tried to find out about the baby from Gerda? Was his child so unimportant compared to the rest of his life and career?

For Mother, the combined shame of being rejected by her lover and disowned by her parents was probably more than she could bear. Knowing how she had been so aware of people's opinions—she must have been very unhappy at her exclusion. Motherhood and marriage to Father were probably not her first choice, but perhaps her only choice. Her parents were so unforgiving; they could have tried to reconcile with her once she was a proper married woman, but they had no interest in that or even in meeting their grandchild. Ada couldn't understand how they could be so heartless.

Ada leaned back in Father's desk chair, the birth certificate still in her hand. The proof was right there in writing—but the document offered no hint about how she was supposed to include the new information into everything she had assumed until now.

How had Father managed to live with the ups and downs in their household, especially when Mother directed her anger towards him? He was perhaps a safe target who would never fight back. He had never complained or said a word against his wife—and he had encouraged both daughters to respect and obey her wishes. Father must have loved her a great deal; he worked hard to create calm in a disordered household. Maybe that was also an indication of how much he had loved her and Lina.

Ada put the certificate back in the box and closed the cupboard door. There was nothing she could do to change any of it. Her parents had their reasons to keep secrets from their children, but they must have known she would eventually look in this box and find out. Now it was too late to discuss it with them or ask the many questions that were running through her mind. How would Lina react to this news?

Back at the kitchen table, Ada opened Gerda's letter with a kitchen knife. The paper was slightly yellowed—the stationery had probably been stored in a desk drawer, unused during the war years. Her hands shook as she held the letter. The paper on which Gerda had written with a fountain pen was as light as air.

Dear Ada:

I am so happy you wrote to me. I have often wondered about you and hoped that you have survived these war years in good health. I hope that you will write me again and tell me more news. I miss your mother a great deal. There are friends you make in life that are irreplaceable, and your mother was one of those.

I realize that you have many questions about your family. I don't know if it would be possible for you to come to my apartment, but I would love to have tea with you so that we could talk further about these important matters.

I am housebound these days so you will find me at home. Perhaps that kind Canadian soldier could give you a lift?

Till we meet,

Tante Gerda

Ada put the letter on the table and ran her finger gently over the folds. She was relieved that Gerda was eager to meet and answer her questions, but the relief was mixed with anxious feelings about how the answers might unsettle her life. She had always taken the basic facts of her identity for granted, but now she felt like she was falling through thin ice, unable to grab onto anything solid that would keep her above the water.

She wanted to ask someone about what it meant to have a Jewish father when she had never had any exposure to his faith. What difference would it make to her and to the people around her? Lucas had always advocated for Jewish students, so he wouldn't regard her differently. Gerda was the only one who knew the whole story, and she had kept that secret for decades. It was time to talk to her and try to find answers to the many questions this diary had generated.

50.

ADA

A FEW days later Lykke, the director of the orphanage, invited Ada to come to her office an hour before her scheduled shift that afternoon.

Ada pulled up to the large brick house and pushed her bike into the rack. There was no sign on the building, but it was clear that there were children inside. A few toys were scattered on the front lawn, and the windows were decorated with drawings.

Ada sat in the chair that Lykke had indicated. "I'll be right with you," Lykke said as she wrote a few lines on a page and signed a letter and put it into an envelope.

Ada looked around at the office while Lykke finished her task. The shelves were empty, and the desk was almost completely cleared.

Lykke took off her reading glasses and set them carefully on the desk in front of her. Her sharp blue eyes looked at Ada while she formulated her words. Dressed in a navy-blue sweater and gray skirt, Lykke had a natural authority that was shaped by kindness. Ada guessed that she was in her early fifties. She had a few wrinkles around her eyes, but her skin was otherwise flawless. Her hair was pulled into a French twist. She wore a red coral necklace with a gold clasp and matching earrings.

"Ada, we need to find a home for Benji. He is one of the last children to find a place. They will send him to Germany, and we know what will happen to him there. His identity papers are false."

Ada's heart skipped a beat. She couldn't find any words as she stared at the director. When she spoke, it came out in a squeak. "Me?" Ada wasn't surprised his papers were false—Lykke had told her that his parents were Jewish. Who would tell him about his origins? Here she was, supposedly old enough to understand, and still struggling to accept the news of her biological father. How would she instruct him about his faith? Was this something they could explore together when he was old enough?

The director smiled. "Yes, you. Everyone knows that he has made a connection with you."

Ada felt her palms grow sweaty. She was flattered by Lykke's trust—the director would only send a child to a suitable and loving home. "I have no experience with children," she admitted.

"I've watched you work, and you have a very good rapport with children. I think you'd be perfect for Benji."

Ada's heart was beating loudly. This would be a sudden leap into parenting. There would be no time to learn any skills—it would either work or be a disaster. What if he came home with her and then was unhappy? What would she do? What if he ran away? Ada cleared her throat and tried to speak. She felt a connection with him but worried that it was merely sympathy for his situation instead of whatever was required to become his parent.

Maybe she imagined it, but she did feel like they understood each other even without words. Perhaps he sensed her loneliness because it resonated with his own. Did a child have that ability to sense someone else's feelings?

Her mind fluttered around like a trapped bird. Where would he sleep? What special needs would he have? What did they know about his parents and his origins? Would a relative come and take him when they located him? And, most frightening of all, what would Lina say?

"I know it will be a big change for you, but it will be a good change."

"He's a very sweet boy, but what if I get it all wrong? My sister lives with me, and I suspect she wouldn't be happy about having another mouth to feed when we can barely feed ourselves."

"Think about it. Parenting is not about perfection, but it's about caring enough to pay attention. We all make mistakes, but we realize them, adapt, and find new strategies. As a child grows and matures, you will grow along with them. Nothing stays the same for long—even when everything is going well."

Ada nodded.

"I know it must seem like a frightening responsibility, but I can tell you that as a parent, the love of a child can change your life and make you ready to take on new challenges. I know you want to go back to school, and Benji won't stop you. He'll need to go to school too when the war ends. You can start a new chapter together."

Ada tried to take a breath, but her chest was tight. "Do you think he will learn to speak again?" How would she protect him from the taunts and teasing of school children if he couldn't defend himself with words?

Lykke tented her long fingers and looked at Ada carefully. "He needs the stability and care of a loving home, and then he will progress."

Ada tried to imagine their home as stable. After unexpected searches by soldiers and neighbors breaking in to search Father's study, it hardly seemed like a secure environment. What if Chief Vriend found a way to evict them? They would be homeless and without any help. Lina would go to Paris and find work, and Ada would be alone with a young child. Her situation would be much the same as her mother's but without a friend like Gerda to help her out. If only Father was still alive—he would have been grateful to be a grandfather to Benji, and he would have provided the experience that Ada lacked.

Ada unclenched her hands and saw that her fingers were reddened from her tight grasp. She overheard the staff talking in the hall about an infant that needed feeding. How did they know what the children needed? She had learned from lectures and books, but none of that helped her to care for a child. Her own mother had seemed ambivalent towards her children—maybe Ada would be the same.

The director sat quietly while she waited for Ada's answer.

"I will give it serious consideration," Ada replied, clearing her throat as she spoke, for her throat had become so dry.

"Good," Lykke said with a smile as she stood and shook Ada's hand. "I want you to have plenty of time to consider this, but we are under increasing pressure to close this home soon."

Ada looked up and down the hallway to find Benji. Because he was busy building a tower with wood blocks, she didn't want to disturb him, but she watched him for a few moments.

Before she could decide anything, she wondered again about her own muddled past. Was she about to repeat Mother's history by bringing a child into an unconventional situation? Although she'd been reading Mother's diary slowly, she needed to finish the last part. She couldn't explain why she had taken so long to read the diary, but she needed to absorb it slowly and figure out what it meant to her.

It was impossible to digest it all—she felt confused. Recently, Lina had been looking at her trying to understand Ada's preoccupation.

After she returned from the orphanage, Ada retrieved the diary and sat on her bed to read.

JANNY'S DIARY, SUMMER, 1923

I have not written on these pages for a long time. It was simply too much to get through the days with my feet swollen and my back aching. I had no time to put my experience into words. Silence seemed more appropriate to my station in life.

The starched apron hid my belly for a long time, but it was such a relief when the school year ended. I heard the whispers as I walked past students in the hall, but I tried to ignore them. Father had given a large donation to the school in the fall, and I suspect none of the teachers or administration wanted to anger him by drawing attention to my condition. Still, I knew my presence was awkward for everyone, and some even avoided me as if my condition were contagious.

At Greta's place, I wondered about how I could contribute to the household costs after the baby was born. We discussed how I could earn some money while taking care of the baby. She had applied to a teacher's training course that would allow her to teach domestic science in a high school. My options were limited, and I was angry at myself for wasting the opportunities I might have had.

Watching Gerda have the freedom to make her plans made me jealous. I've never been around babies very much—I had no idea how much care they needed, but Gerda assured me that maternal instinct would guide me. I was not at all convinced.

We continued to attend the student movement meetings and sit on the executive committee while everyone politely ignored my pregnancy. At an executive meeting, I ran into someone I have known since high school. He was two years ahead of me in school, and he served on the executive committee as well. Albert studied history at the university. In school, I had a feeling that he liked me but was too shy to talk to me. He was from a farm after all, whereas my father had a high position in an oil company. He used to bike into the city every day so that he could attend a good-quality school because he was a promising student. In his final year, he won all the academic prizes and had no trouble securing a place at the university.

At one of the regional club meetings that included other colleges and universities, I had to excuse myself because I was feeling dizzy, so I sat outside on the front step. Albert came to check on me. His concern made me cry. When he asked me what was wrong, I told him the whole story. Without hesitation, he took my hand and offered to marry me. He told me he realized that I might never love him in the same way as I had loved Frans, but he hoped we could find happiness together. He offered to help raise the baby as his own. Although his life was that of a student, it was filled with good friends and deep conversation. I thought he was a good man who would honor his commitments, and I accepted.

I wanted to introduce him to my parents, but they had already made it clear that I was on my own. Without their knowledge, a few weeks later Albert—and his university friend Arie Janzen, a theology student—met Gerda and me at the town hall where we were married. We had a simple dinner afterwards at a small restaurant. Arie insisted on paying for the meal, but I am sure he couldn't afford it any more than we could.

I moved out of Gerda's apartment, relieved to be spared the flights of stairs but sad to leave her. Albert's student rooms consisted of a bedroom, small kitchen, living room, and closet. With the help of friends, we acquired a baby crib and a rocker, and they gave us clothes and diapers for the baby. Both of us were stunned by how rapidly our lives had changed. We barely knew each other and were about to become parents. I was sorry for Albert—he was very busy with his studies, but he still felt so responsible for my happiness. And I felt so little happiness. How long would it take until Albert realized he had made the biggest mistake of his life?

Once the baby arrived, I was completely overwhelmed and deprived of sleep. The baby's cries were incessant. I was unable to discern what those cries meant and lacked the ease of interpretation I saw among other new mothers. The frustration built because I could not accomplish the simplest task without interruption. As a result, I was impatient and often snapped at Albert even though it was not his fault. He tried to help and encourage me, but he was working as hard as he could on his schoolwork, and he needed some sleep to be able to function.

Not only was I being punished for that one night with Frans, but I began to see that punishment would continue indefinitely. In some of my dreams, my parents came back to see the baby. We had grown up on the parable of the prodigal son who wasted years of his life and still was forgiven by his father. That parable held no hope for me. Because I had shamed her before her friends, I would never be forgiven. In Mother's world, God's grace was limited to a hardy few, and forgiveness was extended in rare situations—most people, including me, would be subject to eternal damnation. Such beliefs certainly suited her vengeful personality.

We named the baby Ada, after my grandmother. Days and nights ran into each other as I tried to respond to the demands of an infant. Fortunately, Albert adored her, and perhaps that made up for my inadequacies. Sometimes he even dropped hints that he would like to have a child with me. How can I deny him when he has been utterly selfless? I do hope it won't be soon.

51.

JANNY'S DIARY, FALL, 1923

THE days and weeks have passed in a blur. I have had no strength to write in this diary. Albert adores the baby and has become a dedicated father, willing to get up at night to hold her whenever needed so that I can get an hour or two of sleep. He continues to study till all hours to prepare for his graduate exams, and sometimes he does so with the baby in his arms.

I am too tired to pay much attention—the demands of a child have taken over my life. Gerda visited a few evenings to help with the baby so I could sleep. The lack of sleep has often left me wandering through the days, bumping into furniture, and sometimes falling asleep with my head in my arms on the kitchen table until the baby's cries awaken me.

Something deep inside my heart has refused to soften, and I realize I am jealous of Gerda and envy her freedom, her apartment, and her career. Ignoring the fact that Gerda suffered intensely in an unhappy home during her early years or that she worked hard to get her teaching credentials, I convinced myself that she abandoned me, even though I knew it wasn't true. She was my dearest friend, and I pushed her away.

Albert works as hard as he can to finish his studies, but his advisor is a strict man who demands the best. I feel sorry for Albert when I hear the long list of things expected of him, including writing papers, finishing research, and contributing a chapter to a book. All of this is so foreign to me—but studying the past has never held my interest.

As for my own ambitions, every time I think about working in a restaurant or pursuing Cordon Bleu training, I am faced with the reality that there is no one to watch the baby and no extra money to pay for such things.

Sometimes I watch other women fawn over their babies, and I wonder if I lack something essential that turns women into mothers, fascinated by every detail of their child's life. Although I do everything that is needed, I always feel like I am missing something. If only my parents would show some interest in the baby, it would be so encouraging.

Albert helps as much as he can with household chores. He also assists his parents on the farm when needed. He has fully accepted the baby as his own. For me, it is complicated; when I look at her, she reminds me of my weakness that caused me to throw away my future for a night that apparently meant little to Frans. Instead of seeing love in her face, I am reminded of my rejection.

Albert doesn't demand much as he is far too tired and works too late to have energy left for the private side of life. When he approaches me with a tentative invitation that still manages to irritate me, I pretend enthusiasm, knowing that I owe him much more than such half-hearted compliance. I have never dared ask him if he regrets his decision to take me and the baby under his wing. I fear his answer, but I know his heart expands to make room for others, whereas I have always been selfish.

Having Truus as my older sister doesn't help. She always wanted Mother's attention and knew how to make me look bad. I never learned how to fight back against her manipulations. Mother enjoyed the help of a nanny and a housekeeper that together ensured that she need not be troubled by the needs of the children or the demands of a household. I am not sure that would make much difference to my situation, but it might cover up my blatant failure to meet the standards of the domestic science training I somehow passed.

JANNY'S DIARY, FALL 1923

It is impossible to forgive Truus as she sided completely with my parents when they disowned me. When she married a wealthy businessman, her picture was in the society pages of the local paper with detailed descriptions of the event. Mother must have been in her glory. Although I tried not to care that I wasn't invited, I read every detail of the story and couldn't help but compare it to my budget wedding in city hall with two witnesses followed by a meal in a student restaurant.

When my sister showed up at the apartment one morning without warning, I was shocked.

"Truus, what are you doing here?" I took in her new outfit, a yellow dress with matching hat, purse, and shoes. By contrast, I was wearing an old shirt of Albert's and some baggy pants. I still carried considerable baby weight around my middle, and of course my breasts were constantly leaking and making it impossible to wear any decent dresses, not that I had anything that fit.

"Just came to see," she said, acting as if such a visit was commonplace. "Heard you had the baby."

"You took your time coming for a visit."

"Are you going to invite me in?" she asked.

I ran my hand over my hair as I stepped back to let her inside. I don't think I had bothered to brush my hair that morning or even wash my face. The visiting nurse had reassured me that the baby would outgrow the colic that she suffered daily, but these days once the baby started to cry, there was no time for anything else. Most days no one visited anyway. Housework fell by the wayside—there were still dishes on the table from breakfast and a partially read newspaper spread over the table, which Albert had left for me. As if I had time or interest in world events.

When I invited Truus into the living room, I felt ashamed. I had become accustomed to the room but suddenly saw it through her eyes—a humble collection of donated furniture and mismatched colors. Albert's desk stood in the far corner and was covered by piles of books and paper. He seemed to know where everything was and asked me to leave it alone, which I was happy to do.

"Congratulations on your wedding," I said, biting back the comment I wanted to make about not being invited.

Her fingers twisted her bright gold ring round and round her finger.

"Thanks. It was lovely. Do you have any tea?"

"I'll put the kettle on." I got up and tried to calm myself. If only she'd given me some warning, I might have cleaned and bought some flowers or pastries, but then she hadn't brought anything either—no flowers, not even a baby gift. I saw the apartment through her eyes and knew she delighted in my shabby existence.

"Is he a nice fellow?" I asked her. All I knew was that his name was Jaap, and he was wealthy.

"He's grand. Bought me this as a wedding gift." She held up a gold bracelet with diamonds placed at regular intervals that caught the light every time she moved her arm.

"Very nice," I managed to say, although the words sounded a bit garbled, stuck as they were in my throat. I imagined how much it must have cost and how that would cover our rent for a year or more. "Why did you come?"

"I'm your sister," Truus said.

"I'm glad you remembered. How are Mama and Papa?"

"They're fine. Since I will be moving to Eindhoven, I wanted to see you before I left. Jaap has a house there, and he's been promoted to director at the Philips plant."

"I see. Do you know anyone there?"

She tipped her chin up in that way that suggested she didn't care. "I plan to get involved in a few things so I can meet people. Now where's this baby?"

"She's sleeping, but you can take a look." I led her into our bedroom where the crib stood in the corner. I was embarrassed that I hadn't made the bed yet, and Albert's pajamas were still tossed on the bedspread.

Truus bent over the crib and gazed at the baby. "She's quite beautiful," she said. Across her face flew an expression, first of wonder and then of outright envy.

"Maybe you'll have one soon," I said because I had seen the expression on her face. It was hard to believe that Truus, with her new clothes, fancy jewelry, and new house in Eindhoven, was jealous of my baby.

"I'm not so sure," she replied.

"What do you mean?" I asked.

"I had to see a doctor before we married. There is a problem with my uterus, and I won't be able to conceive; and even if I do, the uterus will not be able to retain the pregnancy."

I looked at her in shocked surprise. She had recited that information in such a monotone one would think there was no emotion present, but I knew better. Still, I had never heard of such a thing. "I am so sorry. Is there nothing they can do?" I am ashamed to admit that something in me rejoiced to hear that there was something that all her money could not buy.

She shook her head. "Nothing."

"Does he know?"

"He might have called off the wedding if I had told him that."

"But Truus, when he finds out, he will be very angry that you didn't tell him."

"*You and the doctor will be the only ones to know. Many women have trouble this way. I'll just end up being another one of those.*" She turned back to the baby. "*May I hold her?*" She was already reaching into the crib.

I wasn't keen on anyone picking up the baby while she was sleeping because I had worked so hard to maintain a sleep schedule. Perhaps one exception wouldn't spoil her. At the school they stressed the importance of being very strict with infants and imposing a routine that allowed the new mother to undertake the rest of her household duties during the baby's nap times. "*Put this cloth on your shoulder,*" I said, "*or she might spit up all over your lovely dress.*"

Truus picked her up carefully, and the baby moved her head trying to get comfortable until she found her fist and began to suck on that. "*You're lucky you have dark hair,*" she said to me, "*or everyone would know immediately that Albert is not her father.*"

"*Albert is her father, and people can think what they want.*"

"*I see. Are you in love with Albert?*" she asked.

I didn't know what to say. What was love? Had Frans loved me? Or had he merely taken advantage of my innocence? He had obediently packed up and moved to Paris as his parents demanded. Albert, by contrast, was devoted to the baby, worked hard to support us, and made sure I knew how much I was appreciated. If that didn't meet my expectations of love, that was my problem.

I wasn't about to share my uncertainty with Truus, but she sensed my hesitation and confusion and appeared pleased to know that I would live with the consequences of my actions. The fact was that I was able to have a child, whereas she never would. In some cases that might have bound us closer together, but for us it only forced us further apart.

After Truus left, I was exhausted, but the baby was wide awake and wanting food. When I finished that, I cleaned up the dishes and made the bed, still embarrassed by the state of the apartment this morning. I resolved to do better, but I knew that tomorrow would bring the same chaos. Maybe Albert regretted marrying me—surely the farm women he had grown up with had managed a baby as well as a house and farm chores with much more skill than I did.

I was a failure in more ways than I could name, and I had no idea how to fix it. And despite my failings, he was so patient and so full of care for this child. The other night he told me he loved her so much that he hoped we might have a second child. How will I refuse him that after his generosity to me and the baby? But I know that a second baby is more than I can *bear, and I suspect I will be unable to nurture it properly. Maybe my heart has limits to its ability to care, or perhaps I am deficient in some unnamed way. I wanted a different life for myself and can only blame myself for not achieving it.*

That knowledge sits heavily on my shoulders, a yoke I had never re-quested but was still expected to carry. To whom might I apologize, and from whom might I expect forgiveness?

52.

ADA

Due to her volunteer work, several days passed before Ada managed to take time to visit *Tante* Gerda in The Hague. But in the meantime, her mind swirled with the revelations in her mother's diary. *What would Mother have done if Albert hadn't offered to marry her? Maybe she would have brought the baby to an orphanage.* Ada realized she would have been in the same position as Benji, waiting for someone to take her home.

On her bike ride to The Hague that Thursday, the wind stayed calm. There was something intoxicating about the spring sunshine. Along the path, she saw daffodils growing in the woods, a swath of cheerful yellow among the green. Grape hyacinths emerged from the frozen soil in clumps of purple.

She rehearsed a story about visiting an elderly aunt in case the patrols stopped her, but so far no one interrupted her trip. As she biked, she thought about the diary and the questions she wanted to ask Gerda. To make it more complicated, she also had questions about Benji and wasn't sure if Gerda could advise her. If her own mother felt that Ada's birth had ruined her dreams, would Ada feel the same? After all, children needed to feel welcome by a parent or guardian—no one deserved anything less.

Ada had been tempted to tell Lina about the diary, but she needed to settle things in her own mind first. Although Lina's life wouldn't change after knowing the story, Ada felt like hers had been turned upside down—that was how she justified her delay in sharing the story with her sister.

After climbing the stairs to Gerda's apartment, Ada knocked on the door. She'd brought some of her herbal tea blend and a jar of her home-made jam as gifts.

Gerda moved slowly with the help of a cane. She was an attractive woman whose face retained the youthful characteristics of the photograph that Ada knew so well. While Gerda boiled some water and added the herbal tea with a measuring spoon following Ada's directions, Ada studied her. She had obviously put some effort into her appearance, with her hair fixed in an elegant chignon and gold earrings that matched her necklace. Her dress was of good quality with some evidence of skillful mending in a few spots around the shoulder.

Delighted with the gifts, her smile made her seem much younger. Gerda invited Ada to carry the tray. Ada set it down on the coffee table and took the chair Gerda indicated. The armchair was upholstered in coarse burgundy wool that looked like it had endured several decades of use. The seat was worn, but the oak armrests gleamed. In one corner of the chair, the stuffing had started to escape.

On the wall beside the chair was an elaborate needlepoint showing windmills in various locations throughout the country. She studied it and found the large windmill that stood near the entrance to Leiden. On the opposite wall was a blank space with an empty hook.

When Gerda noticed her looking at it, she shrugged. "I had an oil painting that my grandmother gave me. It was a beautiful landscape. I had to sell it, but the proceeds helped me survive the winter."

Ada nodded as she thought of the copper pots and paintings she had hidden in the attic. Lina had traded silver and linens for food, but the attic treasures were largely untouched. At the beginning of the war, it had seemed so important to preserve those things, but these days they seemed less important than survival itself.

Gerda carefully took the tea pot out of the cozy and poured two cups of tea. She handed one to Ada with a smile. "Perhaps you should open a tea shop after the war," she suggested. "I like your herbal blend very much."

"That would be nice, but I need to finish my degree first."

While Ada waited for the tea to cool, she looked around the living room. Two chairs and a small divan covered in a moss-green velour fabric filled the room, along with the coffee table. Gerda's chair was positioned to take advantage of the light. The wicker basket of knitting and a pile of books on the side table suggested how she spent her days. The bay window provided a view of the small park, and the windowsill held a variety of empty pots and vases that must have been filled with plants and flowers before the war. The furnishings were tasteful, and the room felt cozy. Ada imagined prewar afternoons of reading and knitting, listening to classical music on the radio while having afternoon tea.

Despite the war, Gerda managed to maintain dignity in her appearance and her surroundings. Ada felt almost drowsy sitting in this room, listening to the wall clock tap out the minutes, responsibility temporarily removed from her shoulders.

A familiar photo of Gerda and Janny at the entrance to the domestic science school stood on the mantle, in addition to a baby picture of herself.

Gerda watched her study the pictures without comment.

Ada picked up the cup and saucer and sipped her tea. Where should she begin? Since it was easier to discuss the current situation, she asked Gerda whether she managed to find enough food. They talked about the bombing in the city and the resulting homelessness of the residents.

"I believe you have questions for me?" Gerda asked.

Ada nodded. She looked at Gerda who leaned back into her chair. Ada cleared her throat and tried to find a way to start telling the story.

"Start at the beginning?" Gerda suggested.

Ada placed the cup carefully on the table. She folded her hands in her lap, taking a steadying breath. "When I cleaned out my parents' room recently, I found a box with Mother's diary and some letters from you. I was glad to find your address, and so I asked Owen to drop off a note to you. Have you lived here long?"

"My father bought this apartment for me when I started my studies at the household school, and I have lived here ever since. The stairs are a challenge, but I am fortunate to have a view of the park."

"I read in my mother's journal about her stay with you during her pregnancy."

Gerda nodded. "After her parents threw her out, she had nowhere to go. I was happy to have her live here."

"Did you know . . . him?" Ada clasped her hands together tightly to stop their trembling.

Gerda picked up her teacup and carefully took a sip, pausing for a moment to gather her thoughts. "When we were students, one evening we went to a café to celebrate someone's birthday. A group of medical students joined our table. Your mother met Frans there, and they fell in love. I think it was love at first sight—a real *coup de foudre*. His father was a lawyer, and his mother was a Swiss-trained doctor. They were a prominent family in the city." She took another sip of tea.

Ada had the feeling Gerda wanted to tell the story. She had kept it to herself for far too long.

"In the next weeks, he and Janny met secretly but then found out she was pregnant. When he told his parents, he was forbidden to have any more contact, and they sent him to Paris to finish his studies. Janny's parents were no more understanding—they threw her out and disowned her. She arrived at my apartment with a small suitcase—I told her to stay as long as she wanted. Neither of us imagined that her parents would exclude her permanently. As happy as I was to share my place, I was very sorry that her family turned their back on her."

"That was very generous of you," Ada said. "She probably had nowhere else to go."

Gerda nodded. "It was sad how her parents treated her. I wish they had taken the opportunity to meet you because you have grown into a splendid young woman."

Ada smiled at the compliment. Would they have shared that opinion if they had bothered to meet her? Ada's eyes floated to the photos on the mantle. She looked back at Gerda's dress and manicured fingernails. Even in war, Gerda took care of herself. Ada gathered the courage to ask a question that had bothered her greatly, but stuttered over part of it: "Do you think my parents—Albert and my mother—were in love?"

"I think your parents respected each other and maybe even found love together despite their differences. Albert became a professor at a young age after growing up on a farm. Janny had grown up in the city with servants, cultural events, and an active social life. Finding herself in a student apartment with no help and no money was a challenge, especially when caring for a baby involved more work than she had ever imagined."

"How did they manage?"

"They did their best. Albert's parents were very welcoming, and that helped. Janny's parents could have done so much more for the young couple. They missed out on the joys of being grandparents. Your *Tante* Truus kept in touch by occasional letter. In my opinion, she enjoyed being the favored child who fulfilled parental expectations by marrying a rich businessman. I must be honest—I never liked your aunt. She always struck me as a bully who felt she never had enough of anything and was jealous of her sister."

Ada nodded as that fit her memory of her aunt as well. "I went to their house one summer for a holiday, but I was relieved to get home again. When Lina visited her one summer, she returned home early and refused to go back there. I remember they had a big fight after Lina returned. After that, my parents seemed to lose contact with them. I just remember a lot of discomfort and silence when their names came up. My Father did not seem to care much for *Tante* Truus or *Oom* Jaap, but he never said anything directly."

"I think you are right—he did not care for her at all. She would upset your mother, and it would take a while to get her to calm down again."

"I remember hearing about you, but I don't remember you visiting when we were teenagers."

"I worked for a while in Geneva, and then I was sent overseas to New York."

"That's amazing."

"It was a wonderful opportunity to collaborate with people who wanted to help teenage girls. We published some books, developed curriculum for schools, and then I returned. Your mother had a hard time accepting the opportunities that I had, and she did not want to see me. I was very sorry, but when I talked to your father, he told me that she had been facing challenges."

"That must have been difficult. Were you hurt by her lack of interest in you?"

Gerda smiled. "At the time it stung, but I tried to remember the fun we had when we were young, and I moved on from that."

Ada forgot to drink her tea because she was listening so hard to the story. She took a sip and asked her next question. "What did you do after you graduated?"

"I qualified as a teacher and started my career in a high school teaching domestic science. I also became head of the League for Domestic Science Teachers. Because I was very busy, my visits with your mother were infrequent. When she had a second child, her pregnancy was tough, and she was very tired. I suspect she wanted more from life, but she couldn't identify what it might be."

"I can imagine that my grandparents were not very helpful."

Gerda took a sip of her tea. "Before she met Frans, her mother wanted her to marry someone rich. Permission to go to the domestic science school was only reluctantly given, and even then it was presumed that the household arts might be useful in finding a wealthy husband."

"Other than my grandparents, you and *Tante* Truus were the only ones who knew the story of my biological father?"

"As far as I know, we were. And Frans' family was invested in keeping it quiet. I told your mother many times that she should tell you about Frans when you were old enough, but she was terrified that her daughters would judge her. She forbade me to have contact with you. I regret that, but I didn't want to lose her friendship. In the end, I think we lost it anyway because dishonesty got in the way of honest conversation."

Ada gulped. She studied the pictures on the mantle again. What would Gerda think if she knew that Ada had not yet shared any of this with Lina? Should she admit that? She was just as guilty as Mother had been of keeping secrets.

"Her sister continued to interfere in her life, always boasting about her wealth. She kept control of Janny by threatening to tell you children as you grew older about your mother's behavior that led to pregnancy. Janny believed that the harm such a revelation might do to her family and your father's career required her to try to keep her sister quiet. Truus was a bully who made your mother's life miserable. You must stand up to a bully, I told her many times. Until we stopped talking." She paused to sip her tea. "I'm sure you have many questions."

Ada looked at the carpet and was silent for a few minutes while she gathered her thoughts. "Why did Frans never have any interest in me? Wouldn't he want to meet his child? As for my mother, I am sorry people let her down and she was disappointed in how life turned out for her. There was something missing—I thought it was my fault, but perhaps it had more to do with her. At times she was very angry and lashed out at me. I was often left to parent Lina because Mother was not up to it."

Gerda nodded. "I believe your mother had challenges that were undiagnosed for a long time. She was treated in a clinic, and I think that helped her."

"What happened to Frans?" Ada asked. "I cannot call him father."

"Your aunt told me that Frans and his parents perished in the death camps."

Ada sat quietly trying to absorb her emotions. "That's very sad. Now I will never know him."

"Indeed."

"I thought I knew who I was and where I came from, but now there's a whole side of the story that I can never know."

"The not knowing is frustrating, but perhaps you can find explanations for things that never quite fit. Maybe you have abilities and interests that no one else shares. Frans was a brilliant surgeon who excelled in his training and studies. He was also very musical and played classical piano. I heard that you are a good student, you love science, and your mother enjoyed hearing you play the harmonium."

"In my case, none of those things would ever be described as brilliant." Ada paused. "I just find this all so hard to accept."

"Of course, my dear. It will be a lifelong project to try to understand all that happened. Some secrets sometimes need to be revealed so they can free those held captive by them, but there are other things we'll never know."

Ada nodded slowly. She had secrets too. She changed the subject. "What about you?" Ada asked. "I know nothing about your family."

Gerda was quiet. "My father was not a nice man. He treated us and my mother very poorly. My sister died of diabetes before the war, and my mother passed in the first year of the war.

"I'm sorry," Ada said.

"I blackmailed him for the way he treated me, and I think it was a very small payment for all that he stole from me. I bought this apartment with the money. When he gave me the key, I thanked him and said I never wanted to see him again. I knew I would never marry. My teaching career was my true love, and my students were my family." Gerda stood up and poured more tea in their cups and then sat down to resume her story.

"After I retired from that career, I worked for an organization that provided assistance to unwed and pregnant young girls." She thought about her next words. "When your mother passed, I was so sad. She had been my best friend, and even when she was unwilling to see me, I knew that she still cared. Albert was a fine man who had more integrity than anyone I know. I was so sorry to hear that he died in a camp. He deserved so much more than that."

Ada sat quietly for a few minutes. "He refused to surrender secret papers to the Germans."

"Your father was a man of principle. Please tell me about your sister."

"She's very frustrated that the war hasn't ended, but she's trying to learn more about photography. She's been taking pictures of how the war has affected our area, and the pictures are very powerful. She also helps with the war effort in several ways. When the war ends, her dream is to move to Paris."

"Are the two of you close?" Gerda asked.

"There's always some tension between us. Because I was often put in charge of her, I bossed her too much, and she resented that. I worried that she was reckless and didn't seem to care about her safety, but I have come to realize that she is both clever and courageous."

"What do you think causes the tension between you?"

Ada studied the carpet again. "I've always been jealous of her—she's stunning to look at, and she's athletic and fearless. Everything that I am not. When she was young, I was responsible for her, and I tried to shield her from Mother's outbursts. When she became a teenager, she didn't want to accept my authority. After Father's death, we are working on learning to work together. She finds food, and I put together meals from what we have. I try to treat her like an adult who can make her own choices, but that has been a gradual development." Ada looked down again. "I don't always succeed."

"You compare yourself to her?"

Ada squirmed in the chair. "I resented the fact that Father seemed to let her off so easily from chores or responsibility. I felt like I was carrying all the burdens of the household. Recently, I realized that wasn't fair, and I can't blame her for wanting to be out of the house."

"It sounds like you have both made strides to accept each other and to work together. That's wonderful. You are each other's family, and you will need each other in the years to come. No matter where Lina goes, you will be home for her."

Ada felt her emotions rise at Gerda's words. Could it be true that she was important to Lina in that way? She had only ever heard her say that she could not wait to get away from all that held her back, and Ada had presumed that included her. But what if Gerda was right? She had never considered the possibility that she might be important to Lina.

"There is something else I wanted to ask you," Ada said.

Gerda nodded. "Please ask anything."

"I volunteer in an orphanage that has been ordered to close. There is one little boy who can't speak due to the experiences he had when his parents were arrested. No one is willing to adopt him, partly because they are afraid that he might never speak. He has attached himself to me. The director wants me to take him home. Any children remaining past the proposed date of closure will be sent away. Despite my lack of experience, the director believes that I can be a parent to him. What do you think?"

"That poor little boy. Who knows what he has been through? I know it must be overwhelming, but he will change your life in unexpected and wonderful ways. Children are amazing teachers. What does Lina think?"

"I am afraid to ask. If she says no, then I don't know what to do."

"Try to talk to her and explain why you think this is important."

Ada nodded and then stood up to collect the cups. "I'm sorry I can't stay longer, but I must work this afternoon.

"Will you come again? Maybe you could bring Lina, too."

"I'll be in touch. Thank you for the invitation and for talking with me. I am sorry Mother didn't feel she could tell us her story. We would have loved her anyway."

Ada put her coat on and shook Gerda's hand.

Gerda kissed her on each cheek and let her hands linger on Ada's shoulders.

"I was pleased to hear that your mother saved some of our correspondence. Just remember that love created you, and love tended you as you grew up. There was always love, and it is up to you to continue to bring love to all that surrounds you." She patted Ada's shoulder. "It will take time to let all this settle. Don't be afraid to love, Ada. There are many opportunities to practice economy, but love is not one. When you find it, seize it and cherish it."

Ada waved and walked down the flights of stairs. She biked home with renewed energy, feeling a lightness in her body and her spirit. How could she tell Lina about all that transpired? She needed to keep it to herself a little longer, but when the time was right, she would explain everything that she had learned. She hoped that Lina would eventually understand.

53.

ADA

THE day after her visit to The Hague, Ada stood in the foyer of the or-phanage studying the children's art tacked on the walls. Down the hall, she could hear babies crying. In the playroom, two of the older children worked to build towers with wooden blocks that were demolished by the younger ones as soon as they were built. She smelled vegetable soup simmering in the kitchen. There were just a few children left, and they were waiting to go to their new homes. Several staff members had already left to find other jobs; fortunately, volunteers offered to help with the remaining children.

When Ada agreed to help bring an infant across town to her new foster home as a favor to Lykke, she did not realize at first that there was more to the request. Just before she left, Lykke explained that they want-ed her to make an additional stop on the way, using a pram to transport guns. Ada was reluctant to undertake that kind of mission, but Lykke said it was very important.

Reverend Arie had assured her that courage would come when it was needed—would that assurance apply to this? She didn't feel brave, but she just couldn't say no to Lykke, who had done so much for the children. Even as she waited for the baby to be dressed, she felt her pulse accelerate and her palms grow sweaty.

A staff member asked her to wait while they finished getting the in-fant ready. She took a moment to watch Benji as he listened to a story in the common room. His attention was completely focused on the book the volunteer was reading. Ada imagined filling a bookshelf with his favorite books. She had found some in the basement, and her neighbors offered to donate a selection of well-used children's books from their attics.

Was it possible to know in advance what type of parent one might be? It was something untested that required a lot of faith. For her, it was quite a leap to take, especially since she would parent alone.

"Are you ready?" Lykke called.

"I'm ready," Ada replied, trying to appear more confident than she felt.

An old-fashioned pram stood in the foyer, ready for the trip.

"Here is the address," Lykke said as she handed Ada a piece of paper with the name and address of the adoptive parents, "and this is her identity card."

Ada looked at the address and nodded. "I know where that is," she said. She tucked the identity card in her purse.

A staff member at the home handed her the infant, who was about six months old.

Ada held her carefully and studied her tiny face that looked back at her intently. "Are you ready for your new home?" She hoped the baby wouldn't cry as they walked across town to her new family. A screaming baby would only attract attention.

Benji stood in the hallway and watched her carefully.

"There's a bottle in here and some cloth diapers and two outfits. We don't have a lot to give, so I hope the mother can find more. Thanks for doing this," Ingrid said as she handed Ada the bag.

"I'll make sure she gets there," Ada replied. Before she left, she walked over to Benji and invited him to see the baby. "I'm going to bring her to a new home," she explained, "and then I'll be back to see you."

The children and staff waved at the window as Ada left.

"*Tot ziens*," Ada replied with a wave. Navigating the pram felt awkward at first, but then she gained confidence.

Ada had been instructed to make one stop on the way to the baby's foster home. She was supposed to leave the pram by the back door and take the baby inside with her as if they were there for a social visit. Someone would retrieve the weapons hidden under the mattress and then give her a signal to leave.

Walking through town, she saw two policemen on the opposite corner, so she quickly crossed the street, but then further on a single policeman stood on the next corner. Her heart started pounding, and her throat felt dry. Why had she agreed to this?

She couldn't keep zigzagging without gaining someone's attention, so she kept walking. She practiced what she would say when he questioned her.

Her identity papers were up to date, and the infant had newly made papers. She planned to tell him that she was a babysitter who had taken the baby for a walk and was on her way to return the child to her mother. There was nothing suspicious about that. When he was just a few steps from her, someone called him over, so he gave her a quick glance and then walked towards his colleague.

When Ada arrived at the safe house, she took the baby out of the pram and knocked on the back door. A young woman invited her inside and checked to make sure that Ada had left the pram near the back door. Instructed to sit at the kitchen table, Ada held the baby and looked around the kitchen. There were dishes piled in the sink while a fly buzzed at the window. No one spoke to her, so she talked softly to the baby, and hoped she would stay quiet.

Ada wasn't sure how much time passed—every minute felt like an hour. What if someone discovered her illegal cargo? She thought about trying to survive in prison, but that thought terrified her even more. She was so lost in thought that when a man opened the door behind her, she jumped up holding the baby tightly in her arms. He told her she could leave. There were no greetings and no names exchanged.

Ada took some breaths to calm herself and then pushed the stroller at a brisk pace. What did new mothers look like when they pushed a pram around town? She'd never really looked at mothers as they pushed prams.

While walking, she quietly sang songs remembered from her childhood to entertain the baby. It was amazing how the words were embedded in her memory—did Benji have his mother's voice in his memory as well? What had he witnessed that had silenced him?

Lykke had told her that his parents had hidden him in an attic, but someone had informed the police of their location. Just before they were arrested, his mother packed a bag and took Benji to a neighbor.

She tried to distract herself with other thoughts—she imagined walking Benji to school in the fall. If the local school wouldn't accept him, she might have to find a special program. It would be a challenge to make her class schedule fit his school hours, but perhaps there would be another parent in the neighborhood with whom she could share responsibilities.

Even though she was tempted to look over her shoulder to make sure no one was following, she kept her eyes straight ahead and tried to remember to breathe.

She planned to tell Lucas she wasn't suited for this kind of work—her heart was beating so fast, and despite the cold breeze she felt perspiration cover her face. Anybody would take one look at her and know that she had something to hide. Lina was never anxious, no matter how risky her assignments—in fact, she seemed to thrive on the danger. Some people were just born courageous—but Ada knew she was not one of them.

Ada arrived at a red brick row house with a small front yard. As she pulled the pram up to the back door, a woman came outside. With a big smile, she received the bundle that Ada handed her.

"Hello, Ida. Welcome to your new home." She looked at Ada. "Please come inside and have a cup of tea. My name is Saskia. Thanks so much for bringing her."

As Ada sat at the kitchen table, Saskia carried Ida on her hip while she prepared tea. Ida seemed to be at home with this woman—perhaps her hands communicated a confidence that Ada lacked.

Saskia had a long blonde braid that fell solidly between her shoulder blades and continued almost to her waist. Her red cheeks seemed to be her usual coloration. Her movements were quietly efficient as she brought the tea to the table.

"You have other children?" Ada asked as she studied the drawings pasted to the walls.

"I have three children aged ten, eight, and six."

"Are they excited to have a sister?"

"They've made cards for her." She pointed to the kitchen cupboard that was covered with welcome cards. "Do you have any children?" Saskia asked.

Ada shook her head. "I'm just helping out at the home." She had a sudden instinct to confide in the woman, but she didn't quite dare. What would she think of Ada's hesitation about adopting Benji? Even though she already had three children, Saskia was still willing to take in one more.

"We wish we could do more for those other children," Saskia said, "but we are out of room."

"It's very kind of you to take Ida."

"I hope she'll be happy here."

Together they admired Ida's curly hair and her brown eyes. The baby curled her tiny fingers around the woman's little finger. Although she'd only been in Saskia's arms for a few moments, Ada thought she could see a connection growing between them. How was that possible?

Whatever Ida experienced when she was separated from her mother in her first months, Ada hoped that she would now feel loved and secure. Saskia was oblivious to Ada's presence as she made little sounds and held the baby close.

Ada thought about Benji. He was a bright lad who understood more things than he could explain in words. She knew she couldn't let them ship him to Germany. There was no need to think about it anymore—she had to do this and to find the courage to stand up to Lina's opposition.

Ada stood up abruptly. "I have to go," she said.

Saskia was fully absorbed in the baby. "Isn't she beautiful?" Saskia asked, admiring the infant's tiny toes and fingers.

"She certainly is," Ada said with a smile. "By the way, the orphanage sent along two outfits and some diapers. They are sorry they don't have more to give you, but here's her identity card." Ada placed the card and the bag on the table. She touched the baby's hand one more time. "Goodbye, baby Ida."

"Thank you for bringing her. Good luck with everything."

"You too," Ada said. "Congratulations."

She wheeled the pram to the front and waved to Saskia, who was watching from the front window with the baby in her arms.

When Ada arrived at the main crossroads where she would normally turn right to return to the orphanage, she saw the same German soldier. This time he walked right up to her.

He demanded her identity papers. "Where's the baby?" he asked as he peered into the empty carriage.

Ada cleared her throat; she felt like her throat had gone dry. "She's at the babysitter."

He looked at Ada and then walked away, bored with the whole thing.

Ada's hands were clenched around the handle of the pram, and her heart pounded loudly for the rest of the walk. If she'd left the baby at the sitter, why wouldn't she have left the pram there, too? What if he'd asked that? What if they had found the guns that had been stored earlier in the bottom of the carriage?

She sped up her pace—she wanted to drop off the pram at the orphanage and finish this mission. Typing and editing were jobs with which she felt comfortable, but these missions required a very cool head, and she did not have what it took. If anyone asked again, she would refuse.

When she arrived at the orphanage, people were agitated.

"We've had a change of plans," Lykke told her. "They've ordered us to close us a week early. If you could take Benji tomorrow, that would be very helpful."

"Tomorrow?" Ada said.

"Is that a problem? We want to get the kids out so we can give the place a thorough cleaning."

"No, it's fine," Ada said.

"We won't tell him until tomorrow. He might be up all night if he knows he's leaving."

Ada nodded and then went to help the volunteers clean up the remaining dormitory rooms. By tomorrow she'd bring home a little boy to live with them and be part of their family. Her life was about to change completely, and she hadn't had nine months of pregnancy to get ready. There was no delaying anymore—she had to tell Lina that Benji was coming home.

54.

LINA

Wᴴɪʟᴇ they waited for Ada to return from her work at the orphanage, Lina invited Owen to play shuffleboard in the basement. Lucas said he would prepare dinner, but he wanted them out of the kitchen while he did so.

Once Owen figured out the rules, he played with great enthusiasm. As they competed on the board, the scent of the simmering sauce infused the house with the scent of garlic and tomatoes.

When Ada finally came home, she looked exhausted. Lucas helped her with her coat and said he would serve up dinner. Owen pulled several cans of beer from his knapsack.

"Where do you get this stuff?" Lina asked as she studied the can.

"From the Yanks. They supply beer to their soldiers."

"Do you want a glass?" Ada asked them.

"You'll only make more dishes dirty." Owen lifted his beer. "I'd like to propose a toast."

Lina and Ada looked at him.

"I'd like to salute a new professional photographer whose photograph will be published in an American magazine."

"What?" Lina said. "You heard from your friend?"

"The editor was very pleased and asked for more. Let's drink to that."

"Cheers," they echoed. "To more!"

Lina stared at Owen. She was shocked. His friend was willing to publish her photograph.

"I've got the letter right here. Would you like to see it?" Owen said, holding the blue airmail letter just out of her reach.

Lina grabbed it from his hands and read it. "I can't believe it," Lina said as she scanned the content.

"Congratulations! I knew you could do it," Ada told her. "This food looks really good," Ada said to Lucas. "Thanks for making this."

Over dinner, they talked more about Lina's new assignment. Owen's American friend wanted her to capture more stories to inform the world of events around them.

When the conversation paused, Ada put down her fork. She had hardly taken a mouthful. She didn't want to intrude on Lina's excitement, but she had to reveal her decision. "I have some news, too."

They looked at her. Her face was flushed, and she looked very nervous as she fidgeted with her utensils.

Ada cleared her throat. "As you know, I've been working at the orphanage, which is being forced to close. Most of the children have been placed with families, but there's one young lad, about five, who doesn't have a placement. He's had a rough time and as a result has traumatic mutism, but he still communicates well. The director believes his speech will return eventually."

Lina set her beer down and looked at Ada. What was she talking about? Bringing a child here to live with them? But that made no sense. They couldn't look after a child. When the war was over, she'd be off to Paris, and Ada would go back to the university. Their parents were gone and couldn't help.

Ada refused to look at her. "I've agreed to foster him. The orphanage closure was accelerated by the occupiers, so I need to bring him home tomorrow."

Everyone had stopped eating. When Ada looked up, she saw Lina glaring at her.

Ada was too nervous to eat. She tucked her hands in her lap so no one would see how badly they were shaking. Owen glanced from Lina to Ada but was reluctant to intervene in a family disagreement. The air was thick with tension.

When Lina stayed silent, Owen jumped in. "That sounds like a great idea," Owen said. "You have this big house, and you're good with children. He'd be lucky to live here."

"Not so fast," Lina said. "Who says I want a child here? I live here too." She looked at Ada and leaned forward. "Do you realize what you are taking on? If he can't speak, how will we know what he needs? He's probably had some horrible experiences, and he'll never be right."

"That's not his fault," Owen volunteered. "He deserves a chance like any other child."

"That's easy for you to say," Lina said. "You're going home soon, and this won't be your problem."

"But Lina," Ada protested, "you've always said you plan to go to Paris the minute the war is finished. Why does it matter what I do?"

"But I must live with him until that day comes. If it ever comes."

Owen gave Lina a look that seemed to silence her. "You need to bring him home tomorrow?" Owen asked Ada. "Do you need any help?"

Ada took a breath. "They're closing the orphanage earlier than expected—if I don't take him tomorrow, he'll be sent to a children's detention camp. The occupiers plan to turn the orphanage into a recreation hall and residence for soldiers."

Lina glared at her. "Are you kidding? Tomorrow? I suppose he has false papers because he's Jewish. You're going to get us all killed."

Ada was angry. When she stood up abruptly, her chair fell with a crash to the floor. "You're used to everything revolving around you, but it's time you learn to think of others. If you don't like it, why don't you move out? You can't wait to leave anyway." She left her food uneaten and went upstairs to her room.

Lina sat in silence with Owen. They ate their food, but no one wanted to be the first to speak. Finally, Lina put down her fork and stood up. "Think what you want, this is not a good idea. She has no experience with children, and this one can't even tell her what he needs. This is ridiculous."

"Sit down, Lina," Owen said in a very firm voice. "We need to talk."

Lucas took the opportunity to bring his plate to the sink and say good night.

55.

ADA

Early the next morning, Ada used the ground coffee that Owen had given her. The kitchen filled with the most delicious aroma. Ada smiled briefly with pleasure, but then remembered what this day would bring.

She was too nervous to eat anything—she planned to bring Benji home and show him where he would sleep. Checking her watch every few minutes, she walked around the kitchen straightening things and making sure all surfaces were wiped and clean, knowing that even though it would make no difference to the little boy, it was soothing to her.

When Ada arrived at the orphanage, Benji was waiting for her. They said their goodbyes, and then Lykke walked Ada and Benji to the front door while the remaining volunteers waved goodbye. In the weeks since Ada had started volunteering, the coziness of the orphanage had been peeled away—the children's art had been removed from the gallery wall, the quilts and wall hangings had also been taken down. The windows looked bare without the plants that volunteers had transplanted from their own gardens and placed on the windowsills. All the beds and little tables and chairs were donated to needy families. The staff had done their best to make this house feel like a home for the children, and Ada had no doubt that some of children would miss this place and the caring staff even after they found new families.

Benji waited quietly beside the bike while she put a few things in her pannier and undid the lock. He waved once to the people at the window and then turned his back to them and watched Ada.

She lifted him into the bicycle seat that was attached to the front handlebars and made sure he was comfortable. Last evening, the neighbors had dropped off the seat and a box of toys and books to welcome Benji to his new home. Ada had arranged the items in the bedroom.

"Thanks for your help," Lykke said to Ada as she watched them prepare to leave. "Be happy in your new home," she told Benji.

"No need to thank me," Ada replied. "I really enjoyed working with you."

"Call me if you have any questions."

"Thank you. I will take you up on that."

As Ada began to bike, she had to adjust to the weight of the boy on her front handlebars, but he sat quietly and observed everything. She wondered if he had ever been taken beyond the walls of the orphanage.

Soon it would be warmer and more inviting to be outside—she planned to take him for walks and bike rides every day. Benji might enjoy helping her plant the garden.

At the house, she lifted him out of the seat and put the bike in the shed.

"This is your new home," she said, taking his hand as they walked towards the back door.

Benji looked up at the big house and held on tightly to her hand.

"I'll show you where you will sleep tonight, and then we can go to the park."

When Ada entered the kitchen, she was surprised to see that Lina had hung the banner she'd sewn for her friend's birthday. She looked at it more closely and realized that Lina had left it unfinished so that it spelled out "Happy." Ada was touched that she had made some effort to welcome Benji. Ada wondered what had changed her mind, but there was no time to think about that now.

Upstairs, she showed Benji the cot that would serve as his bed. Beside the bed was a small basket filled with blocks and some miniature cars. He let go of her hand as he looked around in amazement and pointed to the toys in the basket. She had no idea where Lina had found the cars, but Benji was thrilled to see them. He handed her a small handmade card to read.

Ada studied it with a smile. "Those are for you," Ada said. "From your *Tante* Lina."

He picked up the red car and tested the wheels on the floor. He held it up, his face beaming with pleasure.

"You can bring it with you if you like. Do you want to go see the ducks in the pond?"

He nodded.

She looked at the boy that was now her responsibility, and she felt a wave of fear. How was she going to do this? What if she made mistakes? What if she caused him irreparable damage? She had just made a lifelong commitment to care for a child.

Ada was happy to get out of the house and stop the cycle of frightening thoughts. Here in the park, things seemed simpler. Together they watched the ducks fishing for food. Benji was filled with curiosity as he clung to her hand and clutched the small car in his other hand. He found an enormous spider web that stretched across the branches of a tree; they marveled at it together. She loved to see his eyes sparkle with excitement as he shared every new find with her.

She leaned against a tree trunk while he explored every inch of the ground around them. He ran up to her with a small flower and handed it to her with a huge smile on his face. Ada hugged him as her heart expanded, and her arms encircled him. They would figure it out together, and they would learn as they went along.

56.

LINA

AFTER Ada left their dinner abruptly that night, Owen talked to Lina, and his words just stuck with her, no matter how much she wanted to forget the things he had said.

"Listen, Lina, I am part of a very messy and loud family, so you can either accept what I am going to say or ignore me."

Lina looked at him with a mix of irritation and resentment.

"You also are part of a family, and it doesn't matter whether that involves two people or twelve. A family means that everyone has responsibilities to care for each other. In turn, you have a place you can always call home, where people know you and forgive you and accept you. Even when you really make a mess of things." Owen paused to make sure she was listening to him.

She was studying her hands and twisting a thin silver ring round and round.

He tapped the top of her hand lightly. "Your sister has made a brave choice, and it doesn't mean she plans to replace you or to love you less. The heart has the capacity to grow to include others, people who we choose, who become part of our families. You need to be proud of your sister's courage and to support her. Maybe someday you will teach him to ride a bike or to take pictures, and you will be surprised by how much joy that gives you."

A thin smile passed over Lina's face.

"The only way to win this war is for people to take back what has been stolen from them," Owen continued. "By that, I mean everything that makes us human, including the ability to care, to take responsibility, to welcome strangers into our homes. If we hang on to resentment and hate, we become like them."

"But doesn't a person have a right to disagree?" Lina asked in a small voice.

"You can have an opinion, but when you see that someone has made up her mind, you might want to step back and instead ask how you can help. You have a choice to close yourself off and go through life alone and homeless, or you can decide to be welcoming, to invite people in, and to share what you have. You made me welcome in your home, and it has made all the difference for me. When you bring good into the world, it multiplies in ways you cannot predict, just as when evil is unleashed, it can grow and grow."

"But it's my house too. I deserve to have a say in who lives here."

"You do have some say, but you don't have the power to overrule Ada when she is doing something that she feels is very close to her heart. There is a line between having a voice and just being selfish."

Lina looked at him and felt embarrassed that he witnessed her selfishness.

"Let me tell you something. My sister was five years younger than me. She was full of life and mischief and followed me around everywhere. One time when we were swimming, she was caught in a riptide, and I couldn't save her." He paused.

Lina stopped twirling her ring and stared at him.

"You think there will always be time," he warned, "but sometimes the time runs out, and you are left holding some unbearably heavy luggage. Take my word for it, it's not worth it. If you try, you might be surprised by how that little boy can change your lives for the good. I must go now, but I hope you will think about this and do the right thing."

Lina sat at the table long after Owen left. She had only thought of herself—she felt ashamed as she sat with her head in her hands at the kitchen table. Owen cared enough about them to stay late, to talk to her, and to reassure her that she could fix this.

That night, she thought about Jos' death and Father's arrest and death. Benji had lost his entire world in a devastating moment of change and had been shunted from place to place without having a voice to express what he felt. She knew that Ada believed that Benji would speak again someday, and she also knew that her sister would do her best to make that happen. For someone who complained a great deal that no one took her dreams seriously, Lina knew that she had stepped carelessly on her sister's dreams.

At times like this, she missed her father more than ever—he would have listened to her and encouraged her to do better. Owen had talked to her like an equal, and she was certain Father would have said similar things.

She closed her eyes and imagined the scent of pipe smoke in Father's blazer, the sound of his quiet voice, and his reassuring hand on her shoulder. He had never pitted her against Ada like Mother did, but he had encouraged each daughter to develop her unique abilities and try to get along with the other. Any competition with Ada was in her own head. Father had never expected her to have the same capacities as Ada—he had encouraged her to explore different things and find her own way forward.

Owen had been correct in thinking that Lina was jealous that Benji would replace her as the focus of Ada's care and attention. Owen had seen her insecurity but still cared enough to speak honestly with her. Somehow, she had to make this right. By tomorrow Benji would be here, and she hoped that Ada would forgive her. After the deaths of Father and Jos, it felt like their family was held together by a very thin thread—perhaps Benji might help strengthen that thread over time. What was it Father had often quoted about a three-ply cord not being easily broken? It was something from the Bible, but she'd never really understood what it meant. Whatever it was, life was going to change in their house, and she hoped it would be a good change. Owen was a smart fellow, and he thought it was a good idea. Lucas hadn't said much and escaped the dinner as soon as he could, but she was sure that he didn't want to take sides in an argument between Ada and Lina. She hoped he didn't think she was a selfish and uncaring person. She knew that she was both those things but hoped that she could still change that. She needed to give Ada a sign that she intended to change. Lina went to her room and grabbed some paper and colored pencils and the pennant she had made for that party. Sometimes you just had to make do with what you had and hope that the intention was seen clearly enough through the effort.

57.

LINA

THE next morning when Lina got up, the house was quiet because Ada had already left. Lina had just enough time to do some decorating before she was due to bring photographs for identity cards to Lucas' apartment. She'd found some toy cars in the attic and put them in a basket with a card.

Standing on a kitchen chair, she tied the banner she had sewn for Maarten's party to a shelf in the kitchen where it would be visible as soon as they entered the kitchen. She stepped off the chair and admired the letters that spelled out "Happy."

Next, she made a welcome poster with the colored pencils she'd found in her bedroom closet and tacked that to the door that led to the basement. Looking around the room, it looked more festive. It was all she could do for now—Lucas would be annoyed if she were late.

When Lucas had requested a delivery of the photos she'd taken for identity cards, Lina thought it was a perfect opportunity to see where he lived. She didn't want to be nosy like their neighbor Nel, but she wanted to know something more about him. He wasn't exactly forthcoming with personal information. Owen told her more about himself in his brief visit than she had ever heard from Lucas.

She climbed the stairs to the apartment on the second floor of the student house that Lucas shared with another student who was currently away.

Lucas invited her to sit at the table while he made some coffee in a small Italian stovetop espresso pot.

"This is a nice place," Lina said as she looked around. The small kitchen had four mismatched chairs. On the far wall, a travel poster displayed the Acropolis in Greece, and another showed the blue skies and white buildings of Mykonos. She wondered if Lucas was interested in travel. She could imagine someday traveling through those countries with Lucas as a companion.

Against the side wall, a bookshelf was filled with mismatched cups and plates as well as pots and pans. The window that looked over the backyard was open, and a fresh breeze came in. As the water in the pot came to a boil, the scent of coffee filled the kitchen. She didn't bother to ask where he had obtained the coffee—Lucas had connections everywhere.

"When does Benji arrive?" Lucas asked.

"Ada had already left when I got up, so he might be there now," she replied.

"I look forward to meeting him next time I visit," Lucas said. "I hope that you and Ada are in agreement about that choice."

Lina nodded, somewhat embarrassed that he had seen her fight with her sister.

"Are you free to do another job?" he asked.

"I'm free until Friday when I clean the Captain's house." She was relieved he had moved on from that dinner last evening.

Lucas turned the heat down as the water in the small espresso pot started to bubble. "Sorry for the short notice, but I need you to go with someone to intercept a truck. We plan to use the truck to transport a group of airmen who've been waiting to go to Belgium. From there they'll travel to Spain, hike over the Pyrenees, and sail to England. If we can transport them together in one truck, it will be a lot easier."

"Happy to help. What do I need to do?"

"I really appreciate this. Some of my people are sick, and others have been sent to work in Germany."

"Where will the truck be?"

"We have inside information about when and where the truck will be traveling, thanks to the mechanic who's been working on it. I need you to be ready to leave now, and you'll be back tomorrow."

"Now? But I need to tell Ada I won't be home," she said.

"I'll take care of that as it will give me an excuse to meet your new nephew."

Lina nodded. Her mind was racing.

"Now, let's review the map and the plan. You know how to drive?"

She glared at him, somewhat offended. "My father taught us at my grandfather's farm. I can drive tractors, trucks, cars, and motorcycles."

"Good," Lucas said. "That's very useful. Before we start, why don't I make you something to eat? I have enough eggs to make an omelette."

"That would be wonderful. Can I do anything?"

"Just entertain me while I cook."

Lina watched as he cracked eggs and made a perfect omelette with a small slice of rye bread on the side. While he worked, she talked about the photography expeditions she used to make with her father.

When Lucas set a plate in front of her, Lina looked at it in amazement. "How did you learn how to cook like this?"

"My mother insisted that I learn."

"I don't cook, but I'm a very good dishwasher," Lina said. She noticed the shells for two eggs on the counter and one egg left in the bowl. "But where's your food? There's only one egg left."

"You'll need the energy. One is enough for me."

"Where did you find eggs?" Lina took a bite of the omelette. She wanted to put up more protest, but she was too hungry. "This is so good."

"A farmer gave them to me."

After she finished the omelette and the bread, she sat back and sighed. "I can't remember being so full," she said.

"I think it would be best if you go undercover as Hans and wear your cap over your hair. What you're wearing now is good for this trip. In this bag, I have rolled up a nursing uniform, so tomorrow morning just change into the uniform. If you are stopped, tell them you are a nurse returning from a visit to your sick mother, and you're going to work your shift at the TB hospital. Call the driver Dirk, even though that's not his real name."

"Let me get this straight. On the way there I'll be Hans, and even the fellow won't know."

"That's right," said Lucas. "The less you know about each other, the better."

Lina listened carefully as Lucas explained the plan. It was easy to imagine him as a college teacher, lecturing to his students and patiently explaining his ideas. His scruffy beard suited him—and his eyes were mostly serious but could also light up with mischief. As she listened carefully to his instructions, she couldn't help being distracted by his presence across from her at the small table.

She felt an impulse, which she immediately suppressed, to touch his cheek. It was ridiculous and completely inappropriate. He would think she had lost her mind and decide she wasn't fit to take on this assignment.

She wished she had the nerve to ask him if he had any feelings for her. Was she imagining it? At times like this, he was so professional and concerned for the people in the field who took big risks in running a mission. She drew her attention back to what he was saying and wondered how she might break through the distance between them to tell him about her feelings. Did sending her on a dangerous mission show that he cared and respected her, or was he just desperate for a volunteer?

"The road narrows to one lane just before the bridge, and that is where Dirk will stop the car. He will open the hood and pretend he is fixing something while you hide in the ditch on the side of the road. Since the truck won't be able to get around the car, the driver of the truck will be forced to get out and investigate." Lucas looked at her to make sure she was following the instructions.

He continued to explain the plan. "Dirk will surprise him when he's looking at the engine, tie him up, and leave him at the side of the road. Once the soldier is tied up, you will drive away in the small car—Dirk will follow in the truck. Right after the bridge, there's a gravel laneway where you turn right and go to the end. You'll see a farmhouse and a barn. Park your car behind the barn, and Dirk will pull the truck inside. Do you have any questions?"

"No questions," she said. "You trust Dirk?"

Lucas nodded. "Dirk is not afraid. He said afterwards he will hide up north where that fellow will never find him. You will sleep in the barn that night, and then in the morning change into this uniform and drive to the hospital."

"Where should I leave the car?" she asked.

"Leave it near the hospital, go inside, find a place to change into your normal clothes, and leave from another exit. I'll park your bike in the rack closest to the front door, and the key for the bike lock will be taped under the seat."

"That's a lot of switches. Do you think that's necessary?"

"You need to make sure no one is following you. Stay alert. Let's review the plan quickly, and then I'll take you to the car where Dirk will be waiting. I should warn you, he's quite opinionated, and he'll insist on driving, so don't argue with him. Keep your focus on the directions and getting that car to the barn. You don't have to like him or get along with him. In fact, I am going to bet that you won't do either."

"Do you want me to do the dishes?" she asked.

Lucas laughed. Lina was surprised at the change in his face from his usual serious expression. "That's the least of my problems. I'll do them later. But thanks."

"Remember to tell Ada that I won't be home tonight, or she'll be worried."

"I'll ride your bike to see her and say hello to Benji. After that I'll take your bike to the hospital and walk home."

Lina nodded, memorizing the instructions. She gave him the key to her bicycle wheel lock.

"Just follow the steps and don't improvise. Everything will be fine."

His face revealed nothing—she could only hope he was right. She sensed that he was somewhat reluctant to send her on this mission with Dirk. She preferred to work alone rather than deal with a fellow who made his own rules. Was he the only person available? She wished it were someone she knew. If he wanted to take any risks, he was on his own because she planned to follow the plan to the letter.

She had learned to trust Lucas with the details. For a moment, she considered telling him how she felt about him just in case something went wrong, and he might never know; but that seemed overly dramatic.

The last thing she wanted to do was to make things awkward between them. She needed to keep her mind focused on the instructions he had given. This was a professional relationship, nothing more, and she intended to prove that she was worthy of his trust.

58.

LINA

WHILE Dirk drove quickly over bumpy roads, Lina glanced at him as he muttered to himself and smoked a cigarette. After a mere five minutes, Lina was biting her tongue to keep from telling Dirk to shut up. Almost everything he did annoyed her, especially his outrageous opinions.

She was grateful that Lucas had warned her. Dirk drove the car erratically, drummed his fingers incessantly on the dashboard, and blew cigarette smoke in her face. He sang the same song over and over, oblivious to the fact that he was both off-key and a terrible singer. Worse, Lina was forced to listen to him talk. She ignored his thoughts on agriculture and on the rights of women, but when he began to criticize Lucas' leadership, Lina had enough.

"Listen, Dirk, consider yourself lucky to work for someone who spends his time keeping his people safe. He checks out the details, he plans carefully, and he does everything possible to keep the network and its people safe. If you don't like his leadership, go work somewhere else. Although I suspect no one else would want someone who cannot keep his mouth shut for five minutes." As soon as the words were out of her mouth, she regretted them. For one thing, she did not need to defend Lucas.

She should have ignored this guy—he had a short fuse and a deep distrust of women. He saw right through her disguise. He slammed his hand on the dashboard of the car, causing her to jump. He yelled at her, taking his eyes off the road while he lectured her on how females were emotional and unreliable.

Lina gripped the dash with both hands, fully expecting to land in the ditch that lined the road. "Calm down," she said. "You're giving me a headache. Can we just concentrate on what we're supposed to do?"

But Dirk didn't calm down—he increased his verbal attacks on women by arguing that they had less capacity to think under pressure and less courage. From there he ranted about the inadequacies of the Allied troops.

Lina looked out the side window and wished she'd never agreed to this mission. She was sure if there were any soldiers around, they would hear them coming for miles.

He finally shut up when they saw the bridge ahead. He approached the bridge slowly and stopped the car. "Get out," he said.

"Gladly," she muttered under her breath.

Lina exited the car without a backward look and walked towards the ditch, eyeing it carefully before sliding down the bank and getting into position. She heard Dirk turn the car off, and suddenly everything was still. Lina worked to calm herself and to concentrate on listening. What an ass that guy was! Lucas had to be desperate to have people like that working for him. She could imagine that Dirk was more vocal in the presence of women who, he assumed, would be intimidated by his outrageous opinions. She pulled at her cap and made sure it was covering her hair.

She peeked up over the edge of the ditch to confirm that he was working on the engine and ducked back down when she heard a truck approaching.

The driver of the truck, their target for this mission, pulled up right behind the stalled car, attempting to intimidate Dirk by the size of his vehicle. A soldier got out of the truck and yelled at Dirk in German to move his car. Dirk pointed to something in the engine. When the soldier took a closer look, Dirk pointed a gun in his back. He led him to the side of the road and tied him to a tree facing away from the car, so he couldn't see anything.

He waved to Lina to come and take the car away, so she ran up the hill, put the hood down, and jumped in the driver's seat. She was relieved that he had remembered to leave the keys in the ignition. The engine turned over once or twice and then sputtered into life. Lina drove the car away, taking a sharp right after the bridge onto the dirt road. She checked the mirror a few times, but Dirk didn't follow.

Suddenly, she heard a gunshot. Although she wanted to go back, Lucas had been very clear that she should stick to the plan. She reminded herself to follow every detail of Lucas' instructions. He always had very good reasons for the way he planned things. This expedition was not, however, going according to his well-made plan.

After parking behind the barn, she turned the engine off and quietly observed the yard. No one was around. The farmhouse appeared abandoned. Lina climbed the ladder into the loft and waited for Dirk. She leaned back on the hay with her hands behind her head and wondered what was happening.

Something had gone wrong. Maybe there had been another soldier in the truck who shot Dirk, but she couldn't remember seeing anyone. By now, he should have found the gravel road and the car hidden behind the barn. Should she leave the loft or stay as Lucas had instructed? She was strongly tempted to sneak back to the bridge and figure out what had happened. Would the soldiers search the barn once they saw the car parked behind it and felt the still-warm engine?

After a while, she heard the truck's engine and was relieved when Dirk drove the truck into the barn and closed the barn door behind him.

"Where were you?" Lina asked when he climbed up to the loft.

"Stupid *mof* was arguing with me. I took care of him."

"You took care of him? What does that mean?" Lina couldn't believe her ears. She felt a cold flash of fear in the pit of her stomach. Her heart felt like it was racing. Dirk was completely crazy. Maybe he would "take care" of her too. She listened carefully for the soldiers who would surely come to investigate. They would be executed right there by the barn. She knew for certain that Lucas hadn't told Dirk to shoot the guy. He just wanted the truck, and he didn't want them to commit murder to get it. Even though they had procured the truck, if they were seen anywhere near it, they would be shot. "Now what?"

"I'm getting out of here. I don't want to be near here when they find his body."

"Thanks. You put us both in danger. Where will you go?" Lina asked.

"It's better if I don't say, but I have some ideas."

Lina glared at him. "Lucas told us to stay here with the truck."

He was agitated and kept moving around and pacing the loft, rubbing his eyes and running his hand through his hair. "The truck is now unusable. It will have to stay here. I'll go on foot. See how nice I am? You get to keep the car."

She watched him leave and wished she could check in with Lucas. He'd told her to spend the night in the barn rather than take a chance being on the road after curfew. That night she tossed and turned in the hay, afraid to close her eyes with all the rustling sounds around her. The whole thing reminded her of Jos' death on that terrible night. War, it seemed to her, brought out the worst instincts in humans and resulted in devastating destruction. She hoped Dirk would find his way north to escape the anger of the soldiers, but even if he got away, they would find others to punish in his place. She had to get away from this place and hope that no one followed her home. Putting Ada and Benji in danger was not supposed to be part of this plan. What a mess.

Eventually she was so tired that she fell into a deep sleep, but all too soon the light and the sounds of barn swallows woke her. It was time to get back to town. Where was Dirk now? Lucas would not be happy to hear that he had changed the plan and killed someone in the process.

She changed into the uniform and rolled her up other clothes. She wished she could wash her face or have some breakfast—she smelled like the barn.

The area was deserted. She climbed into the car, checked her face in the mirror, and drove down the long laneway.

Lucas had instructed her to take a different route home, so when she came to the end of the laneway, she prepared to turn right. With a sinking heart, she saw Dirk's body tied to the bridge. He was obviously dead; his head had rolled forward. They had shot him several times and tied him to the place where he'd shot the soldier. Lucas would be so upset to hear about this. She didn't see any soldiers around, so maybe they thought he had acted alone. But they would be angered by the disappearance of the truck as well.

She had to get out of the area quickly and hope that no one had figured out that Dirk had worked with a partner. If anyone had seen this car, they might realize it was connected to the attack. The Germans would search everywhere for the truck as well. They were probably planning to punish others in retribution. Why hadn't Dirk followed the plan? Lina felt so frustrated she wanted to cry, but she knew she had to get away from there.

Her hands shook as she gripped the wheel. She was hungry and afraid. She tried to calm herself by taking deep breaths. Turning away from the scene, she took the south road, then headed east, and finally went north. Some of the secondary roads were in rough shape, so she had to slow down. While she drove, she rehearsed her cover story.

When she got to town, she was relieved to be closer to home, but she knew she needed to remain alert. After parking the car beside the hospital, she went inside. No one bothered her, and she tried to appear as if she were hurrying in for her shift.

In the basement, she found an employee locker room where she could change and wash her face. Putting on her own clothes felt good. She rolled up the uniform and put the wool cap over her hair. She reminded herself to walk slowly through the hospital and not raise any suspicions. The guard at the front door appeared bored and didn't pay much attention to the people passing through the entrance.

She silently thanked Lucas when she saw that her bike was in the rack as he had promised. Although she had a strong urge to go to his apartment to tell him what she had seen, he had been very clear that she was to go straight home where he would get in touch with her.

She was not going to do anything to deviate from the plan he'd given her—she wanted his approval, not another lecture on how she lacked discipline. Lucas was going to be upset that the mission had gone awry, and she hoped he wouldn't blame her. She refused to take the blame for something that was not her fault. Hopefully Lucas would understand that the whole thing had gone wrong thanks to Dirk—she didn't want him to think that women couldn't be trusted to follow the instructions for a mission.

59.

LINA

WHEN Lina got home after the disastrous trip with Dirk, she helped herself to a bowl of Ada's broth and then went upstairs to sleep. Ada had left a note that they'd gone to the neighbor's house.

Lina was so anxious after the mission that she didn't think she would be able to rest, but the bed was familiar, and she fell into a deep sleep.

When she got up, Ada and Benji were in the kitchen where Benji was building a tower with blocks on the floor.

Ada introduced Benji to her.

Lina smiled at him and sat down on the floor with him. She handed him a block for his tower, and he nodded.

"Did everything go all right yesterday?" Ada asked.

"There were a few problems. Did Lucas say when he would come? Because I really need to talk to him."

"He should be here soon."

When Lucas arrived, Ada was upstairs putting Benji to bed for a nap.

"How much did you see?" he asked in a whisper. "I never would have put you into a situation like that." His hand rested on her arm, and he looked at her with concern. She sensed that he wanted to hug her but resisted. She wished he would. The last day had been a nightmare. She still felt shaky from fear.

"I did exactly what you said, but when I started driving down the laneway after he had tied up the soldier, I heard a shot. I parked the car behind the barn and hid in the barn, waiting for Dirk to arrive. After he drove the truck into the barn, he told me he had shot the guy and was leaving immediately. I tried to talk him out of that, but he wasn't about to listen to me."

Lucas got up from the table and paced around the kitchen.

Lina watched him pace but didn't say a word. Now that he knew she had survived, she could see him trying to assess the potential damage of this incident.

He stopped in front of the kitchen sink and stared out the window. His shoulders were tense, and his fists were clenched. "Sometimes they kill ten prisoners for every German that has been killed, but last night they killed fifty."

Lina had never seen him this upset. The burden of responsibility had to be crushing. He could not take it out on Dirk because he was dead, but he felt responsible for the retribution unleashed on innocent people.

He had turned away and paced the kitchen. His unwillingness to look at her probably meant he was furious with her too. It wasn't fair— she had followed his instructions to the letter. She could hardly swallow, she felt so anxious. Lucas was clearly struggling to contain his anger. She did what he had told her to do, and if that wasn't obvious to him, she couldn't defend herself.

There was nothing she could have said or done to stop Dirk from following his disastrous course. Surely Lucas knew Dirk well enough to realize he was completely hardheaded and impulsive. Someone that un-stable should never have been assigned to an important mission, but it was not her job to point that out to him.

As the silence grew heavy, Lucas turned and looked at her. "Tell me again," he ordered in a brusque tone.

She did not like his tone, and her voice initially cracked because she was nervous. But then she gathered her resolve and recounted the events again. "I didn't know what to do, but because you said it was important to stay there for the night, that's what I did." She hoped he would get the message that she had faithfully followed his instructions.

Lina paused in case he wanted to ask any questions, but he contin-ued to pace in silence—it was intimidating and uncomfortable. "When I left in the morning, I drove to the corner, looked over at the bridge, and I saw Dirk tied up there. He'd been shot multiple times. Because he was clearly dead, I decided there was nothing I could do for him, but I needed to leave the area right away."

Lucas ran his fingers through his hair and sighed in frustration.

What else did he want to know? "I followed your directions, took a different route home, and made my way to the hospital without being stopped. I changed out of my uniform and biked home making sure I wasn't followed." When Lucas still didn't respond, Lina continued. "I'm sorry about Dirk, but he was an arrogant ass." He could at least acknowledge that she had done her part of the job, taken the risks, and returned safely home.

Lucas turned from Lina and began to pace again. "Why didn't he do what he was supposed to do? Now there will be all kinds of repercussions."

Losing patience with the feeling that Lucas was judging her along with Dirk, she decided to push back. "You knew Dirk was difficult when you gave him the job. He seemed very volatile to me. I was shocked when he showed up in the barn and told me what he had done."

Lucas sat down on the kitchen chair and held his head in his hands. "It is impossible to run this organization without competent help. I don't know how I'm supposed to do the work when I can't rely on people."

Lina tried to console him. "How many successful missions have you had so far? This one did not go as planned, but it's just one out of many."

"And look how many people will pay for that mistake." Lucas held his palms out, wanting her to realize the extent of the disaster.

"I understand—it is terrible that so many people have been punished." She didn't need to be reminded of that. Maybe she could divert his attention by giving him some advice. "You might consider using women for important jobs as they are very competent and reliable. Unless you are too old-fashioned."

He was surprised. "I am not old-fashioned," he argued, looking quite offended, "and women get all kinds of assignments."

Lina shrugged. "I know they are bicycle couriers, but they could do more. Of course, I am not supposed to socialize with anyone, so I don't know much about how you organize the work."

"You have shown that women can be cool under pressure and even follow orders."

Lina wasn't sure if he was being patronizing or sarcastic, so she didn't respond and kept a neutral expression on her face.

Lucas wasn't done complaining about Dirk. "I don't know why he thought he had to shoot that soldier. He had clear instructions to tie him up and get out of there. For the next while, you need to keep your head down and stay out of public view." He turned to face her and asked, "Can you do that?"

Lina nodded. "Of course," she said. She was surprised to hear his concern for her safety, but she hoped he didn't think that she was incompetent. His brow was furrowed, and his shoulders seemed to carry an impossible weight. It had to be a burden to coordinate all this and to carry the worries with him everywhere. At one time he had been a history student, sitting in a pub after class with his friends, and now he was responsible for people's lives. She wanted to be annoyed with him, and yet she felt like he needed some encouragement.

It was confusing to work for him and be his friend. Lina wished she could ask him how he felt about that, but she didn't dare. Had Father asked him to look after them, or did he choose to spend time with them—or more specifically, with her? Were they friends, comrades, or something else? Even if this wasn't the time, did he ever imagine a future in which they might become more than friends?

"What about my cleaning job? It will look suspicious if I don't show up for work."

"Follow your usual schedule, but then come directly home and don't go anywhere else. They will be searching everywhere and will pick up innocent people just to make a point."

She touched his arm briefly. "I am sorry it went wrong, and I hope you can still use the truck."

He still looked upset. "We'll have to wait for a while because they'll be looking for that vehicle and will shoot anyone driving it. It's just too dangerous to use it right now."

"How will you get those pilots to Belgium?"

"I don't know." He sighed and looked exhausted. "Are you certain that no one saw you?" he asked, his eyes showing a deep concern.

"I'm sure. Unless someone was hidden in the forest, that soldier was alone." Lina felt very confident that she would have seen a second soldier anywhere near that truck.

He took a breath and stood up. "Say goodbye to Ada for me. Be careful," he said, placing his hand briefly on her shoulder before turning to go.

He didn't need to remind her to be careful; she planned to watch her back very carefully—thanks to Dirk. The whole mission left her with an overwhelming sense of failure—they had failed to deliver the truck that Lucas urgently needed, and Dirk had killed a soldier for some unknown reason, setting off a cycle of retribution that had already cost many innocent lives and would claim even more.

She hated to disappoint Lucas. Maybe he would always associate her with this failure. This might be the end of any possibility between them— which, she had to admit, had grown in her mind but was not necessarily shared by him. How easily she had become used to his presence in their kitchen, enjoying conversation over any food they could find to share. Somehow, without noticing it, she had become accustomed to looking for him, scanning the streets for him, waiting for his knock on the back door. What a fool she was to invest in something that was probably just an embarrassing schoolgirl crush.

Although it would have been nice to have his approval, she was confident that she had fulfilled his instructions, even if the rest didn't go according to plan. That had to be enough, so she tried not to feel let down by how the events unfolded. If he didn't trust her or approve of her work, then he needed to tell her. Otherwise, she had done what he had asked. If he blamed her for the failure of his mission, she would not accept the blame. But this was not the day to argue with him. They were both tired and upset, and nothing good would come of that.

PART IV

Late Spring–Summer 1945

60.

ADA

A FTER Ada's work at the orphanage ended, she spent a few weeks in March working at the local health clinic where she helped the staff assess the nutritional status of children prior to their evacuation to the northern and eastern parts of the country. Food was still available on farms in those regions, and some host families accepted children for an extended stay.

Her neighbors the Groens were happy to watch Benji during her volunteer hours. Benji loved doing projects in the kitchen with her or in Mr. Groen's woodworking shop. Although it had been years since he had undertaken any building projects, he had kept a bin full of remnants from previous building projects that were the perfect size for Benji to learn to hammer and saw. Weeks had passed, and between her volunteer jobs and caring for Benji, Ada felt happier than she'd been in a long time.

There was some progress on the food relief efforts as Swedish planes dropped supplies of flour and margarine. Ada had heard rumors that liberation of the northeastern part of the country had begun at the end of March. Owen was very busy these days and had missed a Sunday dinner due to work-related travel. Ada noticed increased activity with the Canadians. Both Owen and Lucas seemed optimistic.

Benji seemed to adapt to his new home. Nights were the most difficult for him—he had nightmares and cried out in the dark. Owen gave him a small flashlight to keep him company when he was afraid and a teddy bear. On the nights when Benji wet the bed, Ada changed him, tucked him into her bed, and changed the linens. Now that everything had to be washed by hand in cold water, it was a lot of extra work, but Ada didn't mind. He looked so vulnerable when he awoke in the middle of the night. She hugged him and sang songs from her childhood to put him back to sleep.

Owen and Lucas renovated Mother's sewing room after Lina had packed up most of the fabric and supplies. They added shelving for his toys and books, and Ada placed a cozy reading chair in the corner. He played in that room during the day, and Ada read books to him in that chair, but when it was bedtime he seemed happy to continue sleeping on the cot in Ada's room.

Although Lykke was convinced that time would heal, Ada still planned to take him to a child psychologist for assessment. She wanted to make sure she was doing everything she could to support his learning. There were times when she was so tired and discouraged that she wanted to weep. But he was such an easy child to love—his brown eyes shone when he found something interesting. His curiosity helped her pay attention to things she would otherwise have missed.

Working at the clinic showed her how sustained hunger damaged children. When the children showed up at the clinic in scruffy clothes with sunken cheeks and hollow eyes, many of them had runny noses, coughs, skin conditions, and intestinal problems. Without medical or dental care during the war years, they presented multiple and often complex needs. Ada found it challenging to remain cheerful and positive around these children and their parents, but they needed all the encouragement they could get. The parents worried about how their children would catch up after being malnourished and unschooled for most of their lives. Ada understood their concern and, for the first time, shared it with them.

Sometimes she wondered if the children she saw in the clinic knew how to read, draw, or play. Some of them had been confined to small spaces, hiding from the occupiers, and warned to keep silent at all costs. Others had been put to work searching for food or stealing necessities. She couldn't imagine how they would adapt to a regular schedule of schooling. Teachers would need to find ways to make up for the years of education that had been lost. With so many schools burned to the ground and textbooks destroyed, it would be a challenge to build schools, purchase supplies, and train teachers able to meet the many challenges.

Ada filled in the admission charts for each child that arrived at the clinic, including their height, weight, and age. Her interactions with the children allowed her to make note of suspected developmental delays or other issues related to poor nutrition. One of the nurses, Jakoba, was a very good instructor who taught Ada how to do assessments.

Ada wondered how many calories would support a child's growth if they developed a supplemental feeding routine for each age group. She wanted to ask the clinic doctor, but he was very brusque and unwilling to teach. In her opinion, he didn't have the personality to be a good pediatrician.

While she worked in the utility room to clean dishes and cups, she thought about how this experience had already helped to clarify her future study goals. Once the university reopened, she hoped to study the topic of nutritional supplementation. Famine, war, and natural disasters would probably recur around the world, but countries needed help to be better prepared.

In her experience, the community work was more effective than the efforts by government, but when the demand exceeded resources, the community networks became irrelevant. The needs of children had to be a priority for governments if they wanted to ensure the future of their country.

At the clinic, the nurses sorted the children into two groups—namely, those who required urgent supplements and those who were deemed able to endure the evacuation trip north. She checked her assessments with the intake nurse who praised her work.

"You seem very interested in all this," Jakoba said, "and I'm happy to see a young person excited by this work."

"I would like to study this more when the university reopens."

"We need more research," Jakoba said. "There will always be disasters that affect the food supply, and children are the most vulnerable. When you become a researcher, remember one thing."

"What would that be?" Ada asked.

"Ask the children for their perspective. Too many researchers ignore the people they intend to study. Don't assume that wealthy countries have well-nourished children—there can be hunger and malnutrition in the most unexpected places."

Ada nodded. "I wonder if there will be courses where I can learn those kinds of things."

"You might have to be creative and spend time doing internships in places or with agencies that deal with food issues. Politics will always be a factor during times of food scarcity."

"Our government could have organized a better distribution of available food and a more efficient harvest this fall. The factors that got in the way are very complicated. I wonder how informed the government-in-exile is, or whether their priorities match the needs of the people. But perhaps I know nothing of the situation and should keep my opinions to myself. That's why I try to concentrate on my own small corner in this clinic."

"Do you think the children's evacuation is a good idea?" Ada asked.

"At the moment it seems to be the only idea—if these children go hungry much longer, there will be long-term consequences. But the trip and the relocation will be difficult for some of the children and for their parents. We must trust that they will be treated kindly by their hosts and that they will be returned to their families when the time is right."

Ada knew that several evacuation trips had been completed, but weather and unpredictable bombing raids had delayed others. Neither train nor boat travel was possible, so trucks with willing drivers had to be found. Few drivers were willing to take the risks that were inherent in such a dangerous journey.

That the occupiers provided support to this mission was still a surprise. She'd always thought that people were either bad or good, but this challenged her opinion—the occupiers had donated food and funds to support the transport and promised not to bomb the evacuees.

Ada decided to follow Jakoba's example and focus on the work that needed to be done. She put her cup away and went to the waiting room. Ada gathered the smallest children in a circle. With the finger puppets she kept in the pockets of her lab coat, she created stories about the characters. The mothers looked at Ada with gratitude as they leaned back into the clinic chairs, closing their eyes with relief.

Some parents were reluctant to be parted from their children, but others appeared eager to send children away—the burden of caring for them and others in the family was perhaps too great. Ada knew that if anyone had suggested that she send Benji north to stay with strangers, she would have resisted it with all her might. She would rather deny herself food than force him to travel to another strange location.

Working in the clinic made Ada think about the things she had learned from her mother's diary. Getting pregnant had resulted in her exile from her family home, but she had tried to carry on and do her best. Without family support, Janny must have felt abandoned. Even when she married a brilliant young graduate student who was willing to help her raise the baby, her parents refused to reconcile. Ada couldn't imagine how painful that must have been. Janny's parents didn't see forgiveness as an option. She felt sorry for her grandparents who believed that judgement was more important than love, or perhaps they thought that judgement was love.

Biking home at the end of her shift, she thought about the things she had learned. The clinic placement had helped to clarify the future direction of her studies—if she was lucky enough to resume those studies someday.

As Ada turned into their street, she knew that she had to tell Lina about Mother's diary as soon as possible. She couldn't justify keeping this secret any longer.

Each day that passed would make it harder to explain why she had withheld this from Lina. Her deepest fear was that Lina would reject her as her sister.

61.

LINA

THAT same night, after Benji was in bed, Ada made a pot of tea and brought some cups to the table. Lina thanked her but didn't look up from her sketch. When she finally did glance up from the page, Ada was still standing by the table.

"Lina," Ada said, "there's something I need to tell you. The clinic is desperately looking for a travel chaperone for one of the last trucks to evacuate children, and it will leave in two days. Is there any chance you'd consider going?"

Lina looked up in surprise. "Me?"

"One of the chaperones became ill, and the children can't travel without supervision."

Lina rolled her eyes. "Sounds like a nightmare—stuck in a truck with screaming kids."

"Please, Lina. I can't leave Benji. He just got here."

Lina sighed.

"It might make an interesting story to document the evacuation," Ada suggested.

Lina looked up from her sketchbook. She'd walked around the city with her camera hoping to shoot another series of photos on a relevant subject, but nothing caught her eye. The American editor had requested human interest photographs related to the war—she didn't want to keep him waiting too long, but it was difficult to find an interesting story. The evacuation of children to the care of strangers would have a great deal of emotional appeal.

"For how long?" Lina asked.

"It will take a few days to get there because the driver can only travel at night. Planes from both sides will shoot anything that moves during the day. He will be able to travel faster on the return journey, although he'll still be restricted to night driving. I could cover your shift at the Captain's house," Ada added.

"I would need to talk to Lucas to make sure he doesn't need anything."

Ada smiled. "I ran into him in town today, and he thought it was a good idea. He suggested you get in touch with him when you return. He thought you might appreciate an excuse to get out of town for a few days."

Lina looked at her. "I suppose. What about food on the trip?"

"Volunteers are putting together supplies. The driver will stop at prearranged towns where meals will be served by the locals."

"Small mercies," Lina said. "I hope I survive it." But Lucas was right—it was a good time to leave town for a while.

Lina didn't bring much with her on the evacuation trip—she packed a change of clothes and her camera in her knapsack. She hoped that one of their hosts would let them wash, but she wasn't counting on it.

When she saw the truck near the orphanage, she realized that her worst fears were about to be realized. Some children clung to their parents and refused to get into the truck. Once inside, they were inconsolable. Lina worried about one little girl who appeared listless and feverish, but many others were skinny and lethargic. She hoped she would not pick up an infection from the kids or an infestation of lice. Just the thought of it was enough to make her start scratching her head in fear.

Stepping forward, Lina introduced herself to the other chaperones who stood apart from the children while waiting for someone to tell them what to do. Apparently, the person she'd replaced was supposed to be the team leader. She had no desire to put herself in charge, but the children would soon turn into a crying mess if they didn't sense that someone was in charge. She took a big breath and stepped towards the other volunteers.

Lina gathered them into a circle and explained that they would each be responsible for a small group of children. At every stop, they had to make sure their group was complete before the truck left. They were to report to her any concerns about their charges so they could decide together what action to take. They nodded and appeared to accept her leadership—relieved that they were not the leader.

Before they left, Lina distributed an enamel cup and a travel bag to each child and reminded them not to share the cups. She had a bag full of sandwiches and cookies that volunteers had prepared for them.

At the last minute, two resistance workers joined the convoy to obtain safe passage to the north. Ada had warned her that they might have some extra riders. Apparently, the children's evacuations gave some people who needed to get away a legitimate cover for travel. The couple looked with dismay at the truck as the children were being loaded. Perhaps they had imagined a quiet trip to the north, not countless hours in a truck with crying and unbathed children.

Lina decided to speak to the couple to try to elicit some cooperation. "As you can see, we are very shorthanded, and I would appreciate some help. If you could sit with them and find ways to distract them, it will help this trip pass more quickly for all of us." Shortly after she made that suggestion, the couple joined a group of older children, and Lina turned her attention to the younger ones.

Once everyone was inside, Lina signaled to the driver that he could leave. The sky was dark and without stars. As they pulled away, Lina saw that some mothers had left immediately after they dropped off their children, but others stayed to wave them off. They had to be desperate, she thought, to put their child on a truck with strangers. They would be driven through a war zone and then delivered to a farm to be cared for by people they'd never met before. It took an enormous amount of trust or desperation.

Lina realized they had managed thus far to keep a minimal food supply at home. With food gifts that Owen brought over for their Sunday night dinners and leftovers that Raoul sent home with her, they'd been able to feed Benji and themselves. Things seemed to be changing slowly—Owen assured them of growing cooperation on the food relief front. The occupiers seemed to be willing to allow food drops and other forms of relief. He explained that the Allied generals delayed progress because they wanted to achieve strategic victory before addressing the food relief question. What was the point of military victory if the citizens starved to death? Owen had shrugged and said they all had to do their jobs and leave the rest to the governments involved.

When adults failed to protect children and vulnerable people, Lina believed they committed a crime. The war had gone on long enough and had damaged everything in sight. Her initial hopes to avenge the deaths of her father and of Jos had been naive. Having blown up buildings, hijacked food supplies, and transported people to safe houses, Lina felt like she'd tried to help end the war, but nothing they did seemed to make much difference. Once a war was started, it seemed to have its own momentum, pushing forward like a hurricane in a destructive path.

She would do this assignment, take the pictures, and with Owen's help get them developed through his army contacts. The more she practiced, the stronger her instincts became for getting a good picture. Sometimes her fingers tingled when it was time to start shooting, and the weight of the camera in her hands was so familiar. Some kind of harmony occurred when she was engaged in a shoot, as if she were playing a piece on a musical instrument from memory. Father had often reminded her to listen for the stories behind the images; she wished she could tell him that she was beginning to understand all the parts that worked in harmony to create an exceptional photograph.

Lina put her knapsack under her head and carefully spread the army blanket over her, tucking in the edges to preserve some heat. She trusted the driver to navigate the dangers and get them to their destination.

The children coughed and cried as they wrapped themselves in their Red Cross blankets and tried to sleep. It wasn't easy—the truck bounced and jolted over rough roads. Lina knew the driver was trying to avoid something more lethal than potholes. Driving without lights, he hoped to escape the notice of any aircraft looking for targets.

She wondered if the responsibility weighed heavily on him or if he managed not to think about it. Perhaps he had children at home who were waiting for his return to see if he brought any food from the north.

Lina rearranged the contents of her knapsack so her head wouldn't rest on the edges of her camera body or lens. It was impossible to get comfortable on the floor of this truck. She needed to think about something to distract herself from the discomfort.

What if photography ended up being a career? Perhaps all this misery would have a happy ending. Ada had made a good point—as a professional photographer, she could either set up a studio or travel around the world. She liked travel, and she wouldn't need to pay rent for a fixed place if she kept moving. Ada reassured her that she could always return home.

Bumping around in the back of a truck provided excellent training for life on the road with her camera. If Lucas thought she might have potential as a photographer, she wondered if he had considered that such a path would take her far from home. Maybe he didn't care. He wanted to finish his studies and find a job when the war ended—neither of those things had anything to do with her. Maybe when she returned from this trip, he would welcome her with a big hug. She smiled in the dark at the thought.

But to be a good enough photographer to make a living from her work, she still had so much to learn. She had tried reading Father's books, but ideas didn't stick with her. She had to learn by doing, but she wanted that to happen quickly. Sometimes it was a matter of listening to people's response to her pictures. Owen had suggested that her portraits would be more powerful if she opened herself to her subjects and interacted with them.

At one of their dinners, Owen explained how he felt. "Listen, Lina, you don't have to prove that you are tough. I already know that. When you take pictures, you need to be open to your subject. Something magical might emerge from that. But if you hide behind the lens, you will never discover the spark that connects you to the subject of the photo."

During the evacuation trip, Lina kept a close eye on the food supplies— she even slept near them. Fortunately, kind people along their route provided meals and gave them some respite from the long hours in the truck. Children curled up on the floor of the church halls where they napped until it was time to resume the journey. Others ran around in the churchyard to burn off some energy.

Lina was impressed with the kindness and generosity of the strangers who cooked and served food to them. Although the role of leader had fallen to her, she was surprised to find she was good at it. Sorting out conflicts, reassuring children, directing the other volunteers—she managed it smoothly. Maybe someone would accuse her of being bossy, but it was important to get people organized.

The truck reminded her of the one that she and Dirk had taken from the driver that day. She wondered if it was still hidden in the barn or whether it had been used to get the airmen to Belgium. Dirk's change of plan would never be clear; Lucas said he had been taking Pervitin to stay awake and sleeping pills to calm down. He had been agitated that day they drove to the country, but she had thought that was just his personality.

Many had died after that botched mission. Hopefully the truck had been put into service to rescue others.

She hadn't seen Lucas for a while after that mess with Dirk. Lina had been worried that he held her responsible for the failed mission. When Ada said he had been away the past two weeks, Lina was relieved to hear that he wasn't simply avoiding her.

She was confused about him. She tried to talk herself out of it but without success. Maybe this trip would provide a perfect way to reset her mind and return without the complication of romance. If he didn't feel anything for her, there was no point in wasting another second thinking about him.

The last time she had seen him, he dropped by the house while Ada was at the clinic.

"Lina, do you have a minute?" he asked.

"I don't know, I'm busy." She wasn't sure she wanted to hear what he had to say. Maybe he was about to fire her from the work.

"I want to apologize for the way I spoke after the terrible incident with Dirk. I know that it was not your fault. I was under a lot of pressure to deliver that truck, but that was minor compared to what you had experienced. I should have been more aware of what you risked. Many people depended on me, and it was embarrassing to have things go wrong." He paused to search her face and then continued. "I apologize for being more concerned with myself than with you. I want you to know that you did exactly what you were supposed to, and the rest was not your fault. In fact, I am grateful you stayed calm when things went wrong and carried on with the plan. If you had overreacted, more lives would have been lost."

Lina studied him for a few moments. The apology seemed genuine. "Thanks for saying so. I appreciate that." There was a moment when she thought he might hug her, but instead they shook hands.

When the truck began to slow, Lina pulled herself out of her reverie and looked around. Children were sleeping, and a bit of morning light was creeping in.

They stopped to rest at a farm that had a large barn attached to the house. Women from the village helped to organize the children, separating them into groups of boys and girls. The women were very clear in their instructions, and the children responded without protest to wash in a designated area. After that, the women served them watered-down oatmeal with a small amount of milk for breakfast before they were told to rest in the loft. The leaders promised them outdoor playtime afterwards.

Lina watched a girl who was around ten years of age keep a tight grip on her little brother's hand, probably following her mother's instructions. Lina took pictures of them as they sat at the table. The little girl wore a serious expression as she kept watch over her brother. Were older siblings trained early to take responsibility, or was it built into their character? Had Ada been instructed to keep watch over her? Lina had always assumed that she was just bossy.

Two of the children who had a fever were isolated in a makeshift sick bay where an experienced nurse took care of them. Their hostess advised Lina to leave the sick children with them until they got better. In their place, she chose two others who had recently recovered from influenza. Lina had no instructions on making that kind of trade, but to be safe she noted the children's names on the manifest and hoped that the sick children would soon follow on the next convoy. They had the potential to infect all the others, including the volunteers, and that was not a risk she was prepared to take.

The woman in charge of the farm told Lina that she'd cared for hundreds of evacuated children and was confident that this was the right thing to do.

They ended up staying at the farm an extra night, which was the third night of the trip, because the driver didn't think it was safe to proceed due to the volume of planes overhead. Luckily no other convoys were expected, and the children were relieved to spend another night in the same place, where they were assured of food and beds. The farm also provided a rare opportunity to play outside, whether kicking a ball or playing hide and seek.

On the fourth day, the skies were quiet, so the driver told them they would travel and stop for a meal in a small town. Lina took pictures of the volunteers who fed them—plain-faced farm women with rough hands who knew how to put solid meals on the table with minimal fuss. After chatting with them, she found a corner from which she could take pictures.

The women seemed both shy and pleased at the attention, and they joked with each other as they struck poses for the camera. Lina tried to capture the sense of community she saw in both their laughter and their work. She was more interested in the unposed pictures when they forgot the camera was on them, but she took the posed ones to keep them happy.

When they climbed back in the truck, the children were subdued. Sometimes Lina nodded off only to wake up with a child snuggling close for comfort. Coughing and cries filled the interior of the truck throughout the night, but they'd become accustomed to it. They rolled and bumped together, huddling close to keep warm. Lina felt like she was in a twilight state that was neither fully awake nor deeply asleep. Time seemed elastic as days flowed into nights. It was good to see the children running and having fun at their rest stops. She hoped that their memories of this time would be good ones.

She was on alert in case there was any problem with the truck or with a child. Never would she take for granted her bed at home or the simple food Ada cooked. Lina pictured some of Ada's homemade jam and the stews she crafted with minimal ingredients, and she imagined Lucas having dinner with them. She hoped to see him again when she got home. This trip had not erased him from her heart and mind—instead, she found she missed him more than ever.

62.

LINA

WHEN the truckload of evacuees finally arrived in the center of Groningen, having undergone a few detours and unscheduled stops along the way, the assembled crowd represented various churches and towns. With an atmosphere resembling a Saturday market day, people pushed and cheered, trying to grab children while ignoring the arrangements made for them by the organizers. They had done their best to match children with families of similar backgrounds, but things didn't go as smoothly as planned.

As two women came forward to claim their guests, they checked their small bags for the ration cards and enamel dinnerware that the children were supposed to bring. One woman demanded to know where the girl's clothes were, but the little girl was too terrified to speak and looked to Lina for help. Lina told the woman in a quiet, firm voice that she didn't have any other clothes.

As she watched the children match up with their hosts, Lina wondered if some parents had withheld ration cards before putting their children on the truck, hoping to collect on those supplies while having one less mouth to feed in their household.

They were herded into a church hall where the women had prepared a welcome meal for the evacuees. Lina took pictures of the children who were too shy to interact with the strangers. When the women put huge bowls of mashed potatoes on the table, the children watched in silence, waiting for the signal to eat.

After the local pastor said grace, the children dove into their food. Lina had warned them to go slowly, but the temptation was too great.

They ate as fast as they could, unsure when they would see another hot meal.

It didn't take long before several children were in acute distress from the unaccustomed food. They clutched their stomachs, sat on the floor against the wall, or searched for the bathrooms. Lina wanted nothing more than to go to sleep in some quiet corner, but she tried to smile and reassure the children through this transition. *Make this trip end*, she thought.

When the driver of the truck asked one of the church ladies to direct him to a place where he could get some sleep before he drove home, she showed him a pew in the sanctuary and gave him a pillow. Lina wished she could do the same, but there was still a fair amount of chaos, and she didn't dare walk away until all the children had been matched to their hosts. Some of the smallest children wanted to be picked up and held, but she couldn't do that for all of them. After traveling together, they seemed to trust her. Some of the other chaperones had already gone off to the nearby park to smoke cigarettes and take a break from the children. She couldn't blame them, but she resented it.

Lina overheard several women arguing, so she went to the kitchen to investigate. Two women fought over a little girl who looked terrified. Lina took some pictures and then slung her camera over her shoulder and out of the way.

"Stop this!" Lina yelled as she marched into the fray. "What do you think you're doing?" She put her arms around the little girl and glared at the women. "Can't you see you're scaring her? Now what's going on?"

"Although she was assigned a boy, now she wants this girl. I have confirmation that she is supposed to go with me." The woman waved a piece of paper.

"Let me see the paper." Lina studied it and looked at the little girl. "The agency has arranged for her to go with you." She turned to the other woman. "Where is your guest?"

The woman pointed to a little boy standing in the corner of the room looking forlorn.

"You better go comfort him. His mother would not want him to feel rejected. How would you feel? That little boy trusts you to take care of him."

The woman glared at Lina and realized she'd lost the fight. She turned away in a huff and walked towards the boy. She didn't say a word to him, just waved her hand to tell him to follow her. The other woman crouched down to the little girl's height. "I think you'll like our farm. We have a horse and some bunnies. I'll need your help to collect eggs from the hens. Do you think you can do that?"

The little girl nodded solemnly. It was that easy, Lina thought, to reach out to a child. She took a photograph of the pair and then watched them walk away.

One of the ladies gave Lina a bag for the driver filled with vegetables. "I hope you have a good trip home. Thanks for bringing these children to us. Please know that we'll take good care of them. Here are some sandwiches for the trip."

Lina was touched by her kindness. "Thank you so much."

As she helped the women wash the dishes; she felt lightheaded from lack of sleep, but she knew she'd feel worse if she had a nap. Without their passengers, she planned to sleep in the truck all the way home.

The hall emptied out as the farm families returned home to take care of chores. They left by horse and wagon or bicycle and cart. The children called out to their friends and waved goodbye. Some looked terrified, and others were excited to start a new adventure.

Another woman brought Lina a bag filled with vegetables. "I thought you might be able to use this," she said.

"Thank you." Lina looked in amazement at the onions, potatoes, and carrots. Ada would be very grateful to receive this food.

Lina pictured putting the bag on the kitchen counter and climbing the stairs to her own bed. She couldn't wait to be home again.

The driver returned to the community hall, rubbing his eyes and looking around for his passengers. He was ready to begin the drive home, and Lina was eager to get going as well. She rounded up the chaperones and said goodbye to the women in the church hall.

The couple had already faded away to their next hiding place without saying a word. Perhaps they'd found a safe place to wait out the war, but Lina thought it would have been nice if they had thanked the driver or said goodbye. Maybe they were in some kind of danger and needed to move to a new area.

The volunteers piled into the truck and stretched out with blankets to get comfortable. Lina sat in the front with the driver. Luckily, he was a man of few words who concentrated on the driving. His calm focus made her feel safe enough to fall into a deep sleep, leaning her cheek into the window against which she'd rolled up her jacket to buffer her face on the bumpy roads.

After a night in the truck, they stopped in a small town that had promised to host them on their way back. The driver, Bart, knocked at the door of a small farmhouse.

"Come in, I've been expecting you. I have a big breakfast ready, and then you can sleep in the barn until it's dark enough to leave."

Lina couldn't believe her eyes. In addition to freshly baked bread, their hostess also provided bacon, eggs, and some fried potatoes. They ate without talking, enjoying the food and savoring the freshly baked bread.

Although she'd slept in the truck, she was still tired, so it didn't take long before she was fast asleep in the loft of the barn. When she woke up, her hostess gave her a basin of warm water and a washcloth and towel. They climbed into the truck as darkness fell over the countryside.

That night, the skies were overcast with no planes passing overhead. Without their young passengers, they could travel for longer intervals without stops. Lina hoped the children were sleeping soundly in the homes of their host families. When it was time for them to return home, they would have stories to tell.

As they got closer to town, the driver stopped to let off the two volunteers at the crossroads where they lived.

Lina was grateful when he offered to drop her at the front door of her house.

It was early morning, and the street was very quiet. She hoped that the noise of the truck wouldn't wake the neighbors. A pale streak of pink light was visible on the eastern horizon. Even if other people were waking up, Lina wanted to go straight to bed.

"Thank you for your help," she told Bart as she shook his hand.

"You did good work back there," he said. "Maybe we'll take another load up north soon."

"Or maybe this damn war will end before we need to," Lina said as she closed the door and waved.

As she let herself in through the back door into the kitchen, she thought of the children who were sleeping in strange beds. A long time ago, she'd been in a strange bed far from home. She tried to think of something else, but that unwanted memory pursued her up the stairs and into bed. She had pushed this memory away for a long time, but it demanded her attention now.

Sleep would be impossible, so she got up to sit at her desk and began to write. Perhaps once she put it into words, it would leave her alone.

Writing as if it were about someone else gave her some distance from the events—the details, however, were still as vivid as if it had happened yesterday. She planned to write it out and then burn it so that the memory would no longer have a place in her life.

63.

LINA

THAT summer in 1938, the summer she turned thirteen, Lina was sent to stay with Oom Jaap and Tante Truus in Eindhoven. At the time, it seemed like a better option than staying home where she would be given lists of chores and told to do summer reading for school.

Oom Jaap was a big boss at Philips. Whenever he visited his sister-in-law's house, he ate and drank too much, made stupid jokes, and laughed loudly at them even if no one else did. One time, he even he grabbed the housekeeper who told him in very clear French to take his hands off her. Tante Truus pretended not to notice. She was busy showing off her latest Parisian handbag. Father didn't care for Jaap, but he did his best to be hospitable and not look too relieved when they finally packed to return home. Mother usually collapsed after their visits, having put all her energy into trying to impress her sister.

That summer, because Mother hadn't been feeling well, she decided she could only deal with one child at home, and of course she chose Ada, who would wait on her and do everything she asked. Lina never did that for Mother, but Ada was always happy to oblige. Tante Truus was excited, Mother said, to take Lina to her favorite stores and lunches with friends.

Her aunt and uncle picked Lina up in his big German car and smoked cigarettes the whole way to Eindhoven. She pretended to sleep in the car, but the smoke was making her carsick. Tante Truus talked on and on about stupid stuff, and people that she didn't know; her words were like the tap-tapping of someone on a typewriter. Did she ever stop to breathe? Oom Jaap tuned it out and only made minimal comments or grunts when required.

Watching the dykes and bridges, farms, and barns pass by, Lina felt the car taking them further and further away from home. Flowering vines clung with exuberance to the fences. The neat rows of vegetable gardens were bursting with produce, and red and white geraniums filled the window boxes.

When they sat down to dinner, her uncle had already finished at least two generous whiskeys—his face was quite red, and his conversation very loud. Following her aunt's cues, Lina spoke only when spoken to. She pushed around her plate the rich food slathered with cheese sauces and gravy. At home, the housekeeper cooked French food, but it was fresh and digestible. When the maid took away the plate, she could have wept with relief—at home, Father would have insisted that she finish every morsel, but here they didn't mind tossing food in the garbage.

She slept in a small room on the third floor. The window looked out over the garden, which imitated that of a French villa with a pond and bushes trimmed with symmetry. On a family vacation years ago, she had visited Paris and enjoyed parks filled with children and dogs, but this garden was formal and silent. Still, her room was cozy with gabled walls furnished in white furniture and pink linens like some enchanted cottage.

Although it was magazine perfect, the house made her feel like a stranger. She had never been this homesick—it was such an awful feeling in the pit of her stomach. Trying to read Little Women only made it worse—it reminded her of her room and bulletin board and her poster of Paris. She even missed Ada, and that was saying a lot. Why did Mother agree to send her here? Did she just want her out of the house? Perhaps she thought that Tante Truus would teach her something, but that woman was so full of nastiness, she didn't want to learn anything from her. She had an amazing skill for covering it all with a veneer of sweetness, but underneath was pure rage and jealousy.

Tante Truus had a phony way of complimenting her that ended up as a subtle criticism of her parents. She didn't know how her aunt did it—it sounded fine coming out of her mouth until she added a hook that was just mean. Underneath her fancy clothes and upper-class accent, Truus could never have enough.

She was so proud of her house and all the stuff that was crammed into it—things she took from her parents' house. Lina had once heard Mother tell her friends that her sister took everything from her parents and didn't even give her a spoon. All that stuff made the place feel claustrophobic with heavy furniture, brass or copper pots, and dark paintings set in England *showing people on horses chasing foxes. Who would want that on their walls?*

Tante Truus relished the opportunity to show Lina off to her friends. Lina didn't particularly like the dresses she made her try on. She had never liked those party dresses, and she didn't want to become her project. Clothes had a big way of dictating what a person could and couldn't do—sitting in somebody's living room sipping tea was never going to be as exciting as racing a bike over the polder or learning to sail in her Opa's boat. She was trying to make Lina into someone like her.

Lina had to go visiting with her, drinking so much tea that she thought she was going to wet her pants. What a waste of time. The people were so boring—they gossiped about women they knew in town or in church. Hypocrites, that's what they were. She watched the clock in the evening, and as soon as it seemed reasonable, she excused herself to go upstairs to read until bedtime.

That night, she felt relieved to settle in her small room. Because it was warm, she opened the window as far as it would go. Putting on her pajamas, she counted the days remaining until she could go home.

Lost in a novel, she didn't hear a thing until she looked up and saw her uncle in the doorway. For a big man he knew how to move quietly, but the smell of tobacco and whiskey accompanied him wherever he went.

"Are you in bed already?" he asked in a whisper.

That seemed too obvious to bother replying. She sat up and glanced at the doorway, which he was blocking, and the window, which offered no escape.

"What are you doing here?" she asked.

"Just want to say good night to my beautiful niece."

She covered her chest with the open book—he was staring at her in a way that made her uncomfortable.

He took a few steps into the room and stood over her. Then he nudged her leg aside so there'd be room for him to sit on the edge of the narrow bed. Her heart pounded loudly in alarm. The mattress creaked and sagged with his weight. He paused for a moment to make sure that the sound hadn't carried downstairs.

What was she supposed to do? If she yelled for her aunt, she would be angry and even blame her. He had no reason to be in her room. Lina knew she had to find a way out of this. But how?

Mother had never talked to her about men and their ways, preferring to pretend that nothing ever happened, but she had heard plenty from girls at school. They had warned her about things like this—they told her stories about men, strangers, relatives, or farm laborers who took whatever they wanted.

He was a powerful man with a fierce temper. She had seen him explode at the servants when they didn't do things the way he wanted. At this moment he was hiding that power beneath a veneer of phony charm, which did not fool her at all. It felt very dangerous.

He ran his hand up and down her leg through the cotton sheet. Even though the sheet remained in place, it was a flimsy barrier. Her heart was pounding loudly.

She couldn't breathe. "Stop it," she said. "Leave me alone." Her voice came out in a croak.

"My niece is growing up," he said. "There are so many exciting things for her to discover."

"I want to go to sleep now, so please leave," knowing her voice sounded childish in her own ears. She tried to swallow, but her mouth was dry.

He took her hand and placed it on his trousers. She was completely terrified, frozen with fear. She could feel it through the fabric and folds of his pants, and she could see it pushing against the zipper. She yanked her hand back and tried to slide herself away from him, but there was nowhere to go. She was pinned between the wall and his huge body. Her armpits were slippery with sweat.

"Leave me alone," she begged. "I'm going to scream for Aunt Truus if you don't go right now!"

"Such innocence needs experience. I can show you so much," he whispered. "You'll thank me."

His leering smile made her feel ill. She estimated the distance to the doorway and wondered whether she could leap from under the sheet, jump past him, and run down the stairs. How would she explain the flight from her own room?

"Get out of my room now!" she said in a louder voice. She felt her back scrape against the headboard of the bed as she had backed into it as far as she could to get away from him. Something scratched her back right through her pajamas, but she didn't care; she just wanted distance from this disgusting man.

He looked at her in surprise because no one dared talk to him that way.

His arm reached for her chin. He was breathing into her face, and she was so disgusted. She hoped he wasn't going to try to kiss her. She moved her head quickly and bit his wrist hard.

He pulled back and stood up, furious with her, and rubbed his wrist. When he saw blood on his cuff, he cursed her quietly and struck her across the face. The slap sounded loud inside her head. She blinked to keep the tears at bay.

Bastard, she thought to herself. Every curse word she had ever heard rose in her head.

She heard her aunt call. "Jaap, where are you? Are you coming to bed?"

Oom Jaap glared at her and straightened the collar of his shirt and tucked his shirt into his trousers. He turned and left without another word.

She stayed in bed the next two days pleading an upset stomach. When she didn't seem to improve, her aunt finally called her parents to pick her up. She was probably relieved to have an excuse to send her home—Lina was a disappointment to her.

When they arrived to collect her, Tante Truus pulled Mother into the kitchen. They didn't realize that she was standing in the hallway with her bag, waiting impatiently to go home.

"I'm glad you came to get her. I think it's time she left," Tante Truus said.

"Did something happen?" Mother asked.

She sounded afraid, and Lina knew her only concern was that she might have shamed her in front of them and showed a lack of proper up-bringing. That lack of trust infuriated her.

"You're going to need to be very strict with her. I caught her flirting with Jaap in a way that was very suggestive. Watch out for her, she's going to be trouble. And you know what happens next."

"That's very serious," Mother replied. "I'm very sorry she upset your household. I will speak to her."

She almost choked. Mother wanted her to apologize to him. She was furious. What was she talking about, saying 'what happens next'? Did she think Lina was on the verge of becoming a prostitute or getting pregnant? She wanted to march in there and tell her aunt there was no amount of money in the world that would tempt her to do anything with her disgust-ing husband.

"That's not necessary," Tante Truus said. "We understand that it is your job as parent, not ours. But we won't be inviting her back."

"*Again, I'm so sorry. Thank you for being so understanding.*"

Lina went outside and found a place behind the hedge where she could throw up. She wiped her face and dug into her pocket for a peppermint. There was no way she was going back into that house to get a drink of water, so she waited beside the car. How could Mother believe those lies? In a million years, she would never flirt with him, he was disgusting. Why did her aunt cover up for him? Did Tante Truus know he did those kinds of things?

Adults were disgusting. She felt betrayed by them and especially by her mother. During the drive home neither Mother nor Lina spoke. She had made a choice to defend and support her sister instead of her daughter—so Lina made her choice too. She would never trust her mother again.

64.

LINA

WHEN Lina awoke and realized that she was in her own room, she stretched and pulled the covers up to her neck and exhaled. Why did she have to ruin the night with those horrible memories of her uncle's bad behavior? He was gone now, as was her aunt, and all the possessions they were so proud of had disappeared into the hands of Nazis and looters.

Lina felt somewhat relieved to have written it down so that she could destroy it. She had never told anyone because nothing would be accomplished by sharing that sordid experience. Her friends would probably tell her that she was lucky that nothing more happened. But that was not the point—the whole thing had soured her relationship with her mother and with most adults. They simply could not be trusted to protect those who depended on them.

There were many times she had been tempted to talk to Father about it, but he was so intensely loyal to Mother, it might have been difficult for him to hear. He always defended her mother's behavior and urged them to be more loving and accepting of her.

Ada had worked hard to please Mother, but Lina stayed out of her way. Her moods were unpredictable and often unpleasant. Father was lucky he could take refuge in his study, but as Lina got older she spent time with her friends, and no one seemed to miss her.

She needed to put those memories aside. The mission to evacuate children had succeeded. She had to move forward. Lina washed her face and found some clean clothes. She bundled her travel clothes to wash later.

When she walked into the kitchen, Benji's face lit up, and he ran to hug her.

She squatted down to meet him and felt his small arms encircle her neck. "Hello, Benji. I think you grew while I was gone. We better start keeping track of this. Come over here."

Picking up a pencil from the table where he'd been drawing, she led him to the far wall next to the door, where she made a pencil line to mark his height. "We'll measure you regularly," she told him, "and we'll watch as you grow and grow." Lina stood up and pointed to the ceiling and Benji smiled.

He led her to the table where he held up his half-finished drawing.

"That's excellent." She looked at Ada who leaned against the counter and watched them. "Morning."

"Do you want some breakfast?"

"That would be nice, thank you."

"Glad to be home?" she asked.

"You have no idea," Lina replied.

Ada brought a slice of bread baked with flour from the Swedish air drop and a jar of jam to the table and poured a cup of tea for Lina. Ada seemed different, Lina thought as she watched her. She seemed lighter and happier—she even hummed while she cooked.

Lina sat across from Benji and watched him draw—his entire upper body leaned over the page with total concentration. He carefully outlined the object and then shaded the drawing with his pencil tipped at the correct angle just as she had shown him. His willingness to learn and to listen to instruction touched her. How could she have been so unwelcoming to this boy?

Lina looked at Ada's back and wondered how to begin to say what she wanted to say. She cleared her throat. "Ada, I need to apologize. I could have been more supportive of your decision. I regret saying those things, and I hope you can forgive me."

Ada turned and looked surprised. "I understand why you were upset. I should have told you much earlier. I was afraid you would say no, and I did not know how to explain how important this was to me. I am sorry I left it till the last minute."

"I want you to be able to tell me things that are important to you. We may not agree, but we should be able to listen."

Ada nodded. "I agree. There's room for me to improve."

"Wait," Lina said in mock horror. "I thought you were perfect." She began to chuckle, and Ada joined her, and soon they were laughing together.

Benji looked at them in amazement.

Lina reached over and mussed Benji's hair. "Laughter is a good thing," she told him. She turned to Ada. "What's been happening here? Did you cover my shift at the Captain's house?"

"Raoul was very helpful. The Captain wasn't around—I think he went to Germany for some important meetings. The Groen's enjoy taking care of Benji. They always have some kind of project for him, and he has fun."

"Raoul is a nice guy in a bad situation. I'll go back Monday. What about Owen?"

"He's away until next week. The Allies are on the move now that they can get beyond the Rhine. I heard him say that Canadian troops re-entered from Gendringen and Emmerich, and they are heading north to liberate up to the Wadden Sea. The Russians are apparently on their way to Berlin. Owen is very happy that the First Canadian Army has opened the supply route through Arnhem, and they'll be clearing the western part of the country. I am starting to believe that the end is in sight."

"I hope you're right." Lina finished her tea and bread and put the plate and cup on the counter. "Do you mind if I go downstairs for a while? I'd like to start developing the pictures from the trip. If I don't have enough supplies, I will give them to Owen when he returns."

"I can't wait to see them. Everything is under control here. Benji's becoming quite the artist, so if we can book another lesson with you once you are settled in, that would be great."

Lina smiled at him. "We'll do a lesson later."

He looked at her, his brown eyes wide and sparkling. After all the things he had experienced, he trusted her and believed that good things could happen. He would be waiting for the basement door to open in anticipation of his next lesson. Was it possible, she wondered, for adults to regain trust like that?

As she walked down the steps to the basement, she felt an unusual sensation, something she hadn't felt for a very long time. Did she dare hope that victory was possible? She shook the thought from her head. Until those Allies marched in, she was not going to open herself to disappointment. Still there were signs that progress was being made towards peace.

She found herself humming as she worked with the last of her developer and was touched when she saw the portraits of the evacuated children emerge. Their faces showed hope and hunger, as well as longing and fear. The experience was probably something they would carry with them the rest of their lives. She hoped it would be a memory of care instead of one of abandonment, but there were no guarantees of either.

65.

LINA

ON Monday, Lina biked to the Captain's house for her cleaning job. When she arrived, Berthe nodded and turned to her preparations for lunch. The soup on the stove smelled delicious. Even if Berthe didn't have an engaging personality, she knew how to cook, aided by a regular supply of fresh food. A grocer dropped off vegetables once a week, and a butcher delivered meat. It was a clear case of theft, Lina thought, as local people starved. Having seen firsthand the effects of that theft on children made her angry.

Housecleaning had become automatic—she started on the top floors and ended in the kitchen, which she only entered once Berthe had left for the day. Their coexistence demanded that Lina stay out of her way.

"I have to talk to you later," Raoul whispered as he passed her in the hall. Even though Berthe was hard of hearing, they were cautious in her presence.

When Berthe finally left, he interrupted Lina while she polished the enormous dining room table.

"Hurry, we don't have much time," Raoul said.

She sat in her usual spot at the kitchen table, but this time Raoul didn't bother making espresso.

He seemed agitated, and his fingers drummed the table.

Lina looked at him and waited for him to speak. She kept her hands folded on her lap and sat very still until he was ready.

"Things are happening, Lina. I heard him talking to his wife last night. He told her he'll soon be home."

Lina looked at his face. He looked devastated with his eyelids heavy from lack of sleep. "Home? You mean back in Germany? But . . ."

Raoul nodded. "He's been meeting with some of the generals regularly. They believe Hitler is finished, and they want to leap into the vacuum with a strong plan. The Captain may be a candidate for a big promotion in Berlin."

"When?" she asked.

"Very soon," Raoul said. "He's in a hurry to leave before anyone can charge him with war crimes. He's also anxious to claim the job offered him in Berlin before anyone else tries to take it from him."

"What's going to happen to you? I thought he was planning to move with you to South America?" Lina asked.

Raoul shook his head sadly. "He was sent here from Berlin because some of Hitler's people wanted him out of the way—now he wants revenge when he becomes the leader. I hardly recognize him—he's driven by a combination of ambition and anger. To be acceptable, he'll need his wife and family by his side."

She touched his hand. "I'm so sorry. When you're ready, stay with us for a while until you figure out what's next. I'll give you the address. We have plenty of room."

"Thank you, Lina."

"I'm serious. You need a safe place where you can figure out what you want to do next. Maybe you could work on your portfolio while you stay with us."

Raoul looked at her, his face bleak.

"Do you have any idea what the occupiers plan to do?" Lina asked.

"I overheard something about organizing the troops so that they can surprise the Allies when they come to town. If the battle fails, they'll try to destroy as much of the town as they can, and they'll load everything of value onto the train cars that are at the station."

Lina sat up straight. "I need to let the fellows know so that they can be prepared, otherwise they'll be ambushed when they enter the gates." Trouble lay ahead for all of them, and they had little time to get ready. Lina stood up so quickly the chair almost fell over. "I should go home. Why don't you pack your things? If there's a bike here, take it when no one is looking and come to our place. Just knock on the back porch door, and one of us will let you in. My sister's name is Ada, and the little boy is Benji, but he can't talk. Don't wait till the last minute. The Captain may think you know too much, and that could be dangerous for you."

Raoul looked at his hands on the table. "There's something else," he said.

She looked at him with her hand still resting on the chair.

He wouldn't meet her eyes. His shoulders were rounded, and she saw him wipe his eyes furtively once or twice.

"There is something else," he repeated. "The Captain intends to question you and your sister. They're trying to find some papers, and he's hunted down a long list of professors from the university, but they know nothing. Because your father hid those Hitler papers, he thinks maybe he also had knowledge of this file. But since your father is gone, his next option is to find out what you and your sister know."

Lina kept her face blank. She trusted Raoul, but she knew the Captain wouldn't hesitate to throw him in jail if he suspected anything. None of them were safe if they got in the way of his ambition—and now there was Benji to worry about. Ada had a story ready about how he was a nephew from the north. Benji could pass as a relative of Ada's—they both had dark hair, brown eyes, and olive-toned skin. "Thanks for letting me know. It sounds like things are really heating up. I better get home and warn Ada. Be careful and stay safe."

Lina hurried out the back door, grabbed her bike, and pedaled hard to get home. She had to warn Ada. Maybe Benji could hide at the neighbors for a few days.

66.

LINA

LINA biked as fast as she could, but caution was required because the rain was coming down hard, and the roads were slippery. Her worn bicycle tires did not have good traction on wet cobblestones. The rain impaired her vision, and she had to take care lest she fall. She had to get home to warn Ada and figure out how to contact Owen and Lucas. How could she protect Ada and Benji from the Captain? If he was getting desperate, there was no predicting what he might do.

If the Captain wasn't enough of a threat, she could just imagine Nel and the Vriends plotting to get their hands on the house and its contents after she and Ada were put in jail or deported. She worried about Raoul as well—she had no doubt that the Captain would cast him aside the moment he didn't need him anymore.

When she arrived at the main intersection in town, she noticed a roadblock. She stopped abruptly, hitting her brakes hard while still panting from her vigorous ride. She pulled up beside a man on a bike. "What's happening?" she asked. "Can we get around this roadblock?"

"I'm not sure. They're searching for someone or something, and they won't let anyone pass."

"I hope they hurry up. It's cold." She rested her arms on the handlebars.

Two soldiers approached them. "Give us your bikes," the one ordered.

"But why?" Lina asked before the soldier came up to her face and glared at her.

They led Lina and the other man to the back of a truck and shoved them inside, throwing their bikes in after them.

Lina winced to see her bike treated so carelessly. "Where are we being taken?" Lina asked.

"Shut up," the soldier said.

"I need to get home," Lina said, but she knew that no one was listening. She might be locked up for days or even weeks. How would she warn Ada and Owen of the Captain's plan? Would Lucas have any advance intelligence regarding the battle?

She tapped the knife she always kept hidden in her knee sock. If she had to, she would use it, but she hoped they wouldn't discover it first. Lucas had warned her more than once that it was dangerous to carry a weapon because it could be used against her, but it had already saved her several times, and she wasn't about to give it up.

When she arrived at the jail, she was told to sit on a hard chair in a cell. Two soldiers who she presumed were Gestapo came in and questioned her. Where had she been? Where was she going? Did she know anything about the Allied plans? Was she hiding illegal papers?

Lina concentrated on keeping her story consistent. She explained that she cleaned houses and was heading home after a shift. She denied all knowledge of secret papers or Allied plans. Keeping her eyes on the floor, she spoke quietly and assumed a submissive posture.

When the men didn't extract any information from her, they left looking disgusted. The jailer, who they called Piet, locked the cell door. He glanced at her and took in her general state. As he locked the door, he seemed to wink. She must have dreamed it. Why would he wink? Did he think her situation was funny? Perhaps it was some kind of message.

Lina wondered if the Gestapo knew that she worked for the Captain. Had he set the trap to catch her, or was it just a random arrest of people on that road?

Lina tried to get comfortable on the hard cot in the jail cell. With only a thin blanket, Lina shivered and tried to cover her eyes from the overhead light. Whatever courage she had shown thus far would disappear quickly at the hands of the interrogators, especially if they thought she was hiding something. She had to survive and keep Father's secret work from them. That file would help prosecute the guilty.

She knew Ada would worry when she didn't return from her cleaning job. That brought tears to her eyes, and she realized she had to refocus her thoughts. There was no room for emotion now—she had to prepare for the next round of questions. Working to calm her mind, she told herself not to feel emotions that would leave her vulnerable. The interrogators would be listening for any inconsistency; she had to remain focused and repeat the same story over and over until they were bored with her. There could be no contradiction in her words or her behavior. It was far better to be seen as simple minded than as a threat.

She used her imagination to put herself in another place—she visualized walking on her favorite stretch of beach where the winds from the North Sea blew every word and emotion into the sky, leaving her carefree. The waves crashed and broke onto the water's edge.

Even this moment, as terrifying as it was, would pass; her goal was to survive. The line between survival and surrender was so thin. She was determined that her story would not end in this place that smelled of dead mice and dirty socks. With her entire being, she would fight to survive. Benji was waiting for his art lesson, and Ada needed her to find food. She was overcome with a longing for home—did it take sitting in a jail to realize that she belonged there?

No matter what she told herself, however, she was terrified. The possibility of failure was huge—no one could withstand sustained interrogation. If she revealed secrets, many people would be hurt. Everything that Lucas and Owen had worked for would be jeopardized. Ada and Benji would be at risk as well. If they broke her, she might as well be dead because facing the damage she'd done to those she loved would be unbearable.

She returned to imagining the beach—the fast-moving clouds occasionally opened space to allow the rays of the sun to paint the distant waters with a silvery wash. Ever since she was a young child, she had felt at home at the beach. The constantly changing water fascinated her, and she was always eager to swim in the cold waters.

If she ever got out of this jail, she would return to that beach. She planned to walk barefoot at the water's edge, sinking into the wet sand. She imagined that sand creeping between her toes. If she were lucky, Lucas would be there with her, and they would run and play like children, freed from all the misery of war.

TUESDAY

Because sleep was impossible, she watched the thin strands of pink morning light through the small cell window as they briefly illuminated the sky and then were devoured by thick clouds.

If her life was meant to end here, there was no point in wasting time sleeping. But there was so much of the world she still wanted to see. "Give me strength," she whispered. In case she was heard, it might be worth it to add a few more prayers. "Keep Benji and Ada safe," she added, "and watch over Owen and Lucas and Raoul." Although they were in imminent danger, she had no way to warn them. Somehow, she had to survive imprisonment and return home to warn the men.

If her captors intended to interrogate her, they could snap her like a twig, and it wouldn't take long. That only made her more determined to escape. But how?

That morning passed slowly. The only person she saw was the prison guard who passed as he lazily mopped the floor outside her cell. He stopped there and lit a cigarette. Introducing himself as Piet, he offered her a cigarette. After lighting it, he handed it to her through the bars. He seemed like a regular fellow, grateful to have someone to talk to. He took the job because he had to feed four children. "What did you do to end up here?" he asked.

"You don't have to do anything, and they'll still pick you up and throw you in jail. I was just biking home."

"They're going to lose, and they know it."

"Hopefully soon. I want to live to see that day."

"It's going to be a good day. The parties will go on for weeks."

"Don't let me miss it," she said.

He nodded solemnly and started mopping again.

Lina went back to her cot to finish the cigarette, hiding the butt under the cot. She hoped the smell of smoke would dissipate before they returned. Lina tried to ignore the hunger pangs to get some sleep. No one came to interrogate her, and she felt a huge relief.

As the afternoon grew darker, she heard the boots advance down the hall to mark their return. *I will survive this day.*

Lina asked repeatedly about her bike, trying to appear more concerned about that than anything else. They gradually lost patience with her as they assumed she had nothing interesting to tell them. Perhaps they were anticipating a meal or a beer and were happy to leave the cell.

Piet brought her a bowl of some kind of gray porridge. Although it tasted like paper, she ate it to keep up her strength.

"Did they hurt you?" he asked.

"Not yet," Lina replied.

"Drink this water," he said. "And be strong. They will soon be in prison themselves."

She drank the water and laid back down on the cot. Piet quietly left the cell. She heard his steps move slowly down the hall. His kindness almost undid her—something which she had to resist. She wanted to call him to come back as she felt the panic rising. *Stay calm and focus on good things.*

That evening, the soldiers returned with a tub of water.

Lina glanced at it and had a terrible premonition of what they intended to do. She felt like she might throw up with fear. She kept her eyes cast down and pleaded with any power that might be listening to spare her this fate.

They pulled her to her feet and dragged her to stand in front of the tub, forcing her to kneel.

Here it is, God, you finally got me on my knees. Help me to survive this.

"What about the papers? Where are they?" they asked.

"What papers?" she replied, looking at the men with a blank face. They were fishing for answers, hoping that random inquiries might yield the information they wanted. Maybe they'd been ordered to find a suspect. Anyone who was weak enough to confess would fit the bill.

The one closest to her grabbed her head and held her under until he pulled her back up. She gasped and choked for breath. She lost all sense of time as her body fought to retain enough air to survive the next dunking.

At one point she felt close to losing consciousness—this was more than she could handle. She could picture the edges of what was left of her strength, but beyond that a dark void beckoned. *No,* she told herself, *this would not be the place where my life would end. How long would they continue this madness? If only Lucas would surprise these men and help me to escape. What if I never see him again?*

Her vision was clouded by oily black spots that slid over her eyes. She blinked and blinked again to clear them. Was her brain leaking fluid, or had her vision become impaired by the near drowning? She thought about Benji's inability to speak. The evil perpetrated by these men was incomprehensible—Lina felt a surge of anger. She could not let them win.

She heard someone in the hallway outside her cell who called for the men to come quickly. They threw her onto the cot without another word. Lina curled up in a fetal position and tried to remember how to breathe, but all she could manage was ragged shallow breaths. Her hair was wet, and it made her even colder. She shivered and wrapped her arms around herself, but fear had taken over her body. Her panic escalated—*they would continue until they killed me, and I would be just one more casualty of war. How many others had died at the hands of these cruel men? Where did they dump the bodies?*

She was cold, tired, and hungry. *Help me.*

They didn't return after having been called away on some other matter. Piet came to visit and brought her a ragged blanket and a cup of hot tea. Lina had tears in her eyes when he handed her the tea.

"Are you an angel?" she asked.

Piet snickered. "Men could never be angels. Now drink up and rest. Don't give in to them. The war will end, and they will be rounded up and shot. You just need to survive this."

Lina slept off and on the rest of the day. Piet had left a crust of bread inside her cell at some point, which she gnawed on hungrily.

WEDNESDAY

The next morning, two men arrived accompanied by an older and more senior officer. The cell felt crowded with the three men in their uniforms. They brought in a chair and ordered her to sit.

She kept quiet with her hands folded in her lap. As a simple house cleaner who knew nothing, she averted her eyes from the men and tried to breathe.

They would never expect much from a woman—such preconceived notions might work in her favor. Any sign of resistance might increase their suspicion that she was not who she said she was, so she reminded herself to maintain a servile attitude. She kept her eyes averted lest they see evidence of rebellion. Even a year ago, that would have been impossible to fake, but she had learned a few things while working for Lucas.

The older officer kept his voice very calm and even. He questioned her over and over about the same topics. Another fellow moved behind her, and it made her anxious not to be able to see him. She heard him strike a match as he lit a cigarette, and the scent filled the cell.

The pipe tobacco that Father smoked had a sweetness that this cigarette lacked. On certain days, she thought she could still detect the scent of Father's pipe in his study and in the coat that hung in the closet. As a child, she'd often watched him take out the tin of tobacco and scrape out the pipe before repacking the bulb carefully with the threads of tobacco. When he lit the pipe, his face relaxed with pleasure. The smoke would fill the space above his head and then float towards the door and down the hall.

Thoughts of Father made her throat feel tight, so she forced her mind into a different direction; but she'd lost her ability to focus, and her mind began to panic, flitting here and there, not obeying her attempts to control it. She had to force herself to become calm—her interrogator was experienced; he watched her face, the constriction of her pupils, the pulse in her neck. She tried counting backwards from one hundred, but she kept losing her place.

She heard the senior officer's voice as if from a distance. Over and over the same questions to which she replied with the same answers.

If she died here, it would be one more loss for Ada. She would be sad—they were learning to accept each other's differences. Benji had worked his magic to bring them closer. Together they laughed at the things he did to amuse them. Lina enjoyed getting him ready for bed and reading to him. Because Ada was up early, she took care of breakfast and a morning walk to the park.

One night, in response to their argument over dinner, he had made them hold hands. When they looked at each other holding hands, they began to laugh. "Here we thought we were the grown-ups," Ada had said. Lina had rubbed the top of his head affectionately and noted how Benji managed to fix things without words.

"I know nothing about papers," she replied again.

She sensed movement behind her, and after a slight nod from the primary interrogator, a cigarette burned the skin on her right shoulder. With a sharp intake of breath, she kept from crying out, even though the pain was intense and brought tears to her eyes. The sickening scent of burned flesh circled around her, making her nauseated. If she threw up on that Nazi's leather boots, he'd probably shoot her on the spot. Never had she seen the face of evil so clearly. Father had often claimed that good would triumph over evil, but perhaps he'd underestimated the power of the enemy. Reminding herself to maintain a submissive attitude, she looked down at her feet and tried to keep her face expressionless.

Repressing a primal urge to howl in pain, she clenched her teeth and sat silently with her hands clasped and her head bowed. While part of her mind remained completely alert, the other part burrowed deeper into a place where her body floated freely and was disconnected from her mind. *Think of the beach*, she told herself. *Listen to the roar of the waves. Picture Benji running ahead and then turning to run back. Imagine picking him up and hugging him. Think of Lucas, holding you with your head fitting in that space under his collarbone.*

After every question, the soldier burned another spot on her shoulders. She counted to five as she held her breath and then slowly released it, focusing on control.

She felt Father's presence—comforting her, running his hand softly over her hair, giving her a blessing. Death was not to be feared, he told her, it was like a heron, lifting from the earth's cold surface with a weightless flight to a place of indescribable beauty. He would be there to welcome her someday, and Mother would be healthy and happy again; but he told her that her time had not yet arrived. Father reached out to her, touched her hand, and said in his soft voice, "I am in a place where there are no tears and no hunger. Lina, it is not your time—you must fight and endure. Gather your strength and choose life."

Betraying Lucas or any of the others was not an option—loyalty sometimes demanded a steep price. Jos had been shot in the woods in an unprovoked attack. She remembered his courage in saving her life as he faced his own end, and she knew it was her time to be brave.

Time lost any discernible structure—some moments had no beginning or end, and others provided spaciousness and a brief respite. She thought of Ada at home, looking out of the kitchen window, hoping to see her bike pull up to the shed.

Breathe, she told herself. Finally, the interrogators stood up and left, irritation expressed in the impatient stomping of boots. Although Lina didn't look up, she felt the movement of air in the departure. Had they given up on her? She returned to the bed, the movement making her dizzy and afraid.

As she lay face down on the cot, she didn't even have the energy to weep. There was no part of her body that didn't hurt. This ugly place, these hateful men—was this how her life would end? She hadn't said goodbye that morning to Ada—there was so much she wished to tell her.

If she could just sit at the kitchen table with Ada and Benji, she would be so grateful.

If she didn't return, Benji would wonder where she'd gone. He might not be able to ask questions, but she knew he would eventually learn to speak. The lad deserved to have a loving home, and Ada would certainly give him that. Their family would include new members: the Groens, Lucas, Owen, Lykke, Raoul, and all the others who had been kind to them.

Even now when she felt abandoned, she knew that was not true—Ada was probably sitting at the kitchen table praying silently, worrying, and drinking tea. That someone would keep watch for her through the long, cold nights was humbling.

She imagined walking towards their house, and in the distance she could see a long line of silent watchers including her grandparents, Jos, friends from church and from high school—people who had disappeared or been executed or deported.

The soldiers would wear down her resistance, and she knew she didn't have unlimited powers to withstand it. Their cruelty was limitless—they'd lost their humanity so long ago. Would they take that from her and leave her as a weak shell, begging for mercy and betraying all that she loved? She dug deeper inside herself and tried to find a safe place to rest, a dwelling place for her bruised spirit.

That day in the forest when Ada foraged mushrooms and nuts, Lina had taken pictures. Small birds had fluttered in and out of the birch and oak trees, their habitat disturbed by human visitation. She was hungry to see more of those woods, those trees, and those birds. The woods gave them a sanctuary that provided them with all they needed. Lina wanted to go home and feel all the familiar things around her. Father had given them that house and knew they would care for it and make it home.

THURSDAY

The cell was still dark, but a thin amount of light showed that day was approaching. It was time to move. She had to get out of this horrible place. Rolling slowly to a sitting position, she looked around the cell. Trying to believe in the possibility of escape, she stood up slowly and began to explore every inch.

As she walked around the cell, she stretched out her muscles to distract herself from the burns on her back. Her mind struggled to focus, so she took some breaths to try to still herself.

The jail was quiet. She hoped her interrogators had given up. The guards wouldn't bother with her—she thought she could hear their snores as the sounds traveled down the corridors. Piet's shift seemed to run from early morning till late afternoon.

She had to get out of this cell to warn Lucas and Owen. Although she wasn't sure, she thought that they would return on the weekend. Without receiving some warning, they would walk into a trap.

Lina stalked the cell slowly with the intensity of a wild animal. After checking the locks, she stood on the cot to shake the bars on the window, but they didn't move. She rested her head on the sill, holding on to the bars. There had to be a way out.

67.

LINA

A T her *Opa's* farm, there'd been a small room in his basement separated
from the rest of the cellar by a wooden door. After painting it, he
thought it was in good shape, but later he noticed that the door had disinte-
grated. Lina was fascinated because it had looked fine to her. He had turned
it into a lesson about not being deceived by appearances—things might look
perfect on the outside, he explained, but underneath that perfection, there
could be unseen rot.

Although disguised by paint, dry rot had crumbled the wood of the
door. Her *Opa* took his Swiss pocketknife and dug it easily into the door
to demonstrate how the integrity of the wood had been compromised.
The cool, damp air had provided perfect conditions for the fungus to
thrive, and he had not noticed until it was too late.

Her father had helped Opa remove the door and replace it.

This jail was filled with cool, damp air just like that basement.

The door contained a tiny window to allow the guards to check on
the prisoner. As far as she could see, the guards slept soundly and didn't
bother checking anything.

She ran her hands over the surface of the door, trying to get a sense
of how solid it was. Lina couldn't see any weakness in the integrity of
the wood, but Opa had explained the oil and lead paint would mask the
damage and make it look intact. She pulled her knife out of her sock and
jabbed the door with it, piercing the wood without resistance.

Working slowly and quietly, she managed to hack out large slivers of
wood. She tried to go slowly so that she wouldn't break the knife or injure
her hand in the process. It took a while, but working around the hinges,

she weakened the frame sufficiently to be able to pry the hinges out of the wood. As she worked, she reminded herself to breathe. At one point, she tried to speed up the process and stabbed herself in the hand. Ignoring the blood that dripped from the cut, she freed the last hinge and carefully moved the door from the frame and dragged it to one side. There was no time for pain, she had to make this work.

She slipped out of the cell and turned right, only to find herself at a dead end. She tried to remember how the men approached her cell and recalled that they made a right turn into her cell and a left to turn away, so she returned to her cell opening and then turned left to see if she could find an exit. When they had dragged her into the jail, she had passed a small office area.

Arriving at the intersection of two hallways, Lina paused to listen. She heard the snoring of the guards, one of whom was asleep at his desk. The other guard saw her immediately, but Lina's fear dissipated when she realized it was Piet. He got up quietly, careful not to disturb his snoring companion as he left the office. He beckoned Lina to follow him to a closet where they stored items taken from inmates. He grabbed a woman's sweater, a coat, and a pair of shoes and told Lina to put them on. He looked at her more carefully and looked in the cupboard for a scarf.

"Put this on your head," he said.

She did what he told her. He looked her up and down. "We will walk quickly out of here. Pretend you are my wife and hold my arm. If we are stopped, let me do the talking. I am going to take you to the monastery in town. They will know how to keep you safe."

"What about that other guard?"

"He will sleep for a while yet. He won't even notice that I was gone. But we should hurry. You can tell me how you managed to get out," he said.

"That door is rotten. I dug the hinges out and removed it," Lina said as she donned the scarf he offered.

"I'll be lucky not to get shot for that," he said, appearing unconcerned.

"I hope you won't," Lina said, feeling discouraged.

"Have no fear, I have my ways," Piet grinned, "now, hush."

Walking together quickly, they approached the center of town, where the streets were lined with boarded up shops, a school with broken windows and burned hallways, and a large Catholic church. The monastery beside the church was dark, but the grounds were tended.

Piet knocked on the large wooden door and waited. At first, they heard nothing, so he knocked again. Glancing over her shoulder, she was relieved to see that no one was around. She heard the slow turning of a lock after which the enormous wooden door opened a crack.

"What do you want?" a man's voice whispered.

"Father, this young woman has been interrogated by the Gestapo. She needs to be hidden for a while and then taken home. Can you help?"

The monk opened the door to let her inside, his gray eyes filled with concern and compassion. He lifted a warning finger to his lips, and she nodded to indicate she would be quiet. He waved to Piet who turned and walked away.

"Thank you," Lina whispered.

68.

LINA

Lina followed the monk as he led the way down a long corridor to a small office that opened into an infirmary. A row of six beds against the far wall were made up with clean linen and ready for patients. The room smelled like antiseptic and floor cleaner.

The monk asked her to sit on a chair while he collected some supplies from a cabinet. He examined the cut on her hand, cleaned the wound, and rolled a length of gauze round and round her hand tightly. "What did they do to you?"

She turned and showed him her back.

He inhaled sharply. "I have something that will cool the skin." He went back to the cupboard and took out a brown jar with a thick salve. "We use it on kitchen burns."

She turned her back to him, and he gently applied the ointment to the burns. She winced at the initial application, but soon the cooling effect of the salve eased the pain.

"What else?" he asked.

"I have been kicked and bruised and nearly drowned, but I don't think any of that needs fixing. Forgive me for asking, but I am so hungry."

He nodded. "I'll go to the kitchen and find something for you to eat. I think you should stay in the infirmary for a little while and get some rest. They'll be looking for you, so we will stay put and then get you home later. Where do you live?"

She told him, and he nodded.

"I have a plan. But first, some food and some rest. Tell me, how did you escape?"

When Lina described what she'd done to the door with her knife, the monk smiled. "Well done. Although that jail has been closed for years, they decided they needed more room for prisoners, so they reopened it. It is in terrible condition, but it serves their purpose as prison and interrogation room. We are not happy to have that in our midst, but there's not much we can do. When the war ends, someone should demolish that place."

He stood up and looked at her. "Try to get comfortable in that chair. I'll put a pillow behind your lower back to keep your shoulders from any pressure. Here's a blanket to put over your legs. I'll be right back with some food."

Lina settled into the chair as best she could and pulled the blanket around her legs. Now that she was safe, she felt exhausted. It would take an effort to lift a finger, so it was better not to try to walk home until she'd rested. If only she could send Ada a message to tell her to warn Lucas and Owen.

The monk, who had shared that his name was Father Henri, returned carrying a tray which he set down on the small table. He'd brewed a small teapot of herbal tea and prepared a slice of brown bread with a piece of cheese.

"Thank you so much."

"Please eat. Once you have some food in your stomach, I will give you a light sedative that should help you to sleep for a few hours and ease your discomfort. I'll come and wake you later. I would rather the others don't learn about your presence for their safety and for yours." He moved around the room with efficiency, tidying up and pulling back the sheets on the infirmary bed.

After eating the bread, she used the small toilet in the alcove and then climbed into bed, turning onto her side to spare her burned back. Even though the ointment had cooled down her burns, she didn't think she'd be able to lie on her back for a long time. Everything in her body ached.

"Thank you, Father."

"Rest well," he said as he quietly left the room, shutting the door behind him.

Lina fell into a deep sleep. When he came to wake her, she felt like she could have slept all day. She got up, straightened the bed sheets, and put her shoes on. He gave her an old sweater to wear, but first he tied a thin linen towel over her shoulders like a shawl to protect the burns. The thick wool of the sweater warmed her immediately. Folding her fingers into fists, she tucked them inside the long sleeves. There was comfort in the familiar scents of damp wool and wood smoke.

When they left the building, the halls were dark and quiet. He closed the heavy door carefully behind them, and they walked quickly to the shed, where a bike with a wagon attached stood ready to go. He helped her climb into the wagon. It was dusk, and no one seemed to be around.

"I know this will be uncomfortable, and I'm very sorry." He covered her with a blanket, then a tarp, and placed a basket of onions, potatoes, and a braid of garlic beside her.

Curled up to protect her back, she tried not to make a sound when he hit the inevitable bumps and potholes on the road. Father Henri biked consistently, and no one stopped or challenged him. If she were arrested again, she didn't know what she would do.

After biking steadily for a long time, he slowed down. She heard him open the gate and pull the bike and wagon into the backyard from the alley that ran behind the house. Helping Lina out of the wagon, he said "I hope your sister has not been too worried," he said.

"Thank you for everything," Lina said as she shook his hand. Her words felt so inadequate when she considered the risks he had taken for a stranger. He nodded and pushed his bike out of the yard and closed the gate.

She looked at the house. She had been gone for days, but everything looked unchanged.

As she walked to the back door, she had an overwhelming sense of relief that made her weak in the knees. *Home*, she thought, *I made it home*. She hoped Piet would make it back to the monastery and face no consequences for helping her. Two complete strangers had helped her escape and get home safely. If she ever had a chance, she would have to find a way to thank them. Maybe they'd been an answer to her prayers. Did such things happen? Before this, she would have scoffed at the notion, but now she wasn't so sure.

Opening the back door slowly, she left her shoes in the sunporch and tiptoed into the kitchen. Ada was at the table, head resting on her arms, fast asleep.

When Lina saw her, she wanted to weep. Ada had kept watch. She probably was exhausted from sitting up and waiting. Lina blinked away the tears and tapped her gently on the shoulder.

69.

LINA

"Have you slept at all?" Lina asked.

Ada lifted her head and tried to focus on Lina. "I slept off and on. Are you all right? I was so worried." Her voice broke with emotion as her eyes took in Lina's disheveled appearance. "Where have you been? It's been days."

"I was detained," she replied.

Lina sat at the kitchen table and looked around as if she'd been on a very long trip and needed to reacquaint herself. But everything was still the same—the tea pot stood on the counter as usual. "Where's Benji?"

"He's next door with the neighbors."

The house was quiet—only the sound of a few mourning doves filled the silence. Ada waited for the water to boil. "Do you know what that sound means?"

Lina looked at her. "What sound?"

"When mourning doves linger around your house, they bring a message of love from the departed."

Lina nodded as she considered that idea. *There is yet another mystery that I need to respect.* She held the cup close and sniffed the scent of mint and lavender in the cup.

Ada brought the tea pot to the table and joined Lina. "What happened?"

"Tell me first if everything is all right here."

Ada sighed. "Yesterday, I took Benji to the park. Even though it was raining and cold, he seemed to want to go. When we left, we saw a big black car parked near the entrance. The Captain told us to get in. He drove us very fast down the farm road past the city limits. I was afraid he was going to crash the car into one of those ditches."

"What then?" Lina asked.

"I was sitting in the front, and he had one hand on the gun that was on the seat. He talked to Benji about the car and how fast it could go. He told me that if I had papers related to war crimes, he knew I wouldn't be so stupid as to keep them in the house. I have until morning to surrender them to him."

"Oh no, what did you do?"

"He dropped us back at the park and told us to get out. Just before I closed the car door, he told me that he would be back for Benji if I didn't surrender whatever information I possessed."

"I'm so sorry. Then what?"

"I didn't know what to do, and Owen and Lucas are both out of town. I decided I had to keep Benji safe, so I brought him to the Groen's house, and they promised to keep him busy inside and all the blinds down. I stayed here all night and waited for the Captain to show up. I had the gun. Lina, I would have shot him."

"But he didn't show up?" Lina asked.

Ada wound a piece of her hair round and round her finger. "Instead of the Captain, Raoul came and wanted a place to hide. He said things had blown up at their house, and the Captain had gone on a rampage. He sounds quite unhinged. Raoul was afraid for his life, so he decided to run."

"I guess they didn't miss their cleaner," Lina said with a wry smile.

"I think it's chaos over there, and the Captain isn't home. He sits in the windmill in town and drinks, while he waits for the Allies to arrive."

"Raoul is here now?"

"He's still sleeping in the basement because he hadn't slept for quite a few nights. Things have not been good there."

"I hope the Captain doesn't know that Raoul came here to hide."

Ada shook her head. "I told him to hide in the darkroom if he heard anything, but he never showed up. Apparently, it's a mess in town because the occupiers are fleeing. They heard that the Allied troops are coming to liberate us. They are looting and burning everything on their way out. The Captain tried to get control of the deserters, but he was unable to do so.

"Are the remaining troops sufficiently organized to mount a surprise attack on the Allied troops?"

"I am not sure. There is too much chaos to tell. And the Captain has lost control. But tell me, what happened to you? I was so worried."

"I am so sorry, but there was no way to get a message to you. On my way home from cleaning, I was stopped at a roadblock on the main road. The soldiers threw me and another man into the back of a truck and drove us to an old prison. I was put in a cell and interrogated by the Gestapo."

"Did they hurt you?" Ada asked. She put a cup of tea in front of her.

Lina cradled the cup in her hands, feeling its reassuring warmth, and kept silent. How could she describe the experience? "They asked a lot of questions."

Ada glanced at the gauze dressing on her hand. "Do you know what they wanted?"

"It was, as far as I could tell, a random checkpoint that I happened to pass through. They wanted to know where I had been and if I had any knowledge of a file containing war secrets."

"Are we in immediate danger?"

"There's enough going on that they might not have time to pursue that investigation. We are heading for a final battle I think, and I must get the news to Owen and Lucas, or they will be ambushed. They're still out of town?"

"I'm not sure exactly when they will return. What kinds of questions did the Gestapo ask?"

"They kept asking about papers and war secrets. I played very dumb and told them I was a cleaner returning from a job. I didn't mention my name nor did I say that I worked for the Captain. He may have told them to arrest me. I don't know for sure. One fellow glanced at my identity card, but it didn't trigger any interest. I think I just got caught in a random search."

Lina pulled the sweater off, undid the pin that held the cloth, and showed Ada her back.

"No!" Ada said. "I'm so sorry. That must hurt so much. What can I do?"

"They beat me and almost drowned me, but you know what? I didn't tell them anything." She shivered and quickly put the towel back over her shoulders.

Ada shook her head. "You were so brave. How did you get out?"

"I carved up the door to the cell. And I had some help. I'll tell you about it later, but first we must decide what to do."

"Maybe you'd like to sleep for a little while after breakfast," Ada suggested.

"I need to get a message to Owen and Lucas. They may walk into an ambush if they are not warned. Do you have any idea how to reach them? It's urgent."

Ada nodded. "Why don't you write it out, and Benji and I will try to figure out how to get it to them? I'll go see Lykke because she has many contacts. In the meantime, you need to get some sleep. I'll lock the house up and hope no one disturbs you. I will tell Raoul you are safely home."

"This is of extreme importance. You must be very careful. Wear a hat and keep an eye out for the Captain. I hope those papers are safe. For everyone's sake, we must keep them hidden until the war ends. We owe it to Father."

Lina turned to look out the window. The blossoms on the fruit trees that lined the side and back of the yard were in full bloom. Father had said they made him nostalgic for the fruit trees on his parent's farm. He had learned to tend those trees, to prune them, and to harvest the fruit. This summer, maybe she and Ada could harvest some fruit in the back-yard. Benji could climb up the ladder and learn to pick, even if Father wasn't there to teach him. She would tell him stories about his *Opa* while Ada helped them to make apple sauce and pie from the fruit.

70.

ADA

A DA knocked on Lykke's door and waited. Finally, she heard footsteps in the hall. She held tightly onto Benji's hand.

Lykke opened the door. "Benji? Are you here to visit me? She bent down to hug him and then hugged Ada. "Please come inside. How are you?"

Benji smiled but didn't let go of Ada's hand as they ventured inside. "We're fine. Sorry to bother you, but I have an urgent message for Lucas and Owen. My sister wrote out some information that they need to see."

Lykke looked at her carefully. "Locating them will be very dangerous. The occupiers are everywhere, stealing what they can and killing whoever crosses their path. People are hiding in their basements or leaving town."

"It's very important. Whoever hasn't already deserted will be organized to attack when the Allies march into town. They will not be expecting any organized resistance, and in their celebratory mood they will not be prepared for this ambush. Someone needs to warn them."

"That is serious. I will do my best to find someone who can help. I am not sure Lucas and Owen are in the same location, so I will alert the Allied commander. Maybe you could write a second message for him? I have some paper and a pen right here." She walked to a small antique desk and retrieved what she needed. Ada sat at the table and wrote a second note.

"How is Benji doing?" Lykke asked.

"We've discovered that he's quite an artist. My sister has been teaching him to draw."

"And she's happy to have him there?" Lykke asked.

Ada decided not to say anything about Lina's arrest and escape. "She's getting attached to him and working with him. He reads people very well," Ada said, smiling at Benji. "And what about you? Are you keeping busy now that the orphanage is closed?"

"There's so much to do. When the war ends, hopefully soon, we will begin rebuilding. Planning is already underway. Social services will be essential as children are behind on everything, including schooling, nutrition, and immunizations. There will be plenty for you to do if you are interested."

"I hope to finish my education first, but I will do whatever I can to support your work."

"I've heard they will open the university as soon as they can—it is such a powerful symbol of freedom. I used to resent the noise from those student apartments, but laughter and parties will be so much better than bombs and planes."

Ada did up the buttons on Benji's coat. "We should get going now. I'm sure you have plenty to do, but thank you for being willing to pass along the message."

They said their goodbyes, and Ada biked home, relieved that Lykke was willing to help. She'd been so afraid that Lina had been captured or killed when she didn't come home. All night she had regretted not sharing the story of Mother's diary with Lina. There was no excuse now—Lina needed to know the family secrets.

71.

ADA

A DA put away the dishes and wiped the counter. A knock on the door interrupted her thoughts. Lykke had told her the Allies might approach the city sometime on the weekend. Lina had been in bed almost continuously since she returned.

"Hello, Nel, how are you?"

"Are you busy? I haven't seen you for a while. I'm sorry for dropping by so late."

"Were you away?" Ada pretended to be interested, but she didn't believe anything Nel said anymore.

"I was in Groningen to help organize child evacuations to Drenthe using the German trains or the ships from the German *Kriegsmarine*. The operation has been a great success."

Nel looked almost puffed up with self-importance. She had found a place with the socialists. Ada told herself to be kind. After all, they had apparently evacuated hundreds of children, maybe more—no one knew for sure. She had heard that mayors had arranged foster homes for thousands, but she was always skeptical of those kinds of reports. Still, she had to give her credit for the work done for children, but if Nel thought that work would lead to a position in the postwar world, she might be disappointed.

Ada was more concerned these days with returning evacuated children to their families when the war ended. Children placed with families with known pro-German sympathies could face suspicion and endure a difficult time while they waited to return home. Ada was proud of the evacuation trip that Lina had assisted, but the focus had changed so that children were being sent to other countries like England, Belgium, Switzerland, and France to recover in camp-like settings.

She warned herself to not anger Nel lest she report them to the occupiers. "I heard that your group was doing evacuations. That's wonderful news. Come in. I'll make some tea." Ada had welcomed Nel's visits in the past, but it was hard to hide her irritation. Owen had reminded her to act normal or Nel would sense a shift in Ada's attitude. She hoped Raoul would stay quietly in the basement; she didn't look forward to explaining his presence there. Nel would run back to Berthe, who would alert the Captain.

"Where is Lina?" Nel asked.

Ada poured the hot water over the mint leaves in the pot. "Lina is resting."

Did Nel report their activities to someone? She certainly had an excellent vantage point from her living room window to see who showed up at their house—except for those who entered from the back gate.

Although Ada was trying to act as if everything was normal, she could not control the shaking of her hands—the cup flipped out of her fingers and onto the floor and smashed into pieces.

"Are you all right?" Nel asked with what appeared to be genuine solicitude.

"I'm fine. My hands were wet, and the cup slipped. Stay where you are while I sweep it up."

Ada picked up the larger pieces first and then swept up the fragments.

"What do you think Lina will do when the war ends?" Nel asked.

Why was she asking that? Ada took a breath to calm herself. "She'll get a job or finish her schooling."

"What happened to Paris?"

Ada felt her face become warm and told herself to keep control. Nel was very persistent. Ada shrugged as if to say that it didn't matter to her. "She'll get there sooner or later; in fact, I'd like to see Paris someday too. Maybe I'll go with her."

Nel appeared taken aback by the that idea.

Had Nel been driving a wedge between her and her sister all this time? If that was the case, then Nel was very clever, and Ada had been obtuse. What did Nel hope to gain from befriending her? If she were working for the occupiers, she might have been sent to find information. Maybe she was spying on Lucas too. Ada felt a chill go through her.

Nel chattered about her son and her grandchildren and didn't seem to notice that Ada only responded in monosyllables. Ada tried to nod and smile at regular intervals as if she were interested. Was Nel talking about her family to make it feel like they were old friends exchanging confidences and gossip? Ada felt sad—she had been wrong about this woman and been blind to the damage she could do to them, *or perhaps*, Ada thought with a chill, *had already done.*

She would pick up Benji before bedtime and hope that the night would be quiet. Ada thought about Owen and Lucas and hoped they had received the message and were making plans for the battle ahead. Owen would tell her that keeping the house secure and protecting those under her roof was enough to worry about, but she wondered what else they might do to help. Hopefully the Captain would be busy in town and would leave them alone.

She wondered what their minister would say if she told him she was prepared to kill the Captain if it meant keeping Benji safe. Was murder ever justified? She listened to Nel gossip about the neighbors and wondered what Nel would say if she knew there was a gun in the sugar cannister, and that Ada was prepared to use it.

72.

LINA

By her reckoning it was Saturday afternoon, and Lina felt like she'd finally caught up on rest, so she got dressed and went downstairs. Shortly after she sat at the table to have a late breakfast, Chief Vriend showed up at the back door with his wife.

When Lina saw them at the door, she took charge. "Ada," she whispered, "take Benji to the basement and stay there until I call you. Tell Raoul to stay down there as well. I'll give you a sign when it's safe."

Lina moved slowly towards the door until she heard that they were safely in the basement. "What are *you* doing here?" Lina asked them.

"Move aside," the chief said as he pushed his way past Lina.

"Sit down," Lina ordered, "and tell me what all this is about."

The chief and his wife sat at the table while Lina kept standing.

Out of his chest pocket, he pulled out a carefully folded piece of paper with two official looking stamps and a fancy signature and handed it to her.

"That looks very nice. Who did you bribe to sign it?"

"This is an official notice of eviction. You must leave this house tomorrow." His wife nodded in agreement.

Lina glanced at the letter and handed it back to him.

"And you support this?" Lina asked his wife.

"I am a patriotic person," Mrs. Vriend said. "My husband will soon be promoted, and a man in his position deserves a larger house."

"If you're counting on the Nazis to promote you, you better hurry because they're leaving town by the hundreds," Lina said.

The chief glared at her, still holding his official paperwork in his hand since Lina had refused to accept it.

"We own this house, and we're not leaving. But I think you should leave," Lina said.

"You use this house to entertain all kinds of men. It's just not right," Mrs. Vriend said. "What would your mother say?"

"I really don't want to hear more of your lies." Lina walked over to open the door to let them out.

The Chief stood up and dropped the papers on the table.

"I mean it. Get out," Lina ordered.

Although Mrs. Vriend expected him to do something to make his point, he got up and left without a word, so she scurried behind him.

Lina locked the door.

"Thanks for defending us," Ada said as she came up from the basement.

"That man is impossible. His wife is just as bad."

Lina tore the eviction notice into small pieces. These people would soon receive their punishment—hopefully Owen and Lucas were getting closer to town. "Where's Benji?"

"He's playing cars with Raoul. I think we have gained a wonderful entertainer for Benji. He's very good with him."

73.

LINA

LATER that evening Raoul and Benji had settled, but both Ada and Lina were too agitated to go to bed. They had hoped to hear some confirmation from Lykke that the message had reached the men, but there was no word. If the Allies returned on Sunday or Monday, as was rumored, they would be met by an army of occupiers, and they wouldn't be prepared for the ambush.

Ada served some chamomile tea. "Let's sit in the sunporch so we don't wake Raoul or Benji." The days were longer, causing the light to linger over the yard, illuminating the white and pink blossoms.

"I don't remember what it's like to live without war," Lina said.

"It will take a long time to return to any kind of normal life—we will have to rebuild everything that was destroyed," Ada observed. "And some things can never be rebuilt."

"We are orphans now," Lina said. "There's no one but us."

"We've added Benji and Lucas and Owen."

"I know, but they are not like family elders who know our history."

"I sometimes wonder how we're supposed to keep memories alive, when there's no one to remember things with." Ada asked.

"On the other hand, not all memories are worth preserving," Lina said.

Ada looked at her sharply. "What do you mean?"

"There are people and things I'd rather forget."

"Like what?"

"*Oom* Jaap and *Tante* Truus, for example. He was so excited to work with the Germans, but when they took over his factory to produce weapons for the German war effort, they didn't need him anymore. The people he thought were his friends sent them to die in the camps."

"He gambled and lost, I guess," Ada said. "As many others did."

"I won't miss that disgusting man," Lina said. "I can't imagine why *Tante* Truus married him, other than for his money."

"I didn't realize you disliked him that much," Ada said. "They did not deserve to die in the camps."

Lina looked at her. "That's true. I just wish he'd been held accountable. I never told you, but . . ."

Ada looked alarmed. "What?"

"He was disgusting. That summer when I was sent to stay there . . ."

"What happened?"

Till now she had never told anyone, but she removed the memory from its power to hurt. "I was invited to be a guest there during the summer because you had to stay home to help Mother. One night, he came up to my room and tried to get friendly. He told me I should be grateful to learn things from him. Disgusting."

Ada shuddered. "What did he do?"

"He didn't get anywhere as near as he wanted. I bit his arm so hard that I left marks. He struck me, and then *Tante* Truus called out to see where he was. He had to wear long sleeves for a while, even though it was summer. And he didn't visit my room again. I'm not sure what I would have done if he'd tried anything more, but I certainly would have defended myself."

"Did you tell anyone?"

"Who could I tell? No one would believe me. I stayed in bed with 'stomach flu,' and when I didn't get better, they called Mother to pick me up. Tante Truus was always worried about catching illness, so she kept me isolated. I even stuck my fingers down my throat to make myself vomit. When I got home, I was suddenly starving and had a miraculous recovery."

"I'm so sorry you went through that," Ada said.

"That's not the worst. *Tante* Truus told Mother that I was being flirtatious with *Oom* Jaap and that she should keep a close eye on me. I was standing near the kitchen door when I heard that, and you know the worst thing was that Mother never tried to defend me. He was a snake, and there are plenty of them around, but Mother should have been willing to hear my side of it."

"She never asked?"

Lina shook her head. "She believed her sister and was furious with me."

"You should have told me," Ada said.

"You wouldn't have been able to do anything. Mother didn't want to hear it."

"Do you think *Tante* Truus knew what he did?"

"I don't know. If he did that regularly, and she knew about it, then she was just as bad as he was. I don't know how she could stand to be with him, but she loved the things his money could buy. Maybe she thought she couldn't live without him."

"Later, the Nazi's took all the contents of their house and burned it down. All the stuff that she took from their parent's house was destroyed."

"Serves her right. She should have shared some of it with our mother."

"I'm so sorry," Ada said. "I wish you could have told me. I hate the thought that you were alone with that all this time."

Lina shrugged. "I could have told a hundred people, but nothing would have happened. It taught me to trust no one. Since that time, I have always carried a knife, and it has served me well. I wrote the whole incident down, and I burned it. It feels a lot further from me now."

Ada studied her hands and then looked up. "Was this why there was always tension between you and Mother?"

"This didn't help. Mostly I didn't live up to her expectations. In fact, I made an art of disappointing her."

"If it helps, I think you're wonderful," Ada said, "I wish I had a small portion of your courage."

Lina sighed. "Maybe I'm just angry or impulsive. Those are words Mother used about me."

Ada sat quietly. She'd been knitting a sweater for Benji out of some recycled wool, but she put that on the table. *Was this the time?* "There's more to her story. I found some new information and have been waiting for the right time to tell you. Forgive me for not sharing this with you sooner, but I needed time to sort it out." Ada cleared her throat.

"What are you talking about?" Lina asked.

"A few weeks ago, I found some letters and a diary in the bottom of Mother's closet. I wrote a note to the address on one of the envelopes and hoped that the author, an old friend of Mother's, still lived at that address. Owen was willing to investigate, and he found Gerda, Mother's best friend, and delivered it to her apartment. She sent me an invitation to visit her there."

Lina nodded but stayed silent.

"I biked to The Hague to meet her. She has lived in the same apartment for decades—a walk-up in a building that has been spared the recent bombing. She's a single woman who never married and who taught school for many years. She and Mother attended the domestic science school together, and she went on to become a teacher. They also attended a Student Christian Club for years that held local and regional meetings and organized camps."

Lina looked puzzled but sat quietly.

"Mother apparently had a male friend before Father."

"What?" Lina exclaimed.

"Frans Josef's parents came from an upper-class Jewish family in The Hague. His father was a well-known legal scholar, and his mother was a doctor. When they found out that Janny was pregnant by their son, the family closed in, sent Frans to Paris to continue his surgical training, and ordered him to have no more contact with her."

"That's crazy," Lina said. "She got pregnant by some guy who took off to Paris?"

"Her parents were furious, so they kicked her out. Luckily, her friend Gerda had an apartment, so she invited Mother to move in with her. Our father—that is, Albert—was a member of the same Student Christian group and served on the regional council. Because Mother was also on the executive committee, she'd known Albert for a while, and he was a friend. When she confided her trouble to him, he offered to marry her. At that time, he was a graduate student. Her parents refused to attend, so they had a simple ceremony. Only Gerda and Reverend Arie attended the wedding."

Ada continued. "*Tante* Truus made sure there was no reconciliation between Mother and her parents, and when they passed Truus got everything. Sometimes she gave Mother some of her used clothes, but it was more a way to show off her wealth than an expression of care."

"What a witch," Lina said.

"She threatened Mother that she would tell us the story of her pregnancy as soon as we were old enough, and that gave her a lot of power over Mother, who was terrified that we would find out."

"Did Father—that is, Albert—love her when he married her?"

"According to Gerda, Father was an honorable man, and he had always been very fond of her. Although he would never take the place of Frans Josef, he trusted that love would grow between them."

Lina took a moment to digest all she had heard. Hesitantly, she asked, "Are we still sisters?"

Ada smiled. "We'll always be sisters, and I will always regard Albert as my father."

"What do you know about Frans Josef?"

"He became a surgeon and had a thriving practice until the Nazis made it impossible for Jewish doctors to practice medicine. He worked for the resistance, helping sick people who were in hiding and writing medical exemptions for those who were going to be sent to death camps. Eventually he was arrested and deported, as were his parents, who had tried to flee to Switzerland. They all died in the camps."

Lina was silent for a moment. Then she asked, "Don't you wish we could talk to Father about this?"

"I do. Father made sure his file box had all the necessary legal documents, and he left some letters in case we wanted to follow the trail; but I have a feeling we were his children and he loved us, and the rest was in the past."

"Mother was always so complicated," Lina said.

"When you were younger, there were many times Mother unleashed her anger on me. She was unpredictable and deeply unhappy. It doesn't excuse some of the things she did, but I think she felt that motherhood robbed her of her future. She wasn't completely well."

"But you were her darling . . . She always praised everything you did," Lina protested.

"I think she did that to upset you. When you were little, I hardly ever left you alone with her. In those days, she'd have an outburst or a temper tantrum and frighten you, but when you were old enough, I knew you could defend yourself or at least tell Father what she'd done. I don't think she was capable of physically hurting you, but her words were nasty."

"Did she lash out at Father too?"

"She did, but he often managed to calm her. And I think she went to a place in the country for treatment for a while. That seemed to help."

"What was her problem? Did she just hate all of us?"

"I think she didn't like herself very much. She never could forgive herself for the relationship with Frans as it caused her to lose her parents, her education, and any chance to find a job. Even though Father made it possible to live in a good house and have the status of a professor's wife, she never felt worthy. She might have had a breakdown at some point, but Father never discussed that with me."

"I never knew," Lina said quietly.

"Watching out for you just became second nature for me, and I'm sorry if I irritated you by hovering too much. Owen helped me to see that I wasn't helping you by doing that."

Lina shook her head. "I know you shielded me, but I just didn't know why."

"Someone once told me that rebellion can be a sign of creativity. I see you as a very creative person," Ada said with a smile.

"That's a nice way to put it," Lina said, "or you could just say I was a rebellious brat."

"Father sometimes reminded me that Mother had been terribly hurt when her parents disowned her and refused to attend her wedding or to see their grandchildren. She lost a lot at a young age, and I think that affected her deeply."

Lina took a sip of tea and set the cup down carefully. She looked at Ada. "What are we supposed to do with all this? I've carried my secret since I was a young girl. There's no one I can confront or forgive, if I even felt like doing that. Which I don't. He was a terrible man, for sure, but the fact that Mother wouldn't listen or defend me hurt the most."

"You have taken steps to let this go, and I hope that will help. These evil people are gone, and none of it can determine who you are now. Your life is about to begin, and you cannot let this get in the way from becoming who you are meant to be."

Lina sat with her arms across her chest. "When I hear your story, it seems that there were more secrets in our house than I could have imagined."

Ada nodded. Lina would need time to absorb it.

Ada went to the study and found the dedication page that Father had written the last afternoon before his arrest. "Read this," she instructed Lina.

"To my daughters, that they may live in freedom. Love, Father."

Lina held her face in her hands.

Ada placed her hand lightly on Lina's arm and stood beside her while they both cried.

74.

ADA AND LINA

O N Sunday, Lykke dropped by in the late afternoon to tell them the messages had gone out to the soldiers. She expected the Allies to enter the city by the end of the day. Lina and Ada looked at each other.

"We must do something," Lina said after Lykke left.

"Raoul, do you feel all right staying with Benji? I don't think it's safe for you to leave the house right now. And Benji enjoys spending time with you, so he'll be fine."

"I'd be happy to stay with him. He has been teaching me a few games. But please be careful as well—it will be dangerous out there. What time is his bedtime?"

"He usually goes at seven thirty, but if he wants to stay up a little later, that's fine."

"Are you ready, Lina?" she asked. "Benji, be a good boy for *Oom* Raoul. You can pick three books to read at bedtime." She hugged him, and he took Raoul by the hand to look at the books.

Lina was dressed in a dark sweater and black pants. She nodded, glancing at the sugar canister, and noted that it had been moved from its original position.

They walked out to the shed to get their bikes.

"Let's review the plan," Ada said. "We'll bike to town and find a place to lock our bikes. We can find a place near the windmill where the Captain spends his time watching the city gates to see if the Allies will march in. If he's there, we will sneak inside. With the element of surprise, we can overpower and restrain him. Raoul said he is drinking so much that his reactions might be very slow. I've got the gun, and we have rope.

Then one of us will go find Owen, and the other will keep guard over the Captain. How's that sound?"

"Sounds good. I'm glad Lykke could give us the estimated time of arrival of the troops, if they're on schedule," Lina replied.

"If he's not in that windmill, we will look for him. I have a feeling he's not going to put himself in the line of fire or serve on the front line. He knows they are defeated, but he wants to pretend to be in charge. We can't let him escape."

"Someone will know where he is."

Ada and Lina biked to town. As they got closer, the noise increased. The center of town was filled with a smoky haze as soldiers were running around in an undisciplined chaos, trying to find transportation out of the city. They called out to each other with panic in their voices, their German loud and insistent. They were soldiers who were accustomed to following orders, but no one was telling them what to do.

Ada and Lina found a store front that provided a view of the windmill. They huddled in the doorway of the old dress shop, hoping that no one would spot them. Lina had pulled a knitted cap over her hair, and Ada had a scarf over hers. From their vantage point, they could see a light coming from the second floor of the windmill and the outlines of a person hunched over a table.

Snippets of conversation floated past them. One soldier yelled, "They've taken Amsterdam!"

Shattered glass sounds filled the air as someone pitched a rock into a store window. Most of the soldiers were on the run—they hurried out of the city gates towards the train station. The sound of boots pounding on the pavement caused the girls to flatten themselves into the wall, but the soldiers weren't interested in them—they just wanted to get out of town before the Allies arrived.

When the crowd dwindled somewhat, they crossed the street and tried the door of the windmill. The circular building had served as a museum until the occupation. Relieved to find that it was unlocked, they pushed the door open. Ada tiptoed slowly up the steps, and she heard the Captain muttering long before she reached the top.

He sat alone at his table with his back to them. His shirt was untucked, and his uniform jacket had fallen to the floor. Flashes of light were visible through the window in front of him. A half-empty bottle of whiskey and a glass stood near his right hand, and a map of the country was open on the table in front of him.

Once Ada reached the top of the stairs, she moved to the right and flattened herself against the wall. The sounds of guns and planes outside provided some cover for her movement over the creaky floorboards.

Lina ascended the stairs and moved to the left of the staircase.

He muttered loudly and swore vigorously. He pounded the table with his fist and poured himself another glass of whiskey.

They watched him for a while from their respective waiting places to try to assess how drunk he was. The desk light that illuminated the map cast additional light around the room. There were no guards, and there were no chairs that might be obstacles on their way to him. His gun was placed on the desk to his left.

Ada pulled Father's gun out of her purse, and Lina got her knife out of her sock, and when she nodded they both crept forward.

Moving swiftly from behind, Lina put an arm under his neck and held her knife to his throat while Ada pointed the gun at his temple. Lina pushed his gun out of reach.

"Aren't you missing all the fun? Your men are running in every direction hoping to find a ride home. But a Captain can't desert his ship, right?"

He tried to speak, but Lina's knife pressed against his throat.

While Ada held her gun to his head, Lina put the knife down and pulled rope from her pocket. She tied his wrists behind his back and secured them to the chair frame. She made sure the rope was tight and silently thanked Father for her sailing lessons and the knots he had insisted she learn.

With the knife removed from his throat, the Captain found his voice and yelled at them. "Set me free. I will win this battle and you will regret this."

Lina leaned forward. "I think you better shut up. You have lost this war through your own stupidity."

"I'll go find Owen," Ada said, "and if I cannot find him, I will try to find someone who has the authority to put him in jail. Use his gun if you need to."

They glanced over as the Captain stomped his feet with rage but couldn't move his arms, nor could he pour himself another whiskey. There was still so much noise outside no one would hear him no matter how he carried on.

"Hurry back. I'll stay here and make sure he doesn't go anywhere. Be careful out there. There are many desperate people."

Ada ran down the stairs and continued down the street in the direction that the Allied soldiers would take to enter town. She grabbed the arm of one who appeared to be an officer, but he said he didn't know where the Canadians were. Ada ran towards the troops looking for the Canadians.

In the windmill, the Captain glared at Lina. "Cut me loose," he ordered. "I can get you anything you want—a flat in Berlin, or a car. You could live like royalty there."

"Thanks, but I'm more interested in Paris. Berlin is a real mess right now after all the Allied bombs."

"Your father was a fool," the Captain said. "He could have saved his life if he had cooperated with us."

"Perhaps he was a man of integrity, but you wouldn't know what that means."

"You think your sister is going to help you, but I know all about her. She has other plans, and she will get rid of you quickly. I know everything that happens in your house."

"You know nothing. This conversation is done. I have no desire to discuss anything further with you."

His face got red, and he exploded with rage, filthy expletives pouring out of his mouth. Lina turned her back to him and started to look at some of the books on the shelves.

He stomped on the floor and tried to wriggle his way out of the knots, but Lina had tied them securely.

Lina chose a book that documented the town's history. The portraits of local citizens were stunning—the women in traditional dress with starched caps gazed at the camera without expression. Distracted by the book, Lina did not notice that the Captain continued to use all his strength to force his arms together and then pull them suddenly apart to put tension on the knots.

When she heard a crack, she looked over at the Captain who had managed to break the dowels of the wooden chair. He jumped up with his hands behind his back, with the remnants of the chair still attached to him, and ran towards her. She grabbed the gun from the shelf where she'd placed it and pointed it at him. He paused his forward movement and glared at her.

"Don't move one step," she threatened.

The door burst open as Ada and Owen entered. Both pointed their guns at the Captain. "Don't move," Owen warned.

"Are you all right, Lina?" Ada asked.

"Just fine. As you can see my excellent knots held, but the chair fell apart."

Owen grabbed the Captain by his arms. "I'll take him to the town jail. We're in charge of that now. Why don't you both go home and get some rest? I may be busy all night, but when we get settled, I'll come over."

"Are you sure there's nothing more we can do?" Ada asked.

"It's under control. Go home," Owen ordered in a quiet voice that confirmed he was the boss, as he had claimed.

"Have you seen Lucas?" Lina asked.

"I have not. I trust he'll be in touch when this night is over. Go home and get some rest now."

Lina picked up the half-empty whiskey bottle and took it with her.

When they arrived home, the house was quiet and dark. Benji was fast asleep in his bed. Raoul had been waiting up for them. "What happened?"

"Let's have some of this first," Lina said as she put the bottle in the middle of the table and took three glasses out of the kitchen cupboard.

Ada blinked as she swallowed the whiskey, and Lina coughed. Raoul sipped his and seemed unfazed.

Ada put the glass down. "I think it's over, but it will take them a while to round up and jail some of the worst offenders. The soldiers were running in every direction trying to get away, and the Captain was sitting exactly where you said he would be, and he was getting quite drunk. He's been taken to jail."

Raoul nodded.

"It's a bit strange. Even though this battle is over, it still feels chaotic out there. I thought I would feel excited, but maybe I'm just too tired. And of course, they must officially surrender, and the peace agreement must be signed. At least that's what Owen said would happen."

"Let's try to get some sleep. The guys are probably going to be busy all night, and Benji will be up early," Ada advised.

"I wonder where Lucas is," Lina asked, peering into the darkness.

"He's probably busy with the battle. He'll come when he can," Ada said, placing a knowing hand on her sister's shoulder.

75.

ADA

A DA was the first one up the next morning. It was hard to believe it was Monday, the days had been so full of unexpected events. She was grateful that Lina had escaped and that Raoul had taken refuge with them. Together they would sort out whatever happened next.

Determined to finish something before Benji got up for the day, she pulled out mixing bowls and the butter and flour that Owen had procured. Although it had been a long time, she felt like she was greeting old friends as she found familiar measuring spoons and cups and the well-worn baking sheets that had belonged to her mother.

They had reached the end of an era. She felt like she was a passenger, sitting in a train car that had finally reached the station where it stood for an indefinite amount of time. Would it stay in place, or would it move forward?

She measured the sugar into a cup and poured it into the mixing bowl.

Out of the wreckage, they would rebuild their lives. But moving forward meant she had to acknowledge all that had been lost. The celebrations would eventually wind down, and then it would be time to face the hard truths that waited in the shadows. They had acquired a terrible knowledge that couldn't be unlearned. With their own eyes, they'd witnessed the horrors that humans could inflict on each other. She would never have the same optimism about the world, but life demanded that she make plans and move forward. She felt guilty doing so, as if she were turning her back on those that were lost. But Benji needed her to walk with him as he moved on from the things that he had experienced.

She measured and sifted the flour and felt a wave of pleasure watching its fluffy whiteness land gently into the bowl. Pouring the melted butter into the flour, she watched how it created little rivers.

"Ada?" came a little voice from nearby, breaking Ada's reverie.

"Yes?" she breathed, scarcely believing her ears. The curly-haired boy tugged on her shirt. She lifted him onto the counter. She wasn't sure what to say next, reveling in the sound of his small, brave voice.

"Help," he offered, pointing to the bowl.

Ada laughed, tears threatening to spill from her eyes. "Yes, of course," she handed him a spoon. "You can help. We need to stir this until all the butter is mixed into the flour."

He took the wooden spoon and began to stir, tentatively at first and then with more confidence.

Ada held on to the bowl so it wouldn't slide off the counter. "Good job, Benji," she said.

When they finished, Benji perched at the table with some milk and his breakfast, Lina came downstairs and ran her fingers through her hair. "Ada, I put my blue shirt in the wash a long time ago. Has it been washed yet?" She leaned over to kiss the top of Benji's head.

Ada felt a flash of irritation and realized she still had a lot to learn about patience. "Your shirt is in the basket, and you might wash it yourself, since I'm busy with other things."

Lina looked surprised. "Fine," she said as she went down to the basement to take care of the shirt.

Ada turned to the baking sheet that she was busy oiling and hid her smile.

She heard a knock on the door, and Lucas walked in with a sling on his arm.

He looked exhausted.

"What happened to you?" Ada asked.

"Gun shot. The last day of the war, and I got shot. That's pathetic."

"You're just looking for an excuse not to finish your thesis," she said. "But you still have your writing arm, so you better get to work."

"Fine, but first, I hope you have some tea."

"Of course," Ada said as Lucas began to play with Benji. "Lina," she called down the basement. "We have company," she said.

Lina came up the stairs and stopped short when she saw Lucas. "What happened?" she asked as she ran carefully into his one-armed embrace.

Ada smiled as she watched him give Lina a one-arm hug.

Benji pointed to him. "Lucas," he said.

Ada nodded. "You are right. That is Lucas, and he's home safe now."

76.

ADA

THE day after the surrender dawned sunny and bright. The fruit trees that lined the back fence were in full bloom. The air was filled with the fragrance of lilacs—a welcome change from the stench of war.

Even from inside the house, Ada could hear the cheering and shouting. Signed peace agreements gave rise to jubilation—celebrations broke out on the streets in cities and towns throughout the country and lasted throughout the night. A church service was planned for the morning in the huge church in town, followed by special events. The town had organized parades, boat races on the canals, and games for children.

Owen invited Benji to ride in the jeep for the official Liberation Day parade in town. He sat proudly beside Owen waving a small Canadian flag in one hand and a Dutch flag in the other.

After the parade, Ada and Lina hurried home to make final preparations for a party at their house. Raoul was accustomed to organizing events for the Captain, and his help proved invaluable. He had been living in the basement, helping with Benji, and working on sketches with Lina. He had started to look happier, and less haggard. They all hoped he would stay while he made plans for his chosen career in design.

Lucas, his arm still in a sling from the bullet wound, watched as they carried extra chairs outside. He grabbed a few with his good arm and carried them to the garden. Owen and Lina placed the kitchen table against the back of the house, and Ada covered it with a red-and-white cloth she'd found in the basement.

While they worked to set up the food table, Ada asked Lina about her recent news.

"Tell me more about that American photographer," Ada asked.

"Owen made the contact for me. She is one of a very few women war correspondents, but she started out in fashion photography. When she saw my pictures of the children's evacuation, she invited me to be her assistant for several months to document the stories of concentration camp survivors and to photograph the camps before evidence is destroyed. She is willing to pay me while training."

"What an opportunity."

"It is intimidating, but it is also a chance to see if this is what I want to do. Owen warned me that it will be emotionally very tough. I hope I'm strong enough for that. But you said once that courage doesn't show up until you really need it, so I'm counting on that. If you're wrong, I'll come back and tell you."

"We'll miss you, but it's very important work. No one should ever forget what happened."

"I'll miss you and Benji."

"We'll be here, making dinner and wishing somebody else would do the dishes. When you're ready, please just come home."

They clinked their glasses. "To home," they said.

77.

ADA

"Do you know where the flag is?" Ada asked her sister. "We haven't used it in years."

"I haven't seen it. Try the closet in Father's study."

Ada eventually found the flag in the back of the hall closet. Standing on a chair on the front porch, Ada tried to insert the flagpole into the metal bracket beside the front door. After her third attempt, she heard a man's voice offering to help. She brushed the flag away from her face to see who was talking to her.

"Can I help you with that?" he asked again.

She didn't recognize him, although there was something familiar about his face. "I almost have it."

"I would hate for you to fall. This is not a good day to go to the emergency department; I don't think anyone is working."

Ada stood with the pole in her hand and studied the man who had somehow turned up on her doorstep. She was unsure about accepting help from this stranger. He quietly took the flagpole from her and inserted it in the bracket. They stepped back from the house to admire it as it unfurled in the breeze.

The man turned to Ada with his hand outstretched. "I'm Simon, Willy's brother."

She shook his hand and stared at him—he looked a lot like Willy. Simon was taller and more solidly built than his younger brother, but he wore a similar pair of gold-rimmed glasses. With the same curly, dark hair and some gray at the temples, he stood very still as Ada tried to absorb his presence and find something to say.

Taking note of her confusion, he began to explain. "I hope you don't mind me dropping by without calling. I was in town for work the last few days."

"I'm glad you did. Why don't you come to the backyard and meet some people? We're having a small party."

"I don't want to intrude," Simon said.

"Come and celebrate with us."

Simon followed her into the yard.

Ada felt like all her senses had gone on alert—she was aware of his presence right behind her as they walked to the backyard. Suddenly she felt terribly self-conscious.

Glancing at the kitchen window as she passed, she remembered all the times she'd stared through that frost-covered window, washing dishes in cold water, scrubbing beets and potatoes, trying to make something out of nothing, and hoping that someday there would be more.

And suddenly there was so much more that she couldn't quite take it in—a yard full of friends, festive food, a child who had chosen her, and now Simon, a thread connecting her to the past and pulling her forward into the future. She saw Owen, Lucas, Jakoba from the evaluation clinic, Lykke, and several volunteers from the former orphanage, as well as their neighbors the Groens. Their minister arrived with his wife, walking with a cane and very frail, yet his blue eyes twinkled with pleasure to see them again. Lina had managed to track down Bart, the driver of the evacuation truck to the north, and he was pleased to attend. Gerda was unable to attend, but they hoped to visit her in the next week, hitching a ride with Owen.

Ada wished she was wearing something other than Mother's old dress and a cardigan that was nearly worn through at the elbows. He probably thought she looked impossibly old-fashioned. She ran her fingers through her hair but then realized he might see the eczema on her hands, so she tucked her hands in the pockets of the dress.

Ada turned to him, pausing for a moment before they turned the corner into the garden. She didn't know what she wanted to say, but she wanted to hold onto this moment when it was just the two of them. The sound of laughter and conversation flowed out of the space and into the trees. "Are you ready to meet everyone?"

He smiled. "Lead the way."

Lucas looked up as they walked into the garden together.

"I'd like you all to meet Simon." Then she took him around to introduce him to each person.

When he came to Benji, he crouched down and took the boy's hand. "Did I see you in the parade today? Waving a flag and riding with the soldiers in a jeep?"

Benji nodded and smiled. He took Simon's hand and led him to the sunporch where he pulled out the box with his favorite cars and pulled out a bright red one to show Simon.

"That's a very fine car," Simon said, "and I bet it goes very fast."

Benji nodded again and showed him the rest.

Ada watched them interact. Something in his posture, the way he crouched to Benji's eye level and let him take the lead, helped Benji to feel comfortable with him.

Ada tapped Simon's shoulder. "I'll check on the food. Will you be all right?"

"Of course," he said. "We have cars to examine."

Ada went into the kitchen where Lina had cut up the bread and put it in a big basket.

"Who's the handsome man?" Lina said, "and where did you find him?"

"He walked in off the street," Ada said.

"What?" Lina looked at her. "I thought I told you not to talk to strangers," she said with a smile.

"Actually, he's the brother of my friend Willy."

"Is he single?" Lina asked as she leaned back against the counter, her arms crossed over her chest.

"I just met him two minutes ago. I have no idea. He said his brother had asked him to visit me when the war ended." Ada stirred the stew. "I think this is ready to go outside. Owen should be here any minute. Lucas has set up the drinks already."

"I'll take care of this, and you go talk to that fellow." Lina pinched her cheeks. "And smile a lot."

Ada was embarrassed. "Stop it. I just met him."

Lina studied her appearance. "That's good. Blushing makes you even more attractive. Be a good hostess and offer him a drink before Benji monopolizes him completely."

Raoul came in carrying a tray of dishes. "Very handsome man," he whispered to Ada. "Don't let him get away."

Ada gave him a light punch to the arm and prepared another tray with refreshments.

78.

ADA

Ada forced herself to walk over to Simon, almost immobilized by self-consciousness. What must he think of her?

He smiled at her in a way that made her heart beat faster. There was so much she wanted to ask. Where had he spent the war? What did he plan to do now that it was finally over?

When Ada brought him a glass of wine, Benji moved away to show his favorite car to Lucas. "Could you tell me about your family?"

"As you know, Willy hid at your grandfather's farm and then moved around for a while until he was arrested and deported. He died in 1942." Simon paused. "My father served on the Jewish Council in Amsterdam, but in 1943 when the Nazis disbanded it, my parents were sent to Westerbork. After that they were transported to a death camp, where they died a few months later."

They were both silent for a moment. "I am so sorry. Willy told me that if they sent him to a camp, his health wouldn't last," Ada said.

Simon nodded. "He was right about that. I am the only one left, and I survived thanks to a resistance group that worked to keep doctors and medical students safe. I was moved around to various safe houses where I continued my medical studies when possible. It was a good distraction and kept my mind active, even though I was confined in small spaces."

Ada touched his arm lightly. There was nothing she could say. They stood together in silence, watching Benji race his cars down a ramp. Trying to absorb the vast space left by all his losses, she couldn't find words and looked at her worn shoes as her eyes filled with tears. She felt silly worrying about her clothing when she considered Simon's losses.

He touched her hand lightly. "We all lost so much."

Ada followed his gaze over the group of people, laughing and talking to each other with glasses in their hands. Worn-out clothes and gaunt figures, survivors of seasons of sorrow. She nodded her agreement.

"Where do you work now?" she asked.

"I'm finishing a residency in cardiology in Amsterdam. I live in my parents' apartment on the *Beethovenstraat*—the same place where Willy and I grew up."

"There must be many memories there," Ada suggested.

"I try not to linger too much on the past. My father was deeply committed to the healing of the world. That's how I choose to honor their memory—by continuing to do that work."

"It's an honorable profession, repairing broken hearts. Willy was so proud of you."

Simon smiled. "I was his older brother. We fought and argued like any other siblings. And sometimes over trivial things."

"I am an older sister. I understand. Willy would have made such a fine professor," Ada said.

"He was much more philosophically inclined. I miss him every day. I miss all of them."

Lina walked over to join them. Somehow, she had repaired her haggard look with some makeup and one of Mother's summer dresses to which she'd added a belt. Even though there was too much fabric for her lean figure, she managed to carry it off with elegance.

A familiar pang of jealousy hit Ada as Simon smiled and shook Lina's hand. They chatted easily about Simon's home in Amsterdam and how the city had been spared compared to Rotterdam, but a bombing at the end of the war had destroyed much of the harbor. Ada felt herself withdraw into her old insecurities as she saw Simon respond with animation to Lina's questions.

"I might go to art school eventually," Lina said, "but for now, I'm going to be an assistant to a photographer who is documenting the camps and survivors. I'm leaving next week."

Ada excused herself to replenish the food. Lina was a much more interesting person. She'd already begun to recover physically from her experiences—her skin looked less sallow, and she'd grown out her hair to a chin-length bob that looked sophisticated. The last time Ada had offered to cut it in her usual short style, Lina said she intended to grow it out to look more French. Lina had not told her the full story of some of the work she'd done for Lucas, and she doubted that she ever would.

"Owen, can I get you something to drink?" she asked.

"I brought some American beer. I'll get myself one, thanks. How are you doing?" Owen asked.

"I'm fine," Ada said cheerfully. "I just want to replenish the food."

Owen took the bowl from her hands. "I'll do that. I wouldn't leave your sister too long with that handsome man."

"If he wants her, then maybe he doesn't want me."

He puts his hand on her shoulder. "I was told he came here looking for you, so the least you can do is not run away."

"I wasn't running." She grinned sheepishly. "I walked."

"Get back out there," Owen commanded. "That's an order. And start believing that someone might be interested in you."

"Canadians are very bossy," Ada said.

"We helped liberate your country. Show your gratitude by following orders."

When Ada returned to the backyard, Simon smiled at her—his brown eyes so warm and welcoming. It was the strangest thing; she felt time stop—it was as if they were alone in the backyard. Lina had gone to talk to Lucas, so Ada stood beside Simon.

"Tell me about yourself. Have you made any plans?"

Ada nodded. "My studies were interrupted when the university was closed, but I'm hoping to restart in the fall with biology and food science. During the war, I worked for the Food Council, and I'd like to continue that work. Benji joined the household not too long ago, and I want to make sure he settles into a good routine."

"Where did he come from?"

"A local orphanage was ordered to close, and he was one of the last children there. People didn't want to adopt him because at the time he couldn't speak. Even now, he will only say a word at a time."

"Traumatic mutism is not unusual when children have witnessed frightening events. He seems very happy and well-adjusted otherwise. I have a colleague who is doing research in this area, if you are interested in meeting with him."

"I would like appreciate that."

"I'll get you the information."

"Because I have no experience with children, I hesitated to take him home. These past weeks, Lina has worked with him using art. We'll soon be on our own, just the two of us. He'll start school in the fall and so will I, so we'll be busy."

"It looks like you're doing a great job."

"I couldn't walk away from him. The occupiers were going to send any remaining children to Germany."

"You saved his life."

"And I think he might be saving mine," Ada said.

"Where do you hope to continue your education?" Simon asked.

"I plan to finish my basic science degree here. My father left us this house, so we have a place to live. The Food Council office in The Hague has invited me to work there next summer.

Simon nodded. "Lina told me you have promising contacts among the food and nutrition scientists."

"She did?" Ada was surprised Lina had mentioned that to him. "I hope that might lead to something in the future. Food issues will continue to challenge people either due to natural disasters or humanly created disasters. As we learned this past winter, food scarcity can become a weapon."

While they ate, Ada expected Simon to move on and talk to others, but he stayed right beside her. Conversation flowed effortlessly as they discussed music and places they hoped to see someday.

"Lucas, I believe you met Simon earlier. He's Willy's brother."

Lucas was startled. "I see the resemblance. I was sorry to hear about him," Lucas said. "We had the best conversations about politics and history. My condolences with your losses."

"Thank you," Simon said. "I've heard about your work. You helped many people."

Lucas nodded. "I wasn't alone." He looked over at Lina, and she smiled at him.

While Ada helped serve coffee and tea, she overheard bits of the conversation. Lucas told Simon about how he hoped to finish his dissertation with a new supervisor. He talked to Simon about preparations for an international court to try war criminals. She was proud that they had rescued the evidence from the hands of the Nazis, but she planned to never speak of that. Others had done so much more and paid a terrible price.

Simon mingled with the guests, listening and asking questions. He occasionally looked across the garden at her and smiled. She felt anchored by his glance as if before this time, she'd been floating aimlessly.

Where did it come from, this sudden infusion of joy? Could it be trusted? Was he was feeling something too? Had Willy set this in motion years ago, predicting that she and Simon would fit together well if he was no longer around?

Raoul, sitting in a chair of honor in the backyard, spoke with Simon, who had pulled up a chair next to him. They talked about how Amsterdam might recover from the war.

Ada served the cake on Mother's plates with the tiny silver forks that had somehow survived Lina's bartering excursions for food.

When people began to leave, the men helped her put the furniture back in place. Lucas and Simon washed dishes while discussing some aspect of the postliberation government powers.

Lina went upstairs to help Benji with his bath and bedtime while Ada helped to put the house back in order.

Ada poured two glasses of wine, and Simon carried them to the sunporch. They sat together in comfortable silence and listened to the sound of birds in the trees. There was an ease between them, as if they were old friends reunited after a long absence. Sipping the wine, they watched the light fade gradually from the sky.

"Ada, would you consider going out with me? I could get tickets to a concert in Amsterdam, or we could go out for dinner—unless you have someone in your life already?"

"I'd love to do any of those things."

"Will you be able to arrange a sitter for Benji?"

Ada smiled. "Certainly."

"I hope it's not too strange for you to go out with me considering that you and Willy . . ."

"Not at all. We were so young and only beginning to know each other."

Simon finished his wine and stood up. "I must work tomorrow, so I should get going. I'm so glad that I stopped by. Would next Saturday work for you?"

"If you come here in the late afternoon, we could walk to town. There's one restaurant that has reopened. They probably have a limited menu, but it would be nice to support them."

"Sounds perfect. I'll come at four. And I'll start looking for any upcoming concerts in Amsterdam."

"Imagine attending a live concert." She walked him to his car parked on the street in front of the house.

"Another time, if you like, we could do something that Benji would enjoy. I look forward to next Saturday. Here's my card with my office and home number on the back."

"Thanks. See you next Saturday." Ada tucked the card in her pocket.

He leaned forward and kissed each cheek.

Ada watched him drive away. It was dark now, but a few lights were visible in houses along their street. This day had turned out very different than she'd expected. She wondered what Simon was thinking as he drove towards Amsterdam.

She glanced at Nel's house, almost expecting to find her watching from the front window, but Nel had been sent to a camp where she would be tried and sentenced as a collaborator, along with the Vriends. There were other people in town who had betrayed their neighbors and friends. They had been shocked to see Maria, with her head shaved, being marched through town to the jeers of people. The Captain would stand trial in The Hague, and the trials would continue elsewhere as well.

Judgement, punishment, forgiveness—those questions were simply too big for her and were better left in the hands of those who were trained in such matters. Seeing the world through Benji's eyes helped her see how the war had broken spirits and stolen people's imaginations. And now that they were at the end of all that, it was time to take stock. Even the worst darkness had not overpowered the light.

Ada walked into the front hall to lock the door and paused as she remembered Father's arrest. If only he could have been with them to celebrate the end of war and to meet Simon and Benji, and Owen and Raoul, as well as the other people they'd met during the war. He would've been so proud of Lucas and Lina's achievements and, she supposed, of her own efforts.

She returned to the kitchen—order had been restored, and the tea towels were drying on the rack. Raoul had taken charge of the cleanup. Silver forks were back in the small wooden box lined with green felt. The kitchen table was clean and ready for another day. How well it had served as a meeting place for the various hungers they had known—not only for food but for purpose and companionship and for laughter.

Pouring the last bit of wine into her glass, she returned to the sunporch to savor the quiet. She wanted to wrap the events of the day around her like a warm shawl.

A lamppost behind the gate shed some light on the yard as white blossoms fluttered from the tree to the ground.

Ada remembered one day when she and Benji had bundled up against the cold and walked to the park. While Benji watched the ducks, a late spring snow began to fall. He ran around with delight, holding out his mittened hands to try to catch the flakes, laughing as they landed on his face and eyelashes. He stuck out his tongue to catch the snow as it fell.

Someday she would tell Benji the story of the ancient peoples who had wandered forty years in the desert, hungry and disconsolate, until fed by mysterious manna and quail. Time was elastic in the face of suffering, and hope was a mirage. Whether for an hour, a year, or longer, suffering happened outside of normal time.

How could she remember the good things without reliving the terrifying experiences over and over? Was forgetting something one chose to do or something that happened gradually over time?

Maybe Benji had the answer. Watching him engage so fully with the world around him despite the pain he had experienced, choosing life seemed possible. Grief and joy could walk hand in hand, just as Benji's small hand found a place in hers. The damaged innocence and the terrifying memories might reside within them forever, but the heart had the capacity to regenerate. By some grace, they had survived, and Ada prayed their lives would be a living testament.

Benji ran towards her and hugged her, freshly ready for bed, his tiny arms reaching to encircle her. Together they would build a home with Lina and Simon, Lucas, Raoul, and new friends whose names they didn't yet know. This thing called hope was a living, beating thing, a heart at the core of the universe.

It took more than bread alone to sustain life, but it was a promise that new beginnings were possible.

79.

ADA

I N the weeks after peace was declared, Ada had expected the celebratory mood to continue, but instead she felt sad and confused by all the changes. As hard as she might try to slow down the rate of change, the transition had begun. Owen was leaving, Raoul hoped to move to Amsterdam, and Lina had already left for Germany.

Simon helped her see the changes in positive ways, but Ada dreaded the prospect of saying goodbye to Owen. He added so much to the household and had become a close friend. Benji would certainly miss having him in his life.

Benji was excited about starting school in the fall. She'd worked with him on recognizing letters, writing numbers, and reading books together. They read books she had collected, but she was eager for libraries and bookstores to open again. She'd taken him to see Simon's colleague, a child psychologist in Amsterdam, and he'd been very encouraging. Healing takes time, he had reminded her. Now that Benji no longer had nightmares, Mother's former sewing room had become his bedroom.

Benji sat at the kitchen table completely focused on his drawing. She wasn't sure if he understood how much their household was about to change; she hoped he wouldn't be bored when it was just the two of them. Perhaps new families would move into their neighborhood and bring new friends for Benji.

He was very patient when she took him along on errands. Although he was content being with her, she knew he needed to engage with a bigger world and make friends his own age. She tried to remind herself to encourage him to use words when he wanted things—it was too easy for her to guess what he wanted.

Watching people move on with their lives, Ada sometimes wondered if she'd missed her moment and was now too old to finish her education. These doubts had plagued her recently as she balanced her need to care for Benji and for the house with the pressures of becoming a student after so many years away.

The university buildings would be the same, and some of the professors might return, but she was a different person. She knew how important it was to continue; Lucas reminded her that it was important to be a good model for Benji as he started out on his educational journey. To eventually land a stable job in her field, she would need a university education.

There was no magical cure for the destruction around them. Returning to some version of normal would take longer than anyone expected. Ever since the spring, when the Allied bombers dropped more than five hundred tons of food supplies and the Canadian military transported a thousand tons more by road, the food situation had improved, but it would take much longer to return to normal. The disruption of agriculture, the inundation of arable land, and the destruction of farm life and families would take a long time to resolve. She had seen the importance of self-sufficiency—she planned to expand her garden in the backyard and to increase production of preserves and dehydrated foods. Ada turned from gazing at the garden and walked towards the living room.

She had begun to bring down some of the furnishings that had been in the attic. The room was still sparse, but she would continue to rebuild the space to make it cozy. She opened the hinged top of the instrument's bench and picked up the large black book that contained the musical arrangements for the psalms. She placed it on the stand and sat down, arranging her skirts so that she could easily pump the pedals.

After a few false notes, she pumped the pedals harder, and the instrument breathed into life; her stiff fingers loosened enough to play some of the quick notes intended for the right hand. As she played her mother's favorite psalm, she imagined deer running and searching for water. She sang the words from memory, her singing voice rusty from lack of use. When she finished the psalm, the room was silent. Expecting her mother's call for yet another favorite, she accepted that she would never hear that voice again.

She studied her hands, reddened from the chores, cold water, and the harsh winter. Smoothing her skirt as it was crumpled over her thighs, she thought about the words. This house had been her refuge, and she hoped it would remain so. Closing the book, she placed it carefully on the holder where she could open it easily whenever she chose to play again.

As she walked towards the study, she thought about neighbors that planned to emigrate to other countries where they would have a chance to start over. Although a new start had its appeal, she planned to stay right here. She didn't want to start over—instead, she wanted to honor the memories embedded in this place and find a way forward.

She walked into Father's study. The air was stale as the room had been closed for a while, and a fine layer of dust covered the desk and the shelves. She sat in the wing chair opposite the cleared desk and remembered the instructions he had written for her.

"Father," she whispered, "I hope I took care of things the way you wanted. Thank you for arranging for us to be secure in this house. I think," she paused as tears began to flow down her face, "that I understand why you didn't tell me the secret. We had too many secrets in this house, and those habits are hard to break."

"You will always be my father, and nothing I have learned will change that. You would be so proud of Lina, she has been very brave in the war effort and has decided to pursue photography. We have learned to work together and to appreciate each other's differences. My life has changed since I brought Benji home from the orphanage—I could tell you about how my heart has expanded as a result, but I suspect you know exactly how that feels. Gerda told me about how you took me under your wing before I was even born. Thank you for being my father."

Ada paused to take a few breaths. "I've learned that a heart, once open, can continue to expand. Willy's brother, Simon, has become very important to me, and we plan to start our life together. It is a miracle that he survived—I will be grateful every day that he did. You would be happy to know that I will register for fall classes at the university. The war has helped me define my goals, and I am eager to begin."

"We took in Raoul who worked and lived in the Captain's house. He will work as a designer of men's clothes, and I believe he will become very successful. He has become an uncle to Benji and visits us regularly from his flat in Amsterdam."

"*Tante* Gerda has been a wonderful aunt to all of us. We try to visit her in her apartment since it is difficult for her to travel. She has been a link to you and your past, and she has been an inspiration in so many ways."

"Our quiet neighbors, the Groens, are quite taken with Benji, and they will help walk him to school or pick him up as needed. They are happy to be *Opa* and *Oma* to Benji, but they promised to tell Benji about you and keep your story alive. Simon also lost his parents, but he has promised to honor their memories and tell Benji about them. We hope that our home will combine the traditions and beliefs of both our families."

"Lucas intends to oversee the publication of your edited volume on fascism so that people can know the full story of this awful war. Together we will move forward and find a way to heal our deepest wounds by remembering and honoring what is good."

As Ada listened to the stillness in the house, she realized that both things could be true and could coexist—deep grief and deep joy were intertwined. Life would bring more of each, but from now on she and Simon would face such things together. The war had taught her so much about survival. Every time Benji took her hand, she learned those lessons over again.

"Goodbye, Father," Ada's throat tightened with emotion as tears ran down her face. She detected the scent of tobacco, much less intense than it used to be, that still hung in the air. They had cleared out Father's things and donated his books to a library. She hoped that Simon would feel at home in his new study. The mourning doves seemed to prefer nesting in the deep heart of the linden tree outside the window. She'd have to tell him that they were singing of loved ones who would stay near them through everything.

Epilogue

AMSTERDAM, 1990

LINA

FROM her favorite red leather reading chair, Lina watched the afternoon sun pour golden light into the living room. Floor-to-ceiling windows provided a view of the canal and the row of houses on the other side—most of which had been subdivided into apartments. Bicycles painted in pinks and yellows, as well as traditional black ones, were locked up in long rows along every available post and bridge.

Inside her apartment on the ground floor, heavy beams crossed the length of the ceiling, supporting the weight of the upper floors. The open living room transitioned into the dining room with a kitchen at the back. The broad wooden floorboards were buffed to a warm glow marked by the occasional scar or shadow remaining from their early industrial days.

When her sister Ada married Simon nearly five decades ago, they had helped Lina invest her share of the family home until she was ready to purchase her own. Under Simon's careful eye, that investment had grown until she'd been able to buy this apartment. After Simon passed, while undergoing surgery for an aortic aneurysm, Ada sold their house and moved in with her. Together they sorted out the business of aging and its challenges.

Their coexistence was mostly peaceful—they had accepted their differences in that long-ago war and were happy to enjoy peace between them now. They still bickered about the same things. Lina, for instance, believed a certain amount of chaos was creative, whereas Ada became annoyed whenever things were out of place. "You're like an old married couple," her grandniece Emily had commented. Perhaps they were, but that relationship contained a deep respect for each other that no circumstance would shake.

Lina had finally convinced Ada to take the trip to Israel that she'd talked about for decades. When Ada protested, Lina had challenged her with "If not now, then when?" That had settled it—Ada knew that her mobility was compromised, and her eyesight was diminished. This was the last chapter, she often said, and she booked the trip with a group of seniors. When Lina reminded her how Gerda had been confined to her apartment due to physical challenges, it gave Ada a reminder to use her time well. Gerda passed a few years after the war's end, but she was a wonderful support in the first few years of their postwar life.

Decades ago, when Lina had first seen this seventeenth-century canal house, she'd stopped to admire the soaring gables and exterior hoisting hook intended for moving heavy items. She knew at that moment that this would be her home. Lucas often teased her that she had more certainty about the house than she did about him.

She was grateful for her career as a photographer but no longer had the desire to travel and carry equipment and deal with delays and obstacles every day. Father had planted the seeds for that career so long ago—Lina had been ten years old when Father gave her a small Kodak camera for her birthday. They often spent Saturdays going on photo excursions and then developing pictures. Father had taught her well—focus on the image and let it speak. His sayings stayed with her, such as "A photographer exists to help the subject tell her story."

On the left wall, by the long, narrow dining room table, a large vertical painting splashed colors of the sea and sky into the room. On the far wall, a series of black-and-white framed prints hung on the exposed brick and depicted street scenes from Africa, Thailand, and Indonesia. Beauty, dignity, poverty—Lina had captured the contradictions in her photographs.

Her work as a photographer over several decades had tested both her physical and emotional limits as she documented the horrors of natural and humanly created disasters. Without Lucas waiting for her at home, she would not have been able to keep working as long as she had. And he had always been waiting for her to return. She was grateful every time she returned home to be with him again. He was present through her nightmares and silences, holding her quietly, absorbing all that she'd witnessed until she was ready to speak, to show her work, and to share what she had documented. Lucas never flinched from what she needed to show him. A lesser man would have turned away or begged her to stop doing this work, but Lucas had a deep commitment to speaking truth whether through her visual images or through his historical research and writing. He had helped her run a philanthropic organization that supported children in some of the countries where she had traveled.

Occasionally on return from her field trips, she'd gone to a nearby monastery for a retreat when she couldn't find her way back to ordinary life. Several of her photos hung in the art gallery that was part of the abbey—gifts of gratitude for having saved her life during the war and continuing to sustain her throughout her career. One of the monks had told her that "it takes courage to look at the face of evil and retain your ability to care." She'd never forgotten that—caring could exact a heavy price, but life was not worthwhile without it. She and Lucas had forged an unusual arrangement, incorporating long absences into deep closeness. It was another one of those contradictions or combinations of darkness and light that she had learned to accept and even value.

While she waited for Emily, Ada's granddaughter, to visit, she listened to the church bells mark the hour—she was grateful for those reminders. Time had always seemed quite simple; on one side was the past, and on the other was the future, and her place was to stand in the middle surveying the whole picture. But it was far more complicated as memories from childhood could be so vivid, whereas the details of yesterday or last week were impossible to recall.

Lina was excited to have Emily visit—without Ada there, she might share more with Lina than she normally did. Ada was so outspoken about what was "proper" that Emily put up fences to protect her privacy. The world had changed in the decades since the war ended, but Ada retained a longing for some of the old ways. Nostalgia was dangerous when it held people back. Emily had moved to Toronto for several years to pursue her art in freedom from her grandmother's judgement, but she had returned when Ada became ill, feeling an obligation to support her grandmother. Lina would have loved to know more about Emily's years in Canada, but she tried to reign in her curiosity and respect Emily's desire for privacy.

The days of endless possibility were finished for Lina—there were no phone calls inviting her to a new assignment. Rather than submerging herself in a trough of self-pity, she chose to remember the opportunities she'd been given. Her memories were rich, and her imagination was vivid—she could recall every detail of swimming on the beaches in Ceylon or hiking to a mountaintop monastery in India.

The heat of the tropics, the quick descent into night, the sounds of unnamed creatures filling the darkness with sound, the clatter of monkeys on the tin roof of her rest house on the tea plantation were things she could not describe to others. She always longed for Lucas during those assignments, wanting to feel him next to her in the night, willing his arms to be there to hold her through terrors that plagued her and kept her sleepless.

If he suffered during her absences, he never spoke of it, and he refused the sympathetic sentiments of friends who wondered why he put up with her travel. Lucas supported her work and her talents, and his belief in its importance gave her the courage to return to the war zones and disasters year after year. After he finished his thesis, he began teaching at the university, carrying on Father's legacy in history. He also spent time writing novels that drew on his experiences during the war.

A few weeks ago, Emily had contacted Lina about a retrospective documentary project dealing with Lina's career in photography. It had caught her off guard—she'd been surprised and uncertain. Having frequently complained that there were so few contemporaries left with whom she could share the stories of the past, suddenly she felt reluctant to open herself and her work to scrutiny.

In contrast to Emily's energetic approach, Lina felt reticent, especially now that work no longer defined her value. Why was Emily interested in her work—what had it accomplished in the larger scale of things? Had the photographs fallen into obscurity, or did they serve as a record, a memory aid to events that should never be forgotten?

Emily wanted to work with educational groups and institutions to provide content that would help people of all age groups to remember the war. Lina had thought that once the horrors of the war were more widely known, no one would ever forget what had been done. But that was not the case. Memory needed to be trained and guided by mentors who understood that the mind would resist apprehension of such horror and would avoid it if possible. On her darkest days, Lina wondered if war would always be with them, repeating over and over the horrors and misery of the past.

So much had changed—not only in the world of digital technology but also in the tastes of the viewers. These days everyone considered themselves to be a competent photographer with compact cameras and computer manipulation of images. Perhaps they were, but Lina believed that nothing was more instructive than a long apprenticeship to master the craft and to understand every step of the technique, including many hours in the darkroom. Her mentor had been tough, and the things they had seen while photographing the camps had nearly broken them both.

The new technologies might make things more automatic, but they made the process fast and disposable. Lina knew that it had taken her years to learn to wait and listen and review—and she wasn't a patient person.

When Emily suggested that Lina cowrite the script and oversee production of the documentary, Lina had been surprised by the request. The young woman was wise—she knew that Lina would want some measure of control over her story, and she was generous enough to offer that to her.

In preparation for their meeting, Lina had pulled out some boxes of photos related to the occupation of the Netherlands during World War II and the famine event that was now named the Hunger Winter of 1944–45.

There were several pictures of Owen, the Canadian soldier, who'd become a friend during that last winter of the war. Owen had stayed in touch over the years, remembering birthdays and sending Christmas letters. Every so often, he returned to the Netherlands with his wife to attend war commemoration ceremonies. At his death two years ago, she felt like she'd lost a brother. Her friends were like the falling leaves of autumn as they fluttered soundlessly to the earth. Did their spirits join with the others who left so long ago? Lina pictured a grand reunion where they could all gather someday. She looked at a picture of Raoul wearing one of his designs, so handsome and proud. He had made a life for himself in Amsterdam and a career that had made him both happy and wealthy.

The sheer curtains danced forward as a puff of fresh air blew through the open window carrying the scent of blossoms that reminded her of their grandfather's farm. She studied a family portrait taken before the war in her grandfather's apple orchard—her father had blonde hair and a long, narrow face. Through his wire-rimmed glasses, he looked directly at the camera. The sleeves of his dress shirt were rolled up as if he had just completed a task. His wife's dark, curly hair was pulled back into a bun. Wearing a belted dress with covered buttons on the bodice, her arms were crossed over her bust, and her eyes looked beyond the photographer, a reluctant subject. Although the harvest had passed, under the tree was a scattering of red apples. They had brought those home, even though they were imperfect, because *Opa* could not sell them. She remembered learning to peel those apples and use an apple corer to pull out the seeds and core of the fruit.

In the photo, Ada and Lina both wore white dresses with shiny dress shoes. Ada resembled her mother with dark, curly hair, whereas Lina looked more like her father with prominent cheek bones and a high forehead. Her very straight and fine hair was cut in a chin-length bob that sported a large white bow on top. Her posture suggested impatience with the slow progress of the portrait. Her eyes were focused on the field where something had caught her interest. She looked ready to spring the moment the portrait was complete, whereas Ada seemed compliant and pleased to smile for the camera.

The photograph displayed no hint of the troubles ahead, nor did it reveal anything about the past. As she studied the picture, Lina was struck by how youthful her parents looked in the photograph. If their lives had not been interrupted by illness, war, and other unexpected events that had changed the trajectory of their lives, their stories might have been very different.

Unable to reveal all that never would be—the photograph presented and preserved only that one moment in time and concealed the rest. Like a scroll that was gently rolled open, some of what was concealed had been revealed, whereas much else would remain secret.

Lina watched as clouds moved swiftly across the sky, allowing the sun to shoot bright shards of light across the canal. She loved being near the water—always changing, always moving, connecting with something essential. They had survived flood and famine, and they'd distributed ashes and replanted inundated fields. Many buried in unmarked graves would never come home from those fields and fires. Lina believed that their spirits would survive no matter how the evil powers had tried to destroy them.

If Emily intended to preserve those stories, Lina knew she was obliged to participate. Neither the evil that was done nor the courage and goodness of ordinary people should ever be forgotten. Good and evil were intertwined like light and dark in her photos.

Her generation had witnessed evil firsthand—a modern plague for which there was no immunity or cure. Although most people acted like it was over forever, she remained skeptical. Evil could burrow underground until conditions favored its emergence. She wished she could tell Lucas about recent events that made it seem as if people had learned nothing.

When Lucas was dying, she had nursed him through long nights of coughing, but he had passed in the hospital. She still felt his presence throughout the apartment. It took a long time before she stopped anticipating his whistling presence and his offer to make coffee or pour a *borrel*.

When the doorbell rang, Lina was shaken out of her reverie. Grabbing the cane that was hooked over the arm of her reading chair, she walked slowly to the door.

The sun's rays lingered briefly on the red leather chair that Lina had vacated, before sliding over to paint the bricks on the far wall with golden light. As the two women talked, the boxes of photographs and albums spread out over the table and onto the floor—a feast of images that would create a story worth telling.

When Emily showed her the outline of a script for the documentary, Lina could see that Emily had already shaped the story she hoped to tell, but she wanted to include Lina in the process. As she watched Emily's excitement, she could see traces of Benji in her eyes and her smile.

When it was her time to leave this life, Lina knew she could entrust her work to caretakers of memory like Emily. She couldn't wait to tell Ada about the project—her pride in Emily would be enormous, as Lina knew it deserved to be. Love had expanded in amazing ways, beginning with Ada's wise choice to adopt Benji and then growing outward in ever-growing circles of connection. Through good and through evil, love had always been with them.

THE END

Appendix A

Reading Questions

1. This book opens with the arrest of the father by the occupiers. How does this event disrupt the lives of his daughters? Compare the reactions of Ada to Lina in response to this traumatic event.

2. *The Hunger Winter* features the point of view of Ada alternating with that of Lina. How would the novel change if it had been told in the voice of just one of the young women?

3. Ada is frustrated with her younger sister because she feels that Lina does not share in the household duties. In your family of origin, how were household chores distributed?

4. Different types of hunger are described in the novel. Name some of the hungers experienced by the characters. Which of these resonate with you?

5. The word *hiraeth* in the Welsh language describes the longing for home. How do the sisters differ in how they view the longing for home? What does the concept mean for you, and what strategies have you employed to realize that longing?

6. Ada feels she lacks courage, whereas Lina seems to have nerves of steel. Ada prefers to do administrative work, whereas Lina wants direct action in the resistance. Yet towards the end of the story, Ada knows where to find Father's gun and is prepared to use it to defend her family. How does Ada's understanding of courage change?

Where does courage come from? Describe a moment where you had courage to confront a situation.

7. Ada visits her local clergyman burdened with sadness and questions about war. What advice does he give her? Do you believe that war is ever necessary?

8. In the novel, local networks provide food for the hungry and vulnerable, and community kitchens serve up meals. In your community, how much does food insecurity affect people? What initiatives have been set up to meet the need? What do you feel should be done to address this need?

9. *The Hunger Winter* describes a relationship between two sisters whose young lives have been interrupted by war. Have you experienced the interruption caused by war, forced or chosen immigration, changed economic or familial circumstances, or illness? Have you ever attempted memoir writing to explore your experiences or share them with others?

10. Ada uncovers a secret that affects her understanding of herself. Lina reveals a secret that has affected her ability to trust others. How do the sisters navigate the revelations?

11. The sisters find their family changed forever by their losses but then are surprised how their concept of family includes chosen friends. How does hospitality contribute to that growth?

12. Ada and Lina eventually find romance. Does romance change anything in their ambitions for their postwar lives?

13. Lina's niece Emily intends to produce a documentary about Lina's career. She is committed to preserving the memory of the war events and educating others. Do you have any intentions to preserve your own or your family history? How do you plan to begin?

Appendix B

Topics for Further Research

- Recent studies on the effects of the Hunger Winter including those on maternal undernutrition as well as diseases associated with famine, such as celiac disease, diabetes, cardiovascular disease, and obesity. What do we understand about epigenetic changes? How is the research conducted on these questions?

- What public health challenges existed during this time? Which of these continue to challenge certain populations today?

- Domestic science and cookery including the *Recipes of the Hague Academy* edited by Anna van Manden (1855–1932) and the *Haagse Kookboek* (1934 edition) edited by Fréderique Mathilde Stoll and Wilhelmina Hendrika de Groot, teachers from the School of Domestic Science on the Laan van Meerdervoort. What did it mean to apply scientific household management to daily tasks? What principles guided household economy? How did these developments in the Netherlands mirror those in the United Kingdom, the United States, and Canada? How did the war affect cooking, diet, and nutritional science?

- Studies on trauma including the work of Jan Bastiaans (1917–97) and the Institute for Medical Psychotherapy in Amsterdam, which opened five days after the Germans invaded. The notion of concentration camp syndrome and transgenerational traumatization changed how research in this area was conducted. The use of LSD with traumatized veterans was controversial, and the debate continues to this day. See Bessel van der Kolk (b. 1943) and Judith Herman (b. 1942) for a contemporary understanding of trauma.

- History of art therapy and aesthetic empathy including the work of Friedl Dicker-Brandeis (1898–1944, died in Auschwitz) and Edith Kramer (1916–2014).

- Relief work of agencies and organizations including Quaker Relief, International Student Service, and the postwar resettlement work of Mennonite Central Committee.

- Changing attitudes and legislation related to child protection, social work, and legislation for single and foster parents in the Netherlands.

- Dissent and rebellion on university campuses during the occupation. See Owen Otterspeer's *Het Horzelnest* (The Hornet's Nest) for a study of collaboration or resistance among students and faculty at Leiden University.

- Women in the resistance during World War II in various countries.

- Documentary photography during the war and occupation. Some of the war photography was exhibited in a New York show called *The Illegal Camera: Photography of the Netherlands During the German Occupation, 1940–1945* in 1996. Photographers such as Ingeborg Wallheimer Kahlenberg (1920–1996) and Fritz Kahlenberg (1916–1996) documented the war and the Hunger Winter, which helped convince the Red Cross to organize food relief.

- Role of churches in the war, resistance, and postwar rebuilding. Student-based relief organizations such as the World Student Christian Federation.

- Changes in education between prewar, Nazi-controlled, and postwar Netherlands.

- Attitudes to war, peace, and nonviolence in the war and postwar period and in current times.

- Emigration and family relations in postwar resettlement of Dutch individuals and families.

- Historiographical questions. Compare the historical treatment by those who lived through the events (Henri van der Zee) to reinterpretations by modern historians (Ingrid de Zwarte).

- Historical empathy is the capacity to perceive, experience emotionally, and contextualize past events. How does historical empathy inform the work of historical fiction writers and historians? Is it possible to imagine characters and contexts different from our own? If you enjoy reading historical fiction, are you drawn to a particular time in history? What sources do your favorite writers consult to build their fictional stories? Are there human qualities to which you can relate that transcend specific historical contexts?